LUST, PLAIN AND SIMPLE

Missy took several steps forward. The glow from the solitary tallow candle suffused her in a warm light. James swallowed again, his breathing an audible rasp in the dead quiet of the night.

"I know you felt something when you kissed me tonight," she said softly.

James nearly groaned aloud, convinced his worst enemy had sent her to test him, torture him.

"Yes, and I believe you felt it too," he replied, his voice harsh.

She displayed no shock or surprise at his crude reference to just how hard he'd been pressed up against her down in the study. In fact her eyes, appearing more gray than blue at present, grew smoky, her lids weighed down by desire. Her gaze dropped to his chest and then to the unmistakable distention in the front of his trousers.

James had nowhere to go. He stood exposed and trapped, caged like a hungry lion with a voracious appetite who'd just come upon his next meal.

"You're very beautiful and I'm a normal male. It's lust, plain and simple. Don't make more of it than that. As I've told you before, any desirable female would elicit the same response."

Again, she said nothing but took another step forward, the light now illuminating the full glorious length of her slim figure, her nipples jutting out impudently from the soft cloth of her nightdress.

"It's more than lust."

BOOK YOUR PLACE ON OUR WEBSITE AND MAKE THE READING CONNECTION!

We've created a customized website just for our very special readers, where you can get the inside scoop on everything that's going on with Zebra, Pinnacle and Kensington books.

When you come online, you'll have the exciting opportunity to:

- View covers of upcoming books
- Read sample chapters
- Learn about our future publishing schedule (listed by publication month *and author*)
- Find out when your favorite authors will be visiting a city near you
- Search for and order backlist books from our online catalog
- Check out author bios and background information
- Send e-mail to your favorite authors
- Meet the Kensington staff online
- Join us in weekly chats with authors, readers and other guests
- Get writing guidelines
- AND MUCH MORE!

**Visit our website at
http://www.kensingtonbooks.com**

SINFUL SURRENDER

BEVERLEY KENDALL

ZEBRA BOOKS

KENSINGTON PUBLISHING CORP.

http://www.kensingtonbooks.com

ZEBRA BOOKS are published by

Kensington Publishing Corp.
119 West 40th Street
New York, NY 10018

All Kensington titles, imprints and distributed lines are available at special quantity discounts for bulk purchases for sales promotion, premiums, fund-raising, educational or institutional use.

Special book excerpts or customized printings can also be created to fit specific needs. For details, write or phone the office of the Kensington Special Sales Manager: Attn. Special Sales Department. Kensington Publishing Corp., 119 West 40th Street, New York, NY 10018. Phone: 1-800-221-2647.

Zebra and the Z logo Reg. U.S. Pat. & TM Off.

ISBN-13: 978-1-4201-0869-9
ISBN-10: 1-4201-0869-7

First Printing: January 2010
10 9 8 7 6 5 4 3 2 1

Printed in the United States of America

This book is dedicated in loving memory of Paul Glasgow

Acknowledgments

There are so many people to thank who dedicated their time and effort to helping me get this book sold.

I owe a huge thanks to my CPs, Devon Gray and Anastasia, for their unstinting support and brainstorming sessions. I'd also like to thank the ladies of Writers of the Roundtable who fostered a forum in which I felt completely at home. And to Avon Fanlit and all of the wonderful women I met there, you have my heartfelt gratitude, because without that event and top-notch writing, I wouldn't have attempted to write a historical romance.

To my family for their support of my writing dream, especially my sister, Dawn, who actually reads my work, I thank you. I would also like to thank my chapter, GRW, for their encouragement, the wonderful mentors, and fantastic writing workshops.

Last but certainly not least, I would like to thank Hilary Sares for pulling *Sinful Surrender* from the slush pile and giving me this incredible opportunity.

Prologue

The morning of the highly anticipated eighteenth birthday of Millicent "Missy" Armstrong—highly anticipated by her, not him—James Rutherford discovered too late that escorting her from the stables had been a monumental error in judgment.

If they hadn't been walking the quarter mile back to Stoneridge Hall, she would not have stumbled and fallen. There would have been no need to assist her to her feet. He certainly wouldn't have been jerked from his own, to land sprawled atop her, her slender arms wrapped tightly about his neck, pulling his head down so she could land an impassioned kiss on lips parted in surprise.

Damn and blast! This was precisely the kind of temptation he could ill afford and had done his best to avoid as this day had closed in on him with the swiftness of the finest pair of blacks in full gallop. A grown up Missy still suffering the pangs of a long held infatuation *and* entering the marriage market was a road fraught with endless pitfalls. One he'd obviously stumbled upon and currently had him cushioned by only the kind of softness and heat a female could render. And yards upon yards of muslin.

For a shameful moment—or perhaps shameless—he didn't extricate himself from her embrace, as surely the friend of her brother would if he at all hoped to maintain the friendship. Instead, he savored the waft of her warm breath against his cheek and discovered the softness of her eager, exploring lips. He discovered she wore the faint scent of lilacs. But the worst of his discoveries was what sprang to rigid attention beneath the front flap of his riding breeches.

Good God, what the blazes was he doing? Armstrong would skewer him clean through if he knew the sorts of thoughts James currently entertained about his sister.

Emitting a hiss then a tortured groan, and with the sweet taste of her still on his lips, he scrambled from atop her, levering himself to a standing position. Never had the ground felt so uneven beneath his feet or his stance quite so unsteady. Swiftly, he turned and offered her his back, drawing in a ragged breath of the cool April air. A sweeping survey across the rolling hills of Dartington revealed not a soul in sight. He should be relieved there'd been no party to the kiss. He wished he could breathe easy. His raging erection made it all but impossible.

Sounds of her scrambling to her feet finally penetrated above the blood roaring in his ears, as did the brisk brush of hands against cloth as she went about ridding herself of dewy blades of grass and the dirt clinging to her green-checkered day dress.

"James?" His name hitched in her throat, the lone syllable seeming to encapsulate a lifetime of yearning.

He briefly closed his eyes, suffering his remorse in silence as he could well imagine the accompanying wistfulness in her eyes and the faint tremble of her pink bottom lip. Ensuring his jacket adequately covered his state of arousal, and with his mouth in a grim line, he pivoted on his heel to face her.

"I thought you might actually like it if I kissed you. Might want me to kiss you." Arresting blue-gray eyes peered up at him from beneath long, sooty lashes, her expression poignant in its vulnerability.

His reaction to her was inexcusable. Reprehensible, really. She was off-limits to him. Armstrong had made that point clear enough when he'd demanded James give her a wide berth, at least during her debut into Society. Her crush would inevitably run its course. Or so his friend hoped. And should Armstrong have his way, she'd marry the much admired and ardently pursued heir to the Wiltshire dukedom, the Earl of Granville. Why shouldn't she marry an exalted title, his friend had reasoned, now that the Armstrong family could no longer be considered impoverished nobility, their fortune regained and currently far in excess of most in the upper stratum of Society?

"Missy," James began, but her name came out hoarse, forcing him to clear the alien object—which he belatedly identified as his tongue—from his throat to begin again. "Missy, you're like a sister to me," he said with a solemnity honed to pitch-perfect sincerity.

Lying to her went beyond prudent, it was now a necessity. Unfortunately, for him—for them both—any sisterly feelings he'd had toward her hadn't been able to withstand her breathtaking emergence into womanhood. Her previously tall and thin frame had developed enticing, feminine curves, and the promise of beauty he'd first seen in the ten-year-old chestnut-haired child had far exceeded his expectations.

A look of hurt flitted across her face that had his heart constricting in painful response.

"I am Thomas's sister, *not* yours."

As if he needed a reminder. It was his relationship with

Armstrong that kept him from taking what she was offering. Her beautiful body for his delectation. Although, in all honesty, even if her brother wouldn't have him strung up by the noose outside Newgate prison if he ever laid a hand on her, Missy deserved much more than giving away her innocence to a man who could never be the husband she needed him to be. The kind of husband she deserved.

"What I'm saying is that I have no interest in you like that . . . in a romantic sense." Lust was an entirely different matter altogether.

The sad fact was, that truth *had* existed up until the prior year. What he wouldn't give that it should exist again, that he be unaware again.

His innocence was interminably lost.

Chapter One

Devonshire, 1855

Missy quietly observed James perusing a book through the hand-span opening of the library door. An instantaneous burst of anticipation and desire collided inside her. Her breath hitched in her throat.

Consistent with his insouciant observance of societal norms, only a starchy tan linen shirt and dark green trousers graced his lean frame in casual elegance. On his feet, he wore a pair of high black Wellingtons. However, his notably absent waistcoat and neckcloth only served to magnify the aura of power and intrigue about him and enhance his charismatic appeal.

And he was alone.

With James, Thomas and Alex dogging each other's steps, the task of getting him to herself this visit had been one worthy of a spy for the Crown. Such a shame it had come to this, all the sneaking about she'd had to do.

With James constantly jaunting off to one country or the other and coming home for only snatches at a time, they had had scant contact over the past three years. He claimed it was for business but she suspected she had factored largely into his frequent and lengthy absences.

It could have just been a coincidence that his excessive travels had commenced two weeks after the incident. The kiss. She suspected it had been her impetuousness that had earned her the subsequent years of avoidance and neglect. But, it was the news of Miss Adelaide Bash's betrothal that would confirm her suspicions, providing the nail and hammer that would etch it into stone.

Part of the landed gentry, Miss Bash was pretty—though not uncommonly so. And while her family was land rich, over the years their finances had been ravaged by either flood or drought. However, her lack of rank in high society and the paltry sum of four hundred pounds that comprised her dowry didn't dissuade Miss Bash from setting her sights on no less than the handsome, wealthy heir to a viscountcy, Lord Alfred Neville.

Many in the *ton* were amused that a gentleman's daughter would be so presumptuous as to believe she could rise above her station and marry one of their own without what it would cost to pave Westminster Bridge with gold. "*Truly, even those crass American females seeking titled husbands are heiresses of great fortunes*," had been only one of the more generous remarks bandied about by some in the august set.

For the most part, people watched the whole affair with little more than passing interest, certain nothing would come of it save a bruised pride and a broken heart and that was if her heart was truly engaged. Far worse was the waste of the five hundred pounds or more it must have cost to fund her debut.

Missy, however, devoured Miss Bash's methods like a how-to manual, taking note of the way the woman had flirted without being forward and had shown an interest in the young lord without appearing at all humbled by her origins. The gentleman's daughter possessed the poise of a lady accustomed to a life of privilege, and the polish of the star pupil from Mrs. Landry's Charm School—a most esteemed finishing school.

Yet Miss Bash—all of only eighteen—emanated a sensuality that had gentlemen young and old watching her too long, too frequently, and with far too much interest. The recipient of all her attention and efforts was smitten to such a degree he formally requested her hand in marriage three months to the day after their introduction.

Their courtship had illuminated everything Missy, herself, had done wrong. She'd approached James with the over-eagerness of a puppy let loose to run free for the first time. She hadn't flirted, teased, or even coaxed. Instead, she'd crashed down on him like a cyclone, too much in love and too impatient to test her new maturity, as if the stroke of midnight had suddenly given her allure beyond her years.

Her face heated with the memory of just how much cheek she'd had. What had she expected, that the kiss she'd forced upon him would result in a grand declaration of his undying love and a betrothal ring? Such an undertaking required more panache and far more subtlety—as Miss Bash had clearly shown.

Missy could only thank heavens she was wiser now, possessing restraint that would have done her well back then. As this year would commence her fourth foray into the marriage market and her sister waited patiently to make her own debut, Missy couldn't afford another such mistake if she at all hoped to succeed with James.

Straightening to her full height, she smoothed a hand over her loosely pinned chignon before pushing open the heavy oak door. In a rustle of voluminous petticoats and shimmering silk, she entered the grand library of Stoneridge Hall.

Decorated with the lord of the manor in mind, the room boasted floor-to-ceiling walnut bookcases, a rich mahogany escritoire, and two large area rugs sitting atop gleaming hardwood floors. She'd always felt at home here, especially when her father was alive. Today, however, a whole field of butterflies had taken up residence in her belly, and clamored to come out.

Missy gently pressed the door closed with a decisive click. James turned at the sound and stared at her. For a moment something flashed in his eyes, something she could not quite discern. Abruptly, his expression shuttered.

"Hello, James."

"Missy." A perfunctory nod accompanied his greeting.

She saw him so rarely these days—his smile even less so—and the polite one he bestowed upon her now didn't particularly encourage conversation. Her hopes of wedded bliss and dark-haired, blue-eyed babies had faltered under the weight of time passing with no results. But that connection they'd once shared—one she thought occurred once in a lifetime—wouldn't permit her to cast a handful of dirt upon a pine box, or prop flowers against a headstone to signal her dream's demise. At least not just yet.

"Don't you think it best if the door remained open?" he asked, his voice a pleasing blend of polished speech and velvet roughness. She gave a faint shiver. Everything about him was beautiful, including his voice. She'd missed the sound of his deep baritone as much as she'd missed him.

"Why, are you afraid to be alone with me?" she asked lightly, trying to strike the right chord between impudence and timidity. Balance was the key.

James's countenance was severe, as if her presence was something to be endured in tight-lipped silence. His Adam's apple then gave a convulsive bob under a hard swallow. She couldn't be certain whether she had discomfited him or if she had nicked his last frayed nerve. She gathered she'd soon find out.

Mustering up all her courage, Missy closed the distance

between them. When she drew to a stop, only a couple feet from where he stood, he queried with a quirk of one dark brow.

"Are you aware we haven't been alone together since the day I turned eighteen? I'd begun to think you've been avoiding me." Missy paused before asking, "Have you?"

Again, an indecipherable emotion flashed in his crystalline blue eyes, before a potent smile spread like sun-warmed molasses across the chiseled beauty of his visage. No longer polite, this smile engaged. It was the kind of smile that could make a woman swoon. However, a puppeteer's string might well have lifted the corners of that sensuous mouth, for his eyes continued to watch her intently, cheerless and sober.

"I beg your pardon?" He sounded faintly abashed, which was absurd as James hadn't an abashed bone in his entire body.

A surreptitious sweep of his form had her hands tingling with the effort to keep them at her side. She tingled in other places proper ladies dared not think of. But then, had she ever considered herself terribly proper with fantasies that could have her barred from Society had she made even one a reality? No, proper she definitely was not.

"It's just that we used to be . . . close. Now I rarely see you. What else am I to think when you have all but vanished from my life?"

The dimples slashing his bristled cheeks all but disappeared, and through lowered lids and spiky lashes, inky black pupils stared back at her. Her claim had obviously hit a nerve because he remained mute for seconds too long. The James of years ago had never been at a loss for words.

"Nothing could be further from the truth," he began, ending the palpable quiet and speaking in a melodic tone best for soothing babies and small animals. "You must be aware that business interests frequently take me out of the country for long stretches at a time. Believe me, I'm a stranger to many."

So, she was now one of many?

"But even when I see you, like at present, you're so . . . different." He treated her with not even the warmth of an acquaintance, much less a friend of ten plus years. He was a stranger, cold and distant, the antithesis of the James she'd known not so long ago. And all her attempts at resurrecting what little life, if any, remained in the bond they'd once shared had been met with forced smiles and guarded eyes. But sadly, that was not the worst. She'd rather those stilted pedestrian conversations than the sheer nothingness that had grown between them, and existed still.

"My life has been quite hectic these past several years." He didn't quite meet her gaze and made no effort to expound on the nature of this "hectic" life, which now hadn't any room for her.

"Too busy for me?" Despite her efforts to keep things light, all the years of bottled up longing, frustration and anguish managed to seep its way into every word.

Years ago, he'd made it a point to make room for her in his life. When she was twelve, he had taught her to ride astride against Thomas's objections months after she'd been thrown from her mare and broken her arm. And how could she forget how he'd taken the blame when she'd broken her mother's favorite Wedgwood vase? And when her brother and Alex had taken to teasingly calling her "beanpole," he had nicknamed her "peaches." He'd claimed it was for her peaches and cream complexion, and for weeks after Missy hadn't walked, she'd floated. He'd been the man of her dreams come to vivid, intoxicating life.

It had taken only one single misguided moment to ruin all of it, she thought, recalling the deafening silence that had accompanied them on their long walk back to the house . . . after the kiss. Silly girl.

James visibly swallowed as his gaze flitted about the room. After a restless search, his regard returned to settle on her.

"That's not it at all," he said, his voice strained.

"Then what is it?" With a naturalness borne of habit, Missy reached out and touched his arm. James jerked sharply back from her touch.

Even before his arrival that morning, James had known this confrontation was inevitable and had anticipated it like a murderer welcomes his punishment. She'd met him at the front entrance, a new sultry air exuding from her, no doubt affected just to tempt and torment him. As if she hadn't already been desirable enough. She'd had a look in her eye that told him, come hell or high water, she'd trap him alone this weekend. He'd decided to make it easy for her, easily extricating himself from the company of her brother and Cartwright, who remained down at the stables. Best to get the whole thing done with, and hopefully peace of mind— if not body—would be his reward.

But as he stared into her eyes, he silently cursed himself for what he had to do. Causing Missy pain could—and should— put a man to shame. But he had no other choice but to discourage her. Nothing had changed in the years since her debut. Despite the intense pull of attraction he had for her, his future wife would not expect love or fidelity. Missy would expect all that and then the moon.

Then of course he had Armstrong to think of. Although their friendship had met with several challenges over the years, their bond had grown only stronger after each adversity. But the durability of that bond would snap as easily as thread catching on something sharp if he dared to make any overtures toward his friend's sister, even in the name of courtship.

James had been at Armstrong's side and matched him

step for step in living up to the label of unrepentant rakehell. He could hardly blame his friend for his opposition to any match between them. In any case, Armstrong's gratitude to Granville had blinded him to all other suitors. Not that James remotely thought of himself in that light. Quite the opposite. He was as unsuitable for Missy as a man could be.

This all would have been so much easier if he didn't have to see her at all. Lord, if not for the insistence of Lady Armstrong, he'd have dispensed with the visits to Stoneridge Hall altogether. Anything to keep temptation out of arm's reach.

He had to think of her and do the right thing. The gentlemanly thing. Composing his expression, he regarded her somberly. "I'm sorry, my reaction was uncalled for. But truly, I'm not avoiding you. It's simply that in the natural course of life, our relationship was bound to change."

"Yes, *that* I quite understand. What I don't understand is why our friendship should diminish altogether."

The note of hurt in her voice had him clearing the thickness in his throat while reminding himself again he was doing this for her. "But you must understand that we are bound to grow apart. Your thoughts and energies should be directed at finding someone suitable to marry. One of the fine gentlemen of the *ton*." Though the very thought of her directing her attentions at Granville or any of those wild bucks brought him little ease. Ruthlessly, he squashed those feelings.

"Would you consider yourself a fine gentleman?" she asked softly, staring up at him, chestnut tendrils wisping each creamy cheek.

Her question hit James with the precision of a marksman's shot. Missy in all her forward naivete had been hard enough to resist, but Missy flirting, her beautiful eyes flashing the time-old invitation, was like asking a healthy male with normal sexual desires to cease thinking of sex.

Swiftly, he turned away to gather his wits. For several

seconds he occupied his hands, releasing the death grip he had on the book to return it to its place on the shelf while the intensity of her gaze singed the back of his head.

What could he say that wouldn't cause her more hurt? "No."

"I beg to disagree," she countered just as softly as before.

She might not say so if she knew some of the wicked things he wanted to do to her . . . outside the sanctity of marriage. Moreover, she wasn't looking for a liaison, brief or otherwise. What she wanted was ten times worse. She wanted permanency—marriage and children. What sane man would submit to tying himself down like some hapless fool? None, if he excluded his father from what surely had to be an endless list.

"It doesn't matter what you believe." Or what she said or did, he would remain strong.

She advanced toward him until she stood near. So close that the ruffled flounces on her yellow skirt brushed his trousered legs, and the tips of her breasts hovered only inches from his chest. Her high, firm—

He gave his head a mental shake in an effort to stop the direction of his lurid thoughts. Lusting after Armstrong's virginal sister wasn't only highly inappropriate, it was dangerous. No woman was worth the sacrifice of the friendship with a man as close to him as a flesh and blood brother.

"Do you know what I believe we should do?" she asked, all innocent seduction. She regarded his mouth with such stark desire, had he been tinder he would have burst into flames.

Tamping down a surge of unwanted lust, James wished the sight of her didn't remind him just how long it had been since he himself had enjoyed the pleasures of the flesh. Something he fully intended to rectify the moment he set foot back in London.

"Nothing. We should do nothing, Missy." Was that his voice, strangled and weak?

Life, at times, was patently unfair, he concluded, taking in the length of her slender body. She was exquisite from her jaw-dropping face, to her small, perfectly shaped breasts, and a waist he could easily span with his hands. Memories of shapely calves and ankles peeping out from beneath her riding habit flitted through his brain. And he could well imagine—*had imagined*—gently curving hips, and long slender thighs beneath the layers of her frothy skirt.

Blast! Why did it have to be this hard? And in every conceivable way.

Smiling as if she knew something he didn't, she reached up with white slender fingers and stroked the taut line of his jaw. He gave an involuntary flinch and took a quick step back to dislodge her hand, his breath a harsh puff of air.

"I believe I spoiled things between us, kissing you like that. I readily admit I was young and foolish. I don't believe I even opened my mouth, did I?"

For a moment, James couldn't think of one sound reason not to pounce on her and take her on the floor. Then reality seeped in to the only area in his brain not listening to his cock.

"That's enough, Missy," he said in a stern, reprimanding voice.

"Enough of what?" she asked and ran the tip of her tongue along the lower curve of her lip, before worrying its cherry lushness in deep concentration.

James stood frozen. Mesmerized.

It required considerable effort, but he managed to drag his gaze from her mouth after a telling pause. He feared if he didn't remove himself from her immediate proximity, his state of arousal would grow too obvious to conceal. And her scent, a faint wisp of lilacs, had already enveloped his senses and was fogging his usually lucid mind with lust.

Crossing the red-and-black Oriental rug spread beneath a small sitting area in the corner of the dome-shaped room, James took a seat in an armchair beside the stone fireplace. He didn't intend to abandon their discussion; she'd just hunt him down, relentless as ever. At least seated, his body's reaction to her would be hidden from view. No need to hand deliver her the weapon to bring about his own doom.

Missy stood where he had left her, perfectly still, her expression uncertain for a moment. Then, as if finding her resolve, she marched over and took a seat on the adjacent blue damask sofa.

She stared him square in the eye. "As I was saying before, I believe my impetuousness has been the cause of our distance. But I believe I've come up with a solution of sorts." Then her expression softened and her voice dropped to a near whisper. "If we were to do it one more time, you know, clear the air as it were, we could end much of the curiosity."

If her suggestion had been issued solely to discomfit him into tongue-tied silence, she could easily claim success. "And whose curiosity are you speaking of?" he finally asked, his tone a quiet rumble.

She had the grace to look sheepish. "Well, I suppose mine."

Proper young ladies did not proposition men. It was unseemly. And entirely too tempting. James was torn. Torn between the desire to haul her onto his lap and have her satisfy the fire raging inside his trousers, or putting her over his knee to give her the spanking she had obviously lacked as a child.

He did neither. Instead, he shifted uncomfortably in his seat. Either option would likely end the same way. With her moaning beneath him.

"Missy, this is complete nonsense." His agitation and her closeness brought him to his feet once again, to cross the length of the room and perch himself against the mahogany desk.

A lengthy silence followed as she thoughtfully regarded him.

"You would not do it for the sake of our friendship?" She rose from her seat.

James steeled himself as she advanced upon him. The cadence of her gait caused her skirt to billow in her wake, and brought to mind the gracefulness of a young gazelle. A young gazelle in heat. Without an ounce of shame, his member twitched again.

"Is it because of my brother?" She peered up at him with those gorgeous slate blue eyes.

He averted his gaze in an effort to cool his ardor, and found himself staring at the large oil painting of the late Viscount Phillip Armstrong hanging on the dark-paneled wall. He must have been in his forties when he sat for the portrait, his dark hair sprinkled with gray and fine wrinkles fanning the corners of his piercing blue eyes. What would he think of his eldest daughter's boldness and her choice in husbands? On both counts, James hardly thought he'd be pleased.

Directing a steely gaze back to her, he said, "You're forcing me to be more plainspoken than I would have liked. As I told you in the past, while I have great affection for you, it has never risen to the level of anything remotely romantic." Unless thoughts of stripping her naked and feasting on her delectable flesh could be considered romantic.

"So are you not curious at all? Your feelings for me have remained the same? That of a sister?"

"That's correct."

He gave the response with the sort of haste only the guilty employ when facing execution. A convincing liar he was not.

"Are you quite certain?"

A look of disbelief flared in his pale blue eyes. He thought her impertinent, but if she failed, she'd seriously have to consider a proposal from someone else if she wanted to marry at all. A more despairing thought she couldn't imagine but sadly a possibility she had to entertain.

"Truly, I've had quite enough of this," he growled, and then made a move as if to brush past her, his face a formidable mask of barely contained emotion.

She made an instinctive move to stop him. Their torsos collided, the tips of her breasts flush with the solid wall of his chest. The pleasure staggered her, the contact exquisite. His hands came up, but whether to push her away or pull her near she would never know, for he seemed to catch himself, dropping them to his sides as he took a cautious step back.

"One kiss, James, how could it possibly hurt?" Missy had never known the motivating power of desperation, fear, and waning hope until that precise moment. Until her audacious dare saturated the air in something thick and fiery hot.

His expression remained impassive and only the tight tick of his jaw conveyed the tenuous hold he had on his composure. Without saying a word, he stared down at her upturned face.

At length, he asked, "And after, what then?"

"I guess that will depend on our response. Were we to enjoy ourselves and be willing to explore the possibility of pursuing a more, er, intimate friendship, then perhaps you'd be in agreement to remain in London and participate in the London Season."

He regarded her with cold, flat eyes. "No."

"I see," she said, only slightly put off by his biting response. If he truly saw her in the light of a sister, surely he would have jumped at the opportunity to prove it. She didn't think a kiss would have been too much of a hardship to accomplish that end. It is not as if they had never kissed before. Perhaps, he was afraid one kiss would not be enough.

His refusal gave her hope.

James's fists contracted spasmodically at his side. Missy was certain at that moment he'd like nothing better than to throttle her. Well, his days of steering the course of their relationship were over. She refused to waste one more year waiting for the man she loved to realize how perfect they would be together. Something potent existed between them. She'd known it since the age of sixteen. And it was that potent, indefinable something that had kept her from losing all hope over the arid years. No, as of today she planned to assume control. Ruthless, seductive control.

"One day you will proposition the wrong man," he bit out coldly.

"Or the right one." Offering him a small smile, she then pivoted on her kid leather heel and quit the room.

Chapter Two

"Armstrong will have you hanged, drawn, and quartered if you so much as touch her."

James's head snapped in the direction of the voice of Alex Cartwright. His friend sauntered into the library and dropped into the rococo-styled winged-back chair.

"I passed Missy as she was leaving," Cartwright elaborated, making no attempt to stifle a highly amused smile.

Sending him a disgruntled glance, James made his way back to his recently vacated chair to settle in with a weary sigh. "It's his sister he need concern himself with. I'm certainly not the problem."

Cartwright chuckled. "So, have you properly discouraged her? Any hope she'll accept Granville's suit—or that of any of the other dozen gentlemen who have requested her hand?"

James emitted a humorless laugh. "I quashed any hopes of marriage between *us*, which is all I can do. I can't very well force her to accept proposals from men she has no desire to wed, even Granville." He detested the way he uttered the man's name as if it were an invective.

"Well as long as you remain unwed, I doubt she'll seriously consider another."

A fact that should have saddened James, but failed miserably in that regard. But truly, a married Missy would be far less dangerous than the one who plagued him now.

"I'll say one thing for Missy, she's certainly loyal and tenacious if nothing else." Regarding him from beneath a shiny black lock of hair, Cartwright remarked, his gray eyes sparking with a speculative gleam. "I must admit, I'm surprised you aren't the least bit tempted. Why, before her debut, the two of you were thick as thieves."

"Yes, my mistake," James grumbled, leaning forward to prop his forearms on his thighs.

"Mistake?"

"Well, isn't it obvious? I took pity on her. She was painfully thin, awkward, shy *and* young when we met. Lord, the poor child had just lost her father. I merely intended to bring her out a bit, put a smile back on her face. If I'd had the slightest notion a little attention would all result in this . . ." And they both were well aware of just what *this* was. Missy still infatuated. Missy still pining for him. And worse still, Missy unwed and going into her *fourth* Season. Lord, she shouldn't have required a third much less a fourth.

Cartwright gave a short, dry laugh. "Well you did an admirable job. Armstrong should be thanking you instead of bemoaning the fact she believes herself in love with you."

Believes? James had to stop the reflexive raising of his eyebrow, quickly thrusting aside his momentary affront at the word. "Regardless, she's an innocent *and* his bloody sister. Each would be a disaster in and of itself, but together it's nothing short of suicide. Anyway, she's hardly my type," James scoffed, flicking a dismissive hand for additional effect. The more he'd repeated it over the years, the easier the lie had rolled off his tongue.

People could say what they would about him, he didn't particularly care, but they could never say with any veracity that he dallied with innocent, well-bred women. And he certainly wouldn't start now, no matter what or *who* the provocation.

Cartwright's brow shot up as he snorted in disbelief. "Except for the ailing and elderly—and even there I'm sure some exceptions could be made—any man who has red or, more importantly," this he said in an arid tone, "blue blood running in their veins would snatch her up if she'd just give the word. She has everything—beauty, lineage, and money. She's any man's fantasy come true."

Experiencing an odd tightening in his chest, James eyed his friend. "Even yours?" The two words felt wrenched from his throat, sounding overly harsh and accusatory to his own ears. He immediately wished he could call back the question. He wasn't some jealous suitor, and certainly didn't want to come across as such.

Cartwright gave a short dry laugh as he rose to his feet and headed toward the sideboard, which held a lone decanter of brandy and several tumblers. "If she wasn't like a sister to me, I'm quite certain she would be."

James's smile touched only his mouth. He had thought much the same until she'd started giving him cockstands. Perhaps the difference being Cartwright had bounced Missy on his knee when she was still in nappies. He and Armstrong had attended Eton together as boys. James had met the men years later while studying at Cambridge, where the three had formed a deep bond of friendship.

The prior day, he and Cartwright had joined Armstrong at his country estate in Devon, the seat of his viscountcy, for the viscountess's annual winter ball. James knew they were not invited solely for the purpose of male companionship or their rapier wit. As one of the most sought after bachelors in all of London (well, certainly since he'd managed to replenish the Armstrong coffers) his friend's motives were purely mercenary. By forcing them to attend his mother's ball, Armstrong effectively deflected some of the attentions of the marriage-minded mothers and their daughters, especially as James would someday become the sixth Earl of Windmere. Out-ranking Armstrong, James was a much more desirable target for those who considered a man's title the height of his distinction. And Cartwright, despite his status as second son to the Duke of Hastings, had enough money to placate many of the socially ambitious mamas, and more than enough good looks to enamor their aristocratic daughters.

Cartwright eyed him and continued. "I believe Missy would make you a fine wife. Certainly a far better one than you deserve," he chided. "But under vastly different circumstances." Picking up the decanter, he jerked his head toward the brandy, and asked, "Will you have one?"

James nodded absently. "Such circumstances as . . . ?" he asked, knowing full well it was a mistake to continue along that particular line of questioning.

"First, I'd have to set aside the fact that your interest in women is notoriously short-lived and Armstrong would never countenance you as his brother-in-law. That said, under the condition you believed in the notion of fidelity, and actually had the capacity to fall in love."

For some odd reason, Cartwright's comments stung. He had the capacity to love. Just not a woman in the "till death do us part" sense. Moreover, he had yet to meet a gentleman who practiced fidelity—and only a handful of women for that matter. At least the married women of his acquaintance.

"Well I have no intention of marrying her. Who are you now, the *ton*'s matchmaker? I daresay I can choose my own wife. And at a time I require one," he said, allowing his sarcasm free rein.

His own father hadn't married until the age of thirty-five and James could not conceive of one reason he shouldn't follow in his example. Which gave him another seven years until he needed to make any such decision. When he did marry, his wife and children would reside in the country, while he discreetly kept a mistress in Town. That was how it was done, his parents being the perfect example.

"Yes, given your views on marriage, I imagine you will choose someone like Lady Victoria, the venerable ice maiden." Cartwright headed back to the sitting area, drinks in hand.

"At least with her, a man knows what he's getting." James accepted the glass from his friend, immediately tipping it to his mouth for a swallow.

He'd rather a passionless wife from the start than have her turn into a cold fish after she'd produced the requisite heir and the spare, just as his mother had done. He'd see the earldom pass to his younger brother, Christopher, before he'd become a man like his father, reduced to beggaring himself for sexual favors from his own wife. He'd never sacrifice his self-respect on the altar of marriage to the illusion of romantic love.

"At least you'd never have to worry about being cuckolded if you married her. I'm sure she'll find the begetting of heirs distasteful enough," Cartwright said with a laugh, settling back in his seat, his long legs stretched wide before him.

Lady Victoria, the youngest daughter of the Marquess of Cornwall, was said to have put the ice in icicle—or so many gentlemen claimed. With countless proposals over the course of five Seasons, bets were being made at White's and Boodle's as to whom her mother would force her to marry and at what age. Others wagered she'd defy her mother and would end up being relegated to the shelf.

James thought the lot of them spiteful and cruel. He personally liked Lady Victoria. Not because she was beautiful, but because she had never displayed an infinitesimal amount of interest in him as a man. Unlike most of the man-hungry misses of the *ton,* she made him feel he could lower his guard in her company. With her, he was safe.

"At least I'd be assured my heir was truly my heir," James said wryly.

"Is that your fear? That your wife will try to pass another man's by-blow off as yours?"

"As it will be the *only* thing I will require of her, it would be nice if I had some amount of certainty the child was mine." James downed the rest of his drink with one long swallow and then pushed to his feet. "Now, if you'll excuse me, I'm going to retire to my guest chamber until supper is served."

Cartwright tipped his glass toward him, a small smile playing across his lips. "I suggest you use the servants' stairs if you wish to avoid a certain miss fairly haunting the halls."

Before James could respond, Armstrong appeared in the doorway, a glove dangling from one hand, while he removed the other with short, deft tugs.

"Good, you're here," he said, pinning James with a green-eyed stare. "We need to discuss Missy."

Good Lord, what now?

Dressed in a hunter green coat and breeches, and a pair of scuffed knee-high leather boots, it appeared his friend had been riding. A fact confirmed once he started toward James, bringing with him a faint whiff of horseflesh and the outdoors.

A sideways glance and a casual inclination of the viscount's head served as his greeting to Cartwright. He halted in front of the low center table and tossed his gloves on the polished redwood surface. Standing opposite him and close enough to note the faint tick of his jaw, James raised one eyebrow in query.

"A change of plans," Armstrong said in that clipped manner of his.

James blinked. "Pardon?"

"This thing with my sister. You keeping your distance until she finds a husband."

"Ah yes, the brilliant plan. It's been a smashing success, wouldn't you agree?" Cartwright—always one who loathed omission from discussions of this sort—chimed in.

James and Armstrong treated him to similar dark glares. In response, Cartwright lifted his shoulders in an innocent shrug while trying to maintain a guileless expression.

With an acute sense of apprehension, James directed his attention back to Armstrong and asked, "What of Missy?"

For a moment, his friend said nothing, merely watched him. When he commenced speaking, he did so slowly, as if a great deal of thought had gone into every word. "After all this time, it's quite obvious your absence has done little to diminish her affections. In fact, I think she believes herself more in love with you than ever. Dug in her heels is what she's done. Do you realize she's turned down over twenty proposals of marriage since her debut?"

That many? A rush of heat suffused James's face as if the blame could be laid squarely at his door. Thrusting his hands deep into his trouser pockets, he widened his stance but didn't respond.

"My mother will not allow Emily to debut this year with Missy still unsettled. If I don't act now, I'll have all three of my sisters out in the marriage market tripping over each other."

"What more do you want me to do? What more can I do? Until yesterday, I hadn't seen her since your mother's birthday celebration, which was almost seven months back. And if you recall, it was at the viscountess's insistence that I attended. Should I now take up residence in France?"

"The Duke has a flat in Paris. He'd never let it to me, his own flesh and blood, but perhaps if you asked him . . . ?"

James ignored Cartwright, finding little humor in his attempt to interject wit into the exchange.

Armstrong's mouth edged up at the corners. "I assure you, nothing so extreme. What I'm suggesting is that we reverse the strategy. Your absence has only made you into a figure in her head. Grander than life, like some fictional romantic hero. She needs to see you out in Society at all those damn events charming and flirting with women. Beautiful and attractive ones. She's never seen that side of you."

James knew what he meant. She'd never seen the rake in him. The charmer. The seducer. Not that he'd ever had to do much seducing. Then of course, months later, when it was over and the thrill of the affair was over, he could walk away without once looking back.

"Perhaps then," Armstrong said, continuing to press his point, "she'll realize how ill suited the two of you are and hopefully cast Granville in a better light. Though why in the world she has done nothing to encourage him is beyond me. I mean, the man's heir to a damned dukedom. And it's not as though he's old and decrepit. Most women would give up their best face cream to be in her position."

Good God, the way he went on about Granville, one would think the man was a bloody saint. Being heir to a dukedom was simply a happenstance of birth, not indicative of a man's core character. And what the hell was Armstrong thinking in asking him to spend an entire Season in such close proximity to Missy? The effort to keep his hands off her was hard enough. Damn hard.

"You've always had a soft spot for her and I know you want her happiness and well-being just as much as I do. I realize I'm imposing on our friendship again, but I want my sister married and settled by year's end. All the better if it's Granville." Armstrong paused, and drew a breath. "Why don't you begin tomorrow evening at my mother's ball?"

Swallowing hard, James met his gaze without blinking. This would all be for her long-term benefit. *His* misery would be short-lived. When put to him like that, he could scarcely refuse. "I will do what I can."

A smile lit Armstrong's face. "Good. I knew I could count on you. And knowing you as I do, I have every confidence you'll succeed."

The evening of the ball, air so cold it would make Jack Frost weep, gave winter a glacial presence. Even the snowflakes long enraptured by the season refused to fall.

Inside the warm, gray stone structure of Stoneridge Hall, Missy remained by her mother's side as they greeted the last recently thawed guest in the queue, the dowager Countess of Stockwell.

For what seemed an eternity, the dowager recounted in excruciating detail every bump and gully she'd encountered on her harrowing journey to Stoneridge Hall. If Missy had not been aware that she lived a short distance down the road on the neighboring estate, she'd have sworn the dowager had traveled days and ridden through Siberia on a hunger-weakened reindeer to get there.

Thankfully, the finely plumed headdress of Lady Bailey, a peer and counterpart of the dowager, captured Lady Stockwell's feckless attention. Halting in midsentence, the dowager's brown-eyed gaze pinned her next quarry. Quickly excusing herself, her steps sure and swift, she hastened toward the refreshment table where Lady Bailey could easily be captured innocently sipping a glass of punch.

In unison, Missy and the viscountess expelled heartfelt sighs of relief.

"I don't believe I have ever met anyone quite so longwinded," the viscountess said. She turned and stared down the long stretch of gleaming marble floors leading to towering front doors. "I do hope all is well with Lucky."

Missy hoped for her brother's sake that the horse would live up to its name. Her brother's prized mare had gone into labor late that morning, but by the afternoon it had become evident there were difficulties with the birth. When the men had heard the news, they had rushed down to the stables where they remained ever since. That had been four long hours ago, and one tortuous hour since their first guests had heralded in.

Fearing if she spoke, she'd reveal the depth of her despair, Missy nodded mutely in response. She desperately hoped to dance with James this evening. When he returned to London, she didn't know when she'd see him, if at all during the coming Season. With only two days at her disposal, she had to make every minute count.

"Now it is time for you to go dance and enjoy yourself." The viscountess smiled and flicked her fingers in a shooing motion. "Claire appears to be having a fine time with Mr. Finley, and I know many of the gentlemen are waiting patiently for you to conclude your hostess duties so they may accompany you to the dance floor."

Missy spotted her friend executing the steps to a quadrille. She looked lovely in her pale blue taffeta gown, a beautiful strand of pearls adorning her neck. Claire, the only daughter of Baron and Baroness Rutland, lived on the neighboring estate to the south. They had become fast friends as children, Claire claiming seniority by one year.

"Lady Armstrong."

With her attention elsewhere, Missy had failed to see Lord Edward Crawley's approach. Broad-shouldered and husky, he topped her five-foot-nine-inch stature by no more than two inches and wore his light brown hair, in her opinion, overly long.

"Good evening, Lord Crawley. I expect you are here seeking my daughter." The viscountess blessed him with a brilliant smile. He responded with a white, winsome smile of his own, his tawny eyes respectfully admiring the viscountess, resplendent in her royal blue satin gown. Her mother looked far too beautiful to have given birth to four children, and certainly too youthful to have a son just three years short of his thirtieth.

Lord Crawley's gaze then arrested on Missy and he did nothing to disguise his romantic interest. "That is, if Miss Armstrong will grant me this dance?" he said, with a gallant bow and a proffered arm.

After a quick glance at her mother, who inclined her head in approval, she accepted his white-gloved hand, allowing him to lead her to the dance floor where a waltz had just commenced.

"You look lovely this evening," he said, drawing her into his arms.

"Thank you," Missy replied, her tone polite. With experienced ease and surprising grace for a man with his muscled stature, he whirled her into the throng of swirling gowns of every conceivable color and hue, and pristine black dress coats, trousers and waistcoats.

Their fathers had been peers in the House of Lords but the frequency of their meetings had seen a marked decrease after her father's death ten years prior of an apoplexy fit. They'd renewed their acquaintance during the course of her first Season. Missy knew with but the slightest bit of encouragement from her, Lord Crawley would ask Thomas for her hand. However, he fell into the vast category of all men other than James—the group who had a better chance of ridding London of its fog than gaining her affections.

As they moved smoothly on the polished floors, Missy began to feel ill at ease under his admiring regard. As they were of similar height, in order to avoid eye contact, she directed her attention over his shoulder and took an idle tour of the hall.

Globe lamps illuminated the three-storied room, its cream walls appearing yellow under their warm glow. Ornamental shrubbery obscured the three-piece orchestra discreetly tucked away near the French doors leading to the walking gardens. A plethora of potted plants and fluted vases containing daisies and lilies dotted the circumference of the room infusing it with a fragrant scent. Her focus drifted toward the double doors to the hall entrance and skidded to a halt. Her heart lurched and her breath hitched softly.

James had arrived.

In that moment, their eyes connected.

James's body instantly responded to Missy's gaze. He wanted to look away but couldn't will his eyes to obey. A feeling of drowning in the fathomless sea of her gray-blue eyes rolled over him in a wave. She was breathtaking—and dancing in the arms of another man. A niggling sense of irritation had him clenching his jaw.

Crawley. A more pompous fool he would never meet. The few times he'd run into him in the halls of Cambridge, Crawley had impressed him as being one of the privileged *ton* who exalted his station over those he considered his minions.

"Missy looks ravishing. Wouldn't you agree, Rutherford?" Cartwright spoke sotto voce, sending him a sidelong glance, the semblance of a smile ghosting his dark features.

James ignored his knowing look and did his level best to keep his expression impassive, helpless to do anything else but continue to watch her.

"Will you look at Missy. She has half the men fairly champing at the bit eager to make her their wife." Arm-

strong said with a sigh worthy of a Shakespearean player at
St. James Theatre.

With the knowledge he had been doing little else since
they'd arrived, James wrenched his gaze away from her and
turned to Armstrong. His friend appeared more at ease now
the ordeal with his horse was over, his features having lost
the strained look of worry. The tired mare had delivered a
healthy foal just the hour before, and they had left the foal
nursing comfortably with its mother.

"I wonder if Granville has shown." Armstrong gazed
about the hall.

"You need only follow the trail of women and he's sure to
be holding court at center stage," James said with a hint of
unintended wryness in his tone. He had nothing against the
man. Granville had certainly been good to Armstrong after
his father had died. It had been he who had introduced his
friend to Lord Bradford, who subsequently aided Armstrong
in his financial recovery.

Granville was exceedingly well liked by both men and
women, and not only because of his rank in Society. What
was not to like? He was amiable, good-looking and intelligent, although somewhat guarded at times. And the latter
certainly wasn't a crime as people had said the same of him.

It was just that . . . James immediately closed off the direction of his thoughts. Further dissecting his reasons would
do him little good.

"Oh yes, there he is," Armstrong said, directing his attention to the south end of the room.

Following his friend's stare, James spotted Granville in
the thick of a mass of hooped skirts and dangling dance
cards, his dark head visible above the throng.

At that moment, Missy danced into his line of vision, instantly knocking thoughts of the earl from his mind completely. Against his will—and going against every bit of

common sense he possessed—her allure drew his attention once again and he sensed danger lurked perilously close.

Her hair, pinned loosely at her crown to allow burnished chestnut curls to brush her neck and bare shoulders, looked soft and shiny, unlike the pomade-laden stiffness of most of the other ladies present. She wore a pale blue gown, the bodice lovingly hugging her slender torso, the cut-off-the-shoulder neckline revealing an expanse of creamy, porcelain skin. In the short, and long, she looked magnificent. And, by the openly admiring stares being cast her way, he was only one of the many men who had taken due notice. Like hounds on the prowl, they circled the periphery and watched as if getting ready to pounce.

Unfortunately, the men's late arrival and relative anonymity didn't last long. Within minutes of making their appearance, they were surrounded by a gaggle of mothers and their debutante daughters. *This* was what James dreaded most about these affairs, the lack of subtlety had become not only accepted by the *ton,* but expected.

Lady Stanton initiated the barrage with her two less-than-comely daughters whose names failed to stay in his memory moments later. And Lady Randall was not to be outdone as she dragged a chubby, sallow-faced girl whom she introduced as her niece, Miss Margaret Crawford. The poor girl only made fleeting eye contact with the three men before resuming her intent regard of the wood planks of the highly beeswaxed floor.

Between polite nods and feigned smiles, James searched the large hall for venues of escape. As eligible, titled gentlemen were not so easy to come by, he had to get away before the crowd grew any larger. Spotting the viscountess at the opposite end of the room gave him the perfect excuse.

"If you will pardon me, ladies, I'd be remiss in my duties if I didn't pay my respects to our hostess."

Quick to seize on the opportunity for a clean exit, Armstrong echoed his sentiments. Before anyone could blink, their long strides had eaten up sufficient distance to leave the growing crowd of crestfallen women behind. A look back revealed Cartwright had been less fortunate. Lightly palming the pale elbow of one of Lady Stanton's daughters, he proceeded to escort the tittering miss over to the refreshment table.

James smiled. It was Cartwright's just deserts for needling him.

James looked spectacular in his formal wear. Like many of the other gentlemen present, he'd opted for white tie and tails. A fine wool coat with a satin collar and lapels further accentuated his broad shoulders. A strip of black satin arrowed down the sides of his trousers, which skimmed long, lean legs. As he and Thomas crossed the room and navigated the treacherous waters of marriage-hungry debutantes, their striking but contrasting good looks and elegant appearance had ladies' necks craning, and their fans and eyes fluttering.

Missy had never been so anxious for a dance to conclude. While she tracked his progress, happily noting it ended at her mother's side, the strains of the waltz played in joyous finality. After declining Lord Crawley's persistent offer for refreshments with an amiable smile, she hastened toward the men, along the way turning down another half dozen invitations to dance.

"As you can see, the men are here," the viscountess remarked, upon her arrival.

"I hardly think we were missed from the bevy of gentlemen vying for Missy's attention," Thomas teased.

"You mean Lord Crawley? You know quite well he is an acquaintance, nothing more." Even as she made light of her brother's comment, her senses were finely attuned to James standing silent at his side. She didn't want him to fear there were rivals for her affections. She was his. Always had been and would always be—if only he'd allow it to be so.

James made a sound in his throat, his narrowed gaze flitting to Lord Crawley, who stood with three other gentlemen, his regard fixed on Missy. When the brawny lord noticed their accumulative regard, he held up his glass in salutation. Thomas nodded his acknowledgment. James's jaw tightened.

"Which gentleman present this evening wouldn't find Millicent absolutely breathtaking?" the viscountess said, her face beaming with maternal pride.

Thomas smiled and Missy flushed. James's gaze flickered to her before he quickly glanced away. All the while, his expression remained impassive.

Taking a swift look around, the viscountess said, "Thomas, I do believe I see Charlotte Ridgeway. That pink gown is quite becoming on her, wouldn't you agree?"

Thomas chuckled wryly. The viscountess was not known for her subtlety, and Missy was certain that her mother's relationship with Lady Ridgeway had something to do with her timely observation. It was well known that Lady Charlotte had a *tendre* for her brother. With a mock bow, a tight smile, and a hard, quick look at James, Thomas obliged his mother and left to seek out the lady in question.

"And James," the viscountess said, turning to him, "since it appears you have frightened away the gentlemen with that glower of yours, why don't you take my daughter on a spin about the floor? She has grown quite accomplished in your absence." The word absence held a note of reprimand, undoubtedly in reference to the prior two years he'd begged off from attending the annual event. Her mother did, however, quirk her mouth in a manner that had a softening effect. Not quite a command, but close.

A dark flush stained James's dimpled cheeks as he inclined his head toward Missy and extended his hand. She could barely contain her joy as he escorted her back to the dance floor. He drew her into his arms, taking one of her hands in his, placing the other one circumspectly on her waist. She fairly shivered at the touch. Keeping his head stiffly erect, he stared fixedly over the top of hers and commenced the waltz.

A peek through a wealth of dark lashes revealed a rather stern-faced James, his gaze directed off in the distance. Then, as if he felt the weight of her stare, his gaze flickered down to her upturned face. Not even a smile broke his granite features. He must still be miffed with her over the incident in the library. Which meant only one thing; she'd simply have to redouble her efforts.

"My mother was right. You look absolutely forbidding this evening." She kept her tone light and teasing.

"You know these are hardly the sort of affairs I enjoy," he said in a remote voice.

"And just what kind of affairs do you enjoy?"

At her question, his hand tightened on her waist, bringing her closer to his hard frame. Something dark flashed in his eyes.

His response was slow in coming. "Certainly none that can be spoken about in mixed company."

"Perhaps it is something I, too, would enjoy."

James, a gentleman known for his grace as a faultless dancer, misstepped. It was a small enough error the casual observer would have overlooked, but not someone who had committed every nuance of his demeanor of the past ten years to memory.

"Yes, it appears you are very eager to learn"—he subjected her to a hard, almost angry stare, dropping his gaze to linger in the vicinity of her breasts a fraction longer than could be considered polite—"the more basic aspects of life."

Heat led a charge up from her chest to her face but instinct and his firm lead glided her across the floor. When the dance concluded, instead of escorting her back to her mother's side, James clasped her lightly by the elbow, and led her toward the arched doorway hidden from the rest of the hall by two oversized potted ferns. With his head high and stiffly erect, he steered her down the hall and into a small study.

Trembling with a mixture of trepidation and excitement, Missy was only too happy to follow his lead . . . once again.

Chapter Three

In the dimly lit study where the soft hiss of a fire dying played its own tune, James placed her solidly in front of him. "One kiss, you said. Well, one kiss is what you'll get if it will end this."

She stared at him with big round eyes. After a moment, a nervous half smile tipped the edges of her lush mouth.

Oh God, her mouth. Oh hell, her mouth.

What he intended was sheer madness. He knew in that moment he should halt this silly game of hers. But it was either this or commit unspeakable acts with her out on the dance floor. He could almost hear the report of the pistol when Armstrong buried a bullet in his chest. At this point, he would do anything to end her flirtation. Her infatuation. The bloody chase. In this instance, the ends did indeed justify the means.

One kiss.

Surely he had enough willpower to remain impassive and unmoved for the duration of one bloody kiss? Good Lord, no matter what other appeal she possessed, Missy was a virgin. He preferred his women with much more expertise in the sexual arena.

But what she'd lacked in experience she'd made up in

passion. He dismissed the provoking voice playing tantalizing games with his mind.

"Well?" Now it was his turn to challenge her.

"Are you not going to kiss me?" She shifted on her feet, looking younger and more uncertain than her years.

"This kiss was not my idea. You're the one who won't stop until we dispel the mystery of whatever you think is between us. Go ahead, dispel away."

They stared at each other for several more seconds before Missy stepped forward and leaned until the silk corsage of her gown met the wool and satin of his jacket. James tried to ignore the shock of desire that pierced him and had him again rethinking his stratagem.

Tipping her head back, she placed her hands upon his shoulders, and when her eyes fluttered close, touched her lips to his. He remained still, afraid to move a single muscle—at least of those he could control. She pressed her lips more firmly against his closed mouth, her breasts flush against his chest. A jolt of lust coursed down to his loins.

Enough! He couldn't draw a decent sanity-giving breath. He lifted his hands to remove hers. There, she'd received her kiss. Now, if God above took pity on him, she'd leave him in peace. But before he could remove the hands from his shoulders, her arms wound tightly about his neck, forcing his head lower. That was when she began the *true* assault.

It was an innocent yet provocative kiss, offered up by soft, closed lips. A primitive hunger twisted his insides into a coiled knot as she moved her mouth sweetly over his. Sweat beaded his temples while he fought for control. Reaching back, he grasped her hands and desperately tried to pry them from around his neck. In response, Missy arched her hips. Through a swatch of cotton and silk, his erection found that inviting notch between her thighs. And just like that, he was lost.

His hands abruptly gave up the fight and cupped the sides of her face, his thumbs stroking the smooth skin of her cheeks. Opening his mouth, he tasted. Heat exploded in him, for what he discovered was she tasted even sweeter than before, her lips soft and luscious. He allowed himself the indulgence of learning the shape and feel of them as he pressed and sipped, his ministrations eliciting tiny gasps and moans. He used that opportunity to ply them apart, plunging his tongue on a voyage of discovery, and reveled when hers swiftly joined. At first, she was tentative in her explorations, but soon participated with a relish that nearly had him completely undone.

She twisted in his arms in mindless abandon, her hands anchored to him like a boat in a turbulent storm, pressing the sweet curves of her breasts against him. James felt branded. He knew he should stop, but the rampaging hunger inside him proved unwilling to cooperate. His hands dropped to grasp her hips and brought her solidly against his throbbing erection.

Soft mewling sounds emerged from her throat on ragged sighs and heady whimpers. He groaned low in his throat, the fires of passion licking close at his heels—no, burning him alive. His hand slid over her quivering stomach up to the underside of her breasts when the distant sound of voices registered in his sluggish senses.

Then awareness hit like a thunderbolt. He was in the study taking untold liberties with the daughter of his hostess and the sister of his friend. The friend who had asked him to discourage her. The consequences of their actions, if discovered, would be enormous.

She stared at him, her eyes unfocused, her lips cherry-red and pouty from his kisses. He hastily set her away.

James tensed as the voices drew closer. After several long moments, they grew distant, eventually dissipating until only the jaunty sounds of a polka and the general rumble of gaiety could be heard. Only then did he allow himself to relax. To breathe. To curse the tent in his trousers. He had far from proven his disinterest.

Guilt gave his voice a hard edge, and unspent lust, a gravelly sound, when he turned to her and said, "There, you got your kiss."

"Yes, I did," she said softly, sounding slightly dazed.

"You're too innocent to know these kinds of kisses mean nothing. It's a man's bodily response to a pretty and willing female."

Her mouth opened, as if to speak, and then snapped shut. She turned and reached for the handle of the door. He closed his hands over her delicate wrists before she could grasp it.

In a hard, cold voice, he said, "I hope you haven't granted other men the same liberties you allowed me tonight. If you have, you'll soon find yourself acquiring a reputation you will not like."

Missy tilted her head to look him square in the eye. "I would never allow just any man those liberties." Her meaning was unmistakable.

James jerked his hand from hers as if he had touched the andiron of a blazing fireplace.

"I expect you to keep your promise, so I expect to see you this Season at *all* the events." The same nervous half smile reappeared on her lips. Opening the door, she checked to ensure no one would witness her departure before slipping out.

James remained rooted in the same spot for another minute, mounting dread consuming him.

Aware that she could not reappear at the ball with her hair mussed and looking as if she'd just been thoroughly kissed,

Missy sought out the ladies' dressing room. It was a room fit for royalty with two large oval gilt-framed mirrors dominating nearly an entire wall. From the corniced ceiling hung a rose crystal chandelier, and beyond the normal trappings was a silk embroidered settee where a woman could take her repose.

Missy observed her reflection and immediately set about smoothing and repinning her hair, then spent several minutes more, grateful for the privacy it afforded to cool the fiery flush in her cheeks.

She reentered the hall feeling somewhat more composed, only to be greeted by the sight of James dancing attendance to Lady Victoria Spencer. The glow of residual passion vanished in that instant. She watched as he leaned down and whispered something into her ear, his dark hair in sharp contrast with Lady Victoria's blond locks. Her throat closed up and a wave of jealousy—the red-hot variety—washed over her.

Her stare should have turned them both to stone. Before she could turn away, his head lifted and he caught her gaze. For a moment, he held her regard, his expression opaque, before turning his attention back to the fair-haired miss at his side.

"I wondered where you had gone."

Missy started at the sound of her friend's voice.

"I see you managed to snag Lord Rutherford for a dance," Claire said, appearing at her side. It was a statement expectant of elaboration.

Missy continued toward the refreshment area, now in desperate need of something to soothe her suddenly parched throat. Claire fell in step with her, their skirts brushing gently as they walked.

"Yes, we danced, but no more beyond that." There was no need to tell her about the kiss and what had occurred in the library the prior day. Since she'd confessed her feelings to Claire at the age of sixteen, her friend hadn't been shy in voicing her misgivings about a match between them and, right now, Missy wasn't in the mood for one of her lectures.

Accepting a glass of punch from the liveried footman posted at the table, Missy offered it to her. Claire declined with a quick shake of her head. "Mr. Finley has already filled my glass twice this evening."

Missy sent her a probing look. Claire remained noncommittal. Unwilling to pry, she took a deep sip of the overly sweet liquid.

After already four years in the marriage-mart, her friend had all but resigned herself to spinsterhood. Why she wasn't married, Missy could not understand. Any gentleman would be lucky to have her as his wife. Claire was pretty, petite and blond. And despite her claims that she could stand to lose a stone, Missy thought her figure lush and curvaceous.

However, after declining a marriage proposal from a baron twice her age in her first Season, a viscount twice-widowed with seven children, and Lord Rudnick, who was rumored to have a penchant for young boys, in the second, Claire had yet to receive another.

"I think you should give up this entire plan of yours. Isn't it enough you've already wasted three perfectly good Seasons pining over a man who, it's obvious, doesn't care a fig about you? If I'd received even half the offers you've received, not only would I be married, but I'd no doubt be expecting my second child by now. For heaven's sakes, at this very moment, you could be the future Duchess of Wiltshire. Isn't it obvious Lord Rutherford is no more ready to settle down than your brother or Lord Alex?" Claire turned and directed a pointed look at James and the marquess's daughter.

While Missy liked Lord Granville very much, she wasn't even close to being in love with him. Moreover, he had yet to actually propose. Oh, he had hinted at it, seeming to deliberate the notion to such a degree, it was clear his heart was not the least involved in whatever decision he should come to.

As for any dalliance between James and Lady Victoria, despite the jealousy still churning her insides, Missy thought it highly unlikely. The woman had never shown an interest in any gentleman since she'd debuted. She was beautiful and excessively refined, but she was cold. Or perhaps cold wasn't the apt term. She was like one of those porcelain dolls, shiny and beautiful with nothing beneath the hard, brittle surface.

"Like most men, James only believes he is not ready for marriage. All he needs is the right woman. I'm sure many thought Lord Neville wasn't destined to marry a gentleman's daughter, then Miss Bash appeared and *voila,* he'll soon be walking down the aisle without a whimper or protest." Which meant, of course, *she* was the right woman for James.

Claire rolled her eyes, shaking her head. "I hope you haven't allowed Miss Bash and Lord Neville to give you false hopes. All things in the matter of the heart are not as simple as their courtship would lead you to believe."

"Whatever is that supposed to mean?"

"That love is not simple."

"How would you know?" Missy asked. Then her eyes widened and she leaned in and whispered, "Have *you* ever been in love?"

Wistfulness clouded Claire's hazel eyes. She studied her blue silk–gloved hands clasped neatly at her waist. After several moments, she peered up at her. "Once—at least I thought I was. It was during my first Season."

The revelation struck Missy momentarily mute. And Claire had not said a word of it to her. "Who was it?" she asked, her tone hushed.

"None of that matters now. What matters is I knew no more about love than I knew about—about midwifery."

"Why won't you tell me who it was? I simply can't believe you would keep it from me."

Claire's winged brow shot up. "I'm sure we don't tell each other *everything*."

A hot blush suffused Missy's cheeks. She allowed the subject to drop without another word.

A moment later, Sir George Clifton claimed Missy for a dance. Like many of the men who had recently returned from the Crimean peninsula, he sported a short beard and a trim mustache. He had gone into the naval services after his attendance at Cambridge, where he and Thomas had become acquainted.

As they glided across the floor, Missy sensed his preoccupation. Although his narrow face wore a smile, a distant quality remained in the fleeting glances he cast ever so often in her direction. This became even more evident as they swept past James and Lady Victoria who, she noted with unwanted rancor, had also taken to the dance floor. For a brief moment, as the two pair glided by one another, the air grew taut as strained glances bumped and then swiveled away. Sir Clifton quickly whisked her in the opposite direction. Their paths never crossed again.

If Missy hadn't had him so consumed with lust and guilt, James might have been able to enjoy the company of Lady Victoria Spencer. But it was all he could do to keep a proper smile pasted on his face and nod in all the right places. After twice being caught staring blankly back at her while she awaited a response to a question or statement she had posed, he'd had to redouble his efforts and be more attentive to her.

James found himself tracking Missy's movements around

the room. Currently she was dancing with Granville, and the fact the knowledge ate away at him in a most unpleasant manner, irritated him. Lust had made a twit of him, he thought in disgust.

Silence.

Lady Victoria regarded him in a particular manner that told him his attention to her had lapsed yet again.

Too embarrassed to ask her to repeat herself for the third time, James merely nodded in hopes that would suffice. In his estimation, most questions asked by ladies could be answered in the affirmative or the negative—that is, with the exception of Missy; her questions were never simple, the answers even less so.

"Really? You appear to protect yours like a gaoler at Newgate," she said.

"Well yes, certainly I do." *What the blazes am I to be protecting?*

"So does that mean you see marriage in the near future? I was under the impression you had no intention of marrying until well into your thirties." Her blue eyes were intent, although her tone conveyed only mild curiosity.

Dear Lord, how had he come to be in a discussion of marriage with the one lady in the room who had expressed little interest in it?

James forced a laugh. "I consider myself too young to be tied down with a wife and children. There will be plenty of time for that when I'm older."

She smiled in response. "Then it would appear we are well suited."

An odd phrasing, he thought, sending her a curious look. However, her expression was as impassive as always. The tension eased from his shoulders.

Lady Victoria's gaze roamed the room. "I am surprised to see Sir Clifton here," she said with an off-handed air. She regarded James. The tilt of her head told him once again, she anticipated some sort of rejoinder.

He obliged. "The man is an M.P., and with his title so recently bestowed by the Queen and his close friendship with Rogers, peer or no peer, no one dares leave him off of their guest list. Do you object to his presence at these Society events? I would be surprised, Lady Victoria, as I never took you for a snob." Her mother, yes. Lady Victoria, no.

She drew herself up, her shoulders back as her spine snapped straight. "Of course I have no objection to his presence. He has just always struck me as a man who loathed the frivolity of the *ton*."

James had to agree with her on that point, but he'd not speculate on the man's motives, so he said nothing. However, the image of Missy dancing in Clifton's arms remained fresh in his mind. Had he, too, been caught up in her spell? It should have alleviated James's guilt about the kiss, knowing he wasn't the first and wouldn't be the last to lose his head, however briefly, over the beautiful minx. Somehow, the thought only served to abrade his already frayed nerves.

Then he heard it, her laugh, light but unrestrained. His head swung in its direction and spied her still in Granville's arms, her head upraised, a wide dazzling smile on her beautiful face. After the kiss they had just shared, she seemed to find it remarkably easy to flirt and turn her considerable charms on another man.

"Miss Armstrong is very beautiful, is she not?"

James turned swiftly. Lady Victoria was watching him closely. If he wasn't careful, people would begin to take notice of his interest.

No! his mind warred in denial. He had no *legitimate* interest in Missy. Just because she'd grown into an utterly desirable young lady and had the misfortune to believe herself in love with him, that didn't mean a thing. He would have to

be insensate not to be tempted. And he was not insensate.
Far from it.

His gaze swung back to observe the lady in question. "To
many, I imagine so," he said, his tone deliberately droll.

Lady Victoria gave a soft tinkling laugh. "Indeed. Lord
Armstrong appears very particular about her suitors. Last
year I heard he discouraged Lord Eldridge and Lord Harts-
mouth."

James chuckled, his spirits lifted for the first time that
evening. He had been present for that particular setdown.
The two men had inquired after her having been introduced
to Missy at some ball. How he'd enjoyed the looks of con-
sternation on their faces when Armstrong had informed
them he'd see them on the field, pistols drawn, before he'd
see either of them courting her.

"I'd have done the same if I had a sister." The men were
nothing but a couple of reprobates out to land themselves an
heiress.

Lady Victoria flicked open her fan, and fluttered it with
an experienced hand. "Well, when Lord Armstrong marries,
I am certain—"

James laughed again, this time tossing his head back and
making enough noise to draw a few glances from the guests
milling about. "You have a better chance of seeing me at the
altar than you do Armstrong."

His friend had become a viscount at the age of seventeen
to an estate mired in debt. He'd had a mother and three
young sisters to support, so perhaps that was why his views
on marriage were even more cynical than James's own. At
least he'd conceded that as heir to the Windmere earldom, it
was his duty to marry at some point. The same couldn't be
said of Armstrong.

Lady Victoria merely smiled while maintaining the gentle
flutter of her fan.

* * *

James climbed the stairs to his chamber in the early hours of the morning after the last of the guests had clambered into their cold carriages spent and weary. He saw no sign of Missy. The relief that washed over him was both humbling and maddening.

The kiss had had him tied up in knots for the remainder of the evening. It was bad enough he had given in to her juvenile game, but not only had he failed, but he'd relived those heated moments repeatedly in his mind while watching as she became the success equivalent of Wellington at Waterloo. To Armstrong's satisfaction, Granville had led the way as gentlemen of every age and rank had vied for a dance, conversation, whatever little attention she had deigned to scatter their way. The whole thing had been quite discomfiting to watch. Painful, even. Disturbing.

He lit the candle by the bed once he entered the darkened chamber. The dim lighting was all he required. Quickly he began divesting himself of his formal attire: jacket, waistcoat, and shirt were tossed wearily over a newly upholstered brocade chair. Despite the fire still burning on the grate, the air in the chamber held the distinct chill of winter's indifference. As he reached to release the clasp of his trousers, an acute awareness prickled the fine hairs on the nape of his neck. The sensation of being watched was tangible. His head snapped and he scoured the dimly lit room.

Then he saw her standing ever so still and quiet in the shadowed corner.

He watched in dazed bewilderment as she stepped forward, her chestnut mane streaming loose and unpinned to the middle of her back. James swallowed. She could have been an angel dressed in the flimsy white nightdress, but he knew better. To him, she was a temptress in disguise.

His desire rose swiftly and violently, clamoring inside him like a volcano on the verge of eruption. Despite the coolness of the air, he was suddenly hot, his nerves protesting the unforgiving confines of his skin.

"Get out," he said, his voice deceptively soft, deceptively low. The air around him had grown so dense, he could cleave it with a knife.

Instead of heeding his demand, Missy took several steps forward. The glow from the solitary tallow candle suffused her in a warm light. James swallowed again, his breathing an audible rasp in the dead quiet of the night.

"I know you felt something when you kissed me tonight," she said softly.

James nearly groaned aloud, convinced his worst enemy had sent her to test him, torture him.

"Yes, and I believe you felt it too," he replied, his voice harsh.

She displayed no shock or surprise at his crude reference to just how hard he'd been pressed up against her down in the study. In fact her eyes, appearing more gray than blue at present, grew smoky, her lids weighed down by desire. Her gaze dropped to his chest and then to the unmistakable distention in the front of his trousers.

James had nowhere to go. He stood exposed and trapped, caged like a hungry lion with a voracious appetite who'd just come upon his next meal.

"You're very beautiful and I'm a normal male. It's lust, plain and simple. Don't make more of it than that. As I've told you before, any desirable female would elicit the same response."

Again, she said nothing but took another step forward, the light now illuminating the full glorious length of her slim figure, her nipples jutting out impudently from the soft cloth of her nightdress.

He throbbed. His whole body throbbed.

"Go back to your chamber," he said, his voice strained and barely recognizable.

She took another step closer, bringing her within inches of his tightly wound form.

"It's more than lust." It came out a feathery whisper. Slowly, she ran her fingers over the hard, stubbled plane of his cheek and square jaw.

He drew in a harsh, labored breath but didn't move, could not move. He was caught in the heady rush of such intense longing and hunger. One move and he feared he'd splinter, his control inexorably lost.

He watched as if in slow motion, as she rose on her toes, angled her head, and pressed her soft lips to his. For several seconds he remained rigid and still, fighting the tumult of lust and desire that crashed down upon him in waves. Then the tip of her tongue pierced the set line of his mouth. Once she gained entry, her tongue boldly sought his out.

James's control shattered. He forgot his promise to his friend. The risk. The consequences. Everything. Rocked by the fiercest passion he had yet to experience, his hands clutched the firm softness of her rounded bottom and pulled her taut against his heated flesh. As if by instinct, her thighs opened to cradle his rampant arousal. The need to be inside her, snug between the tight, wet walls of her feminine sheath consumed him, drove him.

He devoured her, his tongue a well-targeted lance. Missy moaned, her mouth parted wide to receive and to give. Her hands wrapped tightly about his neck as she bucked her hips in an effort to get closer still.

With a few steps backward, James dragged her down onto the bed. She fell atop him in a wanton heap, her slender thighs widened to straddle his hips. He retained his hold on her bottom, his hands flexing to rock her against his steely length. A keening cry escaped her parted lips as her head reared back and her eyes closed.

James had never seen such a beautiful sight in all his life. Only the cloth of his trousers and the thin translucency of her nightdress stood between them. Rising, careful not to dislodge her from where she sat perched riding him, he smoothed the garment from her shoulders. It pooled at her waist. A groan tore from his throat, echoing harshly throughout the room.

For a moment, he could only stare at the stark beauty of the firm, berry-tipped mounds before him. He marveled at their fullness on such a slender, fine-boned torso. Then her back arched. He wasn't even sure that she was conscious of the movement but it spurred him out of his mesmerized daze. Cupping the soft weight with both hands, he raised his head, let out an anguished, hungry rumble, then commenced to feast on her sweet flesh.

Missy thought she would die of pleasure when the raspy tip of his tongue swiped at her nipple. Liquid warmth continued to pool at the delta of her thighs. Clutching the back of his sweat-dampened head, she held him close and urged him to cool the mindless hunger that had overtaken her.

But he continued to tease her, nipping lightly at the bud with his teeth. He pulled it, laved it and rimmed the tip to a ruched peak. Missy's hips undulated helplessly, her lips pressing moist kisses along the curve of his ear and the hard scratchy line of his jaw.

In a sudden, almost violent maneuver, she was on her back, James settled between the spread of her legs. A glimpse of his handsome visage revealed a man on the brink. His expression held a mixture of intense hunger and pain, both to an equal degree. She watched in a bemused fog of passion as he lowered his head to her breast and, much to her delight and relief, parted his lips to take her into his mouth and suckle.

Her back arched off the mattress, her fingers making half-moon crescents on his muscled back.

I love you. The words became an ardent chant in her mind.

The first inkling that something was wrong came seconds later with the abrupt loss of heat, of his touch, while her declaration of love drenched the air. The chill in the chamber finally penetrated her dulled senses.

She hadn't meant to utter the words aloud.

However, she knew the damage had already been done. James was no longer atop her, his mouth no longer at her breasts. She turned, her eyelids almost too heavy to lift. He sat hunched at the side of the bed, hands clenched tightly in the folds of the white bed linen. His shoulders rose and fell with each ragged breath.

Missy reached out, her hand trembling as she lightly touched the naked length of his back. James uttered a curse and jerked to his feet.

"Cover yourself," he said, his back to her.

Slow to obey, Missy lay utterly still for one stunned moment before levering herself up and pushing the tangled mess of hair from her face.

James cast a dark look from over his shoulder and then his head instantly snapped back around. "For God's sake, cover yourself. Have you no shame?"

Responding to the hard tone of his voice, Missy hurriedly pulled up her nightdress and thrust her arms through the sleeves, concealing her breasts.

She came to her feet and stood behind him. If she offered him comfort, he'd reject it out of hand. But he wanted her. In those moments, when nothing had existed but the two of them loving on the bed, that had been as clear as her need of him.

"You're angry."

His breathing stopped for a long second, and then came out in an audible rush. "You are in a man's chamber in your nightwear. Surely, I don't have to tell you that you have more than breached the dictates of Society. Ladies do not behave in this manner."

Missy dropped her hand to her side. If she pressed him anymore tonight, she knew he would bolt. He had already been running the last three years.

He could have easily taken her innocence, but he cared too much for her to compromise her. The knowledge helped smooth the edges of her hurt.

"I am a woman. I never claimed to be a lady."

Missy heard his sharp indrawn breath but he remained with his back to her, his form rigidly controlled. After a pause, she slipped quietly from the chamber.

As Missy readied for breakfast the following day, thoughts of James filled every crevice of her mind. Thoughts of the fiery passion they had shared in the early hours of the morning caused heat to pool between her thighs. The now familiar throb of desire already beckoned.

After the intimacy they had shared, how would he treat her when they met again today? Smoothing the skirt of her peach morning dress, she departed her chamber and headed downstairs to the breakfast room. She would discover soon enough.

Alex and Thomas sat at the long oak table, their plates filled with scones, kippers, eggs, and kidneys. They gave her only a cursory glance when she entered the room, and bid her good morning before digging back into their food, her brother returning his attention to his newspaper.

"Where is everyone?" she asked, hoping she had success-fully managed a casual tone.

Thomas peered up at her, lowering the *London Times*. He probably thought it odd she hadn't yet taken a seat. She was not one to stand on ceremony when it came to food.

"It appears everyone is still abed." He picked up a mug of coffee and took a sip.

It wasn't surprising that her mother and sisters had not come down as yet but James was a notoriously early riser.

"It isn't like James to sleep so late."

Alex leveled her with a curious stare. Missy in turn offered him a benign smile.

"James has gone back to London," he said slowly.

Something fragile inside her shattered into endless pieces. "Gone back to Town? This morning?" The question was choked from her larynx.

"Left with the cocks," Thomas said in between bites, not bothering to glance up from his reading, oblivious to her distress. Oblivious to her heart lying tattered and broken at her feet.

"Apparently he'd forgotten an urgent business matter he needed to tend to," Alex said, still watching her closely.

Missy swallowed a well of despair, disappointment, and wrenching heartbreak. Nodding stiffly, she turned to depart.

"Are you not going to eat?" Alex asked, his tone mild, but his silver eyes sharp.

Turning, Missy reluctantly met his gaze. Summoning up even the pretense of a smile would shatter the tenuous thread she had on her emotions. Her head moved slowly from side to side. "No, I no longer have an appetite."

James was gone. He had run from her . . . again.

Chapter Four

Missy had imagined their first meeting since the moment James had left Stoneridge Hall so abruptly almost three long months ago. Who was she fooling? Since he'd run away, to put it more precisely. She'd assumed that meeting would take place at their residence in Town the following evening, during the small dinner party her mother was hosting.

In her mind, she would be coolly polite, exhibiting not an inkling of interest. Hers would be the mature air of nonchalance and faultless ladylike decorum. She'd not reduce herself to the banality of simpering or the transparency of coquettishness. No, she intended to be every bit the worldly sophisticate he *seemed* to prefer, if the identities of his ex-mistresses were anything to go by: an actress, a dancer, an opera singer, and a widowed duchess, just to name a few. All said to be terribly urbane and beautiful. She had learned all about them in the past month.

This—she stared down in horror at her mauve walking dress—didn't come near to urbane, and was certainly not the way she had envisioned the meeting.

Mud, thick and runny gobs of it, dripped from the ribbon trim flounces of her skirt and speckled the shot silk material in an unlikely pattern. The trickle of something slippery and wet wound its way down her cheek, then a stain of dirt blemished the back of her gloved hand.

With her mouth slack, her eyes wide, and her form taut, she lifted her gaze. James stood across the well-traveled path in Hyde Park barely twenty feet away. And if the sight of her wasn't enough to keep his sides stitched for days, beside him stood none other than Lady Victoria Spencer as yet another witness to her humiliation.

If mortification and disbelief had not kept her frozen in place, she'd have wailed and railed at the unfairness of it. He, naturally, looked dashing clad in a dark brown overcoat and brown and tan plaid trousers, while she—Missy stared down once more at her dress—looked like a mud-spattered wreck. A wave of heat suffused her entire body, her cheeks florid under the brisk breeze of the midmorning air.

"Oh dear, what a mess." Claire, who had luckily missed the damaging spray, removed a white handkerchief from her reticule and began pressing it gently against her face. A giggle escaped her lips as she fought back a smile.

Missy's head jerked up sharply, her slate blue eyes wide, her mouth pursed and tight.

"Forgive me." Claire unsuccessfully tried to stifle another giggle. "It's just that you look so funny with your face streaked with . . ." Missy blistered her with such a look, her friend's voice trailed off. Silence.

Beatrice, her lady's maid, who had been walking several feet behind the pair, busily worked on the polka dot skirt, her handkerchief now limp and soiled from its efforts.

Missy shot a glance down the path at the rider fading over the sloping trail. Did he know he had managed—with one ill-placed horse's hoof and a pool of mud—to not only ruin her dress, but more importantly, leave her utterly humiliated in front of the one man whom she only ever wanted to see her at her best?

She watched James approach, her throat constricted, her pulse racing.

"Good day, ladies." He tipped his hat, brown felt with a high crown, and extended himself in a shallow bow. Although his greeting was all encompassing, his gaze settled on the dishabille that she was. He appeared quite stoic given the circumstances, all patrician concern—damn him.

Beatrice immediately straightened, gave a deep curtsey and murmured her greetings to the two, before sweeping around to Missy's back to check for additional damage.

Sufficiently recovered from her giggles, Claire flashed a gracious smile. "Lord Rutherford. Lady Victoria."

"Oh dear, your beautiful dress," Lady Victoria said, after offering her own greeting. Her gaze sympathetically mourned the loss of the garment. "It is simply dreadful. Horses really should not be permitted on these trails."

All the expressed sympathy in the world could not staunch a pang of jealousy from rising within her to exert its indomitable presence. Did the woman ever act in a manner less than cordial or have a hair out of place? Hair that wasn't the gold blond of Thomas and her sisters, but the ashen blond rarely seen and therefore all the more coveted. Her face hadn't a blemish or a line. It was creamy perfection. And for a woman said to have no interest in men and marriage, she seemed quite partial to James's attention. His company. Her James.

"James. Lady Victoria." Missy nodded curtly, and then lowered her regard with hopes that the shallow brim of her bonnet would keep most of her mud-streaked face from view—his view, more precisely. "You will forgive me, but under the circumstances I'm afraid we must really be on our way."

A drop of mud fell from the brim of her bonnet. Missy's

cheeks caught afire. Directing an icy glare at Claire, she inclined her head stiffly. Keeping her head lowered, she managed a curt nod in the direction of the dazzling twosome. She then spun on her heel and began a brisk walk toward the park's south entrance, forcing Claire and Beatrice to scamper to catch up with her.

They had not gone more than fifteen feet when the low rumble of his rich baritone wafted the distance between them. "I expect I shall see you tomorrow evening." Not one note of inflection in his voice to indicate even a shred of anticipation, or contrarily, dread.

Missy paused, but did not turn to face him. Not with her so disadvantaged by his equanimity. "Yes, I expect you will," she replied before continuing on.

After nearly three months, the sight of Missy covered in mud and looking justifiably annoyed and embarrassed was all it took for his agitation to return with devastating force. He had felt the vein running along the side of his neck pounding in tandem with the accelerated pace of his heart the moment he'd glimpsed her unmistakable figure strolling down the pathway. It took all of his willpower not to glance back to watch her retreat.

Instead, eyes trained forward, James pressed on, his pace steady and brisk, only slowing as Lady Victoria began to lag at his side. In deference to her, he slowed, falling in step with her shorter strides.

Her chaperone, who Lady Victoria had introduced as Miss Fogerty, trailed a fair distance behind, but he could tell by the rigid way she held her head that she was alert to their every move.

"Mother would be thrilled if you called," Lady Victoria said.

James was certain she would. The marchioness would like nothing better than to see her daughter married off to a high-ranking member of the peerage. Naturally, she'd initially set her sights on Granville, being heir to one of the oldest and most powerful dukedoms in all of England. But the marchioness soon saw the futility in trying to snag Granville, as he appeared destined to wed Missy. James had to stop himself from grinding his teeth. Then the marchioness had turned her attention to Lord Chadwick, an earl and the heir to the Marquess of Brunswick. Rumor had it that Lady Victoria herself had discouraged his suit.

An apologetic smile curved his mouth. "If not for another pressing engagement . . ." He enjoyed Lady Victoria's company but coming upon her during his morning stroll certainly didn't warrant that kind of sacrifice. Since the well of eligible future dukes and marquesses had run dry, the marchioness appeared determined to turn their relationship into something much grander than it was.

"Are you certain it isn't the fear that my mother will have marriage banns posted before you exit the house that has you begging off?" Lady Victoria inquired, glancing back at Miss Fogerty, who was distracted by a foursome on horseback passing in the opposite direction.

Lady Victoria's eyes danced with humor, a smile lighting her face, transforming her usually impassive countenance. She was even more beautiful when she smiled. It was a shame she didn't indulge more often.

"You know your mother too well."

"I know my mother better than most," she said dryly. "Even my father, I imagine."

"Then I'm sure you will send her my best and we can leave it at that."

They continued in silence before Miss Fogerty stated in

a dour voice behind them, "Lady Victoria, I think it is time we returned home."

Lady Victoria did not respond, merely stopped and faced him. "Will you be attending Lady Elderly's dinner party tomorrow eve?"

James's interest was piqued. She'd never been inquisitive of his social schedule before. "No," he said, drawing out the word. "I will be attending Lady Armstrong's dinner party."

A contemplative look entered her eyes. "Oh yes, so you said before. I had forgotten that was also the same evening. Mama insists we attend Lady Elderly's. Word has it that Lord Chadwick has accepted."

The reasoning certainly didn't surprise James, although he had thought that the marchioness had beaten that horse to its last gasping breath. A reprieve for him, nonetheless.

"I do wish she would cease thrusting these gentlemen at me, and me at them." Her words were spoken with more emotion he'd ever witnessed from her. She actually sounded peeved, just shy of impassioned. Quite a novelty for a woman known for her unflappability.

"Pick a gentleman and marry and your problem will be solved."

She gave a delicate sniff. "That might very well be the beginning of a much larger dilemma," she muttered.

James simply could not imagine she had a problem more complicated than which marriage proposal to accept or which dress to wear. Young ladies of the *ton* led a life of frightful leisure, wanting little else than to make an advantageous match and produce a passel of children—well, at the very least, an heir.

"But that's neither here nor there at the moment." She executed a small curtsey. "Good day, Lord Rutherford. I expect I shall be seeing you at yet another scintillating social gathering."

James chuckled softly and bid her and the stern-faced Miss Fogerty *adieu*.

Missy checked her reflection in the cheval mirror in her bedchamber. She looked much improved from yesterday. Her face and her dress were free of mud. Beatrice had even managed the curls adorning her head without one singeing mishap.

Satisfied with her appearance, she dabbed some perfume on her wrists and the pulse points at her neck. Her nose wrinkled as she inhaled the light, flowery fragrance. The French did have the best scents on the Continent.

The ormolu clock sat perched on the bed stand, its long hand edging toward the top of the hour. Shortly, her mother would expect her downstairs to greet their guests.

Soon James would be there.

Another glance in the mirror revealed a woman in an ice blue fusion of puffed tulle and silk who, thankfully, bore little resemblance to that mud-spattered creature he had met in the park the day before.

James could have his pick of women. Very beautiful and accomplished women. Tonight she wanted—no, *needed*—to stand out from the rest. Considering her height, she mused wryly, she'd certainly be standing a good head above them.

Currently, he wasn't involved with anyone. This she'd learned from Beatrice, who at the age of nineteen, could tout gossip as her second profession. He'd ended his relationship with his last mistress a few months back. Such an opening would have a multitude of women eagerly vying to be the next to fill the role, maybe with hopes of making it more. Missy's hands skimmed the embroidered flowers adorning the neckline of her gown. This time she intended he acquire a wife.

A knock sounded. Missy turned in time to see her chamber

door open and Sarah sweep in, her golden locks a riot of tight curls pinned up in an unsightly coiffure. It appeared her sister had been experimenting again. A tragic but normal circumstance.

"I'm almost fifteen. I don't understand why I can't attend the dinner party." She stomped over to the bed and plopped down, her mouth pushed out in a pout.

Missy rolled her eyes. "Sarah, there will be gentlemen of marriageable age." The statement itself should have explained everything.

"So?"

"Well, you do remember what happened to Pauline Franks, do you not?" Hadn't she already relayed this story to her just four months back when she'd been grousing about yet another supper party their mother had held? The story had come directly from Beatrice who had gotten it from the kitchen maid at the Franks' residence.

Emerald green eyes stared blankly back at her.

Commencing with a long-suffering sigh, Missy launched into the story again. It certainly bore repeating. "She set her cap for Lord Blake even though she had yet to get a formal introduction. When she finally did during an outing with her sister at Vauxhall Gardens, he paid more attention to her sister than he did her. And her sister wasn't to have her introduction for another two years."

Emily sniffed. "I doubt any of the men here tonight will give me a second glance."

Not give her a second glance? Had her sister looked in the mirror lately or was she blind? "Don't be ridiculous. You're a very beautiful girl."

"But not as beautiful as you or Emmy."

The mention of her sister served as a sobering reminder of just what was at stake. And what her three futile Seasons had cost Emily. But Missy was determined to make it up to her. Her betrothal to James would clear the path for her sister's debut next year. She'd only be eighteen and a half, as young as most of the debutantes. And she'd not have to share it with either her or Sarah.

"Sarah, you are gorgeous. Far prettier than I was at your age. You'll have plenty of time for dinner parties and balls when you are older."

Her sister let out a short puff of air to signify what she thought of Missy's claim.

Another glance at the clock set Missy in motion. "I must be off. Mama will send someone for me if I'm late." She quickly slipped on a pair of soft satin shoes in the exact color of her gown, and hastily quit the chamber with a forlorn Emily still perched on her bed.

She arrived on the second floor to a flurry of activity. The servants were putting the finishing touches on the dining table, attending to even the minutest detail.

Her mother, wearing a bold red confection made of pyramid silk trimmed in lace, stood at the head of the table directing the first footman as he placed the placards at each setting.

"Millicent, you look lovely," she said, turning her attention to her daughter.

Her mother would have declared her lovely if she'd been wearing a cloth sack. "Thank you, Mama."

Missy slowly rounded the length of the mahogany table, which was covered in white linen and decorated with small vases, specimen glasses of lilies and pink roses, and a centerpiece of summer fruit. She searched the names on the embossed placards until she came upon the one with James's name. He would be opposite her but much farther down the table seated between Lady Annabel and Lady Georgette, the eldest daughters to an earl and a marquess. Lucky women.

"Your brother should be arriving momentarily."

Thomas was the furthest thing from her mind. She inclined her head, acknowledging her mother's statement as if it had been of concern to her.

Minutes later, her brother arrived looking golden and dapper in his evening finery. Accompanying him was Miss Camille Foxworth.

Camille, the older sister to her brother's friend currently in military service, looked—well, like Camille always did. She was pale and slender to the point of gauntness, all angles and eyes. And unfortunately, the white gown she wore only added to her wan complexion. Missy always thought it a shame she hadn't a mother with an eye for fashion to give her some direction in that regard.

Thirty minutes after Thomas's arrival, the drawing room overflowed with the bulk of the dinner party, each guest accounted for except James. Not even the attentions of five eligible gentlemen, including some of her most ardent admirers from the prior Seasons—Lord Riley, Lord Crawley and Mr. Townsend—could assuage her acute sense of disappointment. Lord Granville lingered on the outskirts of the circle as if uncertain if he wanted to join the fray.

Where was he? Her ears remained attuned for the announcement of his arrival, while her head bobbed up and down as Lord Riley droned on about something—what, she'd yet to ascertain. But at the moment, she was just grateful it didn't call for her participation.

James appeared at the threshold some five minutes later. Without a formal announcement, she hadn't an opportunity to prepare for the impact dealt every one of her senses. He looked too handsome by far in his dinner attire, a pair of white gloves and a snowy silk shirt throwing all the navy blue into stark relief. Missy toured his body in surreptitious admiration until, with a mental start, she finally noticed the woman pressed too close to his side.

She instantly recognized Baroness Willis with her tight bodice, plunging neckline, and an abundance of light brown hair piled atop her head in an elegant coiffure. The man-hungry widow somehow managed to inveigle even the most sought-after invitations to the most coveted fêtes of the Season. But Missy was almost certain her mother had not issued the woman an invitation. *So what the devil is she doing here? Apart from fawning all over James, that is.*

Missy held her position by the fireplace, Lord Riley and the other gentlemen hovering nearby, while James greeted her mother. And then his gaze roamed the room until it met hers. Something flickered across his sumptuously sculpted features, but his smile—remote, completely disengaged— sent her plunging into a freefall of misery. The wretched man was giving her naught to hang her hopes on.

He began to weave his way through the crowd toward her, Lady Willis close on his heels.

Missy tipped her chin, drew a breath, and pasted a polite smile on her face.

Chapter Five

"Miss Armstrong," he said, all cool and polite. As if they'd never kissed. As if he'd never placed his mouth on her naked breast and laved and pleasured her. But it was hard to mimic his *politesse* when the kiss he placed upon the back of her bare hand caused her heart to perform its familiar somersault.

"Lord Armstrong." She strived for normalcy but it still came out as if she had just caught her breath. She had to force herself not to avert her gaze from the sheer beauty of the azure blue of his eyes.

After she was sufficiently out of sorts, James turned and introduced the baroness. The widow flashed something that might pass for a smile in the cattiest of circles. Missy, not a proponent of blatant artificiality, inclined her head in a less-than-friendly nod. She noted how the woman's gloved fingers trailed down his arm in the sort of propriety manner that indicated an intimacy. Her eyes started to sting.

"Rutherford." The cordial voice came from over her shoulder.

Missy was ashamed to admit she'd forgotten Lord Granville was even there. As usual, the minute James had walked in the room, everything and everyone receded to the background and became mute and nebulous.

"Granville." James nodded to the younger man briskly.

A marked silence ensued. Thankfully, before the tree of unease had an opportunity to take root in the small circle, Thomas arrived with Camille, breaking the tension with his easy smile.

Missy shot another glance at James, who had already returned his attention to the buxom widow at his side. Stifling the urge to surrender to a torrent of tears, she quickly excused herself, leaving Lord Granville to watch her departure, shifting from one foot to the other as if contemplating his next course of action. She was most gratified he did not follow her.

The study across the hall afforded her a temporary sanctuary where she took a moment to collect her composure. She expelled a long, soothing breath and then railed at herself for being weak and foolish. Had she truly expected that after two kisses he would simply fall down on his knee and offer for her hand? Her mother had often said, anything worth having, required work. James was certainly worth having and he was certainly proving to be a great deal of work—years of it in fact.

Stalwart and dry-eyed, she exited the room just before the supper bell summoned the guests to the formal dining room, her mood bolstered. They entered in an orderly queue, chatting, laughing, and ready to satisfy their appetites. It took several minutes before everyone was seated and supper commenced.

As the highest-ranking member at the party, Lord Granville was seated to the left of her brother, closer to James. She sat in the middle, flanked by Lord Crawley and Lord Riley, each trying to draw her into conversation. Missy could offer neither much attention. She was too busy watching as Lady Annabel spoke to Lady Willis. They exchanged a smile and then James was seating the baroness before taking the chair next to hers. Lady Annabel appeared happy to take the seat several chairs down next to Mr. Johns, a handsome young barrister. Missy's heart gave a miserable thump.

This was the type of woman he preferred? She took in the widow's petite figure, her overripe curves, and a sense of despair swept over her. The woman was the opposite of her in every way.

The arrival of the footmen created a flurry of activity around the room, diverting her attention from the pair for the moment. Bearing silver covered dishes and drinks, the footmen stopped at each chair to offer up the food-laden dishes. This activity continued unabated for the next quarter hour until every guest's plate was filled with enough food to satisfy a gourmand.

While Missy endeavored to enjoy her meal, a losing proposition as the food coated her tongue like sawdust shavings, the corner of her vision captured James's profile, the cuff of his dinner jacket, sometimes just the wavy strand of his coffee brown hair. And in her thoughts, she saw him stripped bare to his waist. Beautiful in his masculinity. Impossible to resist.

"Will you be attending Suddernam's Ball?"

Lord Riley's question jolted her from her reverie. Her gaze darted to his. She forced a smile. "Yes, I believe my mother did accept on my behalf."

Turning to converse with Lord Riley placed James in her direct line of vision. Her heart fairly skipped a beat when she caught him watching her with those pale blue eyes, sinfully thick lashes hooding his gaze. When he noticed her regard, he immediately turned away. Pride compelled her to do the same.

"I hope you will save me a dance." Lord Riley offered her a smile, his brown eyes alight with interest.

"As I always do." She smiled, a flash of teeth, casting him a quick glance before giving her full plate her exclusive attention.

By the conclusion of the meal, appetites were assuaged and spirits ran high. *En masse,* the supper party retired to the drawing room, spilling out onto the patio overlooking a modest garden of nodding white pansies and red peonies.

Missy didn't know exactly how she found herself alone in the garden with Lord Crawley behind a line of thick hedgerows. The only thing she knew was that when supper had concluded, she'd desperately required some air and it had been Lord Crawley standing obliging at her side. She required some time to think—or not think as it were. About James. Always about James.

Throughout supper, he had appeared engrossed with the baroness, who had made a habit of leaning over every time she spoke (which had been the majority of the meal), her mouth sometimes dangerously close to his ear, oftentimes their shoulders coming close to touching.

For all the attention he had paid Missy, she might as well have been a discarded landau once the new model had come out. Senses starved for him had found no relief. Except for his polite greeting, he had barely glanced at her, and even the one time he had, his impassive expression had done little to give his thoughts away. Perhaps this whole idea was too foolish to pursue? Maybe Thomas and Claire were right. Perhaps she should give one of the many gentlemen paying her court a real chance. She would have to settle for someone else if she failed with James.

Missy made pains to concentrate on Lord Crawley, who watched her with an undisguised look of appreciation. Clad in a mauve jacket, a green silk embroidered waistcoat, and an elaborate cream ruffled shirt, it was obvious the man was mad about fashion. But he managed it in a manner that took nothing away from his patrician good looks and the elegant air he carried inordinately well on his husky frame.

Now, what had he been saying? Oh yes, he had been telling her of his ear for languages and love of history. Missy flashed a brighter smile than usual: "I, too, have a great fondness for such pursuits." And so she began the task of pushing James from her thoughts.

James told himself for the tenth time he'd come out for a breath of fresh air. It certainly had nothing to do with seeing Missy disappear with Crawley. He forced down a niggling sense of irritation—or perhaps something stronger, something much more basic. Whatever it was, he knew he had no right to feel it. Should not feel it. Then he had to ask himself why he'd excused himself from the clinging Lady Willis, and now stood in a shadowed area on the terrace overlooking the garden watching the movements of the strolling couple.

What the hell was Missy thinking allowing a reprobate and fop like Crawley to escort her alone? He could now see why young ladies were in need of chaperones. Even the bright ones seemed to lack good sense.

James watched quietly as they came to a standstill, Crawley facing her with lascivious intent on his angular face. Something in his gut twisted as the man inclined his head downward to claim hers in a brief kiss. She didn't flinch, didn't cry out in indignation. She did absolutely nothing to prevent it. The twist in his gut became a knot and his breath suspended for an outraged moment. And if his eyes weren't deceiving him, he could swear she'd tilted her head in order to reciprocate.

Unadulterated fury tore a cindering path through him, but before he allowed it to erupt, James spun sharply on his heel and stormed back into the house.

"Ah, Rutherford, there you are."

Never had the sight of the voluptuous widow been more unwelcome. His mood had shifted in the course of the evening, and now a night with her wanton charms held as much appeal as an aria would for the deaf.

The smile he gave her was forced. "I was just coming to collect you: I think it's best we be on our way." Now he regretted that he had offered her an escort home at all.

The baroness instantly brightened, her smile a bit of coyness. "I will have someone retrieve my cloak."

While James awaited her return, he saw Crawley enter the drawing room alone, a pleased smile wreathing his face. Without a thought to what he would do much less what he'd say, James wasted no time approaching him.

"Crawley."

Crawley, who had been helping himself to a drink from a snifter of port at the sideboard, glanced up, his expression easy until he saw the glower in James's eyes and the grim set of his mouth.

"Rutherford," Crawley said, his eyes wary.

Ensuring he kept his voice low, James said, "There is a rumor about Town that your markers have left you broke." James was well aware he could intimidate a man without much effort, much less when he was exerting himself. Tonight he *was* exerting himself thoroughly.

It was a good thing the young lord had yet to take a draw from the glass for he would surely have choked, or so James thought when an indrawn breath brought on a coughing fit. Crawley hastily placed the glass on a side table, no doubt fearing he would spill its contents all over the Oriental rug.

Recovered, he glanced furtively around before subjecting

James to an indignant glare. "My fortune is intact, not that it is any business of yours."

James knew Crawley was lying. It was well known around the *ton* that between his father's drinking, his mother's excesses, and his gambling, he would not have a fortune to inherit, merely a title. The man was a fortune hunter, of that James was certain. And regardless of Missy's behavior this evening—encouraging the man—his friendship with Armstrong as well as his deep affection for the viscountess compelled him to interfere.

"It will be my business if you have a particular heiress in your sight." His voice held a gravity that made him a forbidding foe.

Crawley's brows lifted in surprise, then his eyes narrowed, slyly. "What, after four Seasons you've suddenly taken an interest?"

For a moment James was certain he would hit him. He didn't think he could help but hit him. Then by some fortune of fate, Lady Armstrong came into view, and he remembered in whose house he stood.

"Miss Armstrong is too good for the likes of you. Court her at your own risk." James didn't think he could have made his meaning any clearer.

"I believe that is up to Miss Armstrong," Crawley said stiffly, wearing a look of false bravado.

A harsh laugh emitted from James's throat. "You must be under the mistaken belief duels are no longer fought. They are, just very discreetly. Keep advised, Armstrong is an expert shot and I will gladly act as his second." With that, he turned and walked away.

James collected Lady Willis, then located the viscountess and Armstrong and bid them farewell before departing. He saw no sign of Missy, and with his mood, which draped him in coffinlike darkness, he knew it was for the best.

* * *

James escorted a disappointed Baroness Willis directly to
her door without an apology. The widow had promised a
night of heated pleasure on sweat-dampened sheets but he
had politely but firmly declined. She didn't take the news
well as was evidenced by her pout and the angry glint in her
brown eyes. James couldn't have cared less. After a curt
bow, he turned to make the short walk back to his carriage.

By the time he reached his lodgings, his mood had sunk
to the color of obsidian, the image of Crawley kissing Missy
indelibly etched in his mind's eye. This was her fourth
London Season and he knew he had no right to begrudge
her suitors, but good God, she deserved far better than
Crawley and the like.

After dismissing Smith for the evening, James settled in
the library. He needed a drink more than he needed sleep.
And it wasn't as if he'd be able to sleep with a combination
of anger and lust surging through him. He had no right to be
angry, so his anger was directed at himself. And dear Lord,
Missy had looked beautiful in her blue-green gown, the
neckline exposing a tantalizing glimpse of her sweet breasts.

How different things might be if he and Armstrong weren't
the closest of friends and she wasn't an innocent in search
of a husband. He poured a generous helping of scotch and
savored the burn as it hit the back of his throat.

Dropping into a leather winged-back armchair, he lost
himself in his thoughts. Thoughts he had no right to think.

Tonight it seemed like every unattached gentleman at the
party had been panting after her like unbroken pups. He
brought his glass down on the adjacent table with a loud
thud, the amber liquid sloshing and spilling over the sides.
He had no desire to marry her, nor could he take her as a
mistress. So why did the thought of her with anyone else

raise his hackles and cause him untold aggravation? James slugged the rest of the scotch back as if it were sweet tea.

He lost track of time while he sat drinking, his thoughts pensive and sullen. Images of Missy assailed him from every direction. A glance at the decanter revealed he'd downed a good amount. It was too damn bad he remained stone cold sober, angry, and wanting.

While he contemplated another round, two strident raps of the knocker disturbed the quiet of the night. Pushing himself to his feet, he made his way down the hallway to the front door. He certainly would not be summoning Smith at this hour. Who could be calling close to midnight?

Caution should have had him peering through the peephole before he opened the door, but his mind was still distracted. The moment the door cleared the frame, it was pushed open by a determined hand. James instinctively took a step back and a flash of dark hair under a hooded cloak whirled by him after the door was swiftly pushed shut. He watched in stunned silence as the hood was lowered.

His brows shot up in surprise. "Lady Victoria?"

Yes, even with a dark spill of hair, her features were unmistakable: porcelain skin, dark blue eyes, and an untouchable air that had chagrined many gentlemen of the *ton*.

"I tried to get a message to you earlier to meet me today but you have been impossible to reach," she said, her breath short and choppy.

Bewildered, James continued to stare at her, trying to make sense of what was happening. "What are you doing here? And what, pray tell, is that on your head?"

Still clutching the ends of her cloak together in a vaguely protective gesture, Lady Victoria eyed him and then came in close to sniff, dainty nose in the air, about his person.

"You have been imbibing. Are you drunk?"

"No," he replied tersely.

She retreated several steps.

"Did you come alone?"

"My footman is awaiting me in a carriage nearby." There wasn't another person in sight or within earshot yet she whispered her response as if she was ferreting out secrets for the Crown.

He trailed her uncertainly as she moved quietly down the hall, peeking into darkened rooms as she passed.

"What are you searching for?" Why the hell was he whispering?

"Where are the servants?" she asked, glancing back at him over her shoulder.

"Abed, which is exactly where you should be. I imagine at some point you'll be ever so good as to tell me what has warranted this call? At this hour. In that disguise."

Lady Victoria ignored him, poking her head into the library and surveying the room. With a satisfied nod, she bustled in. James had little choice but to follow. She took a seat on the sofa, briefly releasing her hold on her velvet wrap to jerk off her gloves. Darting a glance at the empty tumbler on the side table, she said, "I do not normally indulge but tonight I am in sore need of a drink."

Wasn't she just full of surprises today. At her request, James changed course and went to the sideboard. Snagging an empty glass, he crossed back to the small seating area. Lady Victoria accepted the glass and held it in a slightly trembling hand while he poured from the half-filled decanter.

"I pray you will not make me drink alone," she said as he sank back into the armchair.

James didn't particularly want another drink but he obliged her, adding a dollop to his glass.

"I needed to speak with you . . . this evening." She spoke softly and haltingly. Her forehead puckered as she fingered the large top button on her wrap.

"To show up like this, I gather is must be urgent." Peering over the rim of his glass, he took a sip of the scotch. Lady Victoria didn't immediately respond, just watched him closely, as if pondering deeply.

And then it came, a torrent of tears, with the suddenness that left him frozen for a stunned moment, before he set down his glass. Gentle sobs shook her slender shoulders.

Pushing himself from his seat, James settled on the plaid sofa next to her. His hands tentatively patted her shoulders in what he hoped was a show of comfort.

"Shush now. You mustn't cry. You'll make yourself sick. Just tell me what is wrong, and I'll try to help as much as I can. "

She lifted tear-soaked blue eyes up at him and whispered, "Oh dear, I'm not sure I can bear to tell you anymore. If word were ever to get out . . . It's all so embarrassing." A shudder shook her slender frame.

He drew her closer, settling her head in the notch of his shoulder. His chin settled on the top of her head, the silky chestnut hanks of hair tickling his nose. Missy had hair this color, with similar streaks of dark red and polished mahogany. But Missy's was richer, warm, and more luxuriant.

"We certainly can't have you risking your good reputation by coming here for naught. Tell me and I promise this will not go beyond us," he soothed.

She tilted her head back and gazed up at him. Suddenly, a strange lethargy stole over him. The effort to keep his eyes open became a task in and of itself. Lady Victoria leaned in, bringing her breasts flush with his chest. Reflexively, he pulled away but there was little he could do to evade the contact as she pressed relentlessly forward, her eyes fixed on his mouth.

"Are you like all the other gentlemen of the *ton*? Do you find me cold and frigid?" Her voice caught on the final word.

James could only gape at her in stupefied silence, his head having become a considerable weight upon his shoulders, his mind swiftly losing its clarity. Too late, he saw her lips ascending to his. The kiss landed softly, like a whisper. James pulled back but she pursued, pressing more firmly. He closed his eyes and he saw her, the scent of lilacs surrounding him. It was Missy. His eyelids grew heavier, his will weakened and the lust he'd kept bottled for so long, fought to reign.

He saw her through a hazy, lethargic fog as she fumbled with the button holding her cloak in place. It fell around her where she sat, partially landing on the sofa, the rest a puddle of blue on his gold-and-green geometric rug. And what it revealed he had no business seeing, for underneath she wore a pink silken nightdress.

He closed his eyes and saw her clear as day. It was Missy in his guest chamber with her chestnut hair and beautiful eyes. His mouth opened, almost helpless to resist her now. An experienced tongue darted forward to stroke his. He felt himself slipping, his anchor to reality eroding away. He was losing the battle he had been valiantly fighting since the day she discovered she was female and he was male and where all that could lead.

His eyes fluttered open once more and he saw slate blue eyes. Filling his hands with warm female, James closed his eyes and surrendered.

Morning proved to be a harsh mistress. It created light where there should be dark and movement where only stillness should exist. James rolled over with a groan, a persistent dull throb holding his head captive.

Shielding his eyes with his hand from the glare of the sun already streaming through the dark green curtains in his— he took a hurried look around—his bedchamber.

His bedchamber!

He skittered to an upright position, hastily throwing off the white bedsheets. He was in his usual sleeping attire, his drawers, but somehow that didn't seem right. James sank back onto the bed, the hazy recollection of the events from the night before slow to filter through his disjointed memory.

There was little doubt he had had several drinks. The woolly taste in his mouth surely attested to that. Oh yes, the dinner party and Missy. And then Missy had appeared at his door. He snapped upright again, his eyes wide as a jolt of alarm shot through him. No, not Missy but Victoria Spencer wearing a dark wig and crying. With a sinking feeling of dismay, the disjointed pieces started to come together in dribs and drabs. They had been in the library and Lady Victoria had started to weep and—bloody hell, the kiss. Oh God, she had kissed him—and he had kissed her back. His stomach gave away in a horrifying thud.

James tossed the sheet off and slowly arose from the bed, still mindful of his head. Who had undressed him and put him to bed? Surely not Lady Victoria? He gave his room a thorough once-over, noting its customary orderliness. No clothes strewn about; nothing out of place.

"Randolph." If anyone would know, it would be his valet.

His valet was prompt in responding to the bellowed summons, appearing at his door within seconds.

"Milord?" he inquired, his short stout form erect in military fashion.

"How did I get to bed last night?" James grabbed the frame of his bedstead, using it for support while pressing the bridge of his nose between his forefinger and thumb in an attempt to dull the pain behind his eyes.

The answer was so long in coming, James was forced to raise his head and drag one eye open. Randolph stood regarding him in a quizzical manner, which was truly beginning to vex him.

"Um—I would assume the way you always do, milord."

James dug his fingers deeper into the bridge of his nose. Well, it appeared that mystery was solved.

"Please bring me some coffee. A whole pot of it. And have my bath prepared." With those instructions, James turned in dismissal.

Could it have been Lady Victoria? What an unsettling thought—no, more like terrifying. He gave a low groan, in part because his head felt like it had been split in two, but mostly because he couldn't remember if he'd managed to put his entire future in jeopardy by compromising the daughter of a bloody marquess.

He sank to the edge of the bed, his head dropping low from the weight of pain and unrelenting anxiety. Surely, he couldn't possibly have had sex with the woman and not remembered. And a virgin no less. He bolted up and peered closely at the white bedsheet. No maiden blood. Certainly that was a good sign?

Despite several more minutes of endeavoring to force his mind to reveal the evening's events, his memory refused to cooperate, remaining stubbornly blank. It appeared the only way he would learn what had occurred was to go to the source. It was embarrassing, humiliating in fact, but he would have to seek out the lady to discover if he had just committed an act of supreme idiocy and sealed his future.

Chapter Six

Normally Missy didn't mind her sisters' inquisitiveness. In fact, most days she welcomed it. Today was not one of those days. Today she wished she could remain in her chamber and while away the day wrapped in a cocoon of her own melancholy.

"Why are you still abed?" Emily asked from the chamber door. Sarah, nearly identical in height and features, stood like a comrade in arms beside her. Setting any feelings of guilt aside, Missy peered over her dusty rose counterpane and sent them what she hoped was her sternest go-away-do-not-bother-me look.

Paying her no mind, they blithely proceeded in, their frocks turning her bed into a profusion of pink-and-white-striped gingham and lavender muslin.

"The flowers started arriving early this morning. The drawing room is beginning to look like a florist shop." Sarah teased, her green eyes dancing with delight. "Mama is thrilled."

Their mother would be even more so when she finally had a ring on her hand and a wedding date scratched on the calendar. But Missy was relieved she had yet to press her on the issue.

Flicking a glance at her younger sister, Missy tried to smile, tried to find some pleasure in the fact that after several years in the marriage market, her popularity hadn't declined as yet. Unfortunately, James's early departure had succeeded in dampening her spirits and shaking her resolve once again.

"I suppose I should rouse and take myself downstairs," Missy said with little enthusiasm and making no effort to do so.

"But first you must tell us about the supper party. How many gentlemen attended?"

The gentlemen could have all been a group of licentious reprobates, but it was the quantity that impressed Sarah. In her youthful opinion, the more men in attendance, the more successful a gathering.

Missy pushed herself up into a sitting position. "It was one of Mama's parties and everyone knows she always throws a marvelous party. But yes," she managed a small smile, "to answer your question, there were many gentlemen present."

Flipping over and sliding down onto her belly, Emily propped her head in her palms. "Did they flirt with you?" The question elicited a giggle from Sarah.

Oh dear, she hoped her sister wasn't thinking about what she herself had missed, being unable to attend the party. "They are men. That is what they do. Don't worry, Emmy, next year you will be inundated with offers." Missy took in her delicate beauty. Both her sisters would have the gentlemen of London on their knees.

"Missy, please, I am not upset that I didn't debut this Season. Frankly, I was quite relieved when Mama told me she wanted to hold off another year. The prospect of being on display like that—" She broke off, shaking her head firmly. "No, it all worked out for the best so not another word about it."

At Emily's assurance, Missy breathed a sigh of relief.

"So did you receive any more proposals?" Sarah seemed intent to remain on point.

Missy immediately remembered the kiss in the garden. "No, but Lord Crawley kissed me," she said, without giving her admission much thought. She shared most things with her sisters—though certainly not everything.

Emily gasped, bolting upright while Sarah emitted a high squeal and clapped a hand over her mouth. "But I thought you were in love with James?" Sarah leveled her with a disapproving stare.

"It was just one little kiss," Missy countered in her own defense. "And James took little notice of me with that— that, Lady Willis fawning all over him."

"Well?" Emily prompted.

"Who is Lady Willis?" Sarah asked, clearly intrigued.

"Well what?" Missy said, directing her attention to Emily. She had no desire to discuss James's "women friends." She now regretted even mentioning the woman.

"What was it like—the kiss?" Emily dashed an errant braid over her shoulder as she leaned forward, her eyes aglow with curiosity.

With a casual shrug, Missy said, "As I said, it was just a kiss." With none of the passion and heat she'd experienced when James had kissed her. But she certainly wouldn't expound upon that with Sarah present. And she saw no reason to divulge why she hadn't slapped the fresh Lord Crawley when he had taken such liberties. Her mother would have a fit if all her daughters went about comparing gentlemen's kisses.

"But what of James?"

Missy sent her sister a sharp glance. Once Sarah got something into her head, she was like the proverbial dog with a bone.

Missy pushed back the counterpane and hopped from the bed, avoiding her sisters' collective and rather avid regards.

"I'd long thought James and I had a . . . connection but now I'm not so certain. Sometimes I don't even think he likes me." Missy didn't miss the disbelieving glances exchanged by the two, reflected back in the mirror as she took a seat on the cushioned brocade chair. Picking up the silver-handled brush from the vanity, she loosed the braid hanging halfway down her back and began brushing the tangles from her hair.

"Not like you?" Sarah bounced off the bed. "That is the most ridiculous thing I've ever heard."

Within seconds, both girls, one on each side, flanked her.

Emily addressed Missy's reflection in the mirror. "I hardly think that's true."

Missy placed the brush down calmly, turned slowly in her chair and tilted her head to look her sister in the eye. "And this you base on what?"

"You have been his favorite since I can recall. Plus, I have two eyes and I can see. He's forever watching you. The moment you look, he turns away. I have read enough novels to know what that means. He is obviously madly in love with you." Her green eyes seemed to challenge her to deny her claim.

Missy sniffed, while a tendril of real hope clung to her words with fierce tenacity. "I have hardly seen him since my debut. You yourself have commented on how rarely he visits anymore."

Emily lifted her narrow shoulders in an artless shrug. "In the novels, that would indicate he is a man of honor. He wouldn't be so crass as to pursue the sister of his dearest friend. And I do see his point. Thomas has said often enough that James is too cynical for marriage. Well, at least to marry for love."

Missy wished her brother would refrain from making such remarks within her earshot. But sadly, however, it wouldn't change the facts. Thomas would never approve of James for any of his sisters.

"What is a rakehell?" Sarah asked.

Missy swung her head to the other side to see her youngest sister's brow furrow. "Where, pray tell, did you hear such a term?"

"I can't remember. I think perhaps I read it in the papers."

Papers? Humph! "You better not let Mama catch you reading those gossip sheets," Missy scolded, rising to her feet and brushing past Emily as she made her way back to the bed.

"So, what do you intend to do?" Emily followed close on her heels.

"Do about what?"

"Do about James?"

"What *can* I do? I cannot very well force him to love me. And he certainly hasn't given me reason to hope he ever will."

"But he must feel something. Why else would he have taken you alone into the study during Mama's ball?" Sarah said with a sly glint in her eye.

Missy spun so quickly on the ball of her feet she nearly tripped over her pink cotton nightdress. Her jaw dropped. She quickly snapped it shut. Heat bloomed in her face. "What?" she asked in a strangled whisper.

Emily joined in on the fun, grinning a Cheshire cat smile. "We saw the two of you going into the study during the ball."

"And just what were you doing downstairs at that time?" She tried for a certain amount of censure but failed miserably, her voice trailing off to a squeak.

"How else were we to know what went on?" Sarah said, exhibiting not an ounce of shame.

Missy let out a soft groan. This should come as no surprise to her. It was just the sort of mischief her sisters would get themselves into.

"Oh don't be such a ninny. We didn't tell anyone. And we won't," Emily added the latter after receiving a sharp look from her.

Missy stared at her sisters long and hard. "You can never speak a word of this to Mama. And most definitely you cannot even breathe—*and I do mean breathe*—a word of it to Thomas. Do you understand?"

Emily and Sarah gave their assurances with fervent nods.

James presented himself at the Spencer residence early that morning, well before normal calling hours. Despite the slight chill in the air, beads of sweat wound its way down past his temple to trickle by his ear. James caught it with a swipe of the back of his gloved hand. Mentally bracing himself, he tapped the brass knocker, which featured a lion's head, on the imposing oak door.

After what felt like an interminable length of time but had only in fact been mere seconds, a tall, thin, angular man clad in black answered.

"May I help you?" he inquired.

"Lord Rutherford to see Lady Victoria." His pulse pounded. He clenched and released his hands to shake off the nerves.

The butler opened the door further for his admittance and James stepped into a high three-storied foyer. It was grand on a scale rivaling his parents' home in Berkshire. Everything gleamed, from the marble floors, the gold-gilded framed artwork, to the bronze chandelier suspended high above. Even the papered walls shone an iridescent silver. Everything appeared oppressively new and overdone.

"Simmons, who—ah, Lord Rutherford, what a pleasant

surprise." The marchioness rushed forward, plump hands outstretched. Lord, how the woman could gush. He had no idea where she'd come from. One moment it had been just he and the butler, the next, in a flurry of dark blue paisley, she appeared.

A wide smile wreathed her plump face as she reached out to squeeze his hands. "Victoria will just be thrilled to see you." Turning to the servant she'd addressed as Simmons, she said, "Please inform my daughter she has a visitor awaiting her in the drawing room."

So, while Simmons went off to do her bidding, the marchioness escorted him to the drawing room, or perhaps more aptly put, shepherded him like one would a sheep to the slaughter.

"Please, make yourself comfortable," the marchioness said, fluttering about. Her brown eyes sparked with girlish excitement. She watched him as if she couldn't believe he was there and, as he had never before called on her daughter, he could well imagine why. He could practically see her little mind furiously working, already planning the betrothal party and the wedding. She would most likely have the grandchildren's names picked before he took his leave. He darted a glance at the drawing room doors and prayed Lady Victoria wouldn't be long.

"Would you care for some tea?" the marchioness asked. Her hand hovered over the teapot on the tray set.

James politely declined and took a seat on the purple-and-red damask settee. Like everything else in the room, it looked and smelled newly bought.

His headache had faded to a faint twinge behind his eyes. However, he had a feeling triggering it again could easily fall to the rather stout woman beaming at him at that very moment. She poured herself a cup of tea and took the seat opposite him.

Even if a man had romantic feelings for Lady Victoria, the thought of forever having the marchioness as his mother-in-law was enough to make him reconsider such a union. James prayed fate would not be so cruel to him. Where the hell was she?

"I was just telling Victoria," the marchioness paused, most likely to stretch the story to its limit, "I believe it was only yesterday—yes, yesterday—I was telling Victoria that I do not think I ever—"

"Lady Victoria." James bounded to his feet the moment he saw her framed in the doorway. He then shot a quick look at the marchioness. Had she taken his interruption as rude? He need not have worried. If anything, Lady Cornwall's smile only grew broader, as her gaze darted between him and her daughter. He could practically hear her little match-making mind whirling faster than a printing press.

Turning his attention to Lady Victoria, James searched her beautiful face for signs of—For signs of what? Embarrassment? Perhaps even chagrin? Wouldn't she appear at the very least—he searched for the word that evaded him—distressed? Yes, wouldn't she be at the very least distressed had she been compromised? That would be the normal reaction for a virginal miss, would it not?

"Lord Rutherford, this certainly is a surprise." She offered him her hand with a gracious but brittle smile.

"Is it?" He accepted her hand, bowing over it, ever cognizant of the marchioness's presence only feet away, her hearing probably as sharply tuned as a canine's.

"Would you care to join me for a ride in the park? I have my carriage waiting outside."

Lady Cornwall set down her cup and sprang to her feet in a motion surprisingly spry for a woman her size. She scurried to her daughter's side. "Well, of course Victoria would love to go for a carriage ride. Do hurry and call for your cloak, Victoria." She shooed her along as if dismissing a recalcitrant child. The woman had all the subtlety of a battering ram and about just as much finesse.

"Shall I send for Miss Fogerty?" Lady Victoria asked, pausing after the three had exited the drawing room and were making their way down the hallway.

Blast! The last thing James needed was a bloody chaperone.

"Oh posh, Miss Fogerty need not accompany you today. It is perfectly respectable for Lord Rutherford to escort you on a ride in the park alone. Really, Victoria, sometimes I do wonder which century you think you live in."

Lady Victoria nodded her assent in that vague, unperturbed way of hers.

Thankfully, it took only a minute for a servant to come with Lady Victoria's shawl, gloves, and bonnet. The marchioness then gave them a rounding send-off, her plump hands fluttering about like the wings of a beheaded chicken. Soon after, they boarded his conveyance and headed off toward Hyde Park.

James gave her his full attention once they were ensconced in the plush velvet-and-leather interior of the carriage. She appeared oddly unruffled, almost serene, given the events of the prior night. She didn't try to evade his gaze but watched him with the same curiosity as he did her.

"This must be important for you to call on me at my residence. You have never called on me before."

James's eyes widened. Perhaps he had actually dreamt the incident.

Shifting his weight so his arms rested on his thighs, he leaned forward, closing the distance between them. "You will forgive me, but my memory needs refreshing."

At first, her expression didn't alter but then a rueful smile tipped the corners of her mouth. "No, it is I who should beg your forgiveness. Last eve I was—well, distraught and not thinking as clearly as I should. It was inexcusable of me to come to your residence." Her voice was soft and she sounded sincere.

At last, he was getting somewhere. He straightened and pushed himself back in his seat, some of the tension easing from his neck and shoulders. "Well, I was surprised to say the least. Now, I know you won't mind telling me what last night was all about? I mean coming to my residence un-chaperoned and at that late hour?"

"I did have my footman with me," came her quick but feeble defense.

"Are you in some sort of trouble?"

Lady Victoria turned and looked out the window, her hands unsteady as she adjusted the bonnet on her head. "A personal matter I thought you could be some assistance with." She turned to look at him. "It is of no consequence now. I have dealt with the situation in my own fashion."

"Which was what?"

"As I already said, it is of no consequence now."

"By God, you came to my home dressed in your under-garments! I am at least owed an explanation." A slight growl crept into his voice.

Her lips pursed in annoyance. "It was a nightdress."

James rolled his eyes. "Well what difference does that make? Undergarments, nightdress, the point being, hardly the proper attire young ladies wear beyond the bedchamber."

"Yes, well, I was hardly going to wake my maid at that hour of the evening to help me dress," she said dryly.

Sarcasm? Lady Victoria? His mind reeled. Night was now day and black was now white. The whole damned world had flipped on its axis. "Damn and blast, are you going to tell me what it was all about?" He didn't make it a habit to curse in the presence of ladies—and certainly not at them—but in this instance, his lapse was understandable. Certainly forgivable.

Her expression grew immediately contrite as she seemed to realize the biting sarcasm in her tone. Staring down at her lap, she idly plucked at her lavender skirt. "All right then, it was really all very silly. Something I had to prove to myself. I'm sure you've heard the talk about me around the *ton*."

James stared at her. "Are you telling me you did all this to prove to yourself that—that—"

"You needn't finish, I'm well aware of what you're trying to say and the answer is yes."

If it wasn't such a serious matter, James might have been amused. But going about proving herself a desirable woman in the manner she had, seemed extreme. She could have gotten a number of men to kiss her without taking such risks.

"Did you see me to my bedchamber?"

Her head jerked up appearing startled by the question. After a pause she replied, "As you were in need of assistance, I merely acted as a guiding hand and a shoulder to lean on. I could never forgive myself if I discovered you tumbled to your death climbing the stairs. And please don't look so alarmed, I left you quite chaste while you tumbled into your bed."

A wave of relief so great swept through him, he became light-headed. He dragged in a lungful of air. He had not compromised her. By the scrape of his teeth, he would retain his freedom.

"You need not look like you were saved your turn at the guillotine," she said. She didn't appear piqued but there had been something in her voice he couldn't discern, something that sent a frisson of uncertainty spiraling through him.

"But who undressed me?" His gaze probed hers.

Lady Victoria gave a slight shrug. "I assure you *that* was not the goal of my mission. You'll be happy to know I left you quite incapacitated on your bed—fully clothed," she added the latter hastily. "Perhaps you undressed yourself."

As he had no recollection of anything beyond the kiss, it was entirely conceivable. That part of the evening was a fog, then nothing. Although he had heard tales of this sort from other men, he had never been one to imbibe to the point of memory loss.

"And the kiss—"

She held up her hand, a fiery blush turning her usually pale visage pink. "Please, let us not speak of it. All of this is embarrassing enough."

James could see for the first time that she was discomfited, and quietly allowed the matter to rest. He was just grateful there would be no consequences from last night's incident.

After a brief trip down Rotten Row, James returned Lady Victoria to her residence. When she disappeared inside, he bound back to his carriage and instructed the coachman home.

As the carriage made its way down Dover Street, he observed ladies in their promenade dresses and parasols dotting the streets, bustling in and out of storefronts. He glimpsed chestnut hair under a yellow bonnet. His head turned as he strained to glimpse the woman's face.

It wasn't Missy, and he was angered by his crushing feeling of disappointment and at how his heart had quickened, his senses stirred when, for a fleeting moment, he thought it was.

Missy.

She was the true cause of what happened last night with Lady Victoria. Through the foggy haze of alcohol, he had closed his eyes and thought it was Missy he had been kissing.

He rubbed a weary hand over his face, cursing his wretched desire for her. He'd come dangerously close to losing the one thing he valued and upon which he put a high premium: his bachelorhood. He'd been just a hairbreadth away from losing it all and being leg-shackled to a woman he didn't want. He sincerely owed Lady Victoria a debt of gratitude. If she'd been one of those unscrupulous husband hunters, she could have easily turned the whole incident to her advantage. She could have demanded marriage. One word of this to her parents would have spelled his doom.

And all because Missy had grown up and turned the coquette.

Chapter Seven

The barouche came to a stop in front of Madame Batiste's shop on Bond Street. One by one, the Armstrong women alighted from the black and silver–lacquered coach with the assistance of Stevens, their footman.

After a slow start to her morning, Missy and her mother had spent most of the day paying calls. They'd returned home to consume a small meal late in the afternoon, and then collected the girls for a promised shopping trip.

Although it had been four years since her brother had turned their fortune around with sound business investments and exemplary financial management, shopping still felt like a decadence, a luxury. Inured in her was years of doing without the latest fashion, the finer fabrics, the better shoes.

However, she hoped this outing would also serve to get her mind off James—at least for a time. As it was, thoughts of him continued to fill her every waking *and* sleeping moment. She too easily recalled the sumptuousness of his touch and the clean scent of sandalwood on his skin. But for a week's worth of his kisses, she'd give up a lifetime of mouth-watering desserts—strawberry ice cream, flaky French pastry, all her favorites.

That he wanted her physically, there was no doubt. But she wanted more—needed much more than that. In this courtship, she couldn't accept anything less than his heart, solely and wholly hers.

En masse, they entered the shop and were immediately greeted by Madame Batiste herself, a tall, robust woman with hair such an unnatural red it shouted hair dye from her brown roots. She held her arms outstretched in welcome.

"Bonjour, Lady Armstrong," she said in a heavily accented singsong voice.

"Bonjour, Madame Batiste," the viscountess responded with a gracious smile. Here, her mother would be able to practice her French, a language every proper member of the aristocracy studied. Missy didn't know why, as she'd found very few places in her life to use it, unless she counted the very same peers who were looking to exercise their limited knowledge.

The modiste greeted Missy and her sisters, warmly exclaiming how beautifully they had grown since she'd seen them last, which had been the prior year. She quickly ushered them into a private dressing area where they were relieved of their shawls, bonnets and gloves. She and her sisters were stripped down to their cotton undergarments and measured. Madame Batiste's assistant, a very young English girl, made a fuss, exclaiming over the tiny span of Missy's waist, which measured eighteen and one-half inches without the use of stays.

The next hour and a half was spent poring over fashion plates and selecting fabrics for walking, morning, and evening dresses. There would be plenty of dresses of pyramid silks, printed muslins, *mousselaine de soie,* and one exquisite evening gown of nankin trimmed in *passementerie.*

When selecting the styles, the viscountess approved with a smile and disapproved with a quick shake of her head and a frown. That part went quickly. By the time they had finished, ten dresses were ordered: six for Missy and two apiece for Emily and Sarah. Madame Batiste promised to have three of the simpler dresses delivered in two days' time and the remaining, four days hence. After the viscountess signed for the purchases, the women filed out of the shop and into the fading light of the late afternoon sun.

"We will stop at the milliner's next and then the cobbler," her mother said as they started down the cobbled sidewalk. They proceeded several shops down to arrive in front of the hatmaker's storefront.

"Lady Armstrong."

All four turned at the greeting. The pudgy figure of Lady Cornwall approached. Missy suppressed a grimace.

The marchioness's face held a shine not a glow, and she wore the most unbecoming violet dress replete with four tiers of flounces. Surely a lady of her distinction knew a woman of her advanced years and size had no need to be puffed out so. And nothing good could be said of her bonnet. It was the oddest piece of frippery Missy had ever seen, adorned with flowers, sprigs and one long ostrich feather. And to make the eyesore a complete and utter catastrophe, it was trimmed in a red lace of sorts. Red of all colors. As if the entire outfit didn't draw attention enough.

It was truly remarkable, given the marchioness's lack of fashion sense, that her daughter was always so attractively turned out. Missy darted a glance around for any sign of Lady Victoria and was relieved to find none.

"Good afternoon, Lady Cornwall," the viscountess said warmly.

"How lovely your daughters have grown," the marchioness tittered. Her smile was wide and her eyes brimmed with something verging on triumph.

"Good afternoon, Lady Cornwall," Missy, Emily and Sarah chorused.

"I had to hurry down to my modiste. I am in need of a new gown for Lady Harrison's soiree." Her smile spread from one long-lobed ear to the other, threatening to outshine the sun.

Ever so polite and always a lady, the viscountess smiled, trying to give the appearance of interest. Missy knew that look well enough.

"Indeed? Well, I shall look forward to seeing you in your new gown." How her mother managed that statement with a straight face was a testament to how long she'd been out in Society.

Their group moved to the left to allow a cluster of ladies to pass without causing a tangling of parasols with bonnets.

"As I'm sure you've already noticed, my daughter is not accompanying me." She paused, her brown eyes alight with anticipation.

The sounds of London life on Bond Street—the clip-clop of horses, the shrill cry of a young child—could not fill the ensuing silence. Seconds elapsed and stretched until Missy finally realized the marchioness expected one of them to inquire upon her daughter's absence.

When it became apparent no such question would be forthcoming, the marchioness continued, excited and breathy. "Lord Rutherford came calling this morning rather early, and they went for a ride through Hyde Park. The poor girl was simply too fatigued to accompany me." By the end of the unsolicited explanation, she looked near to bursting.

Missy's breath caught in her throat. The news had the effect of being pitched from a horse, the landing, nothing short of breath-stealing. Quickly, she lowered her gaze. She would not cry. At least not now.

"How—er—exhausting that must be for her," her mother replied.

But it was clear by the look on Lady Cornwall's face that the viscountess had not displayed the proper amount of enthusiasm. Her smile dimmed in the face of their very sober expressions.

"Well I must be off. I am sure she will be awaiting my return." And with that and a crisp nod, she was on her way, her skirts swaying in tandem with the overgenerous curves of her hips.

The viscountess turned to Missy. "That woman could make a mountain out of a hill," she said with a resigned shake of her head. Missy said nothing.

Emily and Sarah stood mute, casting her tentative, concerned looks. Missy stiffened and looked away. She didn't need their pity. James wasn't interested in marriage, which was the only thing one could expect with Lady Victoria. Furthermore, the woman wasn't interested in him. Not with that touch-me-not air she wore about her like a mantelet.

They entered the milliner's in silence.

A half hour later, they exited. Stevens materialized, collected their packages from the proprietor, and hurried to store them in the boot of the carriage. For Missy, the joy of their shopping excursion was gone. It had left with the words of a certain purple paisley–gowned marchioness. The rest of the afternoon stretched before her like a boat ride on the stench-drenched Thames.

However, she had to endure one more stop at the cobbler. As her sisters and mother shuttled in through the narrow doorway, Missy's gaze idly swept the busy sidewalk. She spotted Lord Crawley exiting a popular tailor's just two shops down. Their gazes met in that brief instant. Missy summoned up a smile. Lord Crawley looked away as if he had not seen her, effectively cutting her.

Disbelief gave way to anger. The blasted man had the nerve

to kiss her the evening before and cut her the next day. Anger welled up inside her like a boiling cauldron. The audacity.

"Mama, I believe I left the swath of material I brought to match the shoes I wish to purchase in the carriage. I will be but a moment."

The viscountess shot a look back at her, and after assenting with a brief nod, followed her younger daughters into the shop.

With quick steps, Missy was able to catch Lord Crawley before he traversed much farther down the sidewalk.

"Lord Crawley, I do believe you saw me."

Lord Crawley's head snapped in her direction as he came to a jerky stop. Missy halted beside him. The red bloom crawling up his neck and spreading mottled across his face was the flush of a guilty man. His Adam's apple bobbed convulsively.

"Why, good afternoon, Miss Armstrong. I'm afraid I didn't see you." His smile was a nervous twitch.

She knew he was lying, and by God, he knew that she knew. Did he think her a fool?

"Truly?" She quirked a brow and managed to dodge the pointed edge of a parasol as a rather rotund matron jostled past.

Lord Crawley's gaze skirted the area around them with narrow, apprehensive eyes. "Is your brother with you today?"

"Why ever would Thomas—no, certainly—"

"I am quite aware of how protective he is of you. It is also well known his shot is both fast and accurate." He laughed. The forced, awkward variety that had no basis in amusement.

Missy shook her head, dazed. Had she heard him correctly? "I beg your pardon? I'm not certain I quite understand your meaning."

He pulled himself up to his full height, all pretence of

lightness and joviality wiped clean from his countenance. "Rutherford has made it quite clear I would not be welcomed as a suitor."

Missy was unable to respond. She snapped her jaw shut when she realized her mouth had been hanging agape, but she continued to stare up at him, her eyes wide.

He took note of her shock and nodded in affirmation. "So if you would be so kind as to not mention our meeting today and this conversation . . ."

"Lord Crawley, I must apologize for Lord Rutherford. He had no right to say such a thing. You have no need to fear my brother," she said, sufficiently recovered enough to speak.

Another nod dipped his chin, this one slower, but his brown eyes clouded over in skepticism. "Yes, well, I do have a pressing engagement. I must bid you good day." And with that, his courtship of her came to a shuddering finale.

Missy stood in the front of the milliner's shop long after she lost sight of him in the throng of shoppers, trying to make sense of what she'd just heard. James was warning off her suitors? He was adamant he didn't want her—at least not to marry—yet he had threatened a peer whose intentions were completely honorable? What did this mean? Suddenly, her heart felt lighter. A jolt of indescribable pleasure chased across every square inch of her warmed flesh. She shivered and let out a wispy sigh. He cared. It was just that simple.

Traipsing back down to the cobbler's store, a check in the front window revealed her mother and sisters still busy examining shoes. Missy schooled her features before entering the shop.

The viscountess was speaking to the owner, Mr. Raphael, her sisters by her side. As she approached, Emily shot her a quizzical look. Missy held a gloved hand up to her temple, furrowing her brows.

When the gray-haired gentleman disappeared into the back, her mother turned to her. "Missy, is something wrong?"

"I fear I have developed a touch of a headache."

"Does that mean we won't be going to Epitaux's?" Sarah's bow mouth had already formed a pout. Epitaux's was a quaint eatery in Pall Mall that offered excellent food and service. The viscountess had promised them they would dine there for supper.

"No, there is no need to change your dining plans on my account," Missy insisted. "I shall have Stevens hail a hackney and accompany me home." This was one of the few occasions Missy was grateful that Sarah's concern to fill her belly overrode that of her sister's malady—feigned though it was.

Almost as if she'd read her mind, Emily gave Sarah a look of censure, which elicited an immediate look of chagrin from the younger girl. "We do hope you feel better soon," Emily said.

Missy managed a faint smile through a properly pained expression.

"Have Mrs. Henderson fix you a hot cup of tea, and then perhaps some rest will take care of it." Her mother's expressed concern flooded her with guilt.

"Yes, Mama. I am certain I'll be fine by morning," she said.

After exiting the cobbler's, Missy found Stevens lounging next to the coach taking in the sea of humanity going about their day. He drew to his full height when he saw her approaching.

Stevens was a young man of no more than twenty years, with brown hair and a sprinkling of freckles across the bridge of his nose and cresting his high cheekbones. He was also trustworthy and able to hold his tongue, unlike her lady's maid.

"Stevens, I will need you to hail a hackney and accompany me on a call."

"Yes, miss." He nodded, agreeing without so much as a question.

With the alacrity that must have secured him his position, he flagged a hackney and in no time at all they were heading south toward Berkley Street.

Fifteen minutes later, Missy climbed the brick steps up to confront the dark wood door of James's townhouse. She'd left Stevens with the hackney, instructing him to hold the conveyance until her return. Whenever that would be.

A sober-faced servant of an indeterminate age answered her knock. She was immediately struck by his bald, gleaming head. She knew she stared at him much too long and hard to be polite, but she'd never seen a man whose head contained not one shaft of hair.

He inclined said head in an austere manner that signified a butler's status. "May I help you?"

"Is Lord Rutherford in?" she asked, her reticule clutched tightly in her hand.

He made no move to further open the door, staring at her politely but not welcoming. "May I ask who is calling?"

How forward she must appear, not only presenting herself at James's residence, but arriving unchaperoned at that. She wondered if those were the thoughts running through the butler's mind as he guarded the entrance much like she imagined Saint Peter tended the pearly gates.

"Could you please inform Lord Rutherford Miss Armstrong is here to see him?" This time he opened the door wide enough to admit her, and then disappeared down the hall.

Twice, when she was much younger, her family had visited James at his parents' estate in Berkshire. However, in all the years she'd known him, she'd never been inside his residence in Town.

Standing in the entryway, she was instantly drawn by the warm masculine tones, and could not help a mild surprise at the tasteful décor. Wainscoting ran along the green silk-papered walls of the foyer, which displayed two large framed scenery oils. Brass wall sconces lit the area and a pair of large brass vases containing green leafy foliage stood on either side of the hall.

Missy made her way up the blue runner to peer past the French doors leading to a room dominated by a rectangular table and an elaborate chandelier hanging from the domed ceiling. She was inching closer for a better look at the dining room when the butler reappeared.

Starting like a guilty child caught committing a misdeed, she hastily backed away from the double doors.

"His lordship will see you. Please follow me." He relieved her of her bonnet, gloves, and shawl, then escorted her to the library.

"Miss Armstrong, my lord," he announced from the threshold, addressing James's back.

Missy barely noted the butler's departure. James now filled her vision. He kept his back to her, standing at the far end of the room swiveling a glass containing a clear liquid.

She regarded the expanse of wrinkled fawn linen covering the breadth of broad shoulders before narrowing down to a trim waist, finally disappearing into a pair of finely tailored trousers of dark taupe.

He took his time acknowledging her, turning to meet her gaze with the languor of a bored aristocrat. Wretched man. If he intended to play the boor that was just fine with her.

Her affront notwithstanding, Missy fairly reeled at the assault on her senses the sight a rather disheveled James presented. His hair, slightly mussed in appearance, made her itch to run her fingers through the shiny dark locks. Dark bristles shadowed his jaw and dimpled cheeks. And his eyes—those pale blue orbs—gazed at her, half mast and penetrating.

Holding a glass up in his left hand, he asked, "A drink, Miss Armstrong?"

In response to the mocking gesture, Missy collected herself and pressed her mouth into a fine line. "Isn't it a little too early in the day to be indulging?"

He ignored her remark and sank into a nearby armchair, motioning casually with his hand for her to do likewise.

Missy crossed the room and chose a seat almost as stiff and rigid as her back. "I just had a most enlightening conversation with Lord Crawley. Apparently, he is under the false notion that Thomas will do him bodily harm, perhaps even fatal damage, should he press his suit. Why ever do you suppose he'd believe such a thing?"

James stared at her for what seemed an eternity, wearing the most inscrutable expression. Then without a word, he downed the last of his drink and rose to his feet to pour another one at the sideboard. Missy's ire began to rise.

"Crawley is a gambler and if his fortunes don't improve, he will find himself penniless." He kept his back to her as he spoke. Her ire rose another notch. Just as she opened her mouth to convey her displeasure, he turned and made his way back to his chair.

"And as for Lord Riley, who has been puttering about you like a pup begging for kitchen scraps, I would be careful not to encourage him. He's still under his mother's skirts. Being married to him would be like having three of you in your marriage bed." He gave a mock shiver and feigned a look of horror, before allowing his mouth to edge into a wicked grin.

Lady Riley, widowed at least ten years now, was one of the most overbearing matrons of the *ton*. And she did cosset her eldest son in a shrill and rather self-serving manner. If Missy were considering a marriage to him, which she was most definitely not, it certainly would be something to keep in mind.

"It is none of your concern who I choose to see, nor is it your responsibility to dissuade any gentleman who should choose to court me. I am not your sister." *Must he constantly be reminded of that?*

His mocking demeanor instantly vanished. With glittering heat in his eyes, he raked her with such a look, a languid, thorough perusal that started at the top of her upswept chestnut curls to the hem of her moss green skirt, lingering with a lack of propriety much too long in the middle.

A tight, throbbing heat unfurled low in her belly and Missy was mindful of the way her breasts peaked beneath her fine ecru muslin bodice. He couldn't possibly see her body's reaction, not with the many layers of fabric covering her bare flesh, but she still had to resist the urge to glance down.

"Believe me," he said with a rasp in his voice, "I'm well aware of that." His gaze dropped to her breasts.

"Then I demand you stop." She wasn't certain now exactly what she wanted him to stop. Stop dissuading eligible suitors or stop watching her with heat enough to set the whole of London afire? Because when he watched her like that, her hopes immediately took flight.

A laugh rumbled from somewhere deep in his throat. It was dark and humorless. He raked her with another searing stare.

"Less than three months gone you came to my chamber, threw yourself at me like a lovesick schoolgirl and today you welcome the attentions of a dandy." Lifting his glass in a jeering toast he said, "Fickle should be the other name for women."

A lump formed in her throat at the scorn in his voice. His look challenged her, almost as if he meant to break her in some way, and it was that knowledge that strengthened her resolve.

"As you said, it is—*was*—the remnants of a young girl's infatuation. But I am over that now—over you." The lie fell effortlessly from her lips, and she tipped her nose in the air to punctuate her point. "You have made your feelings where I am concerned quite clear, yet you are determined to undermine me by rebuffing those who do show an interest. I do not understand you. If I didn't know better, I would say you were jealous."

"Jealous! Over a woman?" James snorted. "Never in my life." He dragged an unsteady hand through the thick strands of dark hair then ran them over the back of his neck, as he seemed to fight for control.

"Then why, pray tell, would you go about threatening Lord Crawley like some common street thug?"

"So you're saying you welcome the advances of the likes of Edward Crawley?" He spat the man's name, anger hardening his features. "I guess you do as you didn't seem to mind him pawing at you at your mother's dinner party."

Missy said nothing for several seconds. When she spoke, she did so evenly, without the slightest inflection. "You saw."

Those two words appeared to infuriate him more. "Yes, I saw him kiss you, and God knows what other liberties you granted him when I left."

The whole thing occurred before she had time to think, the slap snapping his head to the side with surprising strength. Missy's palm burned at the impact.

Stunned, his hand came up to rub the bright red imprint of her hand on his cheek. A storm of emotions swept through her: shock, mortification, guilt, but fury overrode them all. She was on her feet, her form visibly shaking.

"Certainly more liberties than I would ever grant you again," she said, her hands balled at her sides.

Before she could blink, James grabbed her forearms and yanked her hard against him, toppling them back onto the chair, Missy landing square on his lap. "Perhaps we should put that to the test," he growled, lowering his head.

His mouth slanted down on hers, hard, and she fought instinctively against his domination, his ruthless insurrection of her will. Her lips remained tight to his questing tongue. He immediately gentled the kiss, nipping the bowed corners of her mouth and testing the seam with his tongue in firm insistence. A tiny gasp fluttered from her lips and he was in.

James tasted of brandy and passion but it was not enough. She was ravenous for more. Sliding her tongue against his, she discovered the power of a kiss. He jerked and let out a groan. One large hand circled her torso while the other clutched the giving curve of her bottom through the satiny folds of her skirt and layers of petticoats to pull her hard against his erection. A moment later he had her under him.

Her body trembled and throbbed at his thick stabbing presence at the heart of her. The ache, sharp and unrelenting, created a fire that left her gasping. Missy tightened her hold on his neck, pressing her aching breasts up against the muscled wall of his chest.

"God help me," he said on a ragged breath. But it didn't sound like a prayer, it sounded like a hard-fought surrender. His mouth lifted and slanted to take her again, going deeper, getting hotter.

Limp with passion, Missy accepted it all. While one hand squeezed, cupped, and massaged the curve of her bottom, dragging her rhythmically against his hard flesh, his other hand sought the firm thrust of her breast through the soft muslin, plucking avidly at the taut peak.

She heard his name in a breathless chant, unaware the sound emitted from her kiss-swollen lips until his mouth left hers to trail down her neck. With his teeth, he nipped along its creamy length, and then soothed the love bites with his tongue.

Missy felt helpless against the powerful surge of raw unadulterated hunger that gripped her and had her arching her hips, desperately searching for some relief to the sweet pressure building there. Her jerking hips elicited another harsh masculine groan. He abandoned her breast and within seconds, her bodice loosened as his fingers made quick work of the small buttons on her dress. He tugged the bodice from her shoulders, released the front fastenings of her stays and then smoothed the cotton chemise from her torso.

"So sweet and perfect," he murmured, his face tight as his eyes devoured the small, rosy mounds, their peaks pebbled in passionate excitement. With the flat of his thumb, he circled one berry-tipped nipple. Her breath hitched and her hips undulated helplessly.

"Do you like that, Missy?" His voice was hoarse and cajoling, as he continued to pleasure her, tracing the surrounding aureole with his long, tapered index finger.

"Please, James." His name emerged a frustrated sob. Missy forced the lids of her eyes open, still blind to everything except the growing ache building so rapidly and deliciously inside of her, making her hot and damp in that place between her thighs.

"You would like me to please you, wouldn't you?" He lowered his head and she felt his breath, warm and moist, on her before he took her nipple into his mouth. He swathed it with his tongue, two, three times and then clamped down on it, sucking strongly. Missy clenched her inner thighs, her sex contracting so hard she thought she'd explode. Her head fell back onto the cushion, clutching the back of his head, her fingers sifting through the damp, silky strands of his hair, urging him on, holding him.

* * *

Nothing else mattered at that moment but the woman in James's arms. He had never experienced such a loss of control and it frightened him. He knew he could take her now without a murmur of dissent. He moved his hands from her breast to release himself from the unbearable confines of his trousers to do just that when his gaze took in the scene like one would a tableau.

Missy lay suppliant beneath him, her eyes closed, her breasts flushed and shiny from his ministrations while he lay between her legs, her skirt hiked up to her knees. She was an innocent and he had been about to take her like a barmaid with little thought to her comfort or her virginity. With little thought to the consequences, and no thought of her brother, his best friend. Good God, Armstrong would kill him. He was supposed to be discouraging her, not having his way with her. Pulling himself from atop her proved to be a Herculean effort, but he managed it by the skin of his teeth, his cock protesting the entire time. Then he cursed everything on God's green earth.

It seemed to take Missy several seconds to recognize his absence. Her eyes opened slowly, the pupils so large and dark they dominated the slate blue iris. He was already on his feet before she took note of her dishabille. Appearing quite overwrought, she fastened her stays, pulled her chemise and dress into place and then, with shaking hands, struggled to button her dress. A hot pink blush suffused her face, her gaze remaining fixed on the task at hand.

Reaching the sideboard in a few ground-eating strides, James poured himself another glass of distilled water, his hand unsteady. What he needed was a real drink. It was disconcerting, this power she seemed to have over him—this ability to shatter his control so effortlessly.

He downed the contents in a single swallow. A glance over his shoulder revealed Missy was still working with the round pearl buttons. If he hadn't feared he'd ravage her if he got within a foot of her, he might have applied himself to the task.

"You should not have come," he said instead.

She didn't look up from what she was doing, her fingers almost frantic in their haste. At last, with her dress secured but with several glossy chestnut strands dangling about her face, Missy retrieved her reticule from the side table and rose primly from her seat. An action so thoroughly juxtaposed to the wanton of minutes before.

"On that we can both agree," she replied, a slight husk to her voice. "But at least with you, I now have a better idea of where I stand."

James's brows shot up. He couldn't help it. "And where is that? A few kisses and some heated moments and you think to know me so well?" he said disdainfully. "What do you expect when you show up like this alone?"

Missy regarded him silently. Something unfathomable flickered in her eyes. "That's right, any pretty face would cause the same reaction in you. Perhaps then I, too, should discover if any man with a handsome face would affect me similarly."

The rage in him came to a frantic boil. He swiftly closed the distance between them. She smelled like some sweet sexual intoxicant. He dropped back a step. "If you think to play these sorts of games with the *gentlemen* of the *ton*, I warn you, unlike me, they will take what you have to offer."

"I'm certain you are correct."

James inhaled sharply. "Good God, you are shameless."

The look she leveled him with didn't appear the least bit ashamed. "And do you think it is because they want me more than you want me?" Allowing only a heartbeat of a pause, she pressed on. "So why do you think that they would while you will not?"

"What the devil are you talking about?" James asked, baffled. If there was a correct answer to her cryptic question, he was simply agog to hear it.

"I will give you some time to think on it." Missy then issued him a quaint, satisfied nod before quietly taking her leave.

After returning home, Missy remained in her bedchamber awaiting her mother and sisters' return from their outing. She lay on her bed, her lips still tingling from the scorching heat of James's kisses. Memories of what occurred in the library, on the chair, in his lap, evoked an achy, full feeling within her and washed over her like an inundating tide, her nipples puckering in ready response.

Thoughts of his long, tapered fingers and sensuous mouth on her breasts pleasuring her had her pulsing hot and damp between her thighs. James was right. She was completely shameless, but it was his fault. He had given her a taste of passion and it appeared she developed an insatiable appetite for more. But only with him. And his response to her told her he was far from immune. His refusal to take what she'd been unable to deny him told her his feelings *must* go far deeper than simple lust. It was the only reason that explained why he'd deny himself something it was obvious he wanted. Now all she had to do was to figure how she could use this knowledge to her advantage . . . and James's inevitable capitulation.

Chapter Eight

James glanced around the dimly lit interior of White's, the air thick and hazy, carrying with it the pungent scent of cigar smoke and raucous conversation. The swells of Parliament flooded every inch of the prestigious club. An early recess from a day of debates didn't send the members home to the loving arms of their wives; not when there was money to be thrown away gambling and yet more politics, horses, and women to be discussed. An image of his mother's beautiful but bitter countenance came to mind. He could hardly fault the men if their wives were similarly disposed.

Tucked away in the far corner of the main room, James sat indolently cradling a tumbler of brandy in one hand. His other hand drummed a distinctly impatient beat on the smooth hard wood of the table as he drained the remaining liquid from the glass. An hour had already come and gone and another ten minutes crawled by before he saw Armstrong pressing his way toward him through the crush.

Dropping into the chair opposite him, his friend immediately hailed a passing black-clad server. He ordered their best rum, his usual beverage of choice, before settling into the cushioned seat.

"You look like hell," Armstrong said smiling, peeling off his gloves and tossing them on the table.

James shot him a dark glare. "Is it any wonder now that you've kept me waiting for over an hour?" He certainly would not admit his ill temper had more to do with Missy than it did his friend's tardiness. The damned chit had managed to firmly lodge herself in his thoughts since the incident at his townhouse two weeks ago.

He'd convinced himself that his real problem was his three months of unintentional celibacy. The length of time he'd been without a mistress was the reason he found himself particularly vulnerable to Missy's innocent sensuality.

"Sibling duty calls, not that you would know anything about that," Armstrong tossed out with a teasing grin. It had been an ongoing joke of sorts that James's responsibility to his brother, who was a vast twelve years younger, could not compare to those the young viscount had to his three sisters.

"I would hardly call myself an only child," James replied dryly.

"No, not in the literal sense, though you and Christopher have essentially grown up as such."

The server returned and carefully set the drink on the table, putting a momentary halt to their conversation. Armstrong rewarded him by dropping a shilling on the tray. His generosity was met with an appreciative smile and a shallow bow.

James waited until the server moved off to the next table before saying, "Regardless, it doesn't speak of my affection for the boy." Everyone who was acquainted with James knew of his love for his younger brother. There was very little he wouldn't do for the scamp, which Christopher also knew and, at times, had used unfairly to his advantage.

"Of course not, but it's not the same as having nothing but sisters—and beautiful ones at that. If only Missy would finally settle on Granville, I'd at least have some peace until next year." He sounded amused and grim at the same time. "I gather this is what it will be like should I have daughters of my own someday—that is, should I marry." His expression was rueful as he sipped the rum.

"What family duties?" James made a show of nonchalance. "Don't tell me you've again been put in charge of beating away the hordes of suitors begging a place in your mother's drawing room?"

Armstrong chuckled. "Given it's her fourth Season, I'm just relieved she still has prospects. And my mother hasn't changed. She continues to demand a full account of every gentleman who would assume to court my dear sister. My God, the list was as long as my arm."

As beautiful as she was, it certainly wasn't a surprise, but how the very words chafed him. Three heated kisses had apparently sent him into a tailspin.

For years he'd avoided it: the suitors, the lady herself. But no longer. No more running. This Season he'd face the slew of gentlemen, many his own counterparts, out to make Missy their wife. Like a clenched fist, the thought caused a tightening in his chest.

"And just who deems himself fit to be your brother by marriage?" The question came before he could stop it and he silently cursed the need for him to know. He cursed he even cared.

"Riley, Malborough, Essex, and—as you know—Granville, just to name a few," Armstrong replied.

"Good God, I can't believe you would allow Malborough or Essex to come within ten feet of her. Second sons on the hunt for an heiress are all they are. Most doorframes can't accommodate Malborough's girth. And Essex has ears the size of an elephant. Surely, you wouldn't wish either trait on any nephew or niece of yours. Missy would never be happy with them. And, by God, Riley? The man has a spine of a jellyfish.

His mother still leads him around by her apron strings. That accursed woman will make Missy's life miserable."

Pushing his chair back from the table, Armstrong propped a negligent foot on his knee and regarded him, a derisive smile twisting his mouth. "And Granville? I am quite sure you're just dying to tell me why he will not suit my sister as well."

It was as if Armstrong suspected something. Something in James's charge indicating more than friendly concern. But he hadn't intended to comment on the earl's suitability. He was probably as perfect a match for Missy as there could be. The only problem was Missy didn't want Granville. She wanted him.

"I'm surprised you can jest over such a serious matter. As close as you are to your family, I would assume you would be more particular in which gentlemen you would permit to pay her court." He hadn't meant it to be a condemnation but, blast, Armstrong had maddened him with his blasé attitude.

His friend's rejoinder was swift, an ominous tone threading his words. "Never question my devotion to my sisters and their well-being. If I dismissed all of the men based on your exacting criteria, there would be no one left. Every year you find fault with just about all of them. Lord, at this rate it will be a choice between spinsterhood or permitting her to marry you as she so desperately wants."

James's eyes widened with a start, and the words came tumbling out before he could quash them. "Lord, am I such an odious prospect that you'd rather see her grow old alone?" Damn and blast it! He had no desire to court or wed Missy. Pure pride had gotten in the way of common sense.

Several seconds ticked by as Armstrong eyed him silently, his gaze assessing. "Is that to say that you are an interested suitor?" He took another drink from his glass, his eyes never once leaving James's face.

James forced a laugh. "Hardly. I just hate to have myself cast as the worst thing that could happen to a young lady of quality. One day, I'm sure I'll make a fine husband and father."

"Yes perhaps, if the lady wouldn't mind sharing you with half the women of London. Missy deserves better than you and you know it. In any case, you are allowing your inflated opinion of your charms to get in the way of sound judgment. You haven't any interest in my sister, and certainly none in marriage at this stage of your life."

At his friend's confident assertion, James lifted his drink to his mouth, praying the heat flooding his face didn't betray his guilt. "Yes, that's all true but I'm speaking of when I am ready for marriage."

"As I said, perhaps for a certain kind of woman," Armstrong said, with the firm understanding Missy didn't fall into the category of women he referred to.

Armstrong's attention then shifted to rest just above James's right shoulder, and it was at that time he sensed a presence at his back. Lord Clive Essex stepped forward before he was forced to twist his neck to identify him. James could see his friend fighting back an ironic smile as he greeted him.

"Essex, it's been a while. What is it, no less than twenty-four hours since we last saw one another?" Essex, slight and short, reddened at Armstrong's wry tone, causing his pointed nose to appear even larger and longer under the dim glow of the gaslights.

"With your beautiful and charming sister, I would be hard-pressed to stay away," he replied gallantly.

Eyeing the man, James bit back a sharp retort. With Essex's pallid complexion and his bulging eyes—and those ears—the baron could hardly be considered a fine-looking catch.

"Rutherford." The greeting was followed by a brief nod in his direction.

"Essex," James muttered.

Armstrong played the part of the young privileged lord to the hilt, reposed in his seat, hands folded loosely across his chest, legs outstretched. "Yes, I see you're brave enough to throw your hat into the ring."

Essex swallowed nervously while still trying to maintain a winsome smile. "I don't believe bravery has anything to do with it. Your sister is a prize in her own right."

"And no doubt you know exactly how much she is worth," James charged, his hit direct and unequivocal.

Clearly surprised by the attack, Essex sputtered for several seconds before regaining his voice. His stare swung to James. "Just what are you insinuating, Rutherford?"

James pinned him with a narrow, contemptuous gaze. "I don't believe I was *insinuating* anything." The man was nothing but an opportunistic milksop.

The baron's posture appeared so rigid, James was sure that if felled by a blow, he would snap in two.

"You are out of line," Essex said, trying for a certain amount of hauteur but failing miserably when forced to swipe a hand over his face to catch the bead of sweat threatening his rapidly thinning hairline.

Armstrong seemed content to sit back and watch the charged interaction as a quiet observer, his brows raised much of the time.

"And *you* don't have a chance, Essex. My advice to you is to find another heiress to pursue."

Most men knew that if they tangled with James, they would most likely lose—although his intimates held no such fears. Showing the proper amount of affront, Essex mumbled his good-bye to Armstrong and made a hasty retreat.

James watched him until he exited the club. His gaze shifted to his friend, who watched him intently, his expression inscrutable.

"What, dammit?" he bit out after too long under Armstrong's penetrating green-eyed stare.

"You'd better be posting for the position of her protector and not her suitor."

"Don't be a fool," he snapped in response.

Armstrong threw back his head and gave a hearty laugh. "My, you are getting touchy. You must be losing your sense of humor if you can no longer tolerate a little teasing."

Teasing? Nothing about this situation with Missy was remotely amusing.

A shadow crossed their table and once again, James was at a disadvantage as to the identity of this new intruder.

"Clifton," Armstrong called out, as it appeared the man hadn't intended to stop.

James turned to see Sir George Clifton pause. His expression not entirely amiable but it appeared indecision gave way to propriety. He turned to face Armstrong.

"Armstrong," he said before his gaze flickered to James. He gave him a curt nod and muttered, "Rutherford."

"I've been telling everyone how you have taken Parliament by storm." The viscount motioned to the empty chair on his left.

Clifton's smile appeared strained as he shook his head in refusal. "As you know, I am merely trying to make a difference for the working class in the city. Unfortunately, my lords, I must be on my way. I have pressing matters to attend to at home. Good evening." With a brisk nod toward Armstrong, he proceeded on this way.

Was he imagining things, or had the man just slighted him? This was not the first time he'd experienced a vague sense of unease in Clifton's presence. And this was not a normal circumstance as they had all attended Cambridge together. Although Armstrong had forged a deeper acquaintance with him, James and he had been quite amiable in a loose sort of way. But it was apparent matters, perhaps of a personal nature, occupied his thoughts.

He discovered his friend was of a similar mind when he remarked, "He hardly seems himself."

Circling the rim of the empty glass with his forefinger, James nodded in agreement.

"I consider myself quite adept at reading others and I wager he's having woman problems," the viscount continued.

The irony of his statement was not lost on James.

"Oh, before I forget, Mother has requested your attendance next week for supper." An invitation from the viscountess was the equivalent of a ducal command.

"And don't think that your absence this past week has gone unnoticed. For a whole ten minutes I was forced to listen to Lady Melvin complain how you never seem to make her soirees."

James groaned. "One less bachelor for the two daughters she's so desperate to marry off. Yes, I can imagine she was completely distraught."

"And since your absence has coincided with Lady Victoria's, the gossipmongers are having a time. It appears you were seen squiring the lady about in Hyde Park. Then several evenings later, you were both notably absent from Lady Melvin's fete. An invitation that the countess herself insisted you had both accepted." The taunting grin on Armstrong's handsome face made it clear that he took obvious pleasure in conveying that piece of information.

"Let them talk," James said, averting his eyes.

Angling his head, Armstrong quirked a brow. "Should I give any credence to the gossips?"

"Don't be an arse." He grumbled the terse retort.

"Yes, I don't think even you could thaw the ice maiden. But if I didn't know better, I would think you're suffering the same malaise as Clifton. You're downright caustic these days and acting like a man deprived."

It took James only a second to determine that any response would only fan the burning flame of his friend's imagination, so he did the wisest thing—he changed the subject.

"Is Cartwright also expected to make an appearance at this dinner?" As Lady Armstrong's suppers tended to be intimate family affairs, with only a few friends invited, he was hoping to shore up some reinforcements—or at least one.

"Cartwright has been summoned back to Yorkshire by his dear papa," the viscount replied.

James's brows shot up. "It's been a while since the duke has shown any interest in him." Cartwright's father, the Duke of Hastings, rarely had much to do with his youngest son. Though their friend rarely spoke of him, James knew they had been estranged for years.

Armstrong shrugged. "I expect he will return sometime in the next few weeks. He has a new mistress. I'm sure he'll be back by the Derby. The important thing is your presence. I'll inform my mother you'll be escorting someone. And for Missy's sake, the more stunning she is, the better."

"I certainly don't want to see her hurt," James grumbled. Lord, at times it was difficult enough to look his friend in the eye with guilt eating a hole in his conscience. But the whole of it sounded so cold and calculated, for Armstrong had essentially tasked him with breaking her heart.

"Don't you think it would be much crueler to have her rusticating alone in Devon in ten years' time without a family of her own? Believe me, Rutherford, this is not cruelty, this is done out of love."

James lapsed into silence. Funny how something done out of love could make him feel so wretched.

* * *

It was just a small family supper, Missy reminded herself for the tenth time. Since Beatrice had left ten minutes ago, she'd checked her hair and dress repeatedly.

Emily and Sarah poked their heads into the bedchamber with nary a knock—as usual—and then sashayed in with the vivacity of impertinent young misses.

"Isn't my dress absolutely divine?" Sarah twirled twice, rising on her feet with the litheness of a ballerina. The dress, a soft pink silk and satin creation, was indeed lovely with its square neckline and no less than four flounces adorning the gauzy skirt. Emily was content to finger the beads trimming the skirt of her cream dress.

"You both look beautiful." And they both did, each wearing their blond hair pinned up at the back, long ringlets hanging to their shoulders. For Sarah this was a much more sophisticated style than the viscountess usually permitted. Her mother must be feeling generous this evening.

But Missy was to discover the true purpose of their visit. Sarah lifted her skirt and accompanying petticoats, stuck her right and then left foot out, wiggling them all the while.

"Are my shoes not divine also?" Divine, the past week, was *le mot du jour* and one Sarah had been using ad nauseam. If she ate cake she liked, it was divine; a reticule she saw through a storefront window, divine. Everything she took a fancy to was divine and driving Missy divinely batty.

Missy admired the heelless pink, stamped kid leather shoes with the indulgence befitting an older, devoted sister, and gave Sarah a glowing nod of approval.

Sarah preened. Then her eyes widened as she appeared to take in Missy's dress for the first time. "Has Mama seen your dress?" she asked in hushed, scandalized tones.

"Of course she has. It was she who selected it." Missy chided in an attempt to dismiss the question but her heart picked up an anxious beat. Yes, her mother had purchased it for her but it had been Beatrice who had lowered the neckline—but only by an inch.

She glanced down at the lavender dress made of satin, trimmed *en pyramid*, and examined the tight bodice with a critical eye. The tops of her breasts were nicely displayed; not modestly but not immodestly either. Why, she'd seen proper young misses at Society events with a décolletage much more revealing than hers.

Shooting Sarah and Emily a brave look, she then turned back to the mirror where she made a show of smoothing nonexistent ruffles from her skirt, and probing the security of the ivory hair comb holding her mass of hair off her nape.

An impish grin crept over Emily's face. "James will be here tonight."

"And?" she said, but the mention of his name brought forth a flood of warmth all over her body.

"Nothing. I just thought it worth mentioning," Emily replied, her green eyes dancing with anticipation. She then turned and glided elegantly from the room as if she hadn't just been acting like a young mischievous child with a secret to tell. Sarah followed not far behind.

Missy directed her attention once again to her mirrored reflection. Lightly, she pressed a hand to her throat as if that could calm the frantic pounding of her pulse and quell the butterflies fluttering wildly in her belly.

It is only a small family supper, she repeated to herself. With one final check in the mirror, she departed and made her way to the ground floor. Her mother and sisters stood just outside the drawing room with Thomas, who looked exceptionally dapper in a navy blue jacket, waistcoat, and trousers, and an expertly knotted white necktie. He wore his hair precisely placed away from his face, truly appearing the masculine version of his mother just as Emily and Sarah were her image. It was she, with her dark hair and blue-gray eyes amid a sea of golden locks and green eyes, who was the changeling.

Thomas gave a low whistle upon spotting her. "I see I'll have to sharpen my swords and clean my pistols tonight." He leaned down and brushed a kiss on her cheek.

Missy smiled at his teasing. Her gaze then locked with her mother's. Holding her breath, she awaited the very calm censure that was sure to come. Even in her rebuke, her mother was the essence of poise.

"Millicent, you look quite lovely."

Missy blinked twice in quick succession. She wasn't to receive an admonishment for the alteration to her gown? Perhaps her neckline wasn't so very low. "Thank you, Mama." she said, accepting the compliment with more gratitude than aplomb.

"All my girls look beautiful tonight." Looking stunning herself in an evening dress of violet taffeta and a bertha neckline of lace, the viscountess's gaze included all three of her daughters. At her mother's praise, Sarah blossomed like a flower's petal opening under the warm glow of the sun.

The knocker sounded. Within seconds, Missy heard James's low baritone . . . and then another one of the feminine variety. To her knowledge, her mother had invited no one other than James, Alex, and Claire. Her friend had declined due to a previous engagement and Alex was in Yorkshire for a spell.

A large potted fern obscured her view of the front door but there was no mistaking the feminine twitter. James hadn't come alone. The blasted man had a woman accompanying him. Missy swallowed, her hands fidgeting with the skirt of her dress. She felt rather than saw the stares of her sisters as they seemed to bore right through her. Her spirits took a steep dive off a rather high cliff. For the first time that evening, she regretted her decision to lower her neckline.

Thomas, her mother and sisters proceeded down the hall to greet the arriving guests, further blocking her view of James and the hitherto unknown woman. She peeked around the plant and Emily moved to the left to permit Missy a glimpse.

Blond and beautiful appropriately summed up her first impression of James's companion. Her mind shied away from what other role she played in his life. She was voluptuous with a décolletage that made her own appear downright prim. Missy disliked her on sight.

A mere glimpse of James, though, started her heart in a mad staccato beat. Dressed all in dark brown, from his jacket, waistcoat, and soft wool trousers to his shoes, he epitomized male beauty. When his gaze swung to her, the sharp contrast between his dark locks and pale blue eyes held her captive for several heart-thumping seconds. Did he pause in his step and did awareness spark in his eyes, or was it all merely wishful thinking? She quickly broke eye contact.

Tipping her chin, she stepped out from behind the plant and proceeded down toward the group, a smile in place.

He greeted her mother and sisters affectionately, easily, breezing a kiss on their respective cheeks. When he turned to her, he smiled an artless kind of smile, but it did not quite reach his eyes.

"Missy, you look lovely."

"Thank you," Missy replied in her most formal tone.

James had to stop himself from allowing his gaze to drift to the white swells of her breasts, exposed by her stunning off-the-shoulder dress.

"And this must be Millicent—or rather Miss Armstrong." Sophia's voice jolted his thoughts from wandering down forbidden paths. He instantly turned back to her and brought her forward, his hand hovering beneath her elbow.

"Missy, this is Mrs. Sophia Laurel. Sophia, Missy is Lady Armstrong's eldest daughter." He looked at Missy and tried to remember her as a girl, with her thick braid and coltish figure, not as he saw her now. He didn't want to see her as she was now. He kept his eyes trained above her breasts, ignoring the pulsing of his blood and the quickening in his loins.

"Good evening, Miss Armstrong. I see James addresses you as Missy but your mother calls you Millicent," Sophia smiled, nodding. "Tell me, which do you prefer?"

"Miss Armstrong will be fine." Missy said with unfailing politeness.

If it had been any other woman, Missy's response would have elicited more a caustic remark than an amused smile. And it didn't sit well with him that her obvious pique at Sophia's presence there tonight was gratifying—not when he needed to discourage her feelings.

"Indeed. Well I insist you call me Sophia," she said warmly. "James has always spoken of you in the fondest terms. Perhaps you've met my sister, Theresa Barlowe? She is currently enjoying her second Season."

"I don't believe I have." Missy's reply was no-nonsense prim.

"I'll be attending the Laughton soiree as her chaperone." Sophia tilted her head up to him. "Can you believe I am now old enough to chaperone, James?"

James smiled down at her. "Hardly."

At twenty-seven, Sophia was too young to be a widow though she was certainly no innocent schoolgirl. But theirs was a familial relationship made stronger by her tragic loss. And although she was out of her widow weeds, Sophia herself admitted she would never love again.

"Will you be attending?" Sophia asked, directing her attention back to Missy.

"Yes, I believe so." Again, Missy gave a short reply with no amiable verbiage.

His blue eyes fixed on the delectable curve of her lips and was immediately cast back to the hot, passionate moments, in the dimly lit library, where he had licked and nipped them into yielding softness and caressed her firm, plump—

He tore his gaze away and met Armstrong's intent regard. His friend's eyes narrowed, appearing thoughtful. James wondered how long he had been watching him. He wanted to look away but to look away would be an admission of guilt—the guilt of lusting after his sister, so he met his gaze and crooked his mouth into a self-assured grin. He quirked a brow in question as a man who hadn't anything to hide would do.

Armstrong merely smiled a thoroughly frustrating smile. James quickly returned his attention to Sophia.

"—sure to introduce you. I'm sure you'll find you have much in common." Sophia said. Missy nodded, appearing less than thrilled at the prospect, but the smile fixed on her pretty pink mouth never wavered.

"Missy would very much like that," the viscountess said, appearing at his elbow while directing a rather pointed look at Missy. She turned to Sophia. "And I would enjoy meeting your sister as well."

With the weight of her grief and jealousy threatening to choke her, Missy fought the urge to run. To disappear upstairs and into her bedchamber.

She hated him. Hated, hated, hated him. He was worse than a rake, he was cruel and without conscience. When would she learn? How foolish she had been. She'd gone from a foolish young girl to an even more foolish woman. Claire was right, she'd wasted three perfectly good Seasons, ones she could never get back. *Silly, silly, foolish, incredibly stupid girl is what I am.*

Looking down at her dress, the ridiculousness of the situation overcame her. This had all been for him—for James. He had kissed her and touched her in ways she had never allowed any other man, only to treat her like some infectious disease for more than two weeks. And now he had the nerve to bring his latest trollop to their home—to her mother's dinner table.

Emily's tug on the lace of her sleeve snapped her from her tormented thoughts. "Who is she?" her sister mouthed.

"Mrs. Sophia Laurel. Were you not listening?" she practically snapped, endeavoring to keep her voice low. As if by mutual consent, both girls had hung back, lagging a distance behind as the others proceeded ahead of them to the dining room.

"Oh don't be silly. You know what I mean. Is that his lady 'friend'?" Emily stressed the last word.

Just hearing the words caused her eyes to sting, and a tightness to form in her chest. "How on earth should I know?" This time her voice rang loud enough to draw the attention of the five pairs of eyes in front of them. She gave a tight smile and continued on ahead of Emily—dread in every step.

For supper that evening, the viscountess had done it up brown. Missy could not remember the last time they had larded pheasant, wild duck, turtle soup, lark pudding and game patties at home—in one sitting—unless her mother was hosting a supper party. Unfortunately, the grand spread was utterly wasted on her. She picked through the contents on her plate, only nibbling on the few things that managed to make it to her mouth. When she spoke, she did so almost exclusively with her mother and sisters.

Conversation around the table became quite animated when Mrs. Laurel broached the topic of the gold robbery, an event that had held all of London riveted to their papers since mid-May. Everyone was eager to give their theory of who they thought the culprits might be. Only she remained silent throughout the discussion. Not that anyone took notice of the small fact.

It also appeared Mrs. Laurel had an interest in politics, as she expressed her delight in the new Prime Minister. Thomas and James begged to disagree, both having no use for Lord Palmerston's political views. Another lively discussion ensued, with the three participants raising points and counterpoints against the other. Missy fumed in silence. So the woman was intelligent as well as beautiful; yet another reason to dislike her.

"Oh, Mama, this is absolutely divine." Sarah's eyes lit up when the footman appeared with dessert. "Missy, it's your favorite, strawberry ice cream."

Missy forced a smile as the footman placed the dessert tray on the table. "Hmmm, yes, but I fear I can't eat another bite."

"How is that? You've hardly touched a thing on your plate." James was quick to point out.

"Luncheon was quite filling," she said, her voice icily polite.

"I never believed I'd ever see a day when you would turn down your favorite dessert. I remember once, you were ready to wrestle me for it," Thomas teased.

"I suppose I did many silly things as a child. Much has changed now that I've grown." Missy glanced at James. He stared at her, and something dark and dangerous flared briefly in his eyes.

"Then you are very much like me," Mrs. Laurel said, seeming oblivious to the simmering undercurrents, content to chatter on. "When I was a child, I quite adored strawberries. My mother said my appetite for them would send us to the poorhouse. Now, I have no taste for them at all."

Mrs. Laurel's unwitting defense of her vexed her more than she cared to admit. It would be infinitely easier to dislike her if she wasn't being so kind. Perhaps that was why Missy felt the overwhelming urge to lash out. "I pray you are not trying to draw some sort of comparison between us, as it's obvious we are not a thing alike." The insult tumbled from her mouth before she could squelch it. She feared her own expression displayed the same shock rippling around the table.

Chapter Nine

There was silence, and then there was a third-rate horror show complete with dropped jaws and wide eyes. This, Missy acknowledged, was the latter.

She opened her mouth twice to say something, anything to erase the looks of censure from her mother and brother, and the one of discomfiture on Mrs. Laurel's face. Missy could not bring herself to face James's fury.

"Your rudeness toward Sophia is inexcusable. You will apologize this instant." James issued the order between gritted teeth, his blue eyes flaming.

Missy had been about to apologize, profusely, but the anger in his voice and his presumptuous manner sparked her own ire. He was the one responsible for all of this; the wasted efforts on her dress, the misery of the meal, all of it.

"James, it is quite all right," Mrs. Laurel said, laying a calming hand on his arm.

If Missy had been inclined to violence, she'd have slapped her—and then wrenched her hand from his for daring to touch him with such familiarity.

"No, it is not all right. You *will* apologize to Sophia." His tone brooked no refusal.

"You would have me apologizing to one of your women."

Missy heard several audible gasps and a fierce hiss. The hiss came from James.

"Millicent Eleanor Armstrong, you will apologize to both Mrs. Laurel and James at once." Missy had never heard nor seen her mother this angry before, and it was a rare occasion when she strung her three names together. Hers had not been a gaffe but an affront of the worst sort.

Stricken with embarrassment, Missy turned to Mrs. Laurel. "My remark was unwarranted and thoughtless. I beg your forgiveness."

"There is really no need to apologize, Miss Armstrong. My cousin can be very supercilious when he chooses. He was the same way as a child. You would be wise to ignore him during those times, as I have always done." Mrs. Laurel regarded him the way in which a sister would her brother.

His cousin? Mrs. Sophia Laurel was his cousin? If the floor below her had opened and swallowed her whole, she would have been imminently relieved. She hadn't thought it possible but she'd just discovered a whole new depth to her misery.

"Thank you, you are most kind." She managed to sound fairly articulate despite the jumble of her thoughts. Turning to her mother and brother, she asked in a cracked voice, "May I be excused?"

Her mother gave a curt nod and Thomas continued to watch her, his expression impassive. She refused to look at James.

So with the full weight of six pairs of eyes bearing down on her, Missy made an undignified dash to salvation.

Some hours later, a soft tap broke the silence of her bedchamber. Missy, dressed for sleep, sat cross-legged on her bed, her journal open on her lap and her humiliation forever immortalized in black ink. Snapping the book shut, she fully expected her mother to enter, coming to blister her ears as she so richly deserved. She was more than a little surprised when the door opened to reveal Thomas. Once he had surmised that she was properly attired, he entered, closing the door softly behind him.

This was even worse than she imagined. Rarely did her brother have cause to speak to her in a serious manner and his stern expression told her it was serious indeed. Trepidatious, Missy waited.

"I see you're not asleep as yet." He approached her bed, his footsteps muffled by the plush Axminster carpet. He continued to stand, the top of his blond head touching blue gauze of her canopy.

"I know what you wish to say—"

Thomas held up a hand to forestall her. "I am not here to scold you so put your mind at ease." His mouth lifted in a half smile. "I'm here to tell you this will pass."

He finally lowered himself to sit on the edge of the bed.

"I don't know what you mean," she said. But she did, and so did he.

"Your feelings for Rutherford." His tone was understanding, solicitous.

Missy shook her head in quick denial, her mouth poised ready to do the same. But the look on his face stopped her. She closed her mouth. He knew her too well, had loved her too long. Any denial would be met with rightful disbelief.

When she had experienced the first blush of love, she'd been too young and unaffected to hide it. James had known. Everyone had known. And tonight, with her jealousy and cruel words, she had only served to reinforce her feelings and her rank immaturity.

So instead of a grand denial, she shook her head, slowly this time, and said in a thick voice, "I fear this will never pass." Tears stung the corners of her eyes. She valiantly checked their flow.

"You could have your pick of any gentleman. You could have the heir of a duke if you wanted. I'll never understand why you chose to give your heart to Rutherford of all men," he teased, gently pulling her into his arms.

Didn't he know it hadn't been a choice, she despaired as she burrowed into the crook of his shoulder and availed herself to his brotherly compassion as she had done so many times in the past. Thomas, who was closer to her than her father had been when he was alive, and the most influential male in her life, offered her the understanding few could. He was a man and he knew James better than most, creating a bond between them she could not put into words.

His large hands gently grasped her forearms, holding her away to stare down at her forlorn face.

"He is my dearest friend, and I care for him like a brother, but he is not right for you. You deserve so much more. Rutherford and I, we are the same in that regard, perhaps that's why we get on so well. You deserve someone who will cherish you and love you. Rutherford has never been in love. I don't even think he's capable of that kind of emotion." His regard was both serious and kind. "I don't want to see you hurt."

Missy listened and she heard what her brother said but could not merge the James she had glimpsed, his passions blazing, with a man who lacked the ability to experience an emotion as powerful as love.

No, Thomas was wrong but she wouldn't contradict him. As he said, he didn't want to see her hurt.

Missy nodded solemnly. "I suppose Mama is terribly upset with me."

"Mother is not angry—" He broke off at her disbelieving stare. "She is concerned, Missy, just as I am. She does not want to see you hurt and your behavior at supper today . . ."

There was no need for him to finish the statement. Everyone had been witness to her deplorable behavior. Not only did she owe an abject apology to Mrs. Laurel but to James as well. But the prospect of facing him there, in front of everyone had sent her scampering from the room like a coward. She would apologize after she'd given him an opportunity to cool down.

Thomas nudged her chin up with the tip of his forefinger. "My only concern now is that you will end up wasting your life waiting for a man who will never love you. A man who is completely undeserving of your love. Do you think you might afford the gentlemen of the *ton* a chance to win your affections? Perhaps give Granville a real chance? Come, you know you must move on with your life."

Forget James? What she wouldn't give if that were possible. Missy could only offer a tremulous smile in response.

Victoria had long past conceded that her mother was overbearing. Not only was she overbearing but also tended to be extremely ingratiating with her betters (a relatively small group), and snooty to those of an inferior class. Her mother wanted for her the same thing most mothers wanted for their daughters; to marry well. And so in Victoria's fifth Season in the marriage mart, the marchioness had vowed that it would be her last. Victoria would find a husband this Season or the marchioness would die trying, of course metaphorically speaking, although Victoria did sometimes wonder.

"—and I do not understand what happened to Lord Rutherford. It has been three weeks since his last call." Her mother made no effort to hide her pique, her plump face set in a severe frown.

It had been his first and only call, Victoria mused.

Lady Cornwall jostled in her seat and the jar of her fleshy elbow caught Victoria at her waist.

"Ouch!" Victoria squeaked. Cognizant of the other

theatergoers, she shot a quick glance around, afraid her utterance had drawn their attention. To her relief the other occupants were engrossed in their own conversations as they chatted and gossiped throughout the intermission.

The marchioness sent her a look as if to say, what on earth is the matter? Victoria said nothing and turned her attention back to the darkened stage. Better that than begin an exchange with her mother.

"I have told you before, Victoria, and I will tell you again, I simply will not permit you to refuse another suitor. This really is your father's fault. He spoils you so. But what will he do when you are on the shelf and haven't the beauty to attract a decent husband? Why, I would die of shame." The marchioness spoke in hushed tones, leaning to her side so that her mouth was only inches from Victoria's ear.

Victoria did not even flinch. Long used to her mother's barbs and criticism, she continued to stare ahead, wishing she was anywhere else than where she was. Wishing she was with anyone other than who she was with. Wishing desperately she were with him tonight.

A growing buzz on the aisle proved a welcome distraction. Lady Cornwall strained her neck to peer around Victoria in an attempt to see who was causing such a stir. Victoria inclined her head, sharing the same curiosity.

Several rows back, ladies whispered and giggled like schoolgirls. Only a man could elicit such a reaction. And a much sought after man at that, or a very distinguished one.

It came as no surprise when she saw the tall, golden form of Lord Armstrong appear amid the throng of theatergoers making their way back to their seats. He looked altogether too handsome in his black ensemble, which brought out the burnished gold of his hair. She instantly recognized his escort but could not recall her full name. Camille something or the other.

"My word, is that Camille Foxworth on Lord Armstrong's arm?" Her mother said it as though the world had just come to an end. "Why that girl is on the plain side of plain. How on earth did she manage to snag such a man?"

Ah yes, Officer Foxworth's older sister. "I don't believe they are betrothed or that he is courting her, Mama," Victoria whispered as they watched the pair make their way to their seats.

Lady Cornwall drew in a shocked breath, her brown eyes widening. "You cannot mean . . . ?"

Victoria's eyes flashed in annoyance, but her mother was too busy jumping to untold conclusions to note it.

"I believe that Miss Foxworth is the elder sister of a friend enlisted in the Royal Navy. He is currently stationed abroad so I believe Lord Armstrong makes it a point to take her out and about as not to allow her to dwell at home alone. Apparently, she is quite close to her brother and is finding his absence difficult to bear." All this she'd learned from James the prior year.

"Humph," the marchioness snorted indelicately. "There isn't a lady alive who would not try to make more of the situation."

Sorely tempted to tell her mother that not everyone was of her mind, Victoria said nothing.

"Lord Frederick has offered for your hand."

Shocked and horrified, Victoria's head jerked around to stare at the marchioness. *This* is where she was to learn something of this significance, at the intermission of a play? But she knew her mother, how devious she could be. Victoria could hardly make a scene in such a public place.

"I have turned down his suit for the last two Seasons. I shan't marry him. Mother, the man is old enough to be my father."

"Victoria, please lower your voice. We will speak on this later. But I will remind you it will no longer be your decision, nor will I permit your father to interfere this time." Her brown eyes glinted a subtle warning before she turned away.

Victoria faced the stage, her mouth set in a mutinous line. She would sooner marry Lord Crawley, reprobate and fortune hunter that he was, than marry Lord Frederick. The man was much too old for her no matter who in Society deemed it acceptable for men to wed women young enough to be their daughters. And worse than his age was his appearance, with his slight thin figure and pale skin; the thought of having to bed him repulsed her worse than pickled chicken feet.

No, no matter what her mother said, she wouldn't marry him and, thankfully, she didn't have to. If her station dictated she marry a gentleman of rank and money, then she would. She'd taken great pains to ensure it. She now only needed a suitable time and place to tell her soon-to-be intended.

Chapter Ten

A mixture of floral scents permeated the drawing room as bouquets of roses and assortments of lilacs, tulips and lilies grew in abundance fresh on the heel of a soiree, a dinner party, or a ball.

At two o'clock, one week after the dreadful incident with James and Mrs. Laurel, Missy, wearing one of her most fashionable dresses—a caraco bodice, the pleated skirt edged in a sheer lace with decorative embroidered flowers—made her way to the second floor to attend her latest caller, Lord Granville.

Her mother, lovely in a ruby dress with a heart-shaped neckline and gauzy, expansive sleeves, sat on the sofa chatting with Lord Granville in the drawing room when Missy arrived.

"Here is Millicent now," the viscountess said rising, her movement a whisper of feminine grace.

"Good afternoon, Lord Granville."

He swiftly rose to his feet. "Ah, Miss Armstrong, as lovely as always." He had a pitch-perfect voice, low and melodious. Very masculine.

As he bowed over her proffered hand, her mother shot her a look as if to say, *Charming as well as handsome.*

Indeed, the earl could claim all of that in abundance. Clad in an olive green jacket tailor-made to fit his broad shoulders the same way trousers the color of malted barley skimmed the long length of his legs, he did cut quite a dashing figure.

However, a kiss on the hand from him didn't evoke even a tenth of the thrill she experienced when James but looked at her. He did not make her pulse race or the breath hitch in her throat. He did not carry the scent of sandalwood and male essence so sensual, the recollection alone made her tingle in places she herself had touched only once under the cover of darkness. That night she first kissed James.

He was not James.

Lord Granville relinquished her hand and came up to his full height.

The viscountess, ever the diplomat, chose that moment to bid them farewell and quit the room, the lingering scent of vanilla trailing in her wake.

"I'm surprised your mother has never remarried," he commented idly, after the viscountess was out of earshot.

Missy quelled a laugh. Lord Granville also had an eye for beautiful women.

"Is that to say you are offering, my lord?" she asked with a little sauce to her tone.

Chuckling, he didn't respond immediately as he stepped aside to allow her passage to the sofa closest to him. After she'd seated herself, he settled back into his chair.

"If I were to offer, I rather doubt your mother would accept. I'm sure I'm too young and unrefined for her tastes." His tone was all light and teasing, clearly taking none of it seriously.

Lord Granville was a young man—twenty-four only last month—but Missy had yet to meet another gentleman so young who was so completely refined. One day, she was certain he'd make some woman a wonderful husband.

"You, on the other hand, I sense, would more appreciate a man who requires a bit of polishing." His mouth quirked at the corners and his brows rose suggestively.

Unable to determine whether he was teasing or not, Missy opted for a benign reply. "I, my lord, appreciate a good cup of tea. May I pour you a cup?" She turned to the silver tea set on the trolley beside the sofa.

Lord Granville laughed, his shoulders shaking in amusement. "Ah, I see you're going to be a worthy opponent and not make this easy for me. Very well, I shall do it just as they do in those fairy tale novels."

Before Missy fully realized what he was about to do, he dropped smoothly onto one knee and had her left hand clasped firmly in his. "Miss Armstrong, would you do me the honor of agreeing to be my wife?"

She instinctively tried to pull her hand away only to feel his hold tighten. It took a moment for her to understand the implications of his refusal.

"Lord Granville, truly this is—"

"Before you give me your answer, think of how much it would please your brother."

"My lord, I cannot—what?" She shook her head. Had she heard him correctly?

"You know it is his dearest wish," Lord Granville said as if that alone were reason enough for something as life altering as marriage.

Missy slid her hand loose from his grasp and quickly came to her feet. Sidestepping the tea service, she moved to stand by the chiffonier by the entrance. Dear Lord, was he really serious?

"Lord Granville, am I to assume from your proposal you wish to marry me to please my brother?"

On his feet again, he started toward her. "It wouldn't be the only reason."

"And what, pray, are the other reasons you would wish to marry me?"

No doubt he charmed most women wearing the same crooked half smile on his face when he halted in front of her.

"Because it would be a good match." He spoke with a simple directness.

"But not a love match, my lord." She replied with simple honesty.

He stared into her eyes, and as if he saw her sincerity and resolve, splayed his hand in true dramatic fashion over his heart. "Am I to take your response as a refusal?" His mouth twitched, endeavoring to retain a smile.

"Somehow, I think you will recover by evening." Missy didn't even think his ego had been bruised, much less his heart broken.

The sound of male voices halted Lord Granville's reply. He immediately angled his head toward the door.

Thomas. And James. Missy's heart began an erratic dance. Their voices grew closer until they stood outside the drawing room.

The men had a look of surprise as they surveyed the room's occupants. James watched her, his countenance unfathomable, his pale eyes unblinking.

Thomas was the first to speak. "Missy, I didn't expect to find you home. Yesterday Mother mentioned you were to go to the Vauxhall Gardens today." He entered the room, an easy smile on his face.

"Yes, well, that had to be postponed," she replied. But what did it matter if she was home or not? Did his surprised reaction mean he had intended to avoid her? A quick glance at James's stone-faced expression gave her the answer she needed. It had grown apparent over the last week that

James was taking pains to avoid her presence—even more so than usual.

"Afternoon, Granville. Good to see you." Her brother could not have looked more pleased.

James hung back, his blue eyes chilled. "Granville." His tone was just short of curt.

"Good to see you too, Armstrong," Lord Granville said with an affable nod. Shifting his gaze to James, he said, "Something wrong, Rutherford? I've had warmer receptions from my cousin, who'd like nothing better than to see me join the rank of the dearly departed."

Thomas chuckled and Lord Granville grinned. James's strained smile resembled more of a baring of the teeth.

As if attempting to cover the awkwardness of the moment, Thomas quickly changed the subject. "I'm in need of the blacks today. Where is Mother?"

"I believe in the library or the morning room," Missy replied, making every effort not to allow herself to soak in the sight of James as if it might be her last, although it had been one whole week.

"Good." Thomas gave an affirmative nod. Turning to her caller, he said, "Good day, Granville. Good of you to call."

Lord Granville gave a dry smile. "How nice it would be if everyone felt the same." He turned and stared pointedly at James's impassive expression. "Good day, Rutherford."

James issued him another curt nod, uttering not a single word. Missy stared at the empty doorway long after the two men had departed, a bittersweet ache in her heart.

"Miss Armstrong."

Missy nearly started at the sound of her name. James had that effect. Within seconds, he had sent her senses rioting, burying every last reason she needed to forget him.

"Believe it or not, but there was a time when Rutherford was a much more amiable chap."

"James is—"

"Rutherford would do well to take a page from my book," Lord Granville said with a cryptic smile. While she puzzled over his comment, he dropped in a formal bow. "I believe it is time I took my leave. As always, calling on you has been a pleasure. I hope your refusal will not prevent us from remaining friends?"

"But of course not." Had any refusal of a proposal gone so well? She imagined not.

"Wonderful. Good afternoon, Miss Armstrong." With a smile and a wink, he turned and strode from the room. Whistling.

James's mood underwent a complete transformation by the time he exited Six St. James Square. If he had known Missy would be there, he would not have offered Armstrong conveyance to his mother's residence. His friend had all but assured him no one would be home.

His thoughts were muddled, his emotions in shambles by the time he pulled up in front of his townhouse. His plans for this evening involving a comely widow now held little appeal. He had been deep in his cups, well out of the reach of innocents and fair maidens, when he'd thrown out the slurred invitation. She had been eager in her response. He really must stop drinking so much.

He gave his necktie a sharp tug the second he entered the foyer. Smith materialized, ever the efficient butler.

"Milord." He dipped his bald head.

"Smith." He made toward the stairs.

"Will you be dining in this evening?"

"I'm not certain. Have the cook prepare something that can be easily warmed." He paused long enough to toss the curt command over his shoulder, before taking the stairs two at a time.

In his chamber, he tossed the necktie on the bed and shrugged out of his jacket and waistcoat. After a brief knock on the door, it opened to his valet's sober face. The man was nothing if not competent. Like a bloodhound, he could sense James's presence from anywhere in the house, and within a minute, he appeared ever anxious to serve.

"Milord, will you be needing my assistance?"

"Yes, make sure I have hot water for my bath," he replied, his hands releasing the buttons on his lawn shirt.

With a brusque bow, Randolph left to do his bidding, the door closing with a soft click behind him.

Fifteen minutes later, steam wafted over the porcelain tub as James settled in. He had sent Randolph on his way, in sore need of the solitude and soaking. His bunched muscles released its tension into the soothing heat of the water.

James hadn't a clue how things had gotten so bad, but Missy had become a distraction he couldn't afford. He spent considerably too much time thinking about her and worse, measuring every woman he met up against her. That wouldn't have been so tragic if they hadn't all come up wanting. The damned chit had somehow bewitched him.

It was obviously a purely physical attraction that would eventually burn itself out, and until it did he'd be living his greatest nightmare. Wanting her and knowing he could never have her.

God, his reaction to Granville—damn, who was he fooling, his reaction to any man who glanced at her twice—set his teeth on edge.

If she'd only been a pretty face with a delectable figure, the whole situation would have been far more bearable. But she wasn't. She had a refreshing candor, which had always amused him. She was keenly intelligent. Even at the age of fifteen, she'd been well read—more so than some of his own counterparts. It was unfortunate her development into womanhood had cost them their easy rapport and friendship.

If only he could stop the savage stab of lust from overtaking him whenever he came within twenty feet of her. If only he could wipe from his memory the sight of her berry nipples and their exquisite feel and taste as he'd suckled them to hard little points with the hunger of a man long denied.

The hot water didn't stop his cock from growing stiff and straight as a flagpole. A groan of disgust and desire rent humid air as his head fell back onto the rim of the tub, his eyes closed. He cursed the betrayal of his body. He cursed her for being able to so easily bring him to this state. He didn't want to feel this for Missy; didn't want to feel this all-consuming kind of lust for any woman at all. Groaning, he grasped his erection and took his current dilemma in hand.

Chapter Eleven

Twice now she had visited James's residence. If her brother or mother were ever to discover, they would bundle her up like a fattened calf bound for the slaughterhouse and send her back to the country.

Missy's gaze roamed the library while she waited for the butler to summon James. The morose-faced butler hadn't blinked an eye upon viewing her at the door. He had silently permitted her entry and then left to check if his employer was in for callers, returning soon afterward to lead her to the library to await his arrival.

After Missy had begged off from accompanying her mother and sisters to call on her mother's good friend, Mrs. Roland, the need to see James again overwhelmed her. She reasoned she needed to apologize for her atrocious behavior toward Mrs. Laurel in person.

Thankfully, her mother had not deemed it necessary to rake her over the coals the day following the incident, but her disapproval had been duly expressed and noted. Missy had penned an apology to Mrs. Laurel and the viscountess had insisted on sending along a bouquet of fresh-cut daisies from the garden. A thank you note from Mrs. Laurel arrived the following day.

She had intended to apologize the next time she saw him, however, James had never materialized. For a whole week he had been absent from every notable social event. He no longer accompanied Thomas when he called, and had even missed a small celebration her mother held for Sarah's fifteenth birthday.

His appearance at the townhouse earlier that day had made her determined to finally put an end to their estrangement. If he would not come to her, she'd have to go to him. And so here she stood, awaiting him in his library.

The room smelled of James, sandalwood and something else indefinable. Heavy green draperies covered a bank of windows, which lent the perfect view to watch the sun set. Papers littered the desk along with a stack of leather volumes several feet high.

The room lacked the artifice most of their peers tended to display when decorating. Every stick of furniture appeared solid and sturdy, yet fashionable without being coarse.

Despite seeing him hours earlier, Missy started when he entered. She had come prepared for the meeting but still he caught her off kilter, her heart knocking frantically in her chest.

He appeared freshly bathed, his dark hair damp; and he sported a new set of clothes. Missy found it hard to pull her gaze from the glimpse of dark chest hairs revealed by the opening at the neck of his shirtsleeves. Her regard crept higher, only to encounter features formidable in their severity.

"And to what do I owe this pleasure?" he bit out, his tone rank with sarcasm. He remained guarded at the entrance, his tall frame not allowing the double paneled doors to close.

Missy balked and briefly considered leaving right then. It

appeared his anger hadn't abated since the incident with Mrs. Laurel.

"Does your mother or brother know you're here? Did you even have the sense to come with an escort?" His lips twisted in something resembling a sneer.

Her spine stiffened reflexively. "My footman is waiting outside."

A derisive laugh rumbled from his throat. "Apparently, the fair maidens of the *ton* have found yet another task for the overworked footman. Let us hope they know how to hold their tongues."

"I would hardly—"

"Your brother would blister your hide if he knew of your activities." He raked his hand through his hair, leaving clumps of strands spiked in its trail. He regarded her with a narrow and intent focus. Missy shifted, uneasy under the scrutiny. The James of her youth was now a distant memory and in his place was a moody stranger who proved to be even more sinfully attractive, if far more foreboding.

"What are you doing here?" The curt question cut through her musing with a stinging sharpness.

She advanced a step and James retreated almost into the hall, as if threatened by the move. He wore the kind of shocked expression indicating he himself was as surprised by his action.

His unease was palpable. She unnerved him. The knowledge, the indisputable proof in his reaction, gave her a sense of power, going far to equalize their footing, this emotional seesaw she'd ridden for years and years.

"I feared you had dropped out of Society. The ton is abuzz with rumors of your deflection." Hardly the makings of an apology but to issue one so readily would bring a swift end to her call. She intended to prolong it for as long as she could.

"So you're here to make sure I'm still about. You saw

me this afternoon. You needn't have come to my home."
He widened his stance and folded lean-muscled arms across
his chest.

Missy moistened her lips with a sweep of her tongue.
"That is not why I'm here."

James's eyes followed the movement, his jaw tightening.
He gave her a wide berth as he crossed the room to the sideboard, his tread barely perceptible on the rich Aubusson rug.
Missy thought she saw his hand tremble as he poured himself a drink from the decanter.

"Well for God's sake, would you please tell me why
you're here so you can hurry and be on your way." His voice
had lowered to a growl and he kept his back to her while he
took a deep swallow. Slowly he turned to face her.

Missy cautiously approached him. If possible, his face
grew harder, like granite, and his jaw began to tick. As she
stood facing him, she had to forcibly resist the urge to touch
him, trace the bristled line of his jaw. She kept her hands at
her sides.

"I still owe you an apology for my behavior at supper last
week," she said softly. "I would have offered it this afternoon when you were by, but . . ."

He gave her a sharp look. "Yes but you were otherwise
engaged, entertaining. Tell me, has the esteemed Lord
Granville finally asked for your hand in marriage? Am I in
the presence of the future Duchess of Wiltshire?" He took
another swallow of his drink before dropping the glass back
down with a clatter on the dark wood of the sideboard.

She looked away, her face suffusing with heat. He made
a derisive sound at her obvious embarrassment. She had answered his question with just a look.

"And what was your response?"

She could see he attempted to goad her in to an argument.
She hadn't come for that. She'd come here to . . . What had

she really come here for? Because she hadn't been able to help herself.

"I told him I did not want to marry him. Perhaps, I'm not ready for marriage." *Certainly not if I'm not to marry you.*

He laughed darkly. "Yes, perhaps not marriage but you're ready for something." He raked her figure with an angry stare, and then strode past her to throw himself down into the brown leather armchair.

To respond to such a statement would be a mistake, so Missy ignored it and followed him, seating herself opposite him on the edge of the sofa, her fingers plaited together in her lap. James watched her in brooding silence.

"As I said, I came to apologize. I'm terribly sorry for what I said and how childishly I behaved. I had intended to apologize earlier but you've made yourself scarce this past week."

"Ah yes, Sophia did tell me you sent an apology along with flowers. You could have sent a note."

"I tried but—well, it just did not feel right. I felt I owed it to you in person. We are hardly strangers."

His eyes blazed. "Is that the only reason you've come? Because if you've come expecting anything else you will be sorely disappointed. I already have plans this evening." Missy reeled under the cruelty of the inference as a tide of red hot jealousy rose up to envelope her whole.

James finished off the snifter with one last swallow and dropped it on the brushed mahogany side table, where it landed with a distinct thud. He came to his feet in one fluid movement and regarded her, his eyes cold.

"I accept your apology. There, apology delivered and accepted. I believe you can find your way out."

Missy blinked rapidly, taken aback by his abruptness. By the time she opened her mouth to issue a retort, he was halfway across the room. Stunned seconds later, he had disappeared through the arched doorway.

Before she allowed herself time to think, she was on her feet, following him out into the hall. Drat the man, he was impossible. Without looking back, he took the stairs as if he had the devil himself at his heels. He disappeared into one of the upstairs chambers by the time she arrived at the foot of the stairs.

"May I help you, miss?"

Missy turned to find the butler standing by the dining room entrance, disapproval etched around his thin lips, his bald head glinting under the light cast from the elaborate chandelier.

"No-no thank you. I'd forgotten there was something else I needed to give—that is, relay to Lord Rutherford. I will be but a moment." Missy started up the stairs with the prickling knowledge that she would never be able to look James's butler in the face again. However, right now she did not have the luxury of mortification or squeamishness. She needed to clear things with James. Now, before the distance between them became unbridgeable.

By the time she arrived at the top of the stairs, she noticed that one of the chamber doors sat ajar. A flash of movement caught her eye as she approached.

"James?" she said, her voice almost a whisper. She tentatively pushed open the inlaid redwood door and peeked inside. James stood with his back to her near an oversized wooden chest of drawers. Missy advanced into the chamber.

James whipped around, stupefied, when he saw her framed, like a tormenting angel at the door. The quiet click of the door closing resonated loudly in the generous space. She proceeded slowly into the room.

"Have you taken complete leave of your senses?" The words emerged cold and furious.

"James, we need to talk. We need to clear the air between us. Things have not been the same since . . . well things have not been the same for some time."

"You aren't a child any longer as you are so fond of telling me. Things will never be the same between us." His anger had dissipated but when he spoke, his lips barely moved.

She was sultry innocence and hadn't the foggiest idea how close she was to being ravished. Because surely if she knew, she wouldn't be standing in her modest virginal dress, within his reach, tempting him like he'd never been tempted before.

"Then let us at least go forward but not in the manner we've been," she said. She reached up and stroked his jaw. He flinched at her touch but an invisible force had rooted him in place, helpless to move away as he knew he should.

"I know you believe you love me, Missy, but you don't," he said, his voice hoarse, almost pleading.

She lowered her hand; her eyes held a simple entreaty. "Then let us be friends."

James gave a choked laugh. "You know that is impossible."

"Why is it impossible?"

His control collapsed in a heap of thwarted resistance under the unabated pressure of want long denied. He jerked her forward, the softness of her landing against the hardness of him with a jolt. "Because I don't want to do this to my friends," he growled, something violent in him, barely suppressed.

He took her mouth in a fierce display of unrestrained lust. His hand splayed the back of her head, tilting it back as he greedily fed on the sweet fullness of her mouth. His other hand joined to remove the pins securing her chignon, until the heavy mass fell in a curtain of silky chestnut waves.

* * *

Missy closed her eyes, helpless to stop the savage surge of desire that coursed through her body. Her mouth opened to admit the piercing quest of his tongue as it traded thrusts and parries with her own. He tasted of brandy and . . . James—potent, delicious male. She could feel the long rigid line of his erection pressed hard against her belly. Heat bloomed like a runaway fire in her veins and settled in the apex of her thighs, causing a pulsating sensation that grew in intensity with every stroke of his hands as they scored from her waist to the underside of her breasts.

His mouth left hers to hungrily explore the nape of her neck and Missy tilted her head to the side to give him greater access. When he molded the firm roundness of her breasts in his hands, the ragged pants of breath escalated to a high keening sound. A rush of moisture flowed between her legs, causing her to grow slick. With his thumb, he swiped the turgid peaks through the satiny fabric until she was mindless with pleasure. With her hands clutching his hard shoulders in a death grip, she pressed her breasts further into his hands. A harsh moan tore from his throat, his hands flexing strongly on her tender flesh. Missy knew a desperate need to rid herself of the layers of fabric and feel him against her bare flesh.

James's need seemed just as great as he found the long clean line of her spine and began releasing the row of buttons securing her dress in the back. The deftness in which he took to the task spoke of his experience. While his lips played on the delicate line of her neck and the curve of her jaw, his teeth nibbled her lobes, his breath hot and labored. He stripped her down to her white cotton chemise, silk stockings, and garter.

A bemused Missy could barely step out of the circle of satin, muslin, and petticoats at her feet. The tingling in her nipples and the escalating ache in her sex, held her in a spell of desire so strong she thought her legs wouldn't be able to support her much longer.

Her eyes fluttered opened as James lifted her high on his chest and placed her in the center of the bed. He watched her, his blue eyes alive and glazed with a predatory hunger.

His gaze dropped to her breasts. Her nipples pushed hard and pointed against her cotton chemise. His gaze dropped lower still to the brown thatch of hair covering her privates, quite visible through the thin white fabric.

Touch me, she begged silently with her eyes. He swallowed as beads of sweat dotted his forehead and his hands began to shake. Missy had been shaking since she had walked into his room. Now she ached.

He quickly straddled her hips, his fingers tearing at the buttons of his shirt, several falling victim to his frantic haste. When his shirt landed in a heap on the floor, he tackled his trousers.

Without a shirt, James was truly a sight to behold. The dark hair covering his chest was neither thick nor sparse, but landed somewhere nicely in the middle, and narrowed down to a thin line, disappearing below his drawers. The muscles were clearly defined, his abdomen rippled and hard.

"Sweet, sweet, sweet." His rasp was barely audible. He placed one hand to the side of her face as he made quick work of removing his trousers and drawers. Once they were removed, they were added to the growing heap on the carpeted floor.

Missy gave an audible gasp. She had seen penises in books before, but nothing prepared her for the flesh-and-blood sight of one. James's was long and thick, with large veins ridging the sides, and so stiff it prodded his stomach. It did not seem possible that she could accommodate his size. Her thighs clenched together instinctively.

James must have recognized the intimidating sight he

made, for he covered her quickly with his body and began soothing and gentling her with kisses. In no time at all, she opened to him, admitted his tongue and began an exploration of her own, intent on discovering the warm, wet cavern of his mouth. Her hands kneaded his muscled back and shoulders as he wedged a space for himself between her thighs, his erection settling in the dewy notch. The sensation of him hard and hot on the swollen lips of her sex had her arching helplessly beneath him, riding his length through the thin fabric. He surged strongly against her, dragging his erection against her center, her moisture dampening her drawers.

"God, I want you," he groaned against her lips and then proceeded to remove her remaining garments.

With the absence of every stitch of clothing, Missy felt too exposed. Instinctively her hands moved to cover her breasts and her privates. She'd never been naked in front of anyone before, much less a man.

"Shhh," he soothed, gently removing her hands from the places they guarded with soft, moist kisses. Her nipples tightened in painful delight against the light brush of his lips. She thought she'd go mad when he ran his fingers lightly through the thatch of dark curls covering her woman's flesh. Reflexively she clenched her thighs.

"No, let me feel you." His eyes ate at her, hot and dark. Using the tip of his finger, he delved into the moist throbbing flesh, rubbing firmly but gently. His reward, a new rush of moisture. His hands shook. Her hips began to jerk. He gritted his teeth, his face taut with unslaked desire.

His fingers continued to stroke and ply her flesh, parting the tender folds to explore hitherto undiscovered territory, building something inside her she had never experienced. Delving deeper, he found a piece of flesh at the apex of her feminine folds. A nudge of the nub had her hips arching high off the bed. He quickened his movements and the sensation of a band being pulled tighter and tighter gripped her, mindless pleasure growing almost unbearable. Then he lowered his head, pulled the tip of her breast to the roof of his mouth, and sucked. She exploded. The crescendo came in waves, her hips pumping frantically against his ceaseless fingers until, after one last abandoned thrust accompanied by an exultant cry, she slumped, sated, onto the bed.

She was still gasping in the aftermath when James clasped each rounded buttock cheek in his hands, squeezing slowly and using his thighs to spread her legs wider for his scorching presence. Drugged with spent passion, she turned a heavy-lidded gaze to him and watched as he guided his straining erection to her entrance. Slowly he pressed the thick head of his penis in, stretching the tight confines. The sensation of fullness she experienced from his girth was neither painful nor pleasurable, just different, its pressure inexorable.

Sweat trickled down the sides of his face, his teeth clenched, his expression strained.

"Try to relax. This is going to hurt a little." The words came out in a labored groan. Before Missy had a chance to blink, he thrust hard, burying himself to the hilt. The pain, although not unexpected, caused her to flinch and stiffen. Her tender flesh roiled under the assault, causing her muscles to clench spasmodically.

"Oh God, be still," he gasped, his face a picture in torture.

For what must have been a half minute they didn't move, only pants of breaths filled the chamber. In that time, her body accustomed itself to his rigid presence and slowly relaxed, each pulse of his organ no longer discomforting.

James began to thrust, his strokes slow and long. After a minute, the pace quickened and the feel of his erection dragging against her inner walls grew to be quite pleasurable. His hands on her buttocks flexed as he held her still and thrust strongly into her. She could feel herself climbing once more toward the crescendo. Soon his hips were moving furiously, pounding into her, pushing her head and pillow up against the bedstead. Before she could glimpse the summit, he gave a hoarse, anguished cry, drove his hips into her one final time, and emptied himself, before slumping on top of her, his head buried in the crook of her neck.

Several more seconds and she was certain she would have attained the pleasure she'd experienced just a short time before. She would have loved to reach that pinnacle with him inside her.

As Missy lay beneath his heavy but welcome weight, his breath labored and harsh, she breathed in the musky scent of lovemaking. She'd never thought that it had a scent; had never particularly thought about it at all, but it did, and not only was it musky but it was salty and humid. Ambrosia.

After about a minute, when their breathing was almost normal and their heartbeats had slowed, James rolled to the side, sliding out of her in a flood of liquid. He quickly rose, trekking naked from the bed to the wash basin, and came back with a damp cloth. In silence, his expression tight and dark, he wiped the remnants of their lovemaking from between her legs and then began to pick up the strewn garments from the floor.

Missy, an innocent in such affairs, had no idea what to do.

"Here, put this on," he said gruffly.

Not a trace of tenderness softened his tone or eased the tautness of his features. Missy immediately felt as naked as she was. She snatched the chemise from his hand and began dressing. James was dressed in no time at all, leaving her to yank on her petticoats in conspicuous silence. She balked at the idea of asking James to help her with her stays so she'd just have to do without them. Her dress, however, was another matter. She could not manage the buttons by herself. How she now wished she'd worn a dress that buttoned down the front.

She tugged the bodice into place and then peered at him over her shoulder. He watched her with a dogged intensity.

"I can't manage the buttons by myself." A warmth stole over her cheeks as she presented him with her back. "If you would not mind?"

The silence following the request implicit in her statement was as combustible as paraffin oil and fire.

She shot another glance over her shoulder, and nearly started at his expression. There was such a look of carnal desire in his gaze, she thought for a fleeting second he intended to pounce on her. But it was gone in an instant and he approached her with unshakable calm.

He dealt easily with her buttons, but his breathing, ragged and harsh by her ear, indicated the performance of another task far more strenuous. For a moment, when he had finished, his hands grasped her shoulders and squeezed, not hard, but with enough strength to flutter her already sensitive nerve endings. He released her abruptly and retreated several feet back.

"Is that what you came here for?" he asked in a frigid tone.

His question hit her with the force of a felling blow. She stared at him, her eyes wide and disbelieving.

"How can you ask that of me?"

"Why else would you follow me up to my bedchamber?" he bit out.

"You—you left me—I mean we weren't finished," she said, grappling for an answer.

"You just couldn't leave well enough alone. You were determined to have what you wanted and damn everyone else."

Missy sputtered. Whatever warm feelings she'd had in the aftermath vanished at his accusation. He intended to hold her solely to blame for what had occurred between them. He was heartless. Worse, she was weak and supremely stupid.

"I did not force you to make love to me," she replied, tilting her head to stare him directly in the eyes.

He gave a dark laugh. "What we did had nothing to do with love so please don't fool yourself. I'd have to be the bloody Pope to turn down what you've been offering. I was bound to succumb." His voice held a note of self-disgust.

She reeled under the impact of his words. She turned away quickly, tears stinging the corners of her eyes. She would be damned if she would cry in front of him.

"I shall see myself out." She exited the room and crossed the hallway to the stairway with anxious hurried steps.

Once she hit the bottom step, the butler appeared, dour and silent, her shawl and bonnet draped over one arm, her reticule and gloves in the other. She accepted them with a blind urgency, studiously avoiding his gaze.

As she stepped out into the misty London air, she glanced back into the house and a movement at the top of the stairs caught her eyes. She met James's closed expression just before the door closed.

The journey home was a blur, thoughts of the last hour consuming her. She had just made the most foolish mistake of her life. She was ruined. No decent man would have her now. And should her mother discover, she would be positively heartbroken. The viscountess looked upon James as a son. This would be betrayal of the worse kind. And Thomas. She shivered, refusing to entertain the thought.

After Stevens handsomely rewarded the driver for his services, he and Missy entered the townhouse through the servants' entrance in the back. Stevens ventured ahead and made certain the way to her bedchamber was clear. Missy barely managed a strained smile of gratitude before she rushed into her room and turned the lock.

Walking toward the bed, she caught a reflection of herself in the mirror. She had the look of a woman who had been thoroughly tumbled. Her thick hair was mussed, her lips kiss-swollen and red. Between her thighs, the sharp twinges and pleasurable aches reminded her of her lost virginity. Heat spread throughout her body when she remembered how completely abandoned she had been in his arms. How the blind pleasure had turned her into a wanton, arching into his hands as he'd stroked her. And how she'd pressed his head down to suckle her and end the exquisite torture of her nipple. A familiar ache quickened within her, blood surging to pool between her thighs to create a steady thrum.

Dismayed, Missy turned from the mirror and launched onto the bed. He had scorned her afterward, practically accusing her of being some sort of seductress. It was unholy of her to derive such pleasure from the memory of their lovemaking—or whatever he wished to call it.

Like dried leaves at the mercy of a strong gusting wind, her mind whirled. Heartbreak and shame warred with the continual betrayal of her body, as it betrayed her even now. And her feelings for James? To her shame, they weathered the storm of his disparagement and scorn. She wanted to hate him; would will it if she could, but that feeling in her throat, as if her heart had lodged itself there somehow, would soon make a mockery of such sentiments.

What was she to do now? She wouldn't tell a living soul and she imagined, neither would he. He liked his life as it was, *sans* wife. But what if the butler said something or one of the other servants had witnessed her comings and goings? If word got out, she would be ruined. And without a marriage, she would be shunned by Society. No respectable man would ever want her. And her family . . . the shame she would visit upon them would be enormous.

And James.

An anguished sound fluttered past her lips. What would James do? He had compromised the sister of his best friend, a member of the aristocracy. Propriety dictated he do the just thing—propose.

A delicious shiver coursed through her. Marriage to James would be the culmination of every dream she'd ever had. And one he would resent her for, for the rest of his life came another sobering thought. To be thrust upon him like unwanted baggage was not what she wanted. She'd rather face ruination than endure that.

Chapter Twelve

Regret was a crippling emotion, or so James found it to be.

As he'd done for the past ten minutes, he swirled the brandy with a gentle roll of his wrist and watched it slosh and circle until it settled in a serene pool of escape. But it was an escape denied him as there wasn't enough alcohol in the world that could adequately drown regret's effects. Sober in his melancholy, he sat silently contemplating the etched glass in his hand.

With Missy everywhere in his townhouse, James had retreated to the only place he thought to find any solace: White's.

The club was doing brisk business, but the sounds of male revelry did not prove to be as distracting as he'd hoped. Cigar smoke hung thick in the air, glass globes sat on every table, and decorative wall sconces were staggered along the walls, lighting the room in a dim glow. Several acquaintances had approached him for amiable conversation but his marked lack of response had driven them to search out more receptive company.

He had ruined her.

The knowledge stabbed like a hot blade into flesh. He had ruined an innocent. He saw in his mind's eye the vault door shutting on his future. There was no other recourse open to him, no place he could hide from his actions. Her chances at a good match were almost none, although plenty of gentlemen would be more than happy to take her as their mistress. His blood chilled at the thought of Missy vulnerable to the scoundrels and reprobates who preyed upon the vulnerable in Society. And further still at the thought of her being shunned by their peers. Disgraced.

No, he could not allow that; he had no choice but to marry her.

Drained from him was the acrid bitterness of rage. A rage that had caused him to lash out at her, throwing sharp barbs that had fallen with unfailing accuracy. He could not absolve himself of blame in this matter. He had been an active and most enthusiastic participant in what he could only describe as the best sexual experience of his life.

A picture of Missy, her face and lips flushed from his kisses, her hair a tousled mass of chestnut curls, her breasts, soft and firm, and the downy dark hair crowning her very essence glistening with the moisture of her desire, made his pulse leap and caused his erection to throb to life. James was grateful for the protection the table lent his growing condition.

Most men would trade places with him without a thought or a whimper, he mused, scouring the room restlessly. He spotted Caldwell, Soddersworth and Ramsey, all heirs to a title, and each of them known to be courting or had courted the fair Miss Armstrong at one time. He experienced a feeling of smug satisfaction that they would never have her, and silently, reluctantly, identified the word of that emotion . . . possessiveness.

His fate, which had been in question when he walked through the hallowed doors of White's, was now clearly mapped and, oddly, the idea of marriage to Missy no longer appeared quite the prison sentence. It had required many hours and a whole host of tumultuous emotions, but once he'd accepted the new path his life had taken, the road he'd once thought littered with boulders now held only pebbles and gravel. He could do much worse than Missy, and perhaps, might never do better. Of course, they'd have a typical *ton* marriage. At some point, she'd be glad she wouldn't be solely responsible to slake the constant demands of his sexual appetite. In the meanwhile, he would ensure she enjoyed the marriage bed. Certainly, if her enthusiasm that afternoon was any indication, he wouldn't have any complaints in that respect for some time to come—even though he knew, inevitably, the time *would* come.

The real problem was Armstrong. Convincing his friend he'd not only make Missy a fine husband, but the very best husband made a surgeon's job look easy. But James had no choice, for the prospect of losing Armstrong's friendship was more than unsettling, and hung like a pall over the whole affair.

James brought the glass to his lips for his first drink, and took a deep swallow. There was little point in wasting good brandy.

After draining the contents of the glass, he shrugged on his overcoat and headed to the front door. A twinge of awareness prickled the hairs on the back of his neck and the sensation of being watched increased as he neared the entrance. His gaze darted about the crowd of smartly dressed aristocrats until he spotted the source of his disquiet.

Sir George Clifton sat at a corner table hunched over what appeared to be his fourth drink if the three empty glasses lined in regiment fashion before him were any indication. Clifton watched him between squinted eyes, making no effort to hide his scrutiny.

James paused, his brow lifted in a silent query. What had he done to cause the man to watch him with such malevolence?

Clifton raised the half-empty glass clutched tightly in his hand in a decidedly mocking gesture of salutations, before downing the contents. Slamming the glass down, he dropped his head.

His state of inebriation was obvious in the heaviness of his lids and the glassy sheen in his eyes, and for that reason alone James refused to confront him right then, to demand an explanation for his blatant animosity. He sent the still, downcast figure one last lingering look before exiting the club.

Victoria never knew a person's complexion had the ability to take on that particular hue of red—certainly not one so deep and mottled. Her mother put that fallacy to rest.

Turning back to the chamber pot holding the contents of her stomach, she gingerly wiped the sides of her mouth with a damp cloth. She came slowly to her feet, aware a tirade as inevitable as thunder after a lightning strike hovered seconds away.

"Who is the father?" The words were propelled from the marchioness's mouth with a quiet but potent fury. No extraneous questions, no probing preamble. Victoria's body trembled from head to toe. Her mother had gauged the situation within seconds of walking into her bedchamber to find her bent over the chamber pot.

For a moment, she thought to deny the truth. Perhaps, she could still find a way out of the utter shambles she had made of her life. But behind the unbridled fury, Victoria could see a ruthless determination in her mother's brown eyes. Another frisson of alarm coursed the length of her spine.

"James Rutherford." Unable to meet her mother's gaze, she stared down at her feet, watching as her toes curled in apprehension.

A lengthy silence followed her admission. It lasted so

long, she was tempted to raise her gaze to see what kept her mother muted so long. Shock? Murderous rage? Disbelief?

"Does he know?" the marchioness asked in a voice soft and cunning.

Victoria shook her head but still could not bring herself to look up. It would appease her mother greatly if she appeared properly chastised and repentant. Her thoughts briefly went to her older sister Lillian, causing tears to well in her eyes. She blinked furiously to check their flow. At present, tears were a weakness she could not succumb to.

"You must tell him. Naturally, he will then present himself to your father to request your hand." Victoria risked a glance up at the marchioness's flushed, round face. She wore the look of satisfaction, her thin lips tipped up at the corners, her eyes alight with something verging on victory.

Over the years, Victoria imagined countless women had plotted and schemed to get the handsome heir to the altar without success. *She* would have performed a veritable miracle in the eyes of the *ton*. The envy and jealousy of her peers would have her mother fairly chortling with pleasure to be able to grandstand the coveted match.

Victoria managed a stiff but deferential nod.

"When is the child due to arrive?"

"February," she whispered.

The marchioness gave a vigorous nod. "Good. Seven or so months will not have the gossipmongers crying too loudly. But that gives little time to plan the wedding. Three weeks should be sufficient. There must be some sort of courtship and a very public betrothal announcement. Perhaps at one of the grander balls." Her mother's eyes sparked, appearing excited by the idea. "There will be no hushed affair this time around for this family. Everything will go according to custom, however glaring in its brevity." She brushed her plump palms together briskly as if the entire matter was already a *fait accompli*. "He is a fine catch. You should consider yourself a lucky girl." With a rustle of stiff-booked muslin and pyramid silk, her mother swept from the chamber.

Victoria stood in the same spot for several seconds before she clambered onto the canopied bed. Tugging the hem of her nightdress higher, she settled her weight in the center and drew the counterpane up to her chin.

She should be pleased that things with her mother had turned out so well. The scolding she had feared had not come to pass due in large part that her mother had just received one of her greatest desires. It was true, that during her first Season, her mother had wanted the Duke of Kent's son for her, but when Lord Graham had wed a baron's daughter, she had been forced to set her sights elsewhere. And then there had been Lord Chadwick, but the man tended to be a bit of a recluse. Lord Granville appeared destined for Millicent Armstrong, but Victoria had always had doubts about that match. Regardless, he'd never shown any interest in her. That is when her mother's sight had turned to Lord Rutherford, the heir to a fortune surpassing their own and a title no sane mother could find wanting. Yes, for the marchioness, a match with James Rutherford would be most advantageous.

Unfortunately, a more difficult task still lay ahead. Now she must tell the man himself. She had led him to believe that nothing had occurred between them the night she had gone to his residence. It had suited her purpose at that time. She'd hoped to find another way out of her difficulties and had sworn to herself he would be her last resort. As it stood, he was the one she sorely needed now.

What would he say when she told him about the child? Lord, how she hated the deception, but what other choice did she have? None. Thankfully, the one thing she had learned about James Rutherford in the years she had known him was that he was nothing if not honorable. A resigned sigh escaped her lips. He would do the gentlemanly thing, the honorable thing.

The short missive found James still abed the following morning. Randolph handed him the sealed folded piece of paper as he dragged his body into a sitting position.

"I was told it was urgent, and the footman is downstairs awaiting a reply," he said.

James quickly read the note. His brows furrowed. "Tell him I will be there," he said tersely.

"I will have your bath prepared," his valet said upon his exit.

Within the hour James had bathed, dressed and was perched atop his phaeton, headed down Piccadilly toward Hyde Park, the same question running through his head, What did Lady Victoria want? Her note had been short and to the point:

> Lord Rutherford,
>   I need to speak with you. It is urgent. Please meet me in Hyde Park, at the large elm along Rotten Row.
>   Victoria Spencer

He was certain it was connected to the same matter that had driven her to his residence the month before. He had taken pains to avoid her since then, so she must be desperate to have contacted him in this manner.

He found her precisely where she had written in her note. The elm was the largest in the park and often used as a landmark of sorts. The area had little foot traffic at that time of the morning, and even fewer carriages and riders. Drawing his phaeton to a halt in front of her barouche, he alighted.

Lady Victoria wore a blue bonnet, with a dizzying array

of blue and white flowers adorning the crown. Her dress was a soft blue, printed muslin, with short blunted sleeves and a square neckline, and except for her mouth, which was pinched and drawn, she appeared none the worse for wear.

She offered him a hesitant smile on his approach. "Thank you for coming so quickly, Lord Rutherford."

James's return smile was constrained. "How could I ignore such an urgent request?"

"Come, let us go inside the carriage. The air is quite misty."

He assisted her into the carriage. Done in a dark red leather and brass-colored knobs, it was plush and luxurious. He took the seat opposite her once she was seated. The dark, half-drawn curtains on the windows allowed in a weak ray of light.

"Now perhaps you can tell me what was so urgent that I was awakened with the roosters this morning?" Silence greeted his attempt at lightness. Unease began to churn in his gut.

He heard her sigh but there was a catch to it that made it sound like a sob. She had lowered her head, and because of the brim of her bonnet, he couldn't make out any of her features save her mouth, which quivered uncontrollably.

James saw the slow glide of a tear as it slid down her cheek and plopped onto the back of her blue-gloved hand. Until a month ago, he hadn't thought Lady Victoria a woman capable of tears. His unease grew.

He was beside her in an instant, his finger tipping her chin so he could look unobstructed into her eyes. "What is wrong?"

"I—I am with child and the child is yours," she whispered as a fresh wave of tears bathed her cheeks.

James jerked his hand from beneath her chin with such speed her head dropped unceremoniously, her slender neck seeming unable to bear its weight. Making a reflexive move away from her, he sat back slack-jawed on the seat, a quiet stillness enveloping his form.

Lady Victoria watched him, her lips now quivering

violently, her blue eyes wide and shiny. Her hands trembled visibly but his mind had shut down and he noticed little of the woman seated beside him. His world had ceased to make sense.

"That night—that night I came to your residence we did— what I mean is we—" She paused and took a ragged breath as she battled to conquer long familiar words. "I could not bring myself to admit to you that I'd allowed myself to be compromised and—and I didn't want you to feel obligated as I know you don't wish to marry me." She turned her face toward the window, presenting him with the delicate lines of her profile. "But a child has changed everything. I could never bring myself to bear my father a bastard grandchild, and my mother . . . well my mother has already guessed the truth."

James remained frozen, feeling the faintest movement would shatter him. All the while, an all-consuming dread choked the blood to his brain, sweeping aside all logic and reason. He shook his head, as if the small action would somehow negate everything he'd just heard.

"You assured me nothing had occurred." His words came low and strangled.

She turned to face him, her expression haunted. "I was ashamed."

His heart took a crushing blow at the starkness of her statement. His feelings of regret over yesterday's incident with Missy paled in comparison to the emotion swamping him now.

"But there was no blood—" He felt like a fish taking in air, desperate, struggling for its very life.

She sent him a stricken look. "I assure you, my lord, I was a virgin," she said, her tone a mixture of affront and embarrassment.

His eyes closed briefly as thoughts of Missy surfaced. Had it not been just last night when he'd resigned himself to a life with her? An image of her rose in his mind's eye and his chest contracted tightly. He had ruined not one, but two ladies and he could offer only one recompense.

And then the rage surfaced and he cursed the alcohol that had robbed him of the memory of that evening. Surely, he'd have known if he had bedded Lady Victoria. Surely, there would have been some faint memory, have it be hazy or distorted, of having taken a woman's virginity? Lord, he could not even remember leaving the library, why the hell would he remember much else? That night remained as empty as the future before him.

Raking an agitated hand through his hair, James pressed his fingers hard against his skull, the motion jerking roughly on the dark strands. He felt suffocated by the confines of the carriage. He wanted to pace. He wanted to run. As it was, he sat in the tense silence, his breathing deep and measured, pondering his options, while knowing he had none.

"You have confirmed your condition with a physician?" he asked quietly.

Lady Victoria stared at him, a profound sadness in her big eyes, and nodded. "His name is Dr. Samuel Litchfield. I am sure you would like to confirm it for yourself," she said, guessing correctly he'd waste no time in doing so. If he was to be forced into marriage in this manner, it would be negligent of even the most trusting of men not to ensure the validity of a claimed pregnancy—and he'd hardly be considered a man who laid a great deal of trust in anyone. Especially women.

James responded with a curt nod. "Have you told your mother that *I* am the father?"

Lady Victoria's head bobbed her bleak affirmation.

"And your father?" he asked, viewing her downcast head.

She shook her head in vehement denial. A wisp of white-blond hair fluttered about her face.

He supposed he should be grateful a visit from the pow-

'erful Marquess of Cornwall wasn't in his imminent future. No, as it was, he would be seeking the man out to ask for his daughter's hand.

"I will be in contact in a day or two," he said.

A pregnancy meant the wedding would be a rushed affair, which would of course start Society's tongues wagging. He knew quite well that the marriage of Lord James Rutherford would have the gossip mills spinning at breakneck speeds. With his known aversion to the institution, speculation would run rampant and the *ton* would be waiting with bated breath for the announcement of a coming child, and then would be counting the subsequent months with cunning zeal.

Resignation laced his drawn sigh. Defeated, he wiped a fatigued hand over his face. In less than a day, his bride-to-be had changed as well as his life's course. His throat closed and a searing pain burned the walls of his chest and settled into a dull ache as thoughts of Missy again assailed him. He cringed at the thought of her reaction once news of his betrothal to Lady Victoria was made public. He swallowed hard before pushing open the door and alighting the carriage.

With deft expertise, James steered the phaeton at reckless speeds along streets dense with coaches, horses, and people. Some of the corners were taken so sharply the carriage tilted precariously on two wheels, before coming down with a jarring jolt.

The first thing he did upon arriving at his residence was to have his footman request two meetings: one with Dr. Litchfield, and the other with Missy.

What an odd thing to realize that someone could not tell by just looking at you, that you had been debauched.

Her mother, her sisters, and Beatrice hadn't looked at her curiously at all. They had not seen that under her mask of

normalcy lay a seething mass of raw emotions vacillating between shame, dread, uncertainty, and the faintest flicker of
hope. They could not tell that she was no longer a maiden and
therefore, for all intents and purposes, ruined. So the morning
progressed like any other.

It had been after her morning walk in Hyde Park when
Stevens delivered the note to her, right before breakfast. He
had waited until she was alone in the morning room. After
skimming the short note, she had issued him her response.
He then conveyed the message to James's waiting footman.

Her plan of action played out immediately once her mother
and sisters made their appearance. Claiming she needed additional rest before the Florsham's ball, which was that
evening, Missy begged off from going on their scheduled trip
to Vauxhall Gardens. Although the viscountess was disappointed, she allowed her to demur from the day of entertain-
ment. Her mother quite understood the rigors of the social
whirl. Young ladies required sleep if they were to remain sufficiently animated until the wee hours of the morning.

At precisely two o'clock that afternoon, a full thirty minutes after her mother and sisters had departed, James arrived
at their residence. Missy, clad in her most becoming lavender day dress, awaited him anxiously in the drawing room.

With her stomach in a knot and unable to sit still, she was
standing in front of the fireplace when he arrived. Powerless
to resist the pull of his magnetism, she soaked in the sight of
him, her heart choking off her breath. He emanated an earthy
heat, his form tall and commanding in a charcoal gray jacket,
waistcoat, and necktie, black trousers, and a white linen shirt.
The black Wellingtons on his feet were buffed to a brilliant
shine. His countenance however, was closed and cold. The be-
ginnings of a fresh stubble shadowed his square jawline. The
lips that had kissed her in ways she'd never imagined a man
could kiss a woman, were compressed in a severe line. His

eyes were chips of blue ice. Trepidation shortened her already choppy breaths. Slowly, she drew a deep calming breath.

"You wished for us to speak," she said, her gaze direct.

James advanced into the room, stopping by the tea service next to the chintz settee several feet from her. He did not sit and she was not inclined to offer he do so.

"What do you intend to do?" he said, skipping the normal pleasantries, and asking the question as if they were discussing something as mundane as which flowers she'd like best for the garden.

The question itself was so forthright, for an instant, it caught her by surprise. She wavered, trying to come up with an honest response. Lord, she had rather hoped that particular issue would have been taken out of her hands. She had hoped James would decide for her. Her knight come to sweep her off her feet and make everything in her topsy-turvy world steady and lucid. The thought had never occurred to her that he would ask *her* how they should proceed.

Drawing another calming breath, she said, "I expect nothing of you if that is what you are asking. I have no intention of foisting myself upon you."

Brave words, a voice inside her snickered. Now what will you do if he turns and walks away without a glance? A heavy silence followed. He approached until a mere arm span separated them. She was forced to tilt her head slightly to meet his heavy-lidded gaze.

"And what will you do? I have irreparably compromised you. Your prospects now are to become a rich man's mistress, or some reprobate's wife. Or do you intend to rusticate in the country and live your life as a spinster?" His voice held a hard edge of derision as if he very much doubted the latter.

She turned away from his steely regard, and found a spot on the silk blue-and-white floral wall to focus. It prevented her from having to look into the eyes of the man, who at that precise moment had sealed the coffin to a dream that had just lost its already precarious hold on the last gossamer thin thread of hope.

"No one ever has to know," she replied stiffly. It was enough that they would know.

"What of your husband? How will you explain your obvious lack of virginity?"

"It isn't always obvious."

"I do not want to talk to your back," he bit out, touching her shoulder as if to turn her around. But then, as if burned, he pulled his hand back sharply and dropped it to his side. She could hear his breaths coming harshly.

Missy slowly turned to face him once again, an odd calm settling over her.

"What is not obvious?" he asked, his gaze narrowed.

"That a woman is no longer innocent." In her wildest imagination she'd never dreamed she would have such a discussion with a man.

"What the devil are you talking about?" He advanced another step bringing their bodies close in proximity, the tips of her breasts nearly brushing the silver buttons on his waistcoat. Missy inhaled sharply and the fragrant, woodsy scent of sandalwood bombarded her senses. His pale eyes pinned her with a stare so potent and hot, she thought she would melt from the sheer heat of it. She despised that weakness in herself.

She nervously dragged the tip of her tongue across her bottom lip. His eyes followed. "My mother said sometimes one is not able to tell if a woman is a virgin because there are other ways besides the act of intercourse to rid a woman of her maidenhead. She said, on rare occasions, some women are not born with one." If her mother could hear her she would probably faint dead away, and her mother was not a woman who took to the vapors.

His attention, which had locked on the red fullness of her

bottom lip, shifted to her eyes as her words seemed to penetrate. His brows shot up and his eyes widened.

"So you do not intend to tell your husband that you are no longer a virgin? You will have the poor sod believe that he is your first?" His tone dripped with disdain and condemnation.

"What does it matter to you what I do as long as you will not be forced into an unwanted marriage with me?"

A long pause followed her statement. If she'd expected any heartfelt denials or proclamations of love, she would have been disappointed. Instead, he eased back, pulling himself to his full height, his features hard and tight.

"You are right, it should not matter to me what you plan to tell your future husband."

If she'd been alone, she might have sunk to her knees at the devastating impact of his words. As it was, all she could do was turn away and dam up an ocean of tears.

"I hope I have put your mind at ease." She blinked furiously as she choked out the final word. "I will never tell anyone what occurred between us so you needn't worry my brother will one day appear at your door demanding satisfaction. You are safe from me. You have made it clear enough that my attentions are not welcome, so in the future I shan't subject you to them."

The depth of James's sorrow was unmeasured. He tried to speak but the words refused to come, cut by the force of his helplessness. He knew he dare not touch her or he would damage things well beyond repair.

God, she looked so fragile and defeated, her blue-gray eyes glittering with unshed tears, her usually creamy complexion pale.

There, too, was the knowledge that eventually one day she would marry—she was too passionate, too innately sensual to be forever without a man—and it wouldn't be he who would lie beside her at night, or his children she would bear. She would belong to some faceless man who would have rights to her that he never would. The knowledge was like a vise squeezing his heart, making him crazy.

A child. The thought struck him with the force of an expert pugilist's blow. He'd used no protection. Could fate be so cruel and visit yet another crushing blow upon him when he now had Lady Victoria and her child to consider? His mind raced. How long did it take a woman to discover if she was expecting?

"But what will you do if you are with child?" He sank his hands into his trouser pockets to keep them from reaching out to her.

For a moment, he thought he saw a look of fear flash in her eyes and then it was gone. She answered in a monotone voice, "I began my monthly courses this morning. I am not expecting."

James didn't know why her response affected him as it did and he could not explain the incomprehensible feeling of loss that accompanied her assurance. He must surely be losing his mind. He already had one lady claiming he was the father of her unborn child, another would be an unmitigated disaster. He should be relieved he hadn't impregnated them both.

"Then we have been fortunate."

Missy gave a jerky nod.

"I shall take my leave." He raked his fingers through his hair.

Missy averted her gaze and said nothing.

"I shall see myself out." He stopped briefly at the threshold. He wanted to say something, anything that would put the impish spark back into her beautiful eyes, but he knew under the circumstances, there was very little he could say and even less he could do. Without a backward glance, he walked out of her life.

Chapter Thirteen

To date, Missy had attended countless balls, dinner parties, and soirees, but she was still awed into silence every time she passed through the double doors of the entrance of the Devonshire House on Piccadilly.

The Palladian mansion was immense to the point of outrageous. The exterior was somber to the extreme. However, the interior was as sumptuous as one would ever see, housing one of the finest art collections in all of the United Kingdom.

The ballroom teemed with the social elite donned in their evening best. For the gentlemen, it was the standard white tie and tails affair with highly polished shoes, starchy white shirts and neckties, crisply pressed black jackets, waistcoats and trousers. Splendid and bejeweled, the women wore gowns of pyramid silk, satin, taffeta, tulle, and crushed velvet. Each gown seemed to contain more tiers than the last, the necklines running from modest to just short of scandalous.

Attired in a silk turquoise ball gown, the corsage just low enough to make for an enticing décolletage, Missy's three-flounced creation fell somewhere in the middle. A single string of pearls gracing her neck and a pair of earbobs completed the elegant ensemble. In her hands, encased in a pair of matching silk gloves, she clutched a dance card surfeit with the names of eligible gentlemen.

"It appears Lord Clayton has cornered your brother," Claire said. "How long do you think he'll be able to abide Lord Clayton's company before he begs off?"

Having spent the past hour stiffly following the lead of her various dance partners, Missy had been gratified at her friend's arrival. It had been the perfect excuse to beg off when Lord Granville had approached her for a second dance without raising the disapproving brows of her mother and brother. Eligible future dukes were not to be refused by a lady in her fourth Season. Said lady might not always garner this sort of attention. If they only knew, said lady would not be garnering any attention if the truth were known. She'd been well and truly debauched.

Lord Granville had taken her refusal in stride, leaning over to whisper, *Perhaps you are right. We certainly wouldn't want to be accused of having unduly raised expectations.* With a sly wink and a bow, he proceeded on his way to find any of the hundred or more women who would be more than receptive to such an offer.

With her hazel eyes brimming with amusement, Claire eyed the foursome, comprised of Thomas, the viscountess, and Lord and Lady Clayton. Lord Clayton's voice droned on above the jaunty chimes of *Le Pantalon* and the collective murmur of the crush.

"I daresay, talk of ship building or pedigreed horses will have my brother's ear for the remainder of the evening," Missy said wryly. "If anyone is in need of escape, it will be my mother."

Claire chuckled. "Well, as my parents have arrived, I imagine Lord Clayton will seek out Father for one of his tedious political discussions."

Baron Rutland, Claire's father, lived for the political

jousting and wrangling that went on within the pristine walls of Parliament. Save Lord Clayton, he was said to be the most vocal peer in the House of Lords.

Missy shifted her gaze to flit a bored look over the fresh sea of faces flowing through the ballroom doors. The men's faces seemed to blend into one bland, murky blur until one face registered with breathtaking clarity, thrown into sharp and colorful focus against a backdrop of indistinct gray. A breath burst past her lips.

James.

He moved amid the crowd, his height, his dark-haired good looks—just him—riveted her, rooting her in place. A week had past since their last meeting and she hadn't expected to see him here this evening—prayed she would not.

Missy watched as he pressed deeper into the room, the throng thinning as he drew closer. Only then did she spot the woman by his side, Lady Victoria Spencer. Her breath stuttered in her throat before halting altogether.

A quick flick of her wrist brought Claire's fan up in front of her mouth. "It would appear the rumors are true." She spoke *sotto voce* where there was absolutely no need to.

Wrenching her gaze from the pair who elicited the same looks as did the art collection and sumptuous décor— awestruck and envious—Missy directed her attention to her friend. "What rumors?" she asked with an inexplicable sense of dread.

Claire's eyes widened a fraction. She paused, her blond eyebrows furrowed. Lowering the lace-edged fan to just below her mouth she said in a gentle voice, "I thought that was the reason you have been so cast down. I assumed when you were ready, you would talk to me about it."

"About what?" Missy asked again, sharper now.

"That he is courting her. They have attended several operas and soirees together this week past. James has been calling on her almost daily." Claire spoke gently, as if she were telling her a loved one had just died unexpectedly.

Missy bore the news in that exact manner, the pain slicing her heart and reverberating all the way down to the tips of her toes. Her throat closed. She pressed a hand to her mouth. It shook violently. For a week, she'd been lost in a fog of disillusionment, heartache, and shame, barely managing to get through the days. This revelation made the past week feel like a picnic.

Missy looked back at the couple. They were a contrast in perfection, James in black formal wear, Lady Victoria stunning in a pale yellow ball gown, her hair piled atop her head, exposing the elegant lines of her neck and shoulders. Missy couldn't bear the sight of them together.

Before she could look away, James's gaze shifted and met hers over a sea of decorative hair ornaments. For a moment, he and only he existed. His pale blue eyes lingered, until he finally broke their unspoken contact to return his attention to the blond beauty at his side.

Shaken, Missy bit down on her trembling bottom lip. "But that makes no sense. James has no desire to marry." That she knew better than most.

Claire wore the same expression Thomas had worn as he sat on the edge of her bed after the incident with Mrs. Laurel. Pity. Concern. The silk fan collapsed with a snap of her wrist.

"I'm sorry, Missy. I was certain you had heard."

No she hadn't heard. Missy swallowed and looked blindly away. She fought to keep the tears at bay, knowing if one escaped, a deluge would follow.

How naïve she had been. Feelings of jealousy she'd tried to shrug off had not been inconsequential after all, but quite founded in reality. Their appearance together tonight gave the rumor validity.

Unsteady hands struggled with the clasp of her reticule

and hastily pulled out a white linen handkerchief. Inclining her head downward, she dabbed at her eyes as if she had something other than tears to contend with.

Claire moved in closer and Missy felt the prod of her skirt on her own. Replacing her handkerchief back in her reticule, she lifted her head, a wobbly smile in place.

"I thought he didn't want to marry *anyone* at present. It appears I was mistaken. Apparently, his abhorrence to the institution had everything to do with me." A self-deprecating laugh escaped her lips, but the sound caught on her next breath, sending her into a paroxysm of coughing.

"Oh, Missy," Claire whispered, stricken. "Why don't we take some air?"

The coughing fit subsided quickly, but in its wake, the hot rush of heat bloomed in her cheeks. She could only imagine the picture she made, dressed to the nines and hacking like a peasant with consumption.

"Miss Armstrong, I believe this is our dance."

Missy's head jerked in the direction of the male voice. Mr. Robert Chierney stood at her side, his head inclined in a bow, his white-gloved hand extended. Missy remembered his name appeared next on her dance card.

A wan smile struggled to make a courageous showing for the tall, thin gentleman. She sincerely wished she could offer more than *politesse* masquerading as a smile but her mouth felt overstretched by just that small effort.

Dancing would be difficult seeing she'd just had her feet knocked from beneath her. But bowing to stringent social mores, she took his proffered hand.

"Yes, indeed it is," she replied graciously. A glance back revealed an anxious Claire with furrowed brows and plaited fingers amid velvet skirts. Missy managed another difficult smile, hoping to convey to Claire that she would be fine. But it was something she failed to believe herself.

* * *

James spotted her shortly after he entered. He had scoured the room full of elaborate evening gowns until, like an eagle sighting its prey, he found her. He took in the breathtaking sight she made in her blue ball gown, which exposed her shoulders and the creamy expanse of skin just short of the swell of her breasts. The familiar thrum of heat surged through his body. His member throbbed to life, oblivious to the fact it was neither the right place nor time for its resurgence. Though when had it been listening to him these days? At least concerning Missy? Biting down hard on the soft inner flesh of his cheek, he welcomed the sharp sting of pain. It seemed a fair trade tonight, pain for pleasure.

James watched Missy being escorted onto the dance floor. A feeling, though familiar, stabbed at him stronger, fiercer than ever, catching him square in the chest.

Jealousy.

He despised the word, wanting to thrust it from his vocabulary but the emotion worked its way insidiously through him, thwarting his control, and stoking the fire burning within. Jerking his gaze from her beautiful self, he shot a look down to see Lady Victoria watching him with unblinking placidity. His mouth tipped at the corners, in a feigned smile, before proceeding toward Cartwright, who was hailing him from a good thirty feet away. The three met somewhere in the middle.

"Lady Victoria." Cartwright greeted her with a courteous bow.

"Lord Alex." Lady Victoria curtsied offering him a pink-gloved hand, which he accepted, brushing the back with his lips.

"It appears I arrived back in Town at just the right time." Cartwright smiled broadly, raising a black brow.

Heat warmed James's face. He wished he could tell him that while he had taken himself off to Yorkshire, James's life had turned into a farcical tragedy to rival anything Shakespeare could have written. It wasn't enough that he was being forced to marry Lady Victoria, but the marchioness was determined to make the union appear a love match. The damn woman wanted the works: a courtship, a betrothal announcement, and a grand wedding, all in the span of three short weeks. As if anyone would be fooled. Tongues had already begun to wag. But the marchioness was equally determined that unlike Lady Victoria's older sister, Lady Lillian, no scandal would mar her youngest daughter's road to the altar. Evidently, some years ago, Lady Lillian had been compromised by a Frenchman, and the marriage had been a forced affair.

Before he could respond to his friend, the shrill voice of Lady Cornwall—his soon-to-be mother-in-law—fractured, what would undoubtedly be, his last moment of peace for the night. He shivered.

"Why, it is Lord Alex. We must stop and say hello," the marchioness trilled, a triumphant gleam in her eyes. She bustled toward them, her hooped skirt colliding with everyone within several feet of her as the high-pitched squeal of her voice carried to the environs of London far and wide.

Her hand lay on the arm of her husband, a large impressive figure of a man in his late forties with thinning brown hair and a florid complexion. His love of all things sweet was evidenced by his considerable girth. He appeared ill at ease, his large, beefy fingers already tugging at the white necktie.

If Cartwright was in any way struck by her exuberance, he didn't let on. If anything, he appeared mildly amused, an indulgent smile tugging the corners of his mouth as the marchioness dragged her husband toward him. James and Lady Victoria were forced to shift to make room for the couple.

"Lord Alex, I don't believe you have yet to meet my husband, the Marquess of Cornwall. Theodore, this is Lord Alex. Son to—"

"I know who he is," grumbled Lord Cornwall.

"It's a pleasure to make your acquaintance again, my lord." Cartwright executed a courteous bow.

The marquess nodded, pulling a handkerchief from his jacket pocket to dab at the beads of perspiration dotting his temple.

"What a handsome couple the two of them make," the marchioness declared to Cartwright. She then dropped her hand from her husband's arm and stood back as if regarding a famous work of art, her brown eyes gleaming in conceited delight. James shifted under her too-avid gaze. The woman had all the subtlety of a charging ram. By evening's end, all of the *ton* would have them already bedded and wedded—in that order.

Cartwright looked thoroughly perplexed. His gaze darted from Lady Cornwall to James and then Lady Victoria. "Uh—I suppose they are—uh—quite a good-looking pair." He managed with obvious effort, to get the words out.

"And how is York at this time of year?" James could do little else to stem the awkward moment but change the subject. For the first time in memory, his wit failed him, and his charm could not be summoned up with ease. Even the smile that had seduced many females felt strained and wooden. His emotions were already on edge, his only solace—as small as it was—was that his mother was in Italy for the summer and therefore wouldn't witness his folly until after her return. His father was another matter altogether. If he'd heard any rumblings of their courtship in the corridors of Parliament, he had yet to say a word of it to him.

"Rainy," Cartwright replied with a wooden smile.

Several times James saw Cartwright's gaze shift to the

dance floor and he knew exactly where his concerns lay . . .
Missy. His stomach clenched and a burning resentment he'd
managed to keep dormant the past week, seethed to life. What
had happened to Lady Victoria, the safe one, the lady he'd
never have to guard against?

Missy happened.

Had he not been consumed with lust for her and deep in
his cups, he would never have lost his head in a moment of
weakness. A weak moment that would soon have him leg-
shackled to a woman he'd most likely resent for the rest of
his days.

"I believe I saw Lady Randolph about," the marchioness
remarked, her gaze darting about eagerly. It appeared the
marchioness had one goal that evening, and that was to
claim him like some prize she'd won at a county fair. The
evening stretched ahead like a death sentence.

The stone terrace, just off a set of French doors, offered
Missy refuge from the stifling air of the ballroom. She spied
several couples strolling gardens that must have employed
a small army of groundskeepers for the upkeep. They were
a fair distance away, and too agreeably occupied with each
other to notice the solitary figure moving deeper into the
shadows of the night.

Missy had long past given up any hope of experiencing
another moment's pleasure at the ball. Everywhere she
turned, she saw him—she saw *them*. Whether they were
dancing or taking refreshments or conversing, James rarely
left Lady Victoria's side. Jealousy as she'd never experienced in her life before tore through her, leaving in its aftermath gaping wounds. She hated him. She hated them both.

Dragging in a breath of hot florid air, she came to stand

beneath a trellis of yellow daisies, her arms wrapped protectively across her breasts—over her decimated heart.

Missy heard the footfall behind her and knew the identity of the intruder even before she saw the long shadow cast over the flagstones. Instinct and the clamoring of her senses told her it was James. She could feel him in every pore of her body but refused to turn. Seconds later, he was there in front of her, looking darker, more forbidding, and attractive than she should find any man who had caused her so much hurt. Such mind-numbing heartbreak. She hated him all the more.

Missy surveyed him, commencing with the gold, flat-coined buttons of his black waistcoat to his somber features. She shot a glance over his shoulder and then back to his face, which was shadowed in the moonless night. "I hardly think your fiancée would approve of you being out here alone with me."

If possible, the line of his mouth flattened even further. "We are not yet engaged." James watched her, his pale eyes intently focused on her mouth.

"Yes, *yet* being the operative word." Her throat felt tight and dry. He had no right to regard her in that manner. He was practically pledged to Lady Victoria, his intentions plain as day. Yet he stood alone with her where anyone could happen upon them, watching her, the heat in his eyes hot enough to ignite a fire.

"Do you think this is what I want? That this is what I planned?"

Missy turned away, briefly closing her eyes. "I don't particularly care what you do or with whom. Whatever I felt for you died a week ago. You can court Lady Victoria and wed her with my blessing."

James took a step closer, crowding her against the latticed trellis. Daisy petals feathered her cheek, its scent tickling her nostrils. But Missy refused to turn around, keeping her back to him, her skirts crushed against his trousers.

"I don't believe that for a minute," he said with the assurance of a man who knew her better than she knew herself.

Missy spun around, angling her chin high. "You may believe whatever you like, I really do not care. Now, I suggest you go back to your—to Lady Victoria. *We* certainly would not want to be discovered in a compromising situation." She wanted to provoke him. If she could, she would hurt him just as he'd hurt her.

With a swift tug, he pulled her into his arms, and then backed them up against the side of the wooden trellis. His hands clamped down firmly around her, trapping her arms between their bodies. She tried to wrench them loose but his hold was unyielding.

"What do you think you are doing?"

"You enjoyed being compromised more than any woman I've known," he said roughly as his glittering blue gaze dipped to her décolletage. Her breasts immediately peaked at the attention, which only angered her more.

"Yes, I'm sure you have known too many to count," she tossed back.

"Who are you more angry with, me or yourself?"

"*If* I am angry, it is because you are holding me against my will." She tugged hopelessly while trying to control the thundering of her heart. He was too solid and too male. Their bodies met and stirred her in ways she didn't want. He was courting another woman. If she could not claim anything where he was concerned, she could at least claim her own pride and self-respect. He might indeed want her physically, but he didn't love her, and he certainly didn't want her as his wife. No, that role would be filled by the much more poised Lady Victoria Spencer.

"I don't want you to misconstrue what is between Lady Victoria and me," he said harshly.

"What is it that you want from me, my blessing?" Missy stood still for a moment as she gazed up at him. He looked frustrated. "Well if that is what it takes to make you release me, than you have it. Now go court your precious Lady Victoria and leave me alone."

James regarded Missy in silence. He still didn't know what he was doing here in the garden with her. Along with his freedom, he'd obviously lost his mind. All he knew was the moment he had seen her slipping from the ballroom, the compulsion to follow had won the battle waging within him since he'd first spotted her that evening. Lord only knew why he felt he owed her an explanation about him and Lady Victoria. But holding her now, her body against his and his hands secured around her narrow waist, he wanted nothing more than to feel the sweet pressure of her lips against his and the exquisite weight of her breasts in his hands. He wanted to be inside her more than he wanted his next breath.

Awareness coiled within him, his erection pushing rigid and hot against the placket of his trousers. And he knew the moment she became aware of his body's response, because her eyes widened and her attempts to wedge her hands free ceased. She stood breathless and still. She swallowed and her tongue swept her lower lip cautiously, slowly. Contracting his arms around her, James pulled her closer into his embrace, his erection pressing hard and throbbing against her. His nostrils flared and his lips parted as his head began its descent.

"Missy."

He was within inches of his goal—her lips—when he heard the sharp, urgent whisper. He jerked his head up and stepped hurriedly away from her still form.

"Missy, are you there?"

Thankful for the darkness, James turned toward the feminine voice. He instantly recognized Missy's friend, Claire Rutland.

Miss Rutland halted the moment she saw him. "Good evening, Lord Rutherford, I was looking for Missy. I believe I saw her come—"

Missy stepped forward, her expression composed. But even under the dusky hue of the gaslight, he noted the pink of her cheeks and the brightness of her eyes.

"Ah, there you are. I thought I saw you come out here." Miss Rutland treated finding her friend with a man in a darkened area of the garden as if it were an entirely normal occurrence.

"Your mother is looking for you. I believe she is ready to depart." Miss Rutland gave him a small smile before pinning her friend with a rather intense look. Something unspoken passed between the two women, of that he was certain.

Missy gave a thin smile in response. "Yes, I just came out for some fresh air and it seems James was of a similar mind." Her gaze flickered over him without quite reaching his eyes. "It was a pleasure seeing you again." Although she spoke the words, her tone and her stiff posture loudly proclaimed it a lie.

James nodded numbly and the two women made their way to the terrace and through the double-paned doors back into the ballroom. He stood where he was for another minute, fighting an unaccustomed helplessness and a private, wrenching despair and yearning. And then, he too made his way back inside; back to Lady Victoria and the future that tightened like a hangman's noose about his neck.

James had expected the call, he just had not expected it to come so soon, or quite so late in the evening. He himself had only recently returned home from the ball and had not had time to change out of his evening clothes.

In the time it took Smith to summon him from his bedchamber, his friends had made themselves comfortable in the library, so comfortable, in fact, that Cartwright was already ensconced in a leather armchair and Armstrong was in the midst of pouring drinks when James arrived. Apparently, the weak lemonade at the ball hadn't sufficiently quenched their thirst.

His friends must have come directly from the ball, for they, too, still wore their evening garbs, though both had already removed their neckties. Armstrong's hair had the appearance of frequently being run through with his fingers, and his expression was sober—deathly so.

"Somehow, I expected you would give me until morning," he said, strolling over to the sideboard to pour himself a drink.

Armstrong picked up the two glasses, sauntered over to distribute Cartwright his, before installing himself in the other armchair. He took a swallow, his gaze fixed on James all the while. "Somehow I thought I would not be hearing of your impending nuptials from the likes of Lady Cornwall."

"Correct me if I'm wrong, although I believe I understood the situation correctly. Are you in fact paying court to the ice maiden with the intention of marrying her? Your escort made it rather difficult for me to get a word with you alone." Cartwright's shock of hours before had obviously past, for he was his usual dry self.

James gritted his teeth. He carried his snifter of brandy, and took a seat on the sofa, opposite his friends. "Officially, we are not yet betrothed. That will come in another week," he added wryly.

Armstrong lounged back in the chair, his long legs splayed wide. "What the hell did I miss? I hope this has nothing to do with Missy. Because if this is you trying to discourage her, while I'm grateful you're applying yourself so diligently to the task, I think you're taking it too far."

If his friend only knew how very much entwined Missy was with this nightmare that was now his life. James tipped back his head and felt the welcoming burn of the alcohol hitting the back of his throat. Placing the half-empty snifter on the brushed black wood side table, he propped both hands on his splayed thighs. "Lady Victoria is expecting."

Cartwright took another swallow of his drink, his expression unaltered. Armstrong, however, bolted upright in his seat, his eyebrows near his hairline. "And you're the father?" His voice was raised in disbelief.

James inclined his head in dreary affirmation.

Armstrong slowly sank back into his seat. "Good God, when did you take an interest in Lady Victoria like that? I mean, don't get me wrong, she's beautiful and all that, but the woman could be used to keep meat. And you yourself said you could never be attracted to her. "

"I was drunk."

"Ah," Cartwright said as if those three words explained everything. What a man did while deep in his cups could absolve him of almost anything short of murder, so bedding a beautiful, willing female would be the least of his crimes.

"Are you certain she is pregnant?" Armstrong asked.

"Of course I'm certain. Do you think I would allow this debacle to continue if I wasn't? I spoke to the physician myself." And he had, just before he'd met with Missy. The man had pumped his hand, exclaiming his congratulations.

Feeling restless, James rose to his feet and crossed over to the fireplace, propping his elbow on the teak mantel. A log broke and sent sparks of burning embers into the air. For a moment, the fire blazed higher. Too hot. James moved out of the direct line of heat.

"Are you certain it's yours?" Cartwright's left brow edged up.

He jerked his head around to observe his friend. Cartwright lifted his shoulder in a negligent shrug, his look speculative. If it had been anyone else, James would have wondered, but not Lady Victoria. In all the years he'd known her, never had she been linked with a gentleman, or had she shown an interest in any man. If not him, he thought Immaculate Conception a possibility.

"We're speaking about Lady Victoria." James replied, as if no more needed to be said.

"Yes, the same Lady Victoria who apparently saw it fit to bed you," Armstrong said dryly. "It would appear it's not that she lacks the desire or is incapable."

James laughed, a dark hollow sound. "Yes, but I know her well enough. She'd never lie to me about something of this gravity." He returned to his seat, picked up the snifter and drained what remained. His friends said nothing, their expressions similar masks of inscrutability.

"How is Missy?" He wanted to bite back the words the minute they escaped his mouth. He cursed himself silently while watching something flicker in the cool gray depths of Cartwright's eyes.

"Devastated, I imagine. But that is to be expected," Armstrong replied.

James shifted uncomfortably. "I meant—"

"I certainly hadn't expected that you would have managed it in quite this manner. But this is final. Don't worry, she'll recover and soon will be good as new." Armstrong motioned casually with his hand.

His friend's blithe dismissal of the impact of the news on her galled him in a way that set his teeth on edge. James cleared his expression before a scowl settled in.

"I would appreciate it if you wouldn't say anything about the pregnancy," he said.

Armstrong appeared surprised by the request. "You need ask? She has quite enough to deal with now. Although, it will only be a matter of time. A few weeks if you're lucky."

A frown thinned James's lips. He'd take the few weeks. Of course Missy would inevitably discover all, he was just not prepared that it be now.

Armstrong stood. "Your secret is safe with me." Cartwright followed, rising with a pantherlike languidness.

In silence, James accompanied his friends into the foyer and to the front door. Cartwright turned to him, his hand on the knob of the door. "When should we be expecting the official betrothal announcement?" Amusement laced his dry tones.

This time James didn't hold back a dark scowl. He was in no mood for sarcasm. "Go to the devil," he growled.

Cartwright threw his head back, gave a brief laugh, and breezed through the doorway with Armstrong close behind. James pushed the door shut with his booted foot, feeling little satisfaction when it closed with a resounding thud.

Chapter Fourteen

Two days following the ball at Devonshire House, Missy found herself in the unenviable position of sitting next to Miss Jessica Lindley at Lady Brigham's musicale. Miss Lindley was quite happily one of the biggest gossips in Town. She had knowledge of every Society indiscretion well before it was picked up by the gossip sheets—and spread each just as quickly. Claire, who sat to the other side of her, had escaped her fate. She sat near the end of the row next to a busy aisle, contentedly watching the guests filter in and to their respective seats.

Having already exchanged the normal pleasantries with Miss Lindley, Missy hoped that would be the extent of their interaction.

While they waited for the five musicians to take their positions, Missy's gaze toured the bright yellow room, admiring the high shine of the white grand piano sitting center stage in the front, and the dizzying number of framed charcoals hanging on the walls, each featuring instruments in all modes of use.

The gathering was well attended, with more than the usual number of gentlemen occupying the plump cushioned chairs. Lady Brigham had four daughters and, with her twins in their second Season, she could not afford to have them still in need of husbands when the younger two debuted next Season. Not only was husband hunting serious business, it was très expensive, too.

Lord Crawley occupied a seat right in the front, artfully bedecked in a violet jacket, a mulberry sprigged waistcoat and wool trousers in the red family. He was currently burying an enraptured Lady Jane Coverly under a mountain of praises. And it appeared the rumors were true concerning the dismal state of his finances. Lady Jane, who was as wide as she was tall, had a dowry that could support a thriving metropolis.

"I don't recall seeing you at Lady Cresswell's dinner party," Miss Lindley said, fluttering her silk fan furiously. Her pretty face held a smile but it was of the disingenuous variety.

Missy had hoped she would not speak but, alas, she could not very well ignore the woman. She offered a benign smile. "No, unfortunately an illness prevented me from attending." She would certainly not tell her the truth. That the news of James's courtship had so distressed her she'd taken to her bed and cried herself to sleep.

Instead of offering her sympathies, Miss Lindley halted her incessant fluttering, and held the fan spread below her pert little nose. Leaning toward Missy, she whispered in a conspiratorial fashion, "I've heard Lord Rutherford and Lady Victoria's betrothal announcement should come in a matter of days. Their courtship, 'tis all very sudden if you ask me."

Missy ignored the sting of her words. "I don't believe anyone has," she said in a tight voice. Claire snickered softly at her side. Turning to her friend, Missy managed with some effort not to roll her eyes.

Miss Lindley, so intent on her mission, which was to fan the embers—in this case, flame the gossip fire—didn't blink at Missy's words. "But then they have a great need to rush with a child on the way." Her gaze darted between Missy and Claire when she uttered the final words, as she awaited their reaction in breathless delight.

Everything inside Missy went cold. Claire clasped her arm with a gloved hand in a gesture of support. Missy sat motionless in her seat, too numb to move, to speak, to breathe. It took several long seconds to properly school her features into a mask—an impassive mask that conveyed none of the anguish crushing her.

"I heard they will be married within the month. There is only one reason for that kind of haste. My mother said the marchioness is literally over the moon at the prospect of having Lord Rutherford as a son-in-law, and she would not deny that there was a child on the way, although I'm not certain anyone has asked her directly." She flashed a smug and knowing smile. "Mark my words, Lady Victoria will be increasing well before year end." Then her attention shifted to the entrance and she all but chortled in delight. "It seems the happy couple has decided to make an appearance."

Missy instinctively followed the direction of her gaze. Clad in navy blue trousers, waistcoat, and necktie, and a light blue silk shirt, his dark mane swept away from the handsome planes of his face, James instantly commanded the room. Lady Victoria graced his side, wearing a simple but elegant white beaded gown. He was dark and she was light, and they were the perfect foil for one another.

A sharp stabbing pain coursed through her with an intensity that was near incapacitating. Her head felt light and her stomach roiled and for a brief moment she was sure she would empty her stomach right there, in front of the *haute ton*. Seeing them together tonight was simply too much, especially on the heels of the recent news. Turning blindly away, she faced a clearly sympathetic and distressed Claire. Her friend's hand tightened reassuringly on her arm.

"I thought spreading such rumors was beneath you," Claire chided as she peered over at Miss Lindley.

The young miss sniffed and resumed fluttering her fan. "'Tis only a rumor if it isn't true. It will not be a secret much longer."

Missy allowed her gaze to drift back to the couple and watched in dread as they made their way up the aisle to her row. Lady Victoria, turning neither to the left nor right, greeted no one as she passed. James's gaze flitted over everyone. Missy could tell by the change in his demeanor the moment he spotted her. His pale eyes widened and there was a minute pause in his stride. Missy hastily turned away.

Thomas, who had disappeared with Lord Brigham upon their arrival and was her and Claire's escort for the evening, materialized some minutes later. Immediately spying James, he sought him out and the two men retreated to the back of the room to converse.

Missy could offer little in the way of conversation to Claire's obvious but doomed efforts at distraction. However, she could not resist a glance at James as he walked back to his seat. Once again, their eyes met and she immediately looked away.

Miss Lindley's face lit bright as a light when Thomas slid into the vacant chair beside Claire. She quickly closed her fan and smiled prettily at him, fluttering her eyelashes like a simpleton.

Another time Missy might have been impudent enough to bid her to stop wasting her charms on her brother for he was not the least bit interested, but not that evening.

Halfway through the evening, the guests were allowed an intermission. While the band, which in fact was composed of professional musicians hired for the grand occasion, took a much needed break, Missy excused herself to visit the ladies' dressing room. As if sensing Missy needed some time alone, Claire wisely remained behind with Thomas.

Awash in emotions she could not control, Missy used those solitary minutes to come to terms with everything she had just learned. Images of James hung with agonizing and heartbreaking clarity in her mind. James, who now for all intents and purposes, belonged to Victoria Spencer. He would never be hers. The finality of it left her sick to her heart. She stared at the pale, hollow-eyed woman in the mirror, willing her not to cry.

After attaining some semblance of composure, Missy was making her way back down the gilded hallway passing gold framed portraits picturing several generations of Brighams, when Victoria Spencer appeared like an apparition in her pale gown and blond locks.

Missy would have loved to cut her where she stood. But the blasted woman approached her wearing a genuine smile of greeting. Missy forced one of her own. Artificiality did have a purpose, after all.

"Good evening, Miss Armstrong," Lady Victoria said pleasantly.

"Good evening, Lady Victoria." Missy prayed the other woman couldn't hear the underlying strain in her greeting.

The blond beauty halted, forcing Missy to do likewise. Clearly, she intended they speak, which was surprising as they had never spoken before, other than polite words exchanged in the few times they had crossed paths.

"Are you enjoying the musicale?" she inquired.

"Yes, quite." Gazing into the eyes of the woman she'd grown to so thoroughly dislike, Missy disliked her all the more for being so thoroughly amiable.

An awkward silence followed, Lady Victoria making no move to go about whatever business had brought her out into the hall. Missy delicately cleared her throat. "Well then, I really must be getting back inside."

For a moment, it looked as if the woman would say something else to prolong the already torturous exchange, but thankfully, she gave a tentative nod before continuing on her way. Breathing a sigh of relief, Missy started toward the music room, the strains of Beethoven's *Gassenhauer* wafting into the hallway, compelling her to quicken her strides.

When she was mere seconds shy of her goal, out strode James. He came to an abrupt stop upon spotting her. His regard became hooded and his features tensed.

Missy had only a split second to decide whether she would completely ignore him but her pride would not allow her to scuttle away like a coward or play the role of the lady scorned.

"Good evening, Lord Rutherford," she said cool and formal.

"Missy." The utterance of her name was dark and husky. She hated that it elicited a sharp thrill that wound its way up her spine and had her nipples peaking in response. God, she was weak. And too many kinds of stupid to count.

Lady Victoria is expecting his child. The sharp admonishment carried the equivalent of a dousing of ice-cold water on a fire ready to rage out of control. Her senses cooled instantly.

"I believe another round of felicitations is in order. I have just heard your first child is on the way." Missy fought to keep her tone neutral and her expression closed.

Something flashed in his eyes but it was gone before she could discern the emotion. "Perhaps I should have posted banners and then saved the gossipmongers one less breath." Disdain was evident in his voice.

Apparently, with all she had told herself of the hopelessness of her feelings for him, there must have been some minute part of her that had retained a sliver of hope. His lack of a denial dashed them clean and proper. Her heart

gave a sickening thud clear down to her belly, and then tumbled to the floor, shattered and broken.

"Yes, perhaps you should have done so two weeks past
and saved us both."

"Yes," he snapped, after a tension-fraught moment of
silence. "I imagine you would have benefited from such an
act more than I. I pray the next time you will think again
before you go throwing yourself at a man by showing up
alone at his door."

Bastard! He would have to remind her of her folly. "As I
have nothing further to lose, I believe that point is rather
moot."

With two quick strides, he stood looming above her, his
jaw working violently. If she could have done so, she would
have closed her senses off from the scent of him, a scent cit-
rusy and wholly masculine. She took a step back. He might
not be concerned that his soon-to-be fiancée could return in
a moment, but she refused to become fodder for every nat-
tering tongue in Society.

"If I were ever to discover that you are—"

"If you were to discover what?" she interrupted sharply,
while trying to keep her voice low. "That I have visited a man
at his residence? What will you do, James? Tell my mother?
Tell Thomas? What would you tell them, dare I ask? That
you of all people have first-hand experience in what will
happen to me if I do?" Missy did not care that she was goad-
ing him and fueling his temper. His hypocrisy provoked her
to no end.

Ice blue fire blazed in his eyes. He looked like a man
ready to do violence, his hands fisted at his side. "Do not
push me," came his growled warning.

"Then do not think you can tell me how to conduct my
life." With that said, Missy swept around him, angled her
chin high, and returned to the music room.

* * *

Missy, weary in body as well as spirit, climbed into the warmth of her bed in the early hours of the morning following the musicale. Except for the exchange with James out in the hall, they had not spoken again. She and Claire had waited by the front entrance while he and Thomas had spoken before they took their leave.

One thing had become quite apparent as she'd sat through the last half of the event; her feelings for James made it nearly impossible for her to remain in London. Not only would she have to endure his coming nuptials, but a baby soon after. It would be the equivalent of emotional suicide. But what was she to do? He was one of her brother's best friends. She would inevitably have to see him, whether by design or happenstance.

If only she could completely disappear or go someplace far away. Far from James. Then an idea struck her. It came in ripples teasing the corners of her mind, until the practicality as well as logistics made it the perfect solution. She could go to America and stay with her mother's younger sister, Mrs. Camille Rockford.

Ten years ago, her aunt met John Rockford, an American. He had come to England on business and, in two short months, they had fallen in love, married, and returned to New York.

Her aunt had written her mother earlier in the spring extending an invitation for the family to visit, but the viscountess had declined, saying due to Emily and Sarah's studies, this year would not be appropriate for such a trip. But her sisters' studies should not preclude her from going, should it? The real issue would be to get her mother to allow her to take the journey alone.

The only way she could envision her mother permitting her this trip was if Thomas also gave his full support, *and* if she managed to secure a proper chaperone. And by proper she meant beyond reproach and utterly dependable and responsible. If she could come up with someone who had her mother's complete trust, that would work further in her favor. This would require much thought and serious consideration. In the meanwhile, she would speak to Thomas. If anyone could sway her mother, he could.

Her brother lived not far from James. The coach actually passed his street on the circuitous route it took there the following morning. Stevens, who at this point must have thought one of his primary duties was to escort her to and from gentlemen's residences, accompanied her.

Like James, Thomas lived in a narrow, tall townhouse, the front, stone and brick. She climbed the few steps to the oak door and sounded the knocker.

The door flew open so quickly Missy was convinced Arthur must have seen her approaching from the street.

"Good morning, Arthur, is my brother in?" She didn't wait for his permission but simply waltzed past the butler, her eyes darting around the tan-and-green foyer.

Arthur gave a brief, if somewhat belated, bow given she'd not given him an opportunity to do so until then. She heard the door click behind her but kept her ears attuned to the footfall of her brother's arrival.

"Good morning, Miss Armstrong. Regretfully, Lord Armstrong is not at home." He spoke with such impeccable diction, at times she'd wondered if he was in fact truly a servant. Sometimes she sensed in him a hauteur reserved only for the *haute ton*. But here she stood musing about such inane matters when she had much bigger issues to tend to.

Turning back to him, she asked, "Do you know when he is expected back?"

Arthur regarded her for a moment and then said, in his usual stilted tone, "I expect he should arrive home relatively soon as he does have an engagement scheduled for ten."

Missy glanced at the intricately carved rosewood long-case clock in the hall. Only fifteen minutes until ten. She began tugging at her gloves. "Then I shall await him in the drawing room." After her gloves, she removed her bonnet, handed them to Arthur, before making her way down the narrow hall to the cozy drawing room.

Little had changed since she'd been there last year, although she did note her brother had hung several more oils in the entrance and replaced the dark red Oriental rug in the room with a dark tan Aubusson. She slipped onto the sofa, adorned with dark green embroidered pillows.

Missy wondered how much longer her brother would be. It was surprising he was up and out so early. Calling hours were hours away, not that her brother did much calling for that matter, but nonetheless, if he were so inclined, it was frightfully early.

A minute later, Arthur appeared to ask her if she required anything while she waited. As she had just had a breakfast of scones and tea, her appetite was sated for the while. She declined politely and her wait continued.

Earlier that morning, when she was feeling strong and brave, she'd promised herself she would permanently cast James from her thoughts. Two hours later, she'd broken that promise at least two dozen times. Memories of the evening that had irrevocably changed her life played over again in her mind. Sometimes she cringed at her brazenness, ashamed how some could say she'd orchestrated what had happened. Certainly that was how James saw it, she the seductress, he merely a victim of his own physical needs.

And now he was to be married and welcome a child within

a year. Like a vise squeezing her heart, the thought as always, brought pain. Would there ever come a day when it would not?

Missy heard the front door just as she rose to inspect a small woodcarving of a horse resting on a bookshelf near the rear of the room.

Her first thought was that Thomas had finally arrived home but when she heard the low rumble of voices, she thought again. There would be no need for Thomas to ring the bell at his own home. Placing the exquisitely detailed sculpture back on the shelf, she strolled toward the door and poked her head out. She immediately snapped it back and scampered to the sofa. James was advancing down the hall.

Seconds later, his tall frame filled the doorway as he came to a halt. They eyed each other warily. Missy forced even breaths from her lungs and prayed her expression didn't betray her agitation.

"Good morning, Missy."

How cool and reserved he sounded. She surely had it in her to be the same.

"James," she said, tilting her chin. "I'm sure Arthur has already told you Thomas is not in."

An odd smile stretched his mouth. "Indeed he did. But I'm sure he'll be arriving shortly as we have an appointment at ten."

She supposed this is what their encounters would be like—stiff, polite formality. If only she'd listened to her brother and Claire. He was everything he was reputed to be, a cold-hearted rake. Not a glimmer of emotion did he show for the woman he had taken to his bed weeks before. He acted as if it never happened. She must have been a fool all those years, pining and hoping for a man who clearly did not exist. She could scarcely love a man she didn't truly know. And it was apparent she didn't know James Rutherford at all.

Missy stiffened her spine. "Oh, I was not aware Thomas

had a prior engagement." She stood and circled the low mahogany table. "It is probably best if Thomas comes by the townhouse when he has time." She made a move to pass him but he made it difficult because he had not budged from his post at the door. To squeeze past him would require too much brushing and subjecting herself to that didn't seem wise. So instead she stood and waited for him to at least play the gentleman and step aside so she could pass.

But the blasted man just stood there as she burned under the heat of his gaze.

Tipping back her head, she gave him an arched look, hoping she appeared at her most supercilious. But looking directly into his smoldering blue eyes was a mistake. She lowered her regard instantly, maddened that with so little effort he could reduce her to this. She felt her cheeks warming, but with the heat came anger. She remembered Lady Victoria—and then she remembered the coming child, and at that moment she hated him.

"Do you intend to move so I may leave?" she said in a brittle voice.

"Do you plan to tell your brother, is that why you're here?"

Her head snapped back up, her eyes wide and her jaw unhinged. Cheeks recently fiery hot, went cold. Her hands fairly trembled in fury. She snapped her mouth closed. "So that is what worries you? Do you actually believe I would be so stupid as to go to my brother with this and have him know what an utter fool I've been?" She derived some satisfaction when his jaw twitched and his eyes narrowed at her last remark.

"Or do you think so highly of yourself as to believe I am so desperate to have you that I would tell Thomas in an effort to force you to end your courtship of Lady Victoria? Let me assure you, James, I would not have you now if you begged me, and neither Thomas nor my mother could force me to marry you." She resented the thickness that had crept into her voice. She had to show him she was over him. Firming her mouth, she made a move to push past him.

What she didn't expect was for his hand to whip out like a rattler striking to capture her forearm. His grip was not tight enough to bruise but was certainly firm enough to restrain her.

Missy willed away angry, helpless tears pricking at her eyes. "Let go of my arm." She gave two quick decisive tugs, but he didn't relent, continuing to hold her there, much too close.

"Calm down. There is no reason for dramatics. My entire life has been turned upside down in the course of just a few weeks. Do you blame me for wondering?" He kept his voice low as he continued to watch her intently between hooded lids.

"Do you truly believe I want anyone else to know just how big a fool I have been? I would soon marry Lord Crawley and give him the dowry to do with as he pleased than have anyone know my shame."

For a brief moment, something flickered in his eyes, something almost violent. His hand tightened on her arm causing her to wince. He immediately loosened his hold.

"So that is what you plan, to marry the fortune hunter?" His lips pealed back from his teeth in something resembling a snarl.

"Better that than to marry a blackguard like you," she said, tugging to free her arm again.

"Which you wanted desperately enough not so long ago," he muttered before he released her arm only to pull her against him with both hands, locking her tightly to his chest.

The descent of his head seemed to occur in slow motion. She felt helpless to stop what was coming. The silken bond of his possession. Heaven and hell. At the last second, she pulled her head back, a move that only served in aiding his efforts, tilting her head at a steeper angle. His arms, roped with sinewy muscle, remained unyielding around her. His lips caught hers parted and vulnerable, to what masqueraded as a kiss but was really a full assault of her senses.

He made no attempt to be gentle. His lips ate at hers, hungry and demanding. For the first several seconds, she twisted her head in a valiant attempt to dislodge him, his mouth, and the hand anchored to the back of her head, but he retained a steadfast hold. Then an insidious warmth snaked through her body, weakening her, leaving her hot, her nerve endings ultra-sensitive to the stoking passion. As much as she wanted to push him away, knew she should push him away, her arms crept up to his shoulders, the flesh ridged with muscle, firm beneath her fingertips. She slid her hands around his neck urging his head closer, and then closer still.

Her mouth became avaricious, her tongue sliding and stroking his in a desperate bid for surcease to the pressure that had built so swiftly in her loins. Her movements pressed her breasts flush against his chest, tightening her already stiffened peaks. The evidence of his arousal throbbed hard and strong against her belly. A groan rumbled from his throat as one hand slid to cup her bottom and anchor her hips to settle his considerable erection between her thighs— or at least as much as the blasted petticoats would allow— while another hand tracked up to flick over a straining nipple through the layers of silk and muslin. His touch pierced. Her knees buckled, her sagging weight now supported by the hand squeezing her bottom in a purposeful, languid rhythm that caused a rush of moisture to her center.

His mouth left hers to trail down the long curve of her neck, peppering it with tender biting nips and soothing them with the swipe of his tongue. Missy could not think beyond the havoc he wreaked on her body, her senses, leaving her a throbbing, mindless supplicant in his arms.

Suddenly, he was gone; all of his warmth withdrawn in

an instant. If not for his steadying hand, her fall would have been a certainty. But even that support was withdrawn too quickly. Her mind could not grasp what had happened until she heard the distinct roll of the tea trolley on the runner coming down the hall. With her back to the door, Missy scrambled desperately to compose herself. She plucked at the ruffled skirt of her dress and ran a shaky hand to smooth any dishevelment of her hair.

From the corner of her eye, she could see James adjusting his trousers over the still burgeoning swell beneath, and then tugging at his waistcoat.

With composure she did not feel, Missy turned just in time to see the maid crest the doorframe with the silver tea trolley.

"Good morning, me lord, Miz Armstrong." She paused to curtsey before propelling the cart to the side of the sofa.

"That's fine, Molly, we can serve ourselves." Missy feared if Molly lingered much longer she would pick up on what was in the air, all that sexual tension heaped with self-recrimination. The maid curtsied again before quietly exiting.

Missy delicately cleared her throat and retrieved her reticule from the sofa. James, looking wholly composed with only the tautness of his jaw to suggest any inner turmoil, subjected her to one of his half-lidded, blue-eyed stares.

She tore her gaze from him. The man was dangerous. He exuded the kind of appeal that made a woman, against her better judgment, eager to forget herself. She had to leave before she, once again, parted with her better judgment at the sacrifice of her pride.

Under his steady regard, Missy departed, leaving him standing silent and grim-faced in the drawing room. Not a word passed between them, and of course, that was for the best. Little could change all that had occurred and the events that had still yet to unfold. Yes, there burned an attraction between them that, apparently, even his upcoming marriage did little to quell, but for James, as he had said many times, it was just a physical need, easily doused by any attractive, willing female. It was unfortunate she could not claim the same.

Damn him and his lack of control. If it would do James any good to berate himself for the unruly, unquenchable desire he felt for her, he would have gladly done so. As it stood, however, it solved nothing. A bloody rutting steed, that's what he'd become around her. Just a look and a scent and he turned into a man driven solely by his physical needs.

He rammed an agitated hand through his hair. And where the hell was Armstrong? He should have been here a half hour ago. If his friend had been home when he was supposed to, he wouldn't have had to face Missy by himself.

James sank into a nearby side chair. Is that what his life had come to? He couldn't even be in a room alone with her? Were her charms that potent? Good Lord, he had dealt with many women in his life, and none of them had overwhelmed him so much he could not keep his hands off of them when he knew he should.

Then an image of Missy naked and spread before him on his bed tormented his thoughts, instantly causing the flap on his trousers to distend under the growing pressure. He gritted his teeth and closed his eyes but the image grew even sharper. He saw her breasts and his fingers twitched from the recent feel of them, so firm and full for a woman so slender, the gentle flare of her hips and the brown tuft of hair shielding her woman's flesh. The taste of her—

"You look pained."

James's head snapped up and his eyes flew open. He hadn't even heard Armstrong's arrival he had been so lost in his thoughts—thoughts of the man's sister, which made it all the worse.

Armstrong sauntered into the room looking, if not disheveled, then certainly not as immaculate as he was accustomed to seeing him. His neckcloth appeared to have been tied in a rush, lopsided and wrinkled, and the same could be said for his shirt. James could say with a certainty that the man still wore his clothes from the night before.

"And you look like you slept in those," he grumbled. "Where the hell have you been? I expected you a half hour ago. I'm certain we've already lost our place."

His friend dropped in the leather armchair and ran a weary hand over his face. "Oh bloody hell, I forgot all about our match. Lady Jane kept me busy 'til the early hours of the morning." A broad grin accompanied his explanation.

"She's no lady," James muttered, resentful.

Armstrong chuckled, nodding slowly. "That, assuredly, she is not. Don't tell me I'm picking up a note of jealousy? Already pining for your bachelor life and the noose has only just been draped about your neck?"

James found little humor in that remark although it appeared to amuse Armstrong to no end. And the sad fact of it was he was more than resentful.

When he had been old enough to understand what marriage meant, and after watching his father having to beggar himself for his mother's favors, he had felt no rush to bind himself for life to any one woman. Enjoy their charms, certainly, but until he was ready for an heir, he had little use for such permanency. Naturally, when the time did come, he thought he would at least be able to pick his own bride and define his own terms for the marriage. Instead, at the age of twenty-seven, one drunken evening would select the where, when, and who. Never had he imagined fate could be so cruel.

"Go to the devil," he said, rising to his feet. His response only evoked another chuckle from the viscount. "You look like you need a bed or bath or both. Bloody hell, you've made me waste enough time this morning, so I'll be on my way."

"Arthur mentioned Missy was by. Did she say what she wanted?"

James stopped short by the door and shot a sharp glance at his friend. The question itself was innocuous but something in his tone suggested subterfuge. But Armstrong gazed back at him, his expression artless. Apparently, he had grown overly sensitive now to even the mention of her name.

"I'm hardly her favorite person at the moment. She isn't exactly sharing any confidences with me."

There was a pregnant pause before Armstrong said, "I think she's heard rumors about the pregnancy."

"Yes, so she mentioned last night."

"You can't know how grateful I am that the two of you never became involved," Armstrong said, rubbing the stubble on his jaw.

James clenched down on the back of his teeth.

"I know I never let on, but for a time it scared me witless. You find the whole idea unthinkable?" Armstrong asked with a short laugh, quirking a brow. "God, man, Missy is a stunner and you've always had a very discerning eye. Add to the fact she's always been infatuated with you, and you can see why I was worried. All those things could easily have spelled a recipe for disaster. Thankfully, you've been well and truly hooked. Nothing will ever come of it. Maybe now she can truly move on with her life. Marry. Settle down and have a family."

Later, James wouldn't remember how he'd responded to words that riddled him like bullets. Had he nodded stoically? Had he even swallowed or blinked? No matter, he departed the townhouse within a matter of minutes, the fencing match forgotten.

Chapter Fifteen

Missy had never given the piano the time and effort required to ever be considered accomplished. Instead of applying herself to learning F sharp major and C minor scales, she'd applied herself to the art of daydreaming, weaving fantasies where James was the star.

When Thomas made an appearance at the townhouse later that day, he found her seated in front of the black-lacquered piano in the morning room practicing her rusty skills. It was hard to think of James with her mind working furiously to remember which combination of notes would evoke the correct sound.

"Suffering from *ennui*, are we, Missy?" Thomas asked, chuckling as he took a seat next to her on the piano bench. "I can't remember the last time I saw you at the piano." Splaying his fingers, he played a couple of chords.

Missy dropped her hands from the keys and angled toward him. "Which is just as well."

"I agree. You are not very good." He shot her a teasing smile as his fingers flew over the key and a lively tune filled the air. Thomas could certainly play far better than she.

"So what was so imperative you needed to seek me out at my residence?"

Drawing a breath, Missy slid from the bench and stood. Standing made her feel more in control. "Now before you dismiss my request out of hand, I want you to hear me through."

His fingers stilled on the keys as he looked up at her and emitted a long, audible sigh. "I already know I'm not going to like this. Anything prefaced in that distinct manner warrants my immediate refusal."

"Please allow me to finish." she implored, wielding her smile with true expertise.

He heaved another sigh, this time one of resignation and nodded his assent. "I have a feeling I'm going to need a drink."

Missy mulled over her words. She had to phrase it just right if she had any hopes of him agreeing. "I would like to go and visit Aunt Camille."

It took a moment for her words to register. When they did, Thomas shook his head, his refusal emphatic. "To America? Absolutely not!" he exclaimed.

"How can you deny me this when you took a trip around the Continent with Alex when you were just seventeen, four whole years younger than I am now?" The question seemed to catch him off guard for he had no response for several seconds.

"Yes, but I am a man and you are a young lady," he said, finally.

"You were hardly a man nor am I so young. Why, some would say I'm getting into my dotage." She teased, hoping to coax a smile from him. Thomas remained grim-faced.

"You needn't worry, I will find a very able chaperone to accompany me. And I imagine I would be quite safe and well protected sailing on a ship built by Wendel's Shipping."

Her brother could not possibly dispute that, as he was part owner in the ship building company.

Thomas furrowed his brows. "That isn't the point."

"Then what is?"

"You're running away, that's what you're attempting to do, and I won't allow it. What do you plan to do, abandon your Season? You must believe the practice you've made over the years of dismissing eligible, presentable gentlemen will have no negative consequences. Mother's drawing room will not always overflow with callers." He gave a heavy, exasperated sigh. "Surely, England is big enough for you to avoid one blasted man until you acclimatize yourself to the new state of affairs?"

Missy drew in a sharp breath. "For a man who has never had one whit of feeling for a woman who is not a relation beyond lust, this is just the kind of reaction I should have expected. You've never been in love. You have no idea how I feel."

Some inscrutable expression crossed Thomas's face before he slid from the wood bench and came to his feet in one fluid motion. "Oh, for goodness sake, it was not my intent to be callous, but you're asking me to let you go to America—alone," he bit out. His green eyes held a mixture of impatience and a bid for understanding.

Finding it hard to remain in one place while her brother began to wear the tread of the Persian rug with his pacing, Missy began to shadow his movements. "I shall ask Cousin Abigail to go with me. Even you can't find fault with her as a chaperone. Mama just remarked the other day that she recently left her last governess post and is back home in Devon. I'm sure she would be more than eager for a trip to America."

Thomas stopped and regarded her, his forehead creased and his mouth a straight line. "Is he really worth this kind of upheaval in your life?"

Missy gave him a sad smile. "I will not be abandoning the Season. I would leave at the end of August and return well before Christmas. I would only be missing those frightfully boring foxhunt retreats."

Halting, Thomas turned to face her. Missy followed suit. With his forefinger, he tilted her chin to gaze directly into her eyes. "Why him? Of all the marriageable gentlemen in England, why him?" His voice held a wistful quality she'd never before heard from him.

"Does that mean you will permit me to go?" Her smile emerged, hopeful and tremulous.

He lowered his hand but continued to gaze down at her. He gave another weighty sigh, this one less audible but no less resigned. "I won't promise you anything except that I will speak to Mother about it. *If* Mother will consider it, you shall have my support," he said with great emphasis on the word "if." "However, if she should oppose the trip, you know all the cajoling in the world will not change her mind. Agreed?"

Missy nodded, grateful that he would attempt to sway their mother in any respect.

"You know, from the day I brought him home with me I knew he would be the source of some kind of havoc in your life—our lives."

With pursed lips and narrowed eyes, Missy asked, "How on earth could you have known anything? I was only ten at the time."

"Because I saw your face the moment you clapped those beautiful big eyes on him, and I knew it would only be a matter of time. I think you would have been better off falling for Cartwright. Much less jaded and, being a second son and all, he has little pressure of a title to live up to."

Missy could not help but laugh aloud at that wishful statement. "Alex is like a big brother to me. Heavens, he's bounced me on his knee."

"Immaterial, as you were bound and determined to lose your heart to the biggest rake around."

"Perhaps that is why the two of you keep company so well," she said dryly.

He gave a low chuckle. Thomas would be the first to admit his true nature and it didn't disturb him in the least to have such a reputation.

"Now that you've browbeaten me into doing your bidding, I'm off. I have a night of debauchery planned for some poor unsuspecting chit."

Missy folded her arms across her chest. "Humph, the same ones you are usually forced to beat off with sticks?"

"I am not so crude as to use sticks, my dear," he said in mock horror.

"I will be waiting patiently, Thomas."

He elevated one eyebrow. "For what?"

"Your comeuppance. I just hope I am there to witness it."

Smiling, he turned and sauntered out of the room humming the tune she'd been trying to play unsuccessfully on the piano.

Victoria was worried. It had been five days since she had last heard from George. He'd missed their last rendezvous and had not responded to any of her notes. By now, she was certain he had heard about James . . . and her. She had so wished to speak to him before their courtship had become public but her mother had left little time for that. Only word of Napoleon's defeat had spread through the streets of London faster than the courtship of the heir to the Windmere earldom, largely due to her mother's need to boast.

Her heart all but jumped into her throat as she raised the knocker on the door of his flat. All she prayed for now was an opportunity to explain before he saw fit to . . . well, she was not exactly sure just what he would do.

Dalton, his valet, answered and by the surprised look on his face, she could only assume she was the last person he had expected to see, although she'd been there many times before.

"Uh—Lady Victoria—I don't believe Sir George is expecting you." Despite his words, he stepped aside to allow her entrance into the foyer, a small area done in brown, gold, and green.

Victoria entered and cast a hesitant smile his way. "Is he in? It's urgent I speak with him."

For a moment, Dalton looked uncertain, his gaze darting to the closed door of the small library. Then he straightened, gave her a brief nod and said, "I will check to see if Sir Clifton is receiving callers." Brisk strides took him down the short passageway to the closed door. After three sharp raps, he pushed the door open and disappeared inside.

Something was wrong. Victoria could feel it. To be termed a caller meant things were much worse off than she had imagined. And she had imagined things would not be good, especially when the third note to George had elicited no response. The silence was the worst.

When the door to the library opened again, Victoria had moved several feet closer, giving her a brief glimpse inside. His valet came out wearing a stiffly disapproving expression, which she sensed was not directed at her.

"He will see you now." Dalton gestured with a black-sleeved arm to the open door.

Handing him her bonnet, shawl, and gloves, Victoria took a breath, and readied herself to face her beloved.

It became immediately apparent as soon as she stepped into the compact but attractively decorated room, why the valet had acted so curiously.

George looked a mess.

From the tip of his mussed head, his hair spiked in some places and matted in others, to the bottom of his bare feet, he looked a wreck. The mustache and beard he usually kept impeccably trimmed showed days of neglect. He wore a wrinkled, cream linen shirt with oval sweat stains under the arms, and his trousers had fared no better. His eyes, however, made the rest of him appear quite put together as they were red, wild, and bloodshot. They were the eyes of a man deeply tormented. The room held the distinct odor of cigar smoke and spirits, and George smelled as if he'd bathed in a tub of rum.

Victoria blinked three times in quick succession. She had never seen George in such a state before. Not only was it obvious he had been drinking, by the look of him, this was far from the first day.

"Am I to assume you have come to bear good tidings of your betrothal?" His lips curled in disdain as the words spewed from his lips. Clearly, the news of the courtship had hit him hard. Much harder than she'd imagined.

Taking a tentative step into the bowels of his personal perdition, Victoria closed the door. "You must give me a chance to explain," she pleaded.

With a harsh grating laugh, he pivoted on his heel and nearly lost his balance on the edge of the square-fringed rug. He barely managed to evade the ottoman on the way to his desk. There, he retrieved a decanter amid an array of strewn papers and books and, with shaking hands, poured a drink.

"There is nothing to explain. He is a lord, I am not. Heir to a bloody earldom with more money than I will ever see in my life." He turned to face her again, drawing back slightly when he realized how close she stood.

Victoria cautiously reached out and touched his arm. He jerked his arm back and cursed, spilling some of the drink on the carpet.

George had never cursed in her presence.

Lowering her hand, she took a step back. George had a look in his eyes, a look she'd never seen before. She was frightened, but for him, not herself.

"Go back to your precious lord," he sneered. He turned and weaved on unsteady legs over to the bay window overlooking a small park.

"I don't love him. You know you cannot doubt that," she said softly.

"You cannot love me." He did not look at her as he spoke.

"I have no choice in the matter. You know my parents will never allow us to marry. They would send me away, which would do neither of us any good." *And they would force me to give up our baby.* But that was something that went unsaid. If George discovered she was expecting his child, there was no telling what he would do.

He whirled around, nostrils flaring and teeth bared. "You have a bloody choice. You have always had a choice, you just refuse to give up all"—he gestured wildly with one hand, while retaining a hold on the sloshing glass of alcohol in the other—"that you have, to live a life with a man who hasn't your privilege, your esteemed titles."

She closed her eyes briefly as pain exploded in a series of prolonged bursts inside of her. He did not understand the kind of sacrifice she would have to make, all she would have to endure. Things to him were simply black and white but their situation encompassed many shades of gray. Far too many.

"It is not that simple, George. I wish it were but it is not." She dropped her head until her chin brushed the pale blue lace of her neckline. Her fingers curled tightly around the silver handle of her reticule.

"I want you to leave—and make sure you don't come back." He suddenly sounded drained of emotion. She lifted her head and gazed at him. He stared back at her with cold empty eyes. As if something inside him had died.

"I do not love him," she said, as if saying the words again would somehow make things right between them. She could feel the onslaught of tears and was helpless to do anything to staunch their flow.

"He can have you." He was dispassion and ice. "I do not want you anymore. I hope you will now find your way out."

Never had she ever heard him speak with such finality. She had lost him pure and simple. She cast one last look back at him and if the longing, heartbreak and despair she felt was reflected in her eyes, it didn't move him for he turned away.

Tears flowed freely down her face when she exited the flat, her head now shielded by the bonnet she hastily retrieved from George's valet. She took the gray stone steps hastily. Blind to everything but her scraped raw emotions, it was the solid thud of a male body that jolted her briefly from her grief. Strong hands grasped her forearms to steady her.

"Pardon me, miss—"

She glanced up and experienced a strange cessation of breath. When she had thought things could not possibly get worse, they had. It was Lord Armstrong.

"Lady Victoria?" His brows rose in surprise.

"Lord Armstrong, do forgive me. I fear I was being a trifle absentminded." She could think of little else to say.

"Lady Victoria, is something wrong?"

"Please pardon me. I am afraid I am already late in meeting my mother. I really must hurry." She nearly leapt into the waiting coach, bypassing the assistance of the footman, leaving Lord Armstrong standing, his brow knotted, on the cobbled walkway. Fear now surmounted her grief, as a premonition of her world coming unraveled traced an icy finger down the length of her spine.

Chapter Sixteen

"Mama, about Aunt Camille's invitation—"

The viscountess held up her hand. "Your brother has already spoken to me." Her mother sat at a small writing desk in the music room, the letter she penned set aside, forgotten, as she focused her attention on her eldest daughter.

"Your brother seems to think it might indeed do you the world of good, but I am not so certain," the viscountess said.

Missy hurried to her side, taking a seat on the floral chaise next to the desk. "Mama, I thought perhaps Cousin Abigail could act as my chaperone."

Lady Armstrong's expression immediately softened. Missy knew the deep affection her mother held for her niece by marriage and the absolute faith she had in her cousin's judgment and abilities. If she hoped to sway her mother, she had chosen the right person to accompany her.

"Why, by next year I might very well be married and who knows when a trip to America will be possible." It was sometimes frightening how the lies came so easily.

The viscountess gave her a tender look. "As much as I would love to keep you safe and close to me for as long as possible, I do understand your desire to go."

She read the sympathy in her mother's eyes and knew she was speaking of her feelings for James. Missy quickly dropped her gaze to her hands as the heat of a blush stole over her face.

"You have no need to be embarrassed, my dear. I was young once myself, and I know the agony of first love." Her mother's voice held the soothing warmth of the sun on bare skin on a beautiful summer day. Missy raised her eyes to hers and allowed her mother's compassion to soothe her. Her father was lost to her mother forever. James was merely unrequited love.

"So you will permit me to go?"

Lady Armstrong nodded slowly. "Yes, I will permit you to go under two conditions. One, that your Cousin Abigail agrees to accompany you, and the second is that I receive personal assurances from Mr. Wendel of your safety on his ship. Being part owner in a shipping company must afford your brother some sort of privileges."

Missy launched herself into her mother's surprised arms, which swiftly encompassed her in a tight squeeze.

"Thank you, Mama, you will not regret this."

"I sincerely hope not, my dear. Now you must go and write a letter to both your Aunt Camille and Cousin Abigail, and once you receive their replies, I will have Thomas arrange your passage. You will leave after my rout in August and return at the end of November."

Giving her mother one last squeeze, Missy rose to her feet. "I will compose the letters today and send them out to post."

James had never missed the Derby. At least, he had never missed the event since the age of five until this year. He absently rimmed the untouched cup of coffee, his thoughts elsewhere. Cartwright, sitting across the table from him in a small eatery on Regent Street, watched him steadily.

"Will you drink that before it turns to ice?" Cartwright flicked his head in the direction of the earthenware mug.

As the day of the official betrothal announcement drew closer, James knew his disposition soured disproportionately. He was sick to death of squiring Lady Victoria about town and playing the doting suitor. And the marchioness—he didn't have a polite thing to say to the woman, so he wisely remained tight-lipped when in her presence, which was much too frequent for his liking.

"What I need is a real drink," he muttered, setting the cup down and pushing it across the scarred surface of the wooden table.

"I see our match wasn't enough to work off your foul mood," Cartwright said.

James didn't respond, merely turned to view the nearly empty streets through the large window at the front. Most of the masses, aristocrats, gentry, and working class alike, had taken themselves off to the Derby, which is where he should be. But a day standing in the heat of London's June sun held no appeal. The crush of bodies, the scent of horse-flesh and sweat, and the excitement of the races didn't have the pull it normally did.

Cartwright preferred not to attend the Derby most years and this year was no exception. He thought the whole event rather overblown and hadn't a penchant for gambling of any sort.

The door of the eatery opened and James was more than a little surprised to see Armstrong enter. Parliament hadn't met today so he should have gone to the Derby hours before.

Armstrong immediately started for their table, his strides long and swift on the wood floors. Cartwright swiveled in his seat just in time to see him drop into the chair next to him.

"What the devil are you doing here?" Cartwright asked, his surprise evident in his voice and raised brows.

Armstrong didn't even glance at him, his regard intent on James. "Last night I saw Lady Victoria coming from Clifton's residence."

Cartwright sat straight back in his chair. Then two pairs of eyes trained on James, closely gauging his response. The full impact of what the viscount had just revealed was slow to penetrate, but when it did come, the import left him reeling, confused, elated.

He stared at his golden-haired friend for several long seconds, giving his head a mental shake. "You don't believe there is—" He slapped the palm of his hand down hard on the table. "White's! That would explain why he looks at me as if he'd like nothing better than to see me drawn and quartered."

"Now you can't go off half-cocked," Cartwright said, always the voice of reason. "There could be a perfectly reasonable explanation."

"Which I'm sure she will convey to me when I ask her."

The viscount brought his seat closer to the table. "Damn, I still find it rather hard to believe Lady Victoria would risk herself by carrying on with Clifton. The marchioness elevates snobbery to an entirely different level. If it were not for your vast estates and holdings," he looked pointedly at James, "I'm certain even an earl wouldn't be good enough for her."

James nodded his agreement.

"Well if I were you—and I am most happy I am not—I would approach Clifton, not Lady Victoria." Cartwright bore the sage look of a man far more advanced than his twenty-five years. "If she has been lying to you, who says she'll come clean with the truth? Who says she won't come up with some fairy tale for being at Clifton's home?"

"I agree with Cartwright." Armstrong said.

"The man despises me, he won't give me an audience," James grumbled.

Cartwright chortled. "When has that ever stopped you before?"

A half smile tugged the corner of James's mouth. He had a way with people. They would either listen to reason and, if that didn't suffice, he had been known on occasion to apply brute force. But he didn't want to brawl with the man; he just wanted to talk.

"I doubt he will grant me entrance to his lodgings, so I'll seek him out at White's tomorrow evening. I know he fairly haunts the place after his day in Parliament. He can hardly avoid me there."

James found Clifton seated at the very same table, hunched over a glass of alcohol looking just as surly as he had the last time he encountered him. But the circumstances were much changed now, and he was far more knowledgeable. So instead of passing his table, with Clifton's brown eyes bearing down on him with stark animosity, James shouldered his way past many of his rowdy, drunken contemporaries to the table.

If a look of hatred could fell a man, James would be lying dead on the floor. James noted his bloodshot eyes but, surprisingly, the rest of him appeared well put together. His clothes were impeccable, and his neckcloth hadn't lost that crisp starched look.

Coming to halt in front of the table, James cast a long shadow over his seated form. "Clifton, you don't mind if I take a seat, do you?" But it wasn't a question. Before the man could utter a sound, he pulled out the empty chair opposite him and sat down.

Clifton stared at him through glazed eyes, his mouth

twisted in a scowl. "We have nothing to discuss, *my lord.*" He infused the address with venom enough to send a host of small animals darting for cover.

James's intention wasn't to further provoke the man, but he saw his task wouldn't be an easy one. His own ire began to rise, and the only thing that stopped it from spiking right along with Clifton's was the matter concerning a woman. James had never come across a woman he would willingly fight over—fight for—especially if said woman had cunningly plotted to leg-shackle him.

Easing back into the chair, James rested his back against the laddered frame. With a studied casualness, he loosened the buttons on his charcoal gray coat, splaying his legs before him, and folded his arms across his chest.

"It's hard to believe Lady Victoria has the power to reduce you to this. I had thought you above such behavior," he drawled. The brief flaring in Clifton's eyes gave him away. He had hit his mark.

"You don't know anything," Clifton replied, raising his glass and tossing his head back for a deep swallow.

James snorted. "Like bloody hell. She was seen leaving your lodgings in tears the night before last." If he pushed, he was certain Clifton would break. The man exuded an acridness that probably burned right through to his soul.

"What, you're not comfortable marrying soiled goods?" he bit out harshly.

James had known, so no great surprise showed on his face. He had sensed the truth the moment Armstrong had relayed the incident to him. And it had taken so little prodding to get the man to admit to it.

He stared at Clifton, who in turn stared right back at him, glowering and tense, as if he was on the verge of a big explosion. Then Clifton dropped his head. His eyes closed, his shoulders rising and falling rapidly. For a moment James thought he would break down and—God forbid—cry. He shifted uncomfortably at that notion, and sent a singular prayer for that not to occur—at least not while he was sitting there. Seconds later, and with a deep inhalation, Clifton seemed to visibly pull himself together.

"So perhaps you can explain to me why the blazes she set out to trap me into marriage." James's voice was calm, completely juxtaposed to the tumult of his emotions.

Clifton snorted derisively. "Why don't you ask her yourself."

James pushed from the table and rose to his feet. He gazed down at the broken man before him, who, like an animal, lashed out when it was hurt. "Believe me, I intend to."

He gave a curt nod and pivoted on his heels. Before he was out of earshot, he heard Clifton call out, his voice slightly slurred, "Good day, my lord."

James paused before resuming his course. Lady Victoria would have plenty to explain in the morrow.

James could barely believe he'd endured the ten hours that had elapsed since he confronted Clifton, with such incredible forbearance. The marchioness was delighted to find him waiting in the foyer the following morning at nine o'clock sharp. His one wish was she disappeared just as quickly as she'd come.

She ushered him into the drawing room, like a clucking hen, assuring him in the most solicitous tones that Victoria would be arriving shortly. He declined her offer of coffee, tea, hot cocoa, and pastries—French, because they indeed are the flakiest—with a polite but firm shake of his head.

To his undying relief, Lady Victoria arrived just as her mother launched into a monologue in reference to an outing of some sort.

"Lady Victoria, you're looking well." He duly accepted her proffered hand and brought it up to his lips to plant a fleeting kiss on the cool, white flesh.

"I shall leave you two now. I am sure you have many things to discuss," the marchioness simpered. The swish of her heavy skirts as she bustled from the room was one of the most pleasing sights and sounds James had witnessed thus far that week.

"Good morning, Lord Rutherford. What brings you by so early?" Her gaze didn't quite meet his own probing stare. Her eyes were faintly red-rimmed, as if she'd been crying, and she had a pinched look about her mouth.

"Perhaps we could take a seat outside in the garden." He inclined his head toward the doors off the drawing room leading to a lavish garden where yellow daisies ran amuck down the side of the house. He motioned with his hand and she led the way, glancing back nervously as she did. Her blue eyes watched him as if she sensed something unpleasant awaited her.

Humid air met them as they emerged into a day begun with feeble sunlight and ominous gray clouds. Lady Victoria took a seat on the wooden bench, her skirt literally overrunning the smooth, aged surface. James parked himself on a black wrought-iron chair facing her.

Raising her gaze to his, she appeared excessively proper, her pale hands neatly folded in her lap. His eyes caught their tremor.

She didn't look like a treacherous liar, nor did she appear to be a woman who had so little conscience as to trap a man when he was deep in his cups, suffering a weak moment in his life. Amazingly enough, she was both.

"You certainly look serious this morning." An uneasy laugh accompanied her words.

He hadn't realized his expression had altered enough for

her to make that observation. But then, why should he put on a false face? He wasn't pleased and he wouldn't pretend otherwise.

"I want you to tell me what has transpired between yourself and George Clifton."

Lady Victoria stilled and her face went as white as the handkerchief in his jacket pocket. Her eyelids drifted shut. Her slender shoulder lifted and fell.

"Do not bother with any denials because I know you were seen leaving his quarters quite distraught. Also, I have spoken to Clifton. It came as some relief to find out why the man so despises me." His tone gave nothing, hard and implacable.

Several times she opened her mouth, as if to say something, and then snapped it closed. She did at least have the grace to look discomfited; a crimson tide spread from the area exposed by her square-necked morning dress, up to her face. She was unable to meet his gaze. Slowly, she unclasped her hands and held out her palms, imploring. "I was desperate." Her words came out a barely audible whisper, forcing him to strain for every word.

"So I was to be the sacrificial lamb?"

She peered anxiously up at him. "I beg your forgiveness. I know what I did was unforgivable. My only excuse is that I would have done anything to prevent Mother from forcing me to marry Lord Frederick." Clutching herself about her waist, she shivered as if the mere thought was too abhorrent to be borne.

Yes, Lady Victoria presented a pitiful sight, her slender form bowed over in guilt and anguish, her eyes glassy with tears, but James remained unmoved. The damn chit had only been thinking of herself when she cooked up her scheme to trap him. His wishes had not once been considered, so—as sorry as she professed to be—he could not summon up an ounce of sympathy for her quandary.

"I assume I'm not the father of this baby you carry—or does a child even exist?" he asked, a cynical smirk twisting his mouth. "Did you get Dr. Litchfield to part with his ethical scruples to lie for you?"

She shook her head furiously, finally holding his gaze for a length. "No, you mustn't think that of him. He would never do such a thing—not for anything, not for any money. I am with child. I did not lie to you about that. It is what has me in this untenable position."

"Did anything occur between us that evening?"

He saw the truth in her eyes before she responded. "No."

So he hadn't even bedded her. "How then, did I come to wake up in my bed, my head stripped of any memory of the evening events?" he asked through gritted teeth as his ire began to climb.

Her eyes flickered and he saw the fear there.

She swallowed convulsively. "You must remember I was desperate," she implored, dashing a lock of white-blond hair from her face that had been loosed by a gusty breeze. She inhaled a deep breath and continued. "I added some laudanum to your glass when you were pouring my drink. That was why you succumbed to sleep so quickly."

James exploded to his feet. "By God, you used opium on me. You could have killed me. My system has no tolerance for the drug."

That his parents had learned when he was but twelve years old and had broken his ankle. A draught of laudanum had put him to sleep so long his mother had feared he would never wake up. He had the following day with barely any memory of the fall from the tree.

If he had struck her, she couldn't have looked more horrified. "Oh, God. I added a very small amount. Just enough to make you sleep. Please believe me, I never meant to hurt you."

He gave her a look. A look that silently said wouldn't

forcing him to marry be hurtful in its own way. A guilty blush stained her cheeks. "I mean, cause you any physical harm," she amended.

He grunted and subsided back onto the hard chair. "Now you're going to tell me why you did this," he demanded, regarding her coolly, his brow arched as he awaited her explanation for embroiling him in this grossly affair.

Her hands trembled as she smoothed her skirt nervously. The flush had receded from her face, her composure trickling back. "My mother is not an easy woman."

James snickered. So she was going to tell him things he was well acquainted with.

"As you have probably seen, she values rank and money above all else, and insists on a *grand match* for me. If she discovered I carry George's child, I fear my fate would be the same as Lillian's." Her eyes darkened at the mention of her sister, causing her countenance to appear haunted and distressed.

"I thought your sister married a French count and moved to France," he said.

Lady Victoria's mouth lifted in a faint, sad smile. "That is what my mother would have everyone believe. In truth, Lillian resides there in an asylum for the insane."

His brows climbed sky high. "Good Lord, why?"

"She became pregnant in her first Season by the son of a local tradesman in Kent. My mother absolutely refused to allow her to wed David. She sent Lillian away until the child was born, and then forced her to give the child away. Lillian was so distraught at the loss of her daughter and David, she attempted to drown herself. Our gardener was able to pull her from the pond in time but my mother didn't want to risk another occurrence so she had her sent away to the hospital." The story seemed wrenched from her, her breathing quickened, her eyes welled with unshed tears.

James sat stock-still. He remembered the year her sister had all but vanished from Society. If he remembered correctly, the entire family had been gone for a month in the midst of high Season, which at that time had been quite odd, knowing how the marchioness veritably lived for such things. The explanation given and accepted was they had all left to attend her marriage, which had been held in France.

He had been resolved to maintain a cold, hard disposition; after all, Lady Victoria had tried to trap him into marriage with her lies, and pass another man's child off as his own, but at her reasons, an inkling of compassion nudged its way into the corner of his heart—a small part.

"So you fear your mother will force you to give up your child?"

"My mother will not allow a marriage to George and she will not allow her remaining daughter to shame her as my sister did, so . . . yes, I know she would force me to give my baby away. The only possibility of me keeping my child is to marry someone she would approve of."

And sadly, James could see that is where he'd been the perfect dupe. Unfortunately for Lady Victoria, though, he had no intention of being sacrificed for her indiscretion with Clifton.

Almost as if she'd read his mind, she said, "You needn't fear I still expect you to go through with it. And I certainly will not put you in the unpleasant position of refusing me if I were to beg you to do so. I would not expect any man to marry me under these circumstances."

"I'm fairly certain Clifton will marry you." When he remembered the condition he'd found the man in, he thought if she had the ability to reduce him to that, his feelings for her had far from dissipated. She need only make an earnest and heartfelt plea for forgiveness.

Pain flared vividly in her eyes. She slowly shook her

head, swallowing hard, blinking rapidly as she appeared to desperately fight back tears.

"I think you underestimate yourself as well as Clifton. You are a woman of twenty-two. I imagine you can marry anyone you choose so long as you will not require the assistance of your parents. The Queen herself knighted Clifton for his valor during the war. I hardly think you will find a better man among the *ton*."

She regarded him and a tremulous smile emerged as praise glittered in her eyes. "I believe I have. You are an exceedingly kind man, James Rutherford. I wish everyone felt the same as you."

"I am of little consequence here. What is important is how you feel, and what you think of the man." He sensed the war raging inside her as she battled fear and hope in a dueling round.

She laid her slender hand on the back of his. "I would not blame you one bit if you despised me for what I have done to you."

James had never seen her this raw and open, and although he had been angry—explosively so—at her deceit and lies, he understood why she'd done what she did while certainly not condoning any of it. She had quite a battle ahead, and he hoped she proved up for the fight.

"I don't believe you could ever completely warrant my dislike, although I will leave you to tell your parents our courtship has ended and inform your mother it is not my child you carry."

She gave a rueful smile. "I assure you, Lord Rutherford, I will make doubly sure you will be seen as no less than the honorable gentleman you have proven yourself to be."

He stood. "If there is anything I can do for you in the future," he stared pointedly at her waist, "any assistance you require in regard to your—uh, situation, please do not hesitate to call on me."

"Thank you, Lord Rutherford, you are too kind. I will keep your offer in mind." Lady Victoria came gracefully to her feet.

"If you don't mind, I will exit through the gates. I think it best not to risk an encounter with your mother."

She smiled. "I quite understand."

James left the Spencer residence, a weight lifted from his shoulders, his bachelorhood restored. Thoughts of Missy immediately pushed to the forefront of his mind, for he could say she rarely left it these days.

His current predicament would be a tricky maneuver. He *had* ruined her, there was no doubt there. He recalled in vivid detail exactly how exquisitely she'd been ruined. In fact, he had lived on those memories for the past two weeks. And much to his discomfort, a certain rampant part of his anatomy jumped eagerly to life, like present, when his thoughts veered in that direction.

With a sharp tug at his trousers, he settled onto the black cushioned seat of his phaeton and then picked up the ribbons. A firm flick of his wrist sent his blacks off in a canter, their shoes creating a *clip clop* echo along the paved streets.

He would ponder more about what he would do next. He required time to think. Time to plot.

Chapter Seventeen

Mr. Wendel was not at all as Missy had imagined him. He stood at least six feet and possessed a large rawboned frame, that of a pugilist, she imagined. He had a thick shock of light brown hair worn too long to be fashionable, and his face bore a maturity that bespoke a man in his forties, but his smile gave him a more youthful appearance. He was, in fact, quite a handsome man.

Thomas stood by his side, chatting easily when she followed her mother into the library. Both men turned at their entrance but it was the look on Mr. Wendel's face Missy found amusing. His gaze darted between mother and daughter, looking somewhat awestruck, before he settled a very appreciative regard on the viscountess. Then, as if he remembered where he was and who he gaped at like a boy with too little tact and too much appreciation for the fairer sex, he seemed to compose himself, his smile of greeting, polite.

Her mother, long used to such avid male appreciation, sent him a warm smile and extended her hand. "Good afternoon, Mr. Wendel. I hope I haven't put you out with my request, however, I wasn't aware you would be calling in person."

"Lady Armstrong, I saw no other way such assurances

could be given." He took her hand, shaking it slowly, gently, and if he lingered over long in releasing it, her mother was much too refined to comment.

"And you must be the eldest Miss Armstrong," he said, turning his chocolate brown eyes on her. "Your brother didn't tell me that you were such a beauty." He sent her brother a look of mock reproach. Thomas rolled his eyes. When Mr. Wendel returned his attention to her, his gaze held an admiration like that of an art enthusiast enjoying a particularly select *objet d'art*; it lacked the more manly appreciation he'd bestowed upon her mother.

If not for the fatigue she had been suffering the last several days, Missy would have received him with much more enthusiasm but, as it was, she managed only a wan smile as she held out her hand. "Thank you, sir. Without your assurances, my mother would have forbidden this trip, therefore I am in your debt."

He gave her hand a solicitous shake. He didn't hold it a second longer than propriety called for, as he had with her mother. With eyes twinkling, he said, "As I've told Thomas, I will be able to personally ensure your safety and comfort on this voyage. I must travel to America on business, so I will make the crossing with you." His gaze sought out the viscountess's.

Her mother's smile spoke volumes, her relief evident. "Mr. Wendel, you have no idea how that helps to settle my misgivings about Millicent taking this trip. I am in your debt as well. If there is anything I can do for you, please do not hesitate to ask."

Mr. Wendel grinned broadly, revealing even, white teeth. He was even more handsome than Missy had originally thought. She slid a glance at her mother and noticed a slight flush staining her porcelain cheeks.

"I imagine you could start by calling me Derrick."

His response seemed to fluster the viscountess, leaving her at a momentary loss for words. Men and women simply did not call each other by their given names unless they were intimately acquainted. And even then, sometimes not even married couples addressed each other by their Christian names. But apparently either Mr. Wendel was not aware of this, or chose to ignore the fact. "Well—I, certainly if you wish . . . Derrick."

"Nothing would please me more, my lady." Her address came out a caress.

Thomas cleared his throat loudly. "Wendel, I didn't bring you here to charm my mother."

"Thomas," her mother said, shooting him a warning look. "Mr—Derrick was doing no such thing." Mr. Wendel said nothing, which only served to reinforce her brother's claim.

Lightheadedness hit Missy with startling swiftness. Conversation resumed between Thomas, her mother, and Mr. Wendel but their voices grew muted. The room tilted wildly. She shook her head, trying to somehow halt the dizzying whirl, but the sudden move only served to make it worse. Then blackness engulfed her and she knew no more.

Missy struggled to lift her eyelids. Someone held her hand tightly and she discerned her mother's panicked voice and the raw concern lacing her brother's. Her eyes fluttered open.

"Oh, thank goodness," her mother said, bringing Missy's hand up to her mouth, pressing the back against her right cheek. Worry etched fine lines on her forehead and around her mouth, but a hesitant smile tipped the edges of her lips at Missy's return to consciousness.

Thomas stood by her—Missy eyes darted quickly around the room—her bedside. The last she remembered, they had been meeting with Mr. Wendel downstairs in the library. She glanced back at Thomas, who hovered above her like an overprotective father. He offered a tentative smile but his green eyes remained dark and solicitous.

"You gave us quite a scare, young lady." He gently brushed stray wisps of hair from her forehead.

"That will teach me to skip supper and breakfast," she replied in a small voice.

Her mother laid her hand back by her side, giving it several pats before removing her own. "Well, we shall have the physician take a look at you and then my worries can be put to rest. Thomas, please send for Dr. Schmitz." Her brother vanished before Missy could protest.

"Mama, honestly 'tis nothing. I'm hungry is all. There's no need to send for Dr. Schmitz." Food was all she required, and perhaps a bit more sleep than she'd been getting of late.

"When did you last see your monthly courses?"

The suddenness and the unexpectedness of her mother's question rattled her, leaving her bereft of a response. Her mind scrambled for a date. It took what seemed a lifetime of frantic thinking and counting to discover she was indeed overdue for her monthlies. Shame suffused her face with heat and with it came the horror of the revelation, of what it might mean.

"Please tell me you did not. Please tell me you are not." Her mother's plea was hushed and fervent, like a prayer but her eyes said she knew. "You have, haven't you? You are no longer a virgin."

Missy didn't even bother to deny the choked claim, lowering her gaze, unwilling to witness the look of disappointment and heartbreak in her mother's green eyes. She shook her head because the words would not come.

Silence held reign far too long. She finally dared to peer

up at her mother. The countenance staring back at her could put dismay to shame.

"Oh, Missy," she said on a whisper-soft sigh.

"I'm sorry, Mama." Her voice was thick with tears.

"Are you with child?"

"I don't believe so. I'm not certain." Dear God, she prayed she was not.

"But there is a possibility, is there not?"

Missy dipped her head in a small nod.

"And the father, who would that be?" her mother asked, blinking rapidly, her eyes shiny with moisture.

Turning away, Missy gave a definitive shake of her head. How could she tell her the truth? James was like a son to her. It would ruin everything and her ruination was enough.

At the muffled sniff, Missy turned back to her mother. The last time she'd seen her mother cry was at her father's funeral, over ten years ago. After that, she had been stoic in her grief, tending to her children's loss rather than her own. Now silent tears tracked down smooth, pale cheeks.

"Millicent, this is hardly something you can keep to yourself. Of course you must tell me, and then I will have to tell your brother. This man has taken your innocence. He must marry you." The viscountess reached for a handkerchief on the bedside table, then proceeded to use it to dab her eyes and cheeks.

Panic widened her eyes as Missy bolted upright and grasped her mother's free hand tightly. "Mama, you can't tell Thomas. You know his temper. He will kill him or get himself killed. And we aren't even certain of my condition."

"Tell me what?"

Neither of them had heard Thomas's arrival but his tall frame filled the doorway with the indomitable presence of a golden warrior. But no one could mistake the menacing tone in his question.

Dread clambered up her spine, leaving her breathless. Her heart jumped into her throat making it impossible to swallow; she could not even blink, her fear was so stark.

"Missy, if you are, this is hardly something you will be able to hide from him. I needn't remind you that your brother is the man of the house and he has every right to know." Having dried her tears, her mother's sadness had been replaced by a look of calm, parental resolve.

He advanced to her bedside, his brows drawn above his eyes like a thunderstorm. "What do I have a right to know?" he asked quietly, enunciating each word with excruciating exactness.

Missy tried not to cower but she found herself shrinking back into the forgiving softness of the pillows. The viscountess rose from the bed to stand in front of him, her stance that of a mother protecting her young.

"I fear Missy may be expecting."

"Expecting what?" Thomas's bewildered gaze turned to her. It took another second for the full import of her mother's words to sink in. His silence didn't last long, nor was his anger slow to build or erupt.

"I'll kill him!" He slammed his fist against the solid mahogany frame of the four-poster bed, the force causing the bed to shudder, as well as its lone occupant.

"Who is it?" he asked in a voice promising retribution of cataclysmic proportions.

"She refuses to say." The viscountess stepped closer to her son and placed a restraining hand on the broad expanse of his chest. "But you mustn't do anything rash. We must all keep a level head."

Ignoring his mother, Thomas continued to stare at Missy over the top of the viscountess's head. "You will tell me." His command brooked no refusal.

But Missy was too terrified to draw a breath much less

speak. His anger, as potent as a deadly storm, struck her immobile and utterly speechless.

The ensuing silence tested them both—her brother's forbearance and her resolve.

"Fine," he snapped after telling seconds passed without the utterance of a word. He spun on his heel and stormed from the chamber.

"Millicent," her mother said, turning to her, "you understand you will not be able to keep this from him, don't you? He will discover the truth."

Indeed he would, Missy conceded, but she owed James at least some forewarning. "What do you think he'll do?"

Sighing, the viscountess returned to sit on the edge of the bed. "Something I'm sure he'll regret. Your brother has such a dreadful temper." Picking up her hand, her mother stroked the back with gentle fingers. "Why won't you tell me before your brother hunts down every man you have so much as spoken to since you arrived in Town."

Before she was again forced to deny her mother, her brother stormed back into the room, his expression coldly furious. "Is it Crawley or Rutherford?" He spat the two names.

Her mother's hand stroking hers immediately stilled. Alarm stole Missy's next breath.

"James?" the viscountess cried.

When Missy failed to respond, Thomas advanced until he stood at the foot of the bed, his hands clenched around the column of the bedstead. "No, don't answer. I already know. If there is one thing I am confident of is that my friend would never ever take undue advantage of you. Therefore, that leaves only that bloody fop, Crawley." He practically growled the man's name.

"Who—how?" Missy found the recovery of her voice did not necessarily mean she could articulate well enough to communicate.

But her brother knew exactly what she asked. "Under the threat of punishment that I would tan their bloody hides, I forced your sisters to reveal what they know. They told me about a kiss with Crawley and an incident with you and Rutherford in the study at mother's winter ball."

Oh dear Lord, they had promised her they would never speak a word of it to anyone, especially Thomas. That's what she got for trusting a seventeen- and fifteen-year-old with such secrets.

"Crawley is a dead man." He gave the footboard a good shake before turning to leave.

"Wait!" Missy shouted, pulling herself into a sitting position.

Thomas halted at the threshold but did not turn to look at her. "What?" he snapped.

"It wasn't Lord Crawley." Her voice was barely audible.

Her mother inhaled a sharp breath. Thomas didn't move and said nothing for a frighteningly long time. Finally, his shoulders rose and fell just once, as if he'd been forced to take a breath.

"Are you telling me my friend of ten years, a man who is as close to me as my own family, has betrayed not only our friendship, our mother's trust, but has taken your innocence?" He spoke with a calmness that belied the current stillness of his form as he remained with his back to her, his hands taut and splayed on each side of the doorframe.

"If you want to blame someone, blame me. All of it was my doing. He only took what was offered." The latter she said, her eyes downcast. It had taken all the courage she could muster to not only admit it to them, but to herself as well. This was a nightmare of her own creation.

From her peripheral vision, Missy saw her brother slowly turn to face her. She shrank deeper into the pillows.

"Now, Thomas," the viscountess said in her most placating tone, rising from the bed to rush to his side. "It will never do for you to confront him in your present state."

"One of my closest friends has ruined my sister, Mother. Just when do you expect I will be in the right state of mind to see him?" he asked coolly. With those words and a narrow, cold-eyed stare at Missy, he was gone.

Missy finally risked a look up. Her mother stood staring at the open door, her anguish evident in her eyes.

"I shall instruct Stevens to send Alex to James's residence immediately," the viscountess said.

"This is all my fault," Missy said in a tiny voice.

Her mother did not disagree, instead she countered with a sad smile. "I have not forgotten what it is like to be young and in love. I only wish that . . . that you had waited, for your own sake, not mine. As it is, from what I have heard, James is all but pledged to Lady Victoria."

Missy couldn't help but smart at the mention of their coming marriage but she couldn't concern herself with them—with him. James could do little to help her regardless of her circumstances.

"If I am expecting, I shall remain in America and have the baby there. I promise you, Mama, I will not allow what I have done to ruin Emily and Sarah's chances of good matches."

"My concern is for you now. I have no desire to ship you off to America to have a baby without your family present . . . without me." Pain etched tiny lines around her eyes and mouth.

"Let us not think of that now. We still don't even know whether I am with child."

Coming back to her side, her mother pulled her gently into her arms and whispered, "We will get through this, no matter how trying. I could never abandon you."

Missy tightly clutched her mother to her, drawing strength from her seemingly bottomless well of wisdom and love.

* * *

It was amazing that once a significant weight was removed from one's shoulders—namely his—how different the world appeared. Somehow, the sun shone brighter than all previous mornings, and the gray pall that had clasped the city in its unyielding grip that morning had lifted, allowing its inhabitants to feel the real pleasures of summer.

James enjoyed the hearty breakfast he hadn't been able to stomach before meeting with Lady Victoria. Scones topped with fresh strawberry preserves, eggs, ham, and piping hot coffee, black the way he took it—he consumed it all with a gusto that had been absent for weeks. With the matter of Lady Victoria settled, he'd made a decision regarding Missy.

He would marry her as he'd initially intended. It was that simple.

But that didn't change his position on the type of marriage he would have. It would be a marriage without the promise of fidelity or love. He'd take a mistress if he so desired, for Missy would not take the lead in the matters of the marriage bed. No, he would rule that domain as he pleased. Unlike his father, he'd never plead for a taste of passion from the one person who should give it freely. The fact that he desired her as he'd never desired another was an entirely separate matter that would have no bearing on their marriage. But he would need to curb his insatiable lust for her lest she sense that chink in his armor. Lust and desire were weaknesses easily exploited.

Sated from the large meal and quite satisfied with his decision, James had only settled in the library for five minutes before Smith appeared at its entrance. "Lord Armstrong to see you, milord," he intoned.

"See him in," he instructed, setting down the morning edition of the *Times*.

He rose to his feet, his smile easy and cordial when his friend entered and swiftly approached. What he didn't see was the fist that came sailing at him with the force of a gale wind, but he felt its impact all the way down to his toes. It slammed into his right eye, sending him staggering back.

A kaleidoscope of colors exploded in his head. "What the—"

"My own goddamn sister. You bastard."

Oh God, he'd found out about him and Missy. Another blow caught him beneath his jaw, slamming his lower teeth into the soft skin of his upper lip. The coppery taste of blood filled his mouth.

He glimpsed his shocked butler scurrying from the doorway, undoubtedly to bring back suitable reinforcements to break up the melee.

James pulled himself up, just as Armstrong was bringing his arm back for another powerful blow, and managed to evade that one, momentarily unbalancing his friend. James took that opportunity to hurry behind the desk, creating adequate distance to keep him out of Armstrong's reach. He couldn't very well fight back—not under the circumstances. He knew he had it coming—every single blow—but that didn't mean he had to like it and that certainly didn't mean that he wouldn't do everything in his power to minimize the damage.

"I'm not marrying Lady Victoria," he said, panting, his hands clutching the cushioned back of the leather chair.

"I don't give a damn," Armstrong said, pushing aside an ottoman with his foot in an effort to get to him. "You're intent on despoiling every woman I care about," he growled, ending in a roar.

With an agile leap to the side, James wound his way around the desk, trying to maintain a distance that would keep all of his body parts clear of Armstrong's large fists.

Oh Lord, Armstrong was also referring to Lady Louisa,

whom his friend had thought himself in love with six years
back. Bloody hell, she had kissed him, not the other way
around. Surely, Armstrong didn't still hold that against him?

"I didn't despoil Lady Louisa. I didn't even touch her. I'd
thought we had put that whole matter behind us."

When his friend had caught his would-be fiancée trying
to seduce him in the gardens at a ball, Armstrong hadn't said
a word, hadn't reacted overtly. James hadn't even known
Armstrong had seen them until a week after he'd ended all
communication with her. Given that James had politely but
firmly declined her offer to make her his future countess,
his friend had found him exempt of fault.

Or so he'd thought.

Armstrong's only response was a low grumble in his
throat. The man wasn't going to listen to reason.

"And I plan to marry Missy." He could only pray that
those words would do the trick, and cool the fire burning
hot and green in Armstrong's narrowed eyes and contain his
bared teeth.

He laughed. The bloody man had the audacity to laugh.
It was humorless, hollow, and mocking. Affront softened
James's stance, leaving him unprepared for the assault that
came when Armstrong pitched himself across the desk, the
jarring impact of his hands on James's shoulders thrusting
him back into the sideboard.

"Oomph!" His lower back took the full brunt of the
impact, sending him sliding to the floor. The pain in his back
now eclipsed the pain in his eye and jaw, which only told him
how badly it hurt. And he must suffer this all because he was
the one in the wrong. Damn chivalry and honor, right now
he'd rather be a reprobate and defend himself.

As much as it pained him, he sprang to his feet, not in a
remotely lithe or particularly coordinated manner but at
least it got him there—his hands raised in defense. He and

Armstrong were evenly matched in their pugilist abilities but he didn't have rage on his side. Rage counted a great deal when it came to fighting—and winning.

Armstrong charged at him shoulder down, a fury of flesh and lean muscle. Seeing no avenue of escape, except with him lying bloodied and pummeled to a pulp on his own library floor, James made a swift side step and brought his forearm down on Armstrong's back with the weight of his body. Armstrong staggered and fell with a thud on the parquet floors. But on his way down, he grasped James by the legs, yanking him from his feet to land in a heap, his legs pinned underneath his friend's broad chest.

"What the hell is wrong with you?" James shouted, grimacing, trying to free himself from the incredible hold Armstrong had on his legs. His jaw was swelling rapidly, making speech an effort. "I told you I'm going to marry her."

"Over my dead body." Armstrong launched himself forward, now straddling his chest, and caught him with another blow, this time to his left jaw.

Pain exploded like the blast of a cannon in his head, and he braced himself for what was to come.

Then, just as swiftly as the onslaught had begun, it ended, the weight on his chest gone. James opened the other eye—the one that still could—to see Cartwright struggling to stop Armstrong from pouncing on him again. James's breaths came pained and ragged as he tried to lift his head from the floor.

"Let me go, dammit." Armstrong struggled in Cartwright's grasp but with the assistance of James's very able-bodied footman they were able to wrestle him to the floor.

"What the hell is going on?" Cartwright rarely raised his voice, his cool, even temper seemingly always held in check. Today, however, he shouted the question while trying to control his friend's attempts to wrest himself from his grasp and that of the footman.

James sat up as quickly as the pain throbbing in his jaw—both sides—his eye, and his back would allow. If he feared that Armstrong would break hold of his captors, perhaps he'd have acted with more haste. But he seemed relatively secure, lying facedown still twisting hopelessly on the floor, his hands secured at his sides, Cartwright's knee pressing solidly in the center of his back.

With the back of his hand, James swiped at the blood trickling down the side of his mouth. On top of everything else, a steady dull throb penetrated through to the back of his skull. He groaned harshly as he pulled his broken body to his feet.

"Would someone mind telling me what the hell is going on?" Cartwright asked, with exaggerated patience.

Armstrong made one final attempt to free himself. When he failed, he sank down and rested the tip of his forehead on the area rug, resigned. "Ask that bloody bastard," he bit out.

Cartwright inclined his head toward James. James, on the other hand, was too cognizant of the footman, his valet, and his housekeeper standing at the library entrance, their expressions revealing the kind of rapt mortification and curiosity one would see in the audience of a traveling circus featuring a two-headed man. He certainly wasn't going to discuss his personal business with his servants present. Before the sun set, the gossip mill would spin with delicious abandon and Missy's reputation would be forever sullied.

Motioning with his hands, James issued a brief nod for his servants to depart. They did so slowly, Mrs. March glancing back several times before she disappeared from view, her curiosity trailing behind her.

"I'm sure Armstrong would not like me to air our personal business for all to hear," he said, pain punctuating every word. "If I have his guarantee that he won't take the first opportunity to lunge at me again, perhaps we can discuss this like civilized human beings."

The viscount pulled his head up, his neck muscles taut, and turned to observe him between narrowed eyes. He then glanced at Cartwright who was watching him pointedly, one thick brow quirked.

"I won't touch him," he agreed in a growl. "Now would you get the hell off me?"

Although he received the begrudging assurance, James was careful to give him a wide berth, circling the threesome warily and then collapsing onto the sofa with a sigh and a grimace.

Cartwright removed his knee from the viscount's back, and his footman released the clamping hold he had on his legs. Armstrong pulled himself up, shaking his hands out as if trying to revive the blood flow.

The footman questioned him with a look. James inclined his head in dismissal. The young man quit the room without a word, making certain to close the door firmly behind him.

"He had it coming and more." Armstrong's glare was one of pure loathing.

Cartwright moved to position himself between the two men, as if he feared Armstrong would go back on his word. "What the hell did he do? You look like a madman."

"Go ahead, James, why don't you tell him? Tell him how you ruined Missy and left her to bear your bastard."

Chapter Eighteen

The physical blows he had so recently endured compared little to the mental blow dealt by Armstrong's words. James's sharp indrawn breath rent the quiet stillness of the room. As the charge registered in the cognizant area of his brain, he stared—slack-aching-jawed—at the man who had just delivered it.

Armstrong, appearing oddly at ease for the first time since he had barreled in, fist swinging, stood braced on his heels, his arms crossed, wearing an expression mixed with smug satisfaction and unbridled fury. That he gained some sort of perverse pleasure from James's shock was clear.

"Missy is expecting?" James said softly, dazed and confused.

"What do you think has her fainting about the place?" Armstrong's voice resembled a feral growl.

"Good God, you didn't." Cartwright turned to him, wide-eyed and incredulous.

Any pleasure Armstrong had derived from shocking him with Missy's predicament quickly melted away. He gave Cartwright a terse nod.

James said nothing, still too stupefied to speak. She'd lied

to him. When he had asked her about the possibility of a child,
she'd assured him there would be no such consequence. But
so too had Lady Victoria, assured him similarly. It seemed the
two women had more in common than their penchant for
sneaking about calling on gentlemen. They were both excessively good liars.

But what he had done, regardless of the provocation, had
been reprehensible. And that she was the sister of one of his
closest friends lent the deed an even more unsavory air. No,
there was little he could say in his defense. And this new revelation only strengthened his resolve. Without a doubt, he
would take Missy as his wife. There was no other recourse.

"I plan to marry her," he said with such simplicity one
would think the matter required no consideration.

Armstrong stiffened, his hands dropping to his side in
clenched fists. His eyes darkened and he looked as if he was
ready to do battle—again. "I trusted you. You were supposed to cure her of it, not take her to your bloody bed."
Amid his anger, James heard a note of hurt in his friend's
voice at his betrayal, and it cut him to the quick.

"You must know I didn't mean for this to happen." It was
as close to an apology as James could manage at present.

The viscount blistered him with such a look, James's
guilt quite easily superseded his physical pain. "I will see
you in hell before I permit you to marry her."

Cartwright looked at Armstrong as if he'd gone mad. "Although I realize these are not ideal circumstances, and certainly not what you would have wished for Missy, but
considering she is *enceinte,* I don't see that you have any
other choice."

James was more than happy to allow Cartwright to talk
some sense into him. As he was not presently high on Armstrong's list of favorite people, it was probably best he said

as little as possible. The man would soon be his brother-in-law, whether his friend wished it or not.

Armstrong snorted. "Ideal? Really?" he said, his tone growing dry with derision. "Who the bloody hell says he's the only choice she has?"

James's one good eye narrowed instantly. What the hell was Armstrong talking about? Of course he was the only choice she had. Who else would be willing to marry her now that she was expecting his child? Unless . . .

"What does that mean?" The left side of his mouth had swelled to such a degree his speech came out partially muffled.

"Exactly what I just said. She doesn't have to marry you if she doesn't desire. As far as my sister is concerned, you are as good as married to Lady Victoria, who incidentally is carrying your child."

"Well, she'll discover quite differently soon enough." James bore the stab of pain every time he moved his mouth to form a word.

Cartwright, who drank infrequently—his father had a great affection for the bottle—moved to the sideboard during their exchange, and poured himself a tumbler of brandy.

James could have done with one himself.

"I'm sure Granville would take her without question." One dark blond brow rose as if to challenge him.

James bolted to his feet, forgetting the pain in his back, his anger palpable. "I'll be damned if I allow her to wed Granville." Another kind of pain exploded inside him.

"She doesn't require your permission," Armstrong said, regarding him with disdain.

James shot a glance at Cartwright as if to compel him to intercede. But his raven-haired friend continued to sip his brandy, his expression excruciatingly neutral. A sound closely resembling disgust rumbled from James's throat. He turned his attention back to Armstrong.

"It's my child she carries." He said it loud enough to reach the ears of the upstairs servants but at this point, he didn't give a whit. He didn't care if the whole neighborhood heard—it might even force her hand and the hand of her very angry and obstinate brother.

"Do not remind me," Armstrong bit out tersely.

James could see the futility in arguing with him. Armstrong's emotions ran understandably high and his capacity to see reason was greatly diminished. Tomorrow would be soon enough to deal with this matter. At present, he required the attentions of his physician to ensure the blasted man hadn't done him permanent damage.

"This is hardly the end of it." James sent him a meaningful glance before he hobbled from the room.

Lord Rutherford to see you, miss. He's waiting in the drawing room.

The footman's words rang in her mind repeatedly as Missy made her way downstairs the following morning. They set her heart off in a wild gallop as she traversed the hallway and drew ever closer to the source of all her inner turmoil. James had called frightfully early, arriving at minutes to nine. What did he want? What could he want? And where was her brother?

Pausing just before the entrance of the room, she drew a deep breath, smoothed her hair, patted her carmine percale skirt, and then advanced another step. She stood framed in the doorway feeling as vulnerable as a chicken once the call for fowl had been made for supper.

Missy was surprised to find her mother seated on the chintz settee adjacent to James, who sat ensconced in the winged chair. There were no raised voices, which should have been a good sign; however, there was a severity to her mother's countenance she'd never seen before. Conversation ceased abruptly upon her entrance.

James came immediately to his feet and when he turned to her, she nearly stumbled back in horror.

"Oh my heavens, your face."

"You can be certain I will be speaking to Thomas about this," her mother said, her displeasure evidenced by the firm line of her delicate chin.

"Even you cannot deny the man's right to defend his sister's honor." Although his response was directed to her mother, his attention remained wholly focused on Missy. The corner of his mouth lifted—at least the side that still could—in a self-deprecating smile.

"I will allow you a moment alone with Millicent," the viscountess said, preparing to exit. She turned just as she breeched the threshold to shoot him a look. "We will conclude our conversation before you depart." Not a request, it had been a command. The scent of vanilla wafted behind as she swept from the room, her carriage regal and tall.

Missy still marveled at the damage done to his too-handsome face. His left cheek resembled an overstuffed sausage, puffy and misshapen. And his right eye sat amid swelled and discolored flesh. The sight alone appeared painful.

"We need to speak." He made no move to take his seat again, continuing to pierce her with his steady regard.

She met his gaze calmly. "I had hoped Thomas's anger would have cooled by the time he found you. It appears that was not so." She was surprised that she could sound so self-possessed when his presence stirred feelings in her she'd hoped would be more muted since the last time they'd met. And despite the condition of his face, his looks drew her, still with the power to heighten her awareness of him.

He gave a dismissive shrug. Gesturing toward the seating area, he said, "I hope you don't mind if we sit. My back is still rather sore."

Missy took the seat recently vacated by her mother as James reclaimed his. He eased into the armchair with a wince of discomfort.

"Lady Victoria has ended our betrothal."

Shock occurred first, and then a choir of angels began to sing a rendition of "Hallelujah." But Missy managed to suppress any overt reaction. His regard became ferociously intent.

What had he expected, that she would swoon at his feet? She had more pride than that. He'd denied her enough times; she wouldn't give him the opportunity to do so again.

"Do you expect an offer of condolences?" she asked with an arched brow.

She heard what she thought was an expletive uttered under his breath. "Why did you lie to me when I came the next day? You told me there was no possibility of a child."

"What was I to say? It was apparent you didn't want me. I certainly wasn't going to force you to the altar."

The tightening of his jaw made it clear he was reining in his temper. "We will be married as soon as I can procure a special license." His tone indicated he considered the matter not up for discussion. If his arrogance had not been so infuriating, she probably would have found some humor in his presumptuousness.

"While I do indeed find your *order* that I marry you romantic, I fear I will have to decline." The nerve of him, *telling* her they would be married as if he was instructing a servant to a task.

Tears, James had been prepared for, even petulance. But the coolness she exhibited proved far more disconcerting. It was hard to discern whether it was her pride in action or, if in the course of several weeks, her feelings for him had altered so drastically. But given the situation, not even that mattered.

"Well given the circumstances, I thought you would have seen right through any romantic gesture, and as I have only just gotten myself extricated from one impending marriage, it would have been unseemly of me to propose while courting another. As it is, I only just learned of your condition from your brother." If his tone and words conveyed an abundance of sarcasm, he didn't much care. Missy was being difficult. He could understand Armstrong's anger, but she had brought this on herself.

A fire lit her eyes and despite his anger, he instantly grew hard. Bloody sod.

"So that you understand this situation correctly, I have no wish to marry you, so please do not feel honor-bound to do so. I've already made arrangements to—"

With lightning quick speed, he was beside her, securing her forearm tightly with his hand. He leaned toward her until she could clearly see the blooded veins in the whites of his swelled eye. "If you think I will allow you to marry another man and sit idly by while *he* raises my child, you are very much mistaken. It would also be evidence that you don't know me and all that I am capable of."

She took a brief inventory of him, from his boots right up to his neckcloth. At last she looked at his face. "You're right about one thing, I never knew you. I loved a figment created by my quite vivid and romantic imagination."

James stiffened at her words. While he had given little credence to her professions of love, hearing her affirm his sentiments caused the oddest ache in his gut.

With his other hand, he exerted just enough pressure on her perfectly rounded chin to meet his gaze. Sooty lashes lifted to reveal her stunningly beautiful blue-gray eyes. He swallowed and was forced to tamp down a rush of lust so fierce, he shook.

"Our marriage will not require we love one another. It is enough that we can sufficiently tolerate each other in and out of the bedchamber." Never had words uttered been so understated as to be labeled ridiculous. "And as you are already expecting my child, I would say those reasons are more than many can claim."

"Firstly, I do not know whether I am expecting or not. One fainting spell does not make me so, despite what my mother and brother would choose to believe. He should not have said anything to you until I was certain. And even if I were carrying your child, the kind of marriage you've just described might be fine for you and the kind you desire, but it is not the kind I seek." She wrenched her chin from his hand and tilted it in an impudent manner that only further aided in depleting his small reserve of patience.

He released her arm and pushed to his feet. If he touched her now he wasn't sure if he could stop himself from shaking some sense into her—or at least trying to. She gave a whole new meaning to the word stubborn.

"Why didn't you make that clear from the beginning?" Because she wanted him to look the fool, carrying on about a child that might not even exist.

"Because, whether I am or not is immaterial. I will not marry you."

"I'm not going to beg," he growled. "So if that is what you expect, you will be sorely disappointed."

Missy rose to her feet. "What I expect from you is the exact thing you offered me when it happened. Nothing. It would appear the notion eludes you."

James restrained himself—but only just. He took several deep breaths. "If you think you will marry another man,

I can assure you I won't allow that to happen. If I have to, I will claim the child publicly. You'll find yourself immersed in a scandal the likes of which you've never seen." He turned from her and stalked over to the fireplace, where he braced his hand against the intricate hand-carved black wood mantel.

He loathed that she'd forced him to resort to the level of such threats, but damn, she hadn't given him much choice. And unfortunately, he didn't have the support of not even one member of her family.

Her expression held one of shock when she turned slowly to stare at him. "You wouldn't," she said, her tone hushed in disbelief.

"I beg you, do not try me."

"That is unconscionable."

"Any more so than depriving me of my child—perhaps my heir?"

"I just told you I'm not even certain I am pregnant. And I have no plans to marry anyone else. What do you take me for? I am going to America to stay with my aunt. Anyway, what do you care? Yesterday you were to marry Victoria Spencer. Go back to her and convince her to marry you. She already carries your child."

"She does not carry my child," he all but shouted, advancing toward her, halting a foot away.

Instinct told Missy to retreat, which she did. He looked angry—or perhaps it was frustrated—enough to throttle her.

So the child Lady Victoria carried was not his. Obviously this had to be something he'd only recently learned and it explained why the courtship had ended so abruptly. It also suggested that it was he and not she who had initiated the break, and he had allowed her to cry off to save her from the disgrace of being jilted. But when her belly burgeoned with child in the months to come, surely the truth would emerge?

"So you will have me in her stead, is that how it is?"

"Think on what I've just said, Missy, and before you allow your pride to rule your head, at least consider the child you *may* carry. Doesn't he deserve better than to be born a bastard without the name and protection of his own father? I hope your selfishness doesn't extend to the sacrifice of your own flesh and blood."

Missy glared at him. How like him to use the club of reason to beat her about the head and leave her feeling the guilty party. Now if she ran off to America, she would indeed be the villain. Did her child not deserve to have everything being born to the heir to an earldom entailed? Could she in all good conscience deny her child its father and the benefits of such a life? Drat the man, he had succeeded in putting her in an untenable position.

As if sensing his words had started a war raging within her, he straightened to his full height. How he still managed to exude an air of command and magnetism with his face battered like the loser of a pugilist match was beyond her.

"I will be back tomorrow for your decision."

"My answer won't change." Although she spoke bravely, she was not feeling at all as certain of the course of her future as she'd been when she awoke that morning.

"I shall summon my mother if you have said your fill," she said, moving to the room's entrance, ever conscious that his gaze followed her every step with an intensity that seared her. She fought and won the impulse to glance over her shoulder for one final look.

The viscountess had just exited the music room when Missy encountered her in the foyer. "James is waiting for you in the drawing room."

"I take it by your expression, his proposal was not accepted."

"If you mean his *demand* that I marry for the sake of a child we still are not certain even exists? I have declined. However, James is not a man who takes kindly to refusal."

"And you are not a woman who takes kindly to being ordered about, of that, I am quite aware." The viscountess's mouth quirked in a sage smile.

"Yes, but he will be back tomorrow in hopes of a different answer."

Her mother took Missy's hand in hers, patting it lightly. "Then perhaps you should think heavily on this. Decisions made when tempers are still high as well as emotions are usually those we come to regret."

Missy sighed wearily. "Not only must I think about my welfare and that of the family, but I may also have a child to consider."

"No," her mother said, her tone adamant. "Your foremost concern should be that of yourself and your child. Thomas and I are more than capable of taking care of this family. *All* of my daughters will have a debut." The viscountess spoke in firm tones. The rigor with which she protected her children was a sight to behold. At least half of the ladies of the *ton* would be hesitant to make her an enemy, and cutting any of her children would assuredly do that. But an illegitimate child had the power to change things . . .

In a mesh of ruffled petticoats, silk, and muslin, Missy threw her arms around her mother and placed a soft kiss on her cheek. "You are the best mother a girl could ever ask for."

"Whatever your decision, my dear, I will try my best to do what is right by you," her mother said, her voice slightly choked. "Now, enough of all this blathering. I imagine I have kept James waiting long enough."

The warmth of her mother's embrace remained with

her long after she disappeared down the hall and into the drawing room.

Worse than the day she'd discovered she was expecting a child, was the morning Victoria had to tell her mother there would be no spectacular Spencer wedding to dazzle the *ton*. That all preparations would have to stop.

Perhaps she could tell her there was no child; that she'd made the whole thing up and duped Lord Rutherford into accepting responsibility. Then on the morrow, she'd book a passage to somewhere halfway around the world.

Victoria regarded her reflection in the silver-framed mirror in her dressing room. Her blue eyes appeared much too large for her narrow face and her mouth had that drawn look brought on by nerves. She pinched her white cheeks and then slid from the vanity chair. Her rose morning dress also received a smoothing hand to eliminate nonexistent creases. She drew in a breath as if it were her last before she began making her way down to the breakfast room.

Rivers, their second footman and her co-conspirator to her torrid affair, stopped her at the foot of the stairs. He had a wide-eyed look about him that immediately alerted her already overwrought senses.

"Milady." He spoke in a low, furtive voice, as would any good co-conspirator. "Sir Clifton begs an audience with you outside."

Victoria stood stock-still. George had not come to call since his last ill-fated attempt five years ago when he had been turned away by their butler under her mother's directive. He could easily have sent her a note to meet as they had always done in the past. Why would he risk coming here?

Victoria slid a cautious glance down the foyer, checking to ensure they were not being closely observed. "Tell him I will be out in a moment. I will make my excuses to my mother but I will need you to accompany me. I can hardly speak with him in such close proximity to the house."

Rivers gave a crisp nod and disappeared through the front door. Victoria found her mother in the morning room partaking in a mid-morning meal. She informed her she'd need an escort for a brief shopping trip to Bond Street. The marchioness had no quibble with that, her spirits high with how smoothly preparations for the betrothal party were coming along.

Donning her gloves, bonnet and silk shawl, Victoria met Rivers by the front door and they took the carriage precisely two blocks up the street where George's landau sat parked on the side of a dead end street. The Thompsons owned the house on the left, but they were presently in France.

Victoria alighted, too eager to wait for the footman's assistance. The door to the landau was opened from within and she cautiously approached to peer inside.

In an interior illumed by only the hazy light let in by the open door, George sat tall and straight like a seasoned soldier. He looked terribly good to her famished senses, his beard and mustache not quite as closely cropped as he usually kept it. His face appeared leaner, his brown eyes set deeper in their sockets, and his attire, consisting of a dark brown overcoat, navy trousers and waistcoat, and a tan cambric shirt, hung looser on his frame.

He offered his hand, which Victoria accepted and she slid into the seat opposite, hesitant and uncertain. "I never imagined this sort of cloak-and-dagger melodrama was your thing," she said lightly, hoping to make him smile.

"It would not have been necessary if I knew I'd be received in your home," he said stiffly, no answering smile lifted the corners of his mouth. He regarded her intently. "I received a visit from Rutherford."

Victoria forced herself not to drop her gaze while her heart skipped a beat. She swallowed. "Yes, he told me."

"Am I to conclude the nature of your relationship has changed?" The tightening of his jaw and the rigid set of his shoulders belied his nonchalance.

"As you can imagine, he has broken it off. When you arrived, I was on my way to inform my mother."

His nod was an indication he knew how daunting a task that must be, and his lips lost the stern line, softening his expression somewhat.

"And whose child are you carrying?"

No prevarication, no insinuations—he broached the subject with such forthrightness, it was staggering to anyone well used to the spurious nature of the *ton*. Victoria immediately dropped her head and felt the heat of guilt suffusing her face. It was inevitable that he would discover her condition at some point and that he would probably wonder at the child's parentage, but by then she was supposed to have been securely married to Lord Rutherford.

"Am I the father?" he asked not quite as coolly as before.

Victoria gazed at him. "It is yours," she whispered. "I never—never had sexual relations with Lord Rutherford. Not ever." She said the latter emphatically; it was the least she owed the only man she'd ever loved—would ever love.

George abandoned all pretense of indifference, swiftly moving to sit beside her and grasping both of her gloved hands in his. "Then why would he offer for you when it was clear he had no desire to wed you?"

Haltingly, the story spilled from her lips and by the end, his confusion had given way to anger, which had then finally given way to steely resolve.

"This is utterly ridiculous and we both know it. There isn't a law in the country that bars us from marrying. I earn more than enough to keep a wife and a family, although not in the luxury to which you are accustomed."

She swallowed and as tears pricked the corners of her eyes, her heart fluttered.

"I don't care about a dowry or contracts. All I want is you and my child. I will only ask you this final time, Victoria, will you marry me?" Sincerity, love and uncertainty shone from his soulful brown eyes.

He did not have to wait long for her response. Victoria turned and pitched herself into his open arms, her hands capturing the back of his head to pull him down. "Yes. Yes. Yes. Yes," she said, peppering his face with a string of kisses, before sealing his lips in a long, passionate proclamation of love.

Chapter Nineteen

James arrived at the Armstrong residence for his answer as early as he had the morning before. He had spent the remainder of the prior day, and a good portion of what should have been his sleeping hours, consumed with thoughts of Missy—and her refusal.

She had refused him.

The fact ate away at his insides. For years he'd been the recipient of her childish affections, and weeks ago she'd given him the gift of her virginity. Why did her admission that what she had felt was infatuation unsettle him so? How often had he not said the exact thing? The truth was that his feelings for Missy were as complicated as they were simple. He knew he desired her more than he had any other woman he'd ever met, but that certainly didn't equate to love.

Regardless, the one thing he did know was he could not let her go. He had ruined her and she could be carrying his child. For those reasons alone he intended to wed her. And then of course there was Armstrong. The thought of losing his friendship frightened him nearly as much as losing Missy. But how he could make things right between them remained a mystery.

Creighton, the butler, greeted him with a bow, and then led him to the drawing room before he left to summon Missy. James chose to stand. Although he was resolute, his nerves were threadbare. His would-be bride was headstrong. Short of abducting her and forcing her to wed him at gunpoint, there was little he could do if she continued to refuse. Yesterday hadn't gone at all the way he planned. He had dictated instead of cajoled. He could only pray his call for reason, that she think about what was in the best interest of the child—if there proved to be one—had gotten through to her.

His breath caught as she swept into the room, her chestnut curls secured up at her nape, wearing a dress of green silk and lace. His throat closed up.

Closer inspection revealed faint shadows under her big, slate blue eyes, a clear indication that she had received as little sleep as he had. And the way she was fidgeting with the folds of her skirt showed her agitation.

"You look beautiful." The utterance slipped out without thought.

Something flared in her eyes, but it was gone just as quickly as it came. "Good morning, James. Calling so early again?" She slid onto the gold balloon-backed chair, daintily spreading her skirt so it flared perfectly about her.

James took the seat opposite. "Why, have I broken some cardinal rule? You know I care little for what Society deems acceptable."

"Yes, that much I have learned," she said, clasping her hands together in her lap, where they twisted briefly.

"I advised you I'd be back today for my answer."

She nodded, her gaze never wavering from his. "Yes, you did, however nothing has changed since we spoke yesterday. I told you I wouldn't marry you then, and I am telling you again now. Hopefully, this time you will heed my wishes."

* * *

James's gaze narrowed. Missy was frankly surprised he had come. Deep inside she was certain he felt relief. Surely, he had appeased his sense of honor and now could go forward without a twinge of conscience impeding his precisely mapped future?

"When Thomas was here last evening, I told him of my decision, and he said it was mine to make." In truth her brother thought her crazy. The man she'd adored almost half her life had offered her marriage and she had refused. She'd had to listen to her brother lecture her for fifteen minutes while he had railed on the vagaries of the female mind.

"Well I don't give a d—fig what your brother thinks at this point." He still looked like he'd been on the losing end of a pugilist match, his handsome face still colorfully swollen, contorted in frustration and anger. It was clear that this rift with her brother caused him significant distress but she knew he had too much pride to admit it—at least to her.

"Which is obvious," she said, tongue firmly in cheek, but he seemed too preoccupied with other thoughts to note her sarcasm.

"We will be married as soon as I can procure a license," he said.

Had he lost his hearing? She had just refused him and yet he blithely went on as if she'd consented. "I am not marrying you. Lord, the way you used to guard your freedom, I would think you'd be relieved." She moved toward the entrance of the room, willing him to follow with hopes he'd find the front door. She could not properly think with him there.

Missy stole a glance over her shoulder to find James had not budged, his face, an implacable mask.

"What if you are expecting? What will you do then?"

"I will cross that particular bridge if need be. But, as that has not been determined yet, I have no desire to create an intolerable situation for us that would be difficult for us to extricate ourselves from if we married in haste and then discovered there was no reason for such a sacrifice. I for one, still hope to marry for love."

His blue eyes turned stormy, the pupils the black of oblivion, and his frame fairly bristled at her words. He came to his feet and advanced toward her, his movements stalking and dangerous.

"How faulty your memory must be. You *are* getting a love match or have you forgotten so quickly how much you love me?" His voice was silky smooth, knowing and taunting. He now stood close, the scent of him tormenting her. Bewitching her.

"I would hardly call a schoolgirl crush the kind required for anything as long-lasting as a marriage. It didn't even endure an evening of sex," she scoffed, determined to hold her ground and not give an inch. If he thought she would ever be that girl again—the one who had perched him high on a pedestal—her brother had more than bloodied him, he'd also knocked the sense right out of him.

He watched her like a predator watches his prey. A smile spread slowly across his handsome face, and a chuckle emerged soft and low. "Well then, I will make it my first duty as your husband to make sure it endures much longer than that."

A crimson blush washed her face as an image of them lying entwined and naked on his bed, James kneeling between her legs. She gave her head a hard shake to banish the image.

"Don't shake your head no, Missy. *When,* not if, we are married, there will be very few nights when I'll leave you be. Before too long I will know your body even better than I know my own." His voice had lowered to a purr, setting off twinges of sensation that lanced down from her peaked nipples to the moisture collecting at her center.

It was really disgraceful how easily he managed to reduce her mind to absolute mush and her body to a quivering mass of flesh. She took a deliberate step backward, in an effort to create some distance between them—physical and emotional.

"That's where you're wrong. I'm not going to marry you and that's the end of it." She tried to match her tone to her words, she was helpless to prevent her eyes from dropping to trace the curve of his bruised mouth. Saliva collected in her mouth.

He watched her until the heat within her became a burn. He took thorough inventory of her body, lingering over the thrust of her breasts and the nip of her waist. As his gaze traveled farther south, she was almost convinced he could see right through the layers of petticoats and muslin to her bare flesh pulsing hotly below. Missy fought the urge to squirm beneath his gaze.

His lips curved farther upward, revealing even white teeth. "As you wish, my dear." It was not a tone meant to pacify.

Missy wanted to stamp her feet in a childish tantrum and wipe that smug, wolfish smile from his face. He made no effort to hide the fact that he was patronizing her and he knew damn well there was little she could say about it. But say nothing was exactly what she would do. He'd find out rather shortly she meant every word she said.

"Just as long as we understand each other," she replied, her stare unwavering. "Because I hope you will abide by my decision."

Suddenly, a glint appeared in his blue eyes as his smile faltered. Then it was back in place but the glint lingered. "I will abide by any decision you make," he said in dulcet tones.

"Good." She gave a brisk nod with an assuredness she

wished she had. His capitulation had come too easy, his demeanor suggesting he was far from accepting of her decision.

"Well, then, I will take my leave."

The abruptness of the conclusion to their discussion had her blinking rapidly as she stared across at him. Hurriedly, she moved to the drawing room entrance.

"Yes, indeed."

Without warning, she was hauled unceremoniously into his arms, her hands instinctively clutching at his shoulders for balance.

"You can fool yourself all you want, but I know this is what you want." He had her plastered against him from head to toe. His hip prodded hers to emphasize the *this* he spoke of. He was rigid and hard against her belly. "This," another nudge of his erection, "is what you've wanted for a long time."

He lowered his head. She felt a moist, warm breath of air on the rim of her ear and thought she would asphyxiate from desire. Her breathing now came in fits and starts.

"And you could have it whenever you wanted." He nipped her lobe with his teeth, then feathered the line of her jaw with kisses. Contrary to the swiftness in which he had pulled her into his arms, he took achingly long to reach her trembling lips.

The first brush of his mouth on hers was soft, almost gentle, as he rubbed and lifted repeatedly, teasing her lips. Soon, however, the teasing brushes were not enough for either of them. Missy's lips parted in a silent demand for more, much more, and he was only too happy to oblige, angling to taste her deeper and more thoroughly.

His tongue darted forward to plunge deep as he sought the recess of her mouth. She moaned softly and reciprocated in kind, her tongue making sumptuous forays of his inner cheeks, the roof of his mouth, the ridge of his teeth, before once again playing with his tongue. James was nearly brought to his knees. He could think of nothing else than pinning her against a wall—any wall—with her legs around his waist and pumping into her.

The taste of her, the feel of her, consumed him with mindless pleasure. As his hands began working on the long row of mother of pearl buttons marching down the long length of her spine, a faint sound near the doorway wrenched him back to his senses.

He dropped his hands and placed her swiftly at arm's length. Her eyes were closed, her mouth reddened and full. Quickly, he turned away from the arousing sight of her, as he tried to cool his ardor and control his breathing.

What on earth had he been thinking? To even touch Missy in her home was asking for more trouble than he could afford. Someone could have easily come upon them. Even worse, it could have been Armstrong. He shook his head as if that would clear him of the lust that seemed to rob him of all logical thought when he was around her.

Missy watched James's shoulders heaving up and down, while she struggled to regain what little composure she had left after his kiss. Her body still tingled and her heart thundered loudly in her chest, leaving her breathing erratic and labored.

Again her body had betrayed her. No sooner had she refused his proposal when, seconds later, she was writhing in his arms. The man was like the most powerful narcotic. Worse than opium, which was said to cause hallucinations and incredible euphoria.

He turned back to face her and only the slight ruffle of his thick locks indicated that only moments before he had been the participant of a rather torrid embrace. "Hmm. That was nice. Now, I gather I will see you soon." It wasn't a question but rather a statement.

Nice? It had been many things—lurid, decadent, delicious—but nice was not one.

He continued as if he hadn't expected her to respond. "You will be attending Lady Langley's ball, won't you?" One dark brow lifted in query, his look all innocence and politeness.

"Yes, but with your—uh—face, I didn't imagine that you would." She prayed he would not or could not. Either would suffice.

"The ball is in three days. I should be good as new by then. If anyone should comment on any bruising that may remain, I'll tell them your brother beat me to a pulp. I don't think anyone would be surprised, do you?"

Except for the fact that everyone knew the men were the best of friends, unfortunately her brother pummeling someone wouldn't come as a great surprise to the members of Society. He had been known to allow his temper to get the better of him every now and again.

"Then I expect I shall see you at the ball." She had no intention of attending now. "Now, if you will excuse me, I have a rather full day ahead."

Amusement lit his eyes and he gave a low chuckle. "Are you asking me to leave?"

"I do believe our conversation is over." Her dark winged brow arched.

He regarded her, a smile still curving his mouth. Then he executed a formal bow. "If I could trust myself—and you, as well—I would bestow a chaste kiss upon the inside of your wrist. But then you know where that would lead."

He seemed to take an enormous amount of pleasure in needling her. Missy bit back a retort. She feared if she began a war of words with him now, he'd resort to an arsenal of weapons against which she had no defense. Better to keep silent and shore up her defenses for later, for she was certain she would need them.

Missy watched him quit the drawing room. Only after she heard the loud click of the front door, did she depart. The man was too sure of himself by far, and the fact that she was partially responsible for his arrogance, melting like ice under the hot glare of the sun every time he touched her, did little to soothe her pique.

"So when should we expect the wedding?"

Missy started at the sound of the quiet query and nearly lost her footing on the stairs as she jerked around.

Thomas stood by the library door in light green shirt-sleeves and dark green trousers, his hands folded neatly across his chest. He advanced closer, his regard steady on her.

"Thomas, I didn't even know you were here," she said with a nervous laugh. She wondered how long he had been there. The library was almost directly across from the drawing room and if he had only stepped out minutes before . . . She did not want to imagine what he'd seen.

But he did not look at all perturbed, his mouth crooked in such a manner as to suggest that he was privy to a private joke—a very private joke as they were the only two present, and she was certainly not amused.

"And what is it you find so amusing?"

"So you agreed to marry the blackguard?"

If he had been at the door, obviously he had not heard correctly. "No I did not."

His brows furrowed, his languid stance grew stiff. "Come, we can hardly carry on a private conversation on the stairs." His tone was curt, his displeasure pronounced.

Scowling, Missy followed him into the library. Glancing around, she noted the morning newspaper lay open on the side table, which confirmed he *had* been here for some time. He must have arrived at the crack of dawn.

"Having known you all of your twenty-one years, you might be willing to concede I know you extremely well, wouldn't you agree?" he asked after they were both seated. He paused a heartbeat and continued, as apparently the question was rhetorical. "In some form or another, you've been in love with Rutherford for practically half your life so please explain to me why you are now refusing to marry him? Dammit, if nothing else, he owes you." His green eyes flashed with anger.

"What do you mean?" Missy cried. "You told me you would support any decision I made."

"That's when I thought you'd come to your senses and accept," he snapped. "My God, he's ruined you and you may be expecting his child. Have you given any thought to what you—an unmarried lady—will do?"

Except for the day Thomas had learned about the indiscretion, she'd never seen him so worked up. Damn him for promising his support when he hadn't meant it.

"He doesn't love me. Would you have me married to a man who was forced to the altar?" She sat rigid in her seat.

"I would have you married to the father of your child rather than disgraced and ostracized from Society." He came to his feet in one fluid motion and began pacing the length of the room.

"As I told James, I don't even know if I am with child. Women do faint for other reasons. It could very well have been from hunger. My appetite has been off for several weeks." Which was the truth. Ever since she had met with James after the incident, food had become a necessity, not a pleasure.

Thomas paused to pin her with a look that told her that nothing she said would appease him today.

"You said you would not force me," she reminded him

again, watching the broad spread of his retreating back, before he spun on his heels and made his way back, his tread quiet and tempered. He halted by the mahogany desk.

"I will say nothing for now, but in the event you are carrying his child, I promise you, we will have this discussion again and I will be far less indulgent."

In other words, he wouldn't rest until he saw them wed.

"I take the blame for what happened and I am willing to deal with the consequences by myself. Judging by what you did to his face, don't you think James has already received his due?"

Missy thought her brother was going to explode as his green eyes flashed like lightning strikes. "You are not the only member of this family. Have you given any thought to Emily or Sarah? And what of Mother?"

"Of course I have and I won't allow anything to damage our standing in Society. I'll leave if I have to."

With a weary sigh, Thomas closed his eyes and shook his blond head. "Missy, the man ruined you. He owes you. Moreover, he had that beating coming and more. If you didn't love the blasted man so much, I would have called him out."

"They do not permit duels any longer. You'd have been jailed or hanged."

"Men have been called out for less," came her brother's dry reply.

Missy gave a small smile. Although famous for his volatile temper, especially if compared to Alex, who was the soul of temperance, she knew her brother was capable of beating James senseless but he loved him too much to actually kill him.

"Well, then we must all be extremely relieved that it didn't come to that."

He grunted and said, "Yes, I imagine we all are. Look,

Missy, I know I've never spoken to you about this, but I want you to know that I will provide amply for you in your marriage contract." He braced against the edge of the desk, his legs crossed at the ankles. "You will be given a monthly stipend in an amount that will keep you and any children you may have," he stared pointedly at her waist, "self-sufficient and in relative comfort for the duration of the marriage. I have also put the house in Dorchester in trust for you. I will also demand a clause be put in the contract that your husband has the responsibility of furnishing you with comfortable conveyance for your exclusive use."

It appeared Thomas had given the matter a great deal of thought. But his gesture, while generous and caring, didn't bode well for her marriage—that is to say, *if* she were to wed.

Reading the surprise on her face, he rushed to add, "This is something I plan to do for Emily and Sarah as well. My intent is to ensure you will always have lodgings to call your own, and enough money to care for yourselves in the event your marriages are not to your liking."

Tears misted her eyes as she stared up at her brother. She could see his anger was born out of love and much of her own pique dissipated. Rising to her feet, she came to stand in front of him. She reached out and took his hand in hers. "Thank you." Tenderness lit the pure green of his eyes, which was the only response she required.

After a loving squeeze, she released his hand and dropped hers to her side. "I wonder what James would make of these demands—if I had agreed to his proposal, that is?" she added quickly.

"I can't imagine I would hear one word of dissension," Thomas replied, grimly. Then he muttered under his breath, "If he knows what's good for him."

But loud enough for her to hear every word . . . and smile.

Chapter Twenty

Missy felt like a wallflower, hugging the wall like it was her only support. She'd declined the third invitation to dance in as many minutes, but when Claire had been whisked away by Mr. Chepley, Missy had thought better of it. She hadn't wanted to attend Lady Langley's ball but her mother had been adamant.

A quick glance around revealed that James hadn't arrived—as yet. But she was certain he'd come. In the three days since she'd refused him, he had attended every event where she'd been present. He had showed up daily in Hyde Park to intercept her morning walks. Even an impulsive trip to Bond Street to procure a new reticule and shoes had triggered an encounter. The man was everywhere! He simply wouldn't leave her alone.

Missy felt hunted . . . and vulnerable, for with every encounter, every look, every touch, she weakened. Until then, she'd never experienced James Rutherford in pursuit. If he had been hard to resist before—and she knew intimately just how much—he was nearly impossible when he utilized the full force of his charm. He kept her on edge, her senses in a constant heightened state. She knew he was determined to wear her down but she was equally determined to resist.

Another sweep across the dance floor revealed Claire enjoying a waltz. Her gaze continued on until she spotted both Thomas and Alex, cups in hand, near the refreshment table at the rear of the room. The last she had seen both men they, too, were on the dance floor. Missy didn't see one young miss pass the pair whose eyes did not linger over long on the sight they made, tall and disarmingly handsome in their evening wear. She started across toward the popular pair, skirting the perimeter.

"Missy."

The sound of her name came from behind her and stopped her dead in her tracks. James said it loud enough for her to hear above the music and gaiety but it held a sensual quality to it; low and gravelly, for her ears alone. She wanted to run and hide but if she did it would give him the upper hand. She turned on the heel of her kid leather boots to confront her tormentor.

Her breath caught in her throat. He was dressed in black evening wear, white gloves and a blinding white cravat. He looked dashing, simply breathtaking.

"Missy, you look exquisite," he murmured, peering at her from between thickly fringed lashes. She saw seduction in his eyes. She had to force herself not to stare like a besotted fool. Composing her features, she affected an air of indifference.

"James." She did not offer her hand but he took it anyway. Impaling her with his gaze, he bent his head and brushed the back of her gloved hand with his lips. Then he turned her hand until her palm faced upward. Too bemused to pull away, she had no idea what he intended until she felt the damp swipe of his tongue on the inside of her wrist.

This time, Missy did jerk her hand back and then glanced quickly around to see if anyone had witnessed his impertinence. She met a couple of curious stares with a cool smile.

She turned her attention back to James. "Just what on earth do you think you are doing?" she said in a fierce whisper.

The smile he sent her set her heart into a mad race and caused her toes to curl. A dull throb started between her thighs. She silently cursed the ease in which he could bring her body to a pulsing state of unwanted arousal.

"Is that not the manner in which men greet women of such dear acquaintance?" he asked, all innocence and light.

"We no longer have that kind of familiarity." She smiled for the benefit of any onlookers and then turned to resume her course.

But she should have known a man like James could not be dismissed. In two swift strides, he was by her side, his hand taking a commanding grip of her elbow.

"I think our familiarity goes well beyond a mere kiss on the wrist, wouldn't you say?"

Startled, Missy instinctively started to jerk her arm away but he clamped his hand down firmly and steered her toward the doors leading outside.

Missy could have struggled if she wanted to make a scene, but she'd no desire to be on the tongue of every gossipmonger, so she allowed him to lead her to the terrace.

"What is it you want, James?" she asked, doing her best to sound as bored as she was flustered, agitated, and hot.

He released her elbow and Missy instantly yanked her hand from his reach, thrusting it behind her back for good measure. But the tingling of her flesh lingered long after the contact ended.

"You have had over a half dozen men paying you court tonight alone. Do I not warrant the same opportunity?" He watched her from between hooded eyes, his mouth a sensuous dream. "I would think given the—uh—intimate nature of our relationship, even more so."

Missy knew that looking into his eyes spelled certain

surrender so she cast her gaze out into the dark, still London night where the scent of floral blossoms mixed with his sandalwood cologne.

"We," she said, with great emphasis, "do not have a relationship."

James moved into the line of her vision. She could tell by the amused glimmer in his eyes that he knew exactly what she'd been trying to do.

"Don't fool yourself. We," he said with the same emphasis, "will always have a relationship. Right this moment you could be expecting my child."

Missy stamped her foot. "Hush!" She made a furtive look around, spying a long row of hedgerows on one side and two couples conversing quietly just outside the terrace door, well out of earshot. "Do you really want the world to know? Is it not enough to ruin me but will you have me shunned too?"

James's pale eyes slit ominously. "You're the one who wishes it this way. Just say the word and we can be married within the week."

He made it all sound so terribly easy but she knew better. A marriage between them would be a disaster.

"Why are you pushing so hard now? You do not want to marry me. You have said so often enough."

"I want you," he said, his voice throaty and deep, his eyes glittering hot.

"You said it was only lust."

"Which is sometimes more than many couples have."

"Yes, but it is not enough—not for me."

James took a step closer and tilted her chin with a gloved hand. "What do you want me to say?"

"I don't want you to say anything," she said, while resisting the urge to wrench her chin from his hand.

"You will be my wife," he said softly but his tone held a hard edge of determination.

"Yes, but will you be my husband? Will you be the kind of husband I want?"

"What exactly is that supposed to mean?"

"Will you pledge your love and fidelity?"

James paused, and it was the kind of pause that, no matter how quick the recovery, was an answer in itself.

"What you are offering me is not a marriage. It is a business arrangement. I will provide you with an heir and I will get . . ." Missy allowed the sentence to trail off.

Nothing is what she would get. A cold sterile union with the benefit of fantastic, mind-shattering sex. And sadly, no matter how well suited they were in bed, it would not be enough to build a good marriage.

"I am offering you a father for our child. I am saving you from the shame of ruination." Missy could tell by the hard note in his voice that his patience had worn thin. The last three days of cajoling had now given way to hard coercion.

"That is *if* there is even a child. We don't know as yet."

"So you would rather wait and then have the *ton* whisper your name when our child comes early?"

"It is done all the time," she said, feigning indifference with a shrug of her shoulders.

"I won't have it done to me or mine."

The possessive tone in his voice startled her. She could almost feel the frustration and anger in his form emanating from him in waves.

"You act as though I belong to you. I belong to no one. Even if we were to marry, you wouldn't own me."

"You would be my wife. That claim alone would be sufficient." He treated her with another hot stare and this time he took his time as he trailed down her figure, his gaze lingering on the pointed peaks of her breasts and the indentation of her waist. She felt a hot blush suffuse her cheeks, and her body, in its usual betrayal, reacted to his regard.

She folded her arms across her chest. As if there was protection against the way her body immediately responded to him in any and every fashion. The knowing smile that curved his sensuous lips told her he was aware of her response.

"I have a proposition to make I believe will suit us both." He gave her one of his coaxing, gentling smiles that she had been subjected to with potent frequency the past three days. Missy wanted to close her eyes against its lure. "Until we have ascertained whether a child has resulted from our love—"

"Our indiscretion. Our mistake," she cut in. Whatever his ploy, she was determined not to lose sight of the stark, brutal reality of what had occurred between them. Embellishing it with words like love didn't change the facts.

The irises contracted within the azure blue of his eyes and his mouth tightened. After a moment, his expression eased.

James continued after her heated correction. "Very well, then if you are expecting my child, you will marry me. If you prove not to be, well then . . ." He deliberately left the sentence unfinished. Let her conclude what she willed from it. Right now he needed her to stop running from him. A lie by omission was a small price to pay.

She opened her mouth to speak, and James could tell by her expression, her response would be anything but agreeable.

"And before you refuse, let me advise you of two things. Not only am I a high-ranking member of the *ton*, but my father is quite influential in the House of Lords. I hope you've come to know me well enough to know I will not allow you to take my child from me. I will not allow you to bear me a bastard. I would exert all my influence and power, and that of my family to ensure that that does not come to pass." He paused, to let his words penetrate. "It's up to you to decide which you prefer, a truce or a fight."

Missy's mouth snapped shut and remained that way while silence held court. She eyed him, as if to gauge his sincerity. Eventually, her shoulders and chin dropped as if understanding that he hadn't issued a groundless threat, but an avowal he would follow through to the bitter end.

"And if I am not?" she asked, suspicion in her voice.

"If you are not, then we'll both be spared, won't we?" he replied, avoiding answering the question directly.

Missy regarded him, trepidation in her eyes. Slowly, almost reluctantly, she said, "Very well. I shall agree to that."

Relief flooded him. Until she'd agreed he hadn't known just how important her acquiescence had been. Thoughts of the child had barely factored into his determination. He wanted her. Craved her. It didn't matter if she was expecting his child or not. And if he was being honest with himself, it was that fact that terrified him.

"Wonderful," he said briskly. "Then come, let us dance. We should at least act the role of a prospective couple."

Missy hung back for a moment, while she considered his latest proposition. Giving a slow nod, she accompanied him back into the ballroom.

What Missy hadn't expected was for James to head directly toward her brother and Alex. Thomas was still sorely upset with him and grew quiet and brooding whenever his name was uttered. Alex, on the other hand, refused to take sides, continuing to treat James exactly as before.

"I see you have decided to brave the lion's den." Alex said, thrusting his hand forward as they halted in front of him. Two dimples creased the slash of his cheeks and one dimpled his chin, loading him down with looks aplenty. His reference to Thomas at any other time would have elicited amused smiles instead of the tension-wrought stretch of silence that followed.

James shook his outstretched hand, clearing his throat uncomfortably. "I'm relieved to see I've managed to retain one of my friends." He stared pointedly at Thomas, who glowered at him before turning his gaze away. Missy was surprised he hadn't already walked away.

Alex chuckled. "As I don't believe my brother has the same appeal as Missy, I can say we are fairly safe from having the same issue mar our friendship."

Missy couldn't help a smile. James scowled and glanced over at Thomas, who stood mere feet away.

Following the direction of James's gaze, Cartwright said, "Don't concern yourself with him, he will eventually come around."

Even above the din of the crowd, Thomas was still well within earshot, and his expression grew fiercer before he pivoted on his heel and stalked away. James instantly stiffened and a red flush washed his cheeks and the bridge of his nose. It was apparent his rift with Thomas sat heavy on his mind—perhaps even on his heart, if he had one.

"I will leave the two of you to enjoy yourselves." Cartwright gave a half smile and a brief nod and then strode away to get lost in the crush.

For the next hour, Missy chatted with a number of the guests, a solicitous James firmly planted by her side. He carried on one rather lengthy conversation with Lord Stanton who, as a prominent peer in the House of Lords, had recently set forth a bill to reassert the Corn Laws almost a decade after they had been repealed. James clearly did not agree with such an action but Lord Stanton seemed just as intent on attempting to change his position. The discussion ended cordially, though in a stalemate.

In those twenty minutes, Missy learned more about Corn

Laws and the plight of the working poor than she could have had she read some dry article in the *London Times*. James impressed her with his passion and thorough knowledge of what he spoke. She had no idea he so strongly sympathized with the plight of the working class nor that he had influenced his father to vote to abolish the Corn Laws nine years before. It appeared there was more to James Rutherford, heir to one of the richest earldoms, than most saw on the surface.

The next time the orchestra struck up a waltz, he swept her into his arms and commenced to sweep her off her feet. He danced as elegantly as he moved. To be led by him was to enjoy an effortless, fluid movement of the body and soul. He had eyes for no one else in the room but her and didn't appear reticent to let everyone know. His face lit up when he gazed down upon her and if she hadn't known it was merely a show put on for the members of the *ton*, she was certain she would have fallen completely under his spell . . . once again.

Lord Feathersby caught an unsuspecting James just as they left the dance floor after their second dance. The way he sprang on them, it was as if the man had been laying in wait. He then embarked on a discussion regarding the ongoing Crimean War. Missy took that opportunity to escape to the ladies' dressing room and remind herself that what was between her and James was not real—at least not on his part.

Upon her return, Missy spotted Thomas. He stood alone on the edge of the dance floor nursing a glass of punch. Missy followed his stare to the opposite side of the room and encountered a slim brunette, resplendent in a breathtaking gold gown. Missy had never seen her before, but Lord Bradford, the man at her side, was one of Thomas's business partners.

"Thomas, who is that?" Missy asked, once she had reached his side. The fact that he hadn't taken his eyes off the young lady since she'd entered the room on the arm of the marquess piqued her curiosity.

Thomas shook his head, obviously distracted, but managed to tear his gaze from the dark-haired beauty long enough to pay her some mind.

"Pardon?"

A sly smile curved her mouth. "I said who is the lady you've been staring at?"

"Harry Bartram's daughter, I imagine. He indicated that he would be escorting her this evening."

"She is very beautiful." Her eyes probed his for a response.

"Quite, but she's young."

Missy gave the woman another assessing look. "I would hardly call her a child. She looks to be about nineteen."

"A year younger," he said.

"Well, then, there you have it. You can hardly call her a child."

Thomas said nothing, continuing to stare at the tall brunette.

"And what exactly are your business dealings with Lord Bradford?"

Thomas's gaze still fixed across the room at the pair—or more importantly, Lord Bradford's daughter. "We both have part ownership in Wendel's shipping company."

Another quick glance over revealed the marquess had spotted Thomas and he and his daughter were now headed in their direction. As they advanced closer, Lord Bradford's daughter revealed herself to be even a greater beauty than she'd appeared from afar. Her hair hung thick and lustrous, brushing her shoulders, held in an elegant twist by a flowered pin, and she had a creamy, flawless complexion.

"Thomas," Lord Bradford said, closing the distance between them, his right hand extended in greeting.

"Nice to see you in attendance, Harry." Thomas gave his hands two firm pumps. He then turned and reintroduced Missy, which was met by the marquess with the kind of exuberance she didn't often find in the aristocracy. Of medium height with a slender frame, the man exuded a joviality that made him hard to resist.

After Thomas finished his introduction, Lord Bradford turned to his daughter. "And this is my daughter, Amelia."

Thomas flashed a smile. Her brother had probably never met a woman he could not charm with that very smile.

"Your father speaks most highly of you, Lady Amelia. I'm delighted to finally make your acquaintance."

Lady Amelia acknowledged Missy with a nod and then shot a look of askance at her father causing him to flush. She then turned her attention back to Thomas and replied, "Is that so? And I've heard you are considered, at best, a rake about town, and at worst, a debaucher of women and maiden sensibilities. I certainly hope you are not going to ply your trade here this evening."

The marquess inhaled a gasp, Thomas choked on his next breath, and Missy swiftly covered her laugh with two rather unconvincing coughs. Never in all her years had she ever witnessed such a setdown. Quite the opposite in fact. Most women fell over themselves trying to gain his attention and affections. This was a most gratifying experience.

Lady Amelia, however, appeared unruffled by the whole thing and not the least apologetic. Who could ever have imagined an eighteen-year-old miss with this much self-possession and nerve?

"Amelia, you will apologize to Lord Armstrong at once," Lord Bradford said, recovered from his momentary lapse of composure.

Eyeing Thomas directly and unflinchingly, she said, "I do apologize *my lord* that you felt the need to lie to me. My father could never bring himself to speak highly of me but, perhaps, that is something you were not aware of, making the lie you just told me quite innocuous. I, however, did not lie, and for that I do apologize. As I have found, there are certain truths that should never be voiced in polite society."

Missy had another fit of coughing and Thomas stood frozen while Lord Bradford looked as though he would surely perish of shame.

"Papa, I believe I have apologized. Are there any other gentlemen you wish to introduce me to?" She stood eye to eye with her father, making her taller than the average woman, but she held herself with the regalness of royalty, which gave her the appearance of possessing more height.

The sarcasm in her soft tones was not lost on her father. The poor man, red-faced with embarrassment, ushered her away before another scathing dulcet-toned remark could pass her lips.

Missy dared to peek up at her brother, her gloved hand hiding her laughing mouth. Thomas was gritting his teeth so hard she swore she actually heard the scrape of enamel against enamel, and his eyes were narrowed to slits. And if he could produce it, she swore she would have seen smoke coming from his ears.

He turned his head, ever so slowly, toward her and pierced her with such a look, she finally understood the term to look daggers on someone.

"I am hardly the one who called you a rake about town." She was forced to stop at this point and contain the mirth that threatened to spill from her lips. After a moment, somewhat composed, she continued. "So please refrain from looking at me like you would like to see me walking the plank." Her laughter spilled forth.

"I would advise you to find more amiable company if you know what's good for you." The words were uttered too calmly, and with too much control.

Lady Amelia Bertram had managed to get the best of her brother and that in itself was a rarity. Shooting her brother a mischievous smile, she said, "A truly charming young woman. Please make sure Lord Bradford brings her by for tea."

She then hastily started across the room still laughing softly, surveying the glittering ladies of the *ton*, hoping to find Claire returned from the dance floor.

What she did find caused her to pause in her steps, for standing no more than twenty feet away near a large, white Greek column adorned with climbing ivy, were James and Lady Victoria Spencer.

They appeared deep in conversation, their visages quite sober, but not containing the kind of animosity one might expect given what had occurred between them. Truth be told, she was surprised to see Lady Victoria present. Rumors of her condition had made her the talk of the *ton,* and now that it appeared there would be no match between her and James, she'd become a pariah in many circles. But even knowing all of this, she could not stop the niggling feeling of jealousy from rearing its head as she watched James's dark head bend to hers in close attention.

Missy pivoted sharply and blindly made her way to the opposite side of the hall.

Chapter Twenty-One

"So what will you do now?" James stared down at Lady Victoria's upturned face. He could hardly believe this was the same woman he had come to know over the past several years. Her countenance held the kind of warm glow that softened her already beautiful features.

"George and I will be married by special license next week. He is currently in Bedfordshire readying the house there for our occupation. Once Parliament is in recess, he will join me." Her blue eyes seemed to soften at the mention of her affiance's name.

"And your parents?" James had already heard that the marchioness had taken to her bed claiming every malady known to man. Her avoidance of Society was as obvious as the eyesores she called her bonnets.

Lady Victoria's smile slipped for an instant. "My mother is, as you can imagine, exceedingly disappointed."

James imagined that was the mildest of understatements.

"However, Papa has been exceptional regarding the whole affair. He is determined that Lillian and I not share the same fate. As there is already a child on the way, he is willing to support my union with George." A wry laugh trickled from her lips. "Also, I fear I was quite serious when I promised him that I would wed George with or without his approval. I believe he was shocked that I was willing to forgo my dowry to marry a man whom Mama refers to as a nobody and a pauper."

James shook his head in bemusement. Clearly, Lady Victoria had discovered she possessed a great deal more inner strength than she'd thought. "Well, it seems things have worked out well for you."

Her expression immediately sobered at his words. "That is why I came here this evening. I knew it would be the only occasion where I could safely speak with you. Despite repeatedly telling him we are not and have never been more than friends, George is still uncomfortable with our relationship." She uttered a soft sigh. "But the truth is, without you none of this would have been possible. I am forever in your debt. You have been a true gentleman despite everything I've put you through. I acted in an utterly selfish manner, and I cannot blithely go on with my life with George without knowing whether I have ruined things between you and Miss Armstrong. But watching you tonight gave me some relief."

James blinked and his heart stuttered. What did she know about Missy? "I pray you will elucidate me on what you're talking about?"

She gave him a knowing look and an amused smile curled her lips. "My dear Lord Rutherford, don't be coy. Are you not courting her? You have already danced twice with her this evening and your eyes practically devour her every move. But, rest assured," she patted his arm lightly, "I was only able to recognize your reaction to Miss Armstrong because George is very much like you when it comes to hiding his emotions. Your interest is probably only obvious to those who know you more intimately."

James felt poleaxed. "I have no such feelings for Missy."

But even as he uttered the words, he knew he was lying. He had done the unthinkable and fallen in love just like his father. Now was he to follow in his father's footsteps and let love lead him around by his nose—or more appropriately, by another part of his anatomy? Well, certainly not if he could help it, for he had no intention of letting on that he harbored such feelings.

Lady Victoria tipped her head back, still wearing that amused, knowing smile. "I am quite certain that is exactly the same thing George convinced himself of before he went off to the Crimean peninsula."

James's scowl only deepened.

Missy should have been riddled with relief when her monthlies came especially given the promise she'd made to James at the Langley ball. Only she wasn't as relieved as she should have been—would have wanted to be.

On that morning, she'd sat on her canopied bed feeling a bottomless emptiness. No baby meant no life with James. It was only then she'd admitted to herself how she'd yearned for a living, breathing link to the man she loved. Would undoubtedly always love.

That morning, though, had come and gone a week ago. Since then they had attended two more balls, one musicale, one opera and supper party. She'd known a whole week and had not said a word because she'd still been clinging to a dream.

One whole week of pretense. Oh, they might have fooled the *ton,* but Missy could scarcely say things had progressed better in terms of their relationship than the day they'd made their pact.

James acted the perfect gentleman in the presence of others. He smiled that roguish smile, charming even the ladies who were thought to be immune to the most handsome visages—which he could claim in abundance. Many times, even she'd succumbed to his feigned expressions of adoration and an attentiveness that had the ladies simmering with envy. And although she'd been loathe to admit it to herself, a secret part of her had desperately wanted to believe something there grew; that his behavior was more than an act worthy of a royal audience.

But the moment they were alone, his mien changed. He kept her at a distance that put arm's length to shame it was so vast. The smiles vanished quicker than bats in daylight, to be replaced by a straight severe line, and that grimness was reflected in the rest of his inscrutable features.

She had been such a fool to give her heart to this man but now she was more than ready to wave the white flag. Men like James never changed. The only reason they married was to acquire an heir; a son to pass on their legacy. And now she knew she wouldn't be the mother to that child, or for that matter, any child of his.

For a week now, he had been appearing on the front door step to escort her on a leisurely sojourn through Hyde Park and today was no different. He was, as usual, unbearably polite but cool, and once they were both seated in the open carriage, his attention turned inward and he'd all but ignore her until they made the turn down Rotten Row, encountering a crush of carriages, horses, and ladies and gentlemen on foot. Only then would he make an attempt at idle conversation, which tended to be stilted at best.

Today she would allow none of that. This pretense would come to an end this very day. She had lost. She was admitting defeat on the grandest scale. She surrendered.

"I am not with child." No preamble, just a flat, toneless declaration.

His head snapped to her, his blue eyes flickering with an

emotion—surprise, perhaps? He stared at her for what seemed an interminably long time, his eyes searching.

"I imagine this comes as an enormous relief to you," she continued, putting on a brave smile. "As I do not want to cause any more problems between you and Thomas, I will make it well understood that you still would like us to be married but it is I who am unwilling."

James just continued to stare at her with not one blink of an eye and not a twitch of a muscle. But his scrutiny grew more and more intense until she was forced to look away.

Disappointment seared him like a newly sharpened sword. And it rendered him mute as he tried to find some counter argument he could rally that wouldn't have him appear as desperate as he felt inside.

Regardless of how this had all come about, he'd long since accepted that she'd be his wife. More than accepted, he now anticipated with a certain possessive relish. *She will be mine.* She would be the woman who would bear his children.

Her family now believed they would marry—even Thomas appeared to have thawed, now not storming from the room when James entered. And the *ton* was eagerly anticipating an announcement before the end of the Season, which was only days away. Yet at the present time, she looked the farthest thing from an eager bride. Quite the opposite, for he sensed a relief there, as if she truly didn't want to marry him.

Did not want to marry him?

Missy?

He wasn't the type of man who went for all that boasting—he really had no need of it as others did the job for him well enough—but the simple fact was that as long as he'd known her, she'd wanted him. Worshipped and adored him. Loved him.

Although there had always been the possibility they had not created a child after that one time, he'd somehow never envisioned it playing out like this. That she would be so keen to give him an out. He didn't want an out. He loved her, but that was something she could never know. The knowledge would leave him crippled. Disadvantaged.

When he finally broke the silence, his voice was raspy. "That will hardly appease your brother." He cleared his throat.

Missy shook her head, her expression impassive. "Don't worry over much with Thomas. As I said, I will make certain he knows it is I who has denied you." A smile tinged with sadness touched the corners of her cherry lips. "You did try to do the honorable thing."

He bit back a rather coarse reply about his damn honor that was being continuously flung in his face. He didn't feel the least bit honorable, he felt adrift and empty.

God, he needed to think. And he didn't think well or with any great result with her near. Her proximity skewed everything in his, until recently, tidy life.

"Then I guess there is nothing left to do but take you home."

Missy gave a brief nod before turning her attention to the lush landscape of Hyde Park. Not that she had expected him to utter even a token protest. No. She had known relief would reign paramount in his response. Then why could she not rid herself of the sense of disappointment stabbing at her already tender heart? She'd prepared herself for this. She'd accepted her love for him would remain forever unrequited, so his response—or lack thereof—should not have the power to hurt her. Nearly cripple her.

Every second dragged like a minute, and every minute like an hour, so by the time the carriage arrived back at the red-bricked structure that she called home when in Town, it felt like they'd spent an eternity in silence. In actuality, no more than twenty minutes had passed, but certainly twenty of the longest minutes of her life.

James leapt from the carriage, rather woodenlike, not at all with his usual grace and fluidity, and assisted her down from the high perch of the phaeton. She wondered idly how much of her legs he could see from such a position. She thought he'd quite liked her legs.

Once she had her feet firmly planted on the ground, he relinquished his hold . . . slowly. Did his hand linger or was that her overwrought imagination and wishful thinking?

"No need to see me to the door. I think we have played this melodrama to the bitter end, wouldn't you say?" She faced him, her head tilted so she could regard him directly without the hindrance the brim of her bonnet might cause.

Not a smile or a frown did he wear on his face. For a man who had just been given a pardon from a life sentence, he looked unusually sober.

"As you wish." He gave a shallow bow.

Missy nodded and proceeded to the front door. Just before she entered, she glanced back to find him exactly where she had left him, his pale blue eyes intent on her, haunted. She turned quickly and hurried into the house.

The end to the Season came with nary a whimper. Missy was thankful for it, truly. The last ball had been Lady Sneldon's and, although Missy had been in attendance, she had problems days later summoning up a clear memory of who'd been present, and even which gentlemen she had partnered with for many of the dances. The one thing she did recollect with any clarity was that James had not made an appearance.

It had been a week since she had last seen or spoken to

him. A week since she'd laid his guilty mind to rest regarding the possibility of a child. Yes, she was certain he was relieved. So relieved, in fact, he had once again vanished from her life.

Missy sighed, her gaze flitting around the drawing room for the umpteenth time. Of all the years she wished her mother had forgone her annual three day rout, it was now. She'd had only a week to prepare for the guests who had taken over Stoneridge Hall commencing earlier that day.

Lady Sneldon was there with her son who, of course, was of a marriageable age, and Lord and Lady Rotheringham were there, accompanied by the heir to their vast fortune. The one thing she was grateful for was that the crowd was at least a small, manageable one of no more than twenty guests.

As she skimmed over their smiling faces, Missy wished for a swift end to the event.

"Unfortunately, Alex and Thomas will not be able to attend," her mother said, coming to stand by her elbow. The viscountess looked youthful in her supper dress, the neckline baring her slender shoulders, and the sapphire necklace adorning her neck accentuated its long, elegant lines. Missy wondered if she would fare as well when she approached her mother's age. She sorely hoped so.

Angling her head, Missy viewed her mother's profile. The viscountess's gaze hovered over the group in the drawing room as if trying to anticipate each of their guest's needs in advance.

"Thomas and Alex never miss the rout."

"Yes, well, your brother sent word at midday that their business dealings with Lord Bradford would keep them in London for several more days."

Missy nodded. James had missed the event the last three years but she could not bring herself to inquire about his status. The pain of heartbreak remained too fresh and raw.

And even while the question clamored in her head, she already knew the answer. Between the narrow escape he'd had with her and the ongoing friction with her brother, she hadn't expected him to put in an appearance.

The supper bell rang. With much gay conversation and peals of laughter, the entire lot scattered about the drawing room managed, with some semblance of order, to make their way to the dining room. Missy trailed behind by her mother's side, a strained smile on her face, the only thought in her mind was that she would endure.

And endure she did. By the evening's end, Missy had managed to escape the rather lustful attentions of four gentlemen, all of whom were wealthy, young, and fairly attractive. Lady Sneldon's son, Viscount Charles Dalworth, was even more so with his handsome countenance and blond locks. She could tell by the determined gleam in her suitors' eyes that the weekend would prove trying indeed, as she endeavored to thwart their pursuit.

It was well past midnight when Missy retired to bed, her lids fighting valiantly to remain open while she struggled with buttons on her gown. If it had been earlier, she would have called for Beatrice but at this time of the night the poor girl was fast asleep. It took only five minutes of twisting and stretching her arms in positions she was sure they were never intended to bend to loosen the gown enough to remove it.

Once she'd kicked off the three layers of petticoats and sent thanks to heaven above that she'd opted not to wear any stays, she stood in a thin cotton chemise and pantaloons. The maid had laid her nightdress on the bed, so she quickly stripped herself of her remaining garments and was pulling the nightdress over her head when she heard the soft click of her bedchamber door.

Her breath caught in her throat as panic assailed her. While she frantically pushed the gown down around her naked body, her eyes peered through the darkness and quickly discerned a figure propped near the door—a large male form.

A scream trembled on the tip of her tongue when the voice said calmly, "It took you long enough."

She bit back the scream just in time to prevent the kind of rousing no one welcomed at that time of the night.

James. Her eyes adjusted well enough to make him out, clad all in black, standing as if on guard.

"What are you doing here?" she croaked, when she found her breath and her voice.

"Waiting for you." He advanced toward her, his movements predatory and smooth.

Missy instinctively skittered back until her legs hit the edge of the bed. "What do you want?" she asked all wary and panicky.

He stopped inches away from her frozen form. His pale eyes pierced the dimness and scorched a trail from the peaks of her breasts to the tips of her toes, so thorough was his appraisal. He looked hungry.

"What do you think I want?" He bent his head, his mouth feathering her ear, his voice a rumbled purr. "I want you."

Missy hated the way he had her body responding without thought or reason to the sound of his voice, the lust in his eyes, but respond it did. Her nipples pebbled and moisture gathered between her thighs as her whole being vibrated like a plucked harp string.

She felt the brush of his body as he stepped ever closer. Turning swiftly, she gave him her back, which helped her not one bit. He settled his erection, full and hard, against the round curve of her bottom, and began a slow grind.

She closed her eyes and bit her lip to stifle a groan. A whimper escaped.

If she dared go down this path with him again, she knew the only thing awaiting her would be heartache and hurt.

"I don't want this," she said weakly, turning her head as he trailed a soft kiss along the curve of her cheek down to her neck. She fought the overwhelming need to give in to the desire and sink onto the bed, but she fought it.

"You're lying," he whispered, his hands coming up to cup the firm, full weight of her breasts over the blue muslin. The feel of his large hands elicited a soft groan from her trembling lips. The sound echoed in the still of the chamber. She was helpless to do anything as he rolled her nipples between his fingers, playing her like the most revered instrument.

With sure hands, he stripped her of the nightdress, Missy watching in partial disbelief and horror as it pooled, whisper-soft, at her feet, leaving smooth creamy flesh for him to feast on—which he did with a carnivorous greed.

"If you knew how long I've wanted you." The words came out guttural, sounding almost pained. His hands reached once again for her breasts and the feel of him now touching the heated flesh caused her to turn and lean into his arms—a weight he accepted gladly, while he bent his dark head to enclose her nipple between his greedy lips.

Reality faded to a distant buzz and Missy could only concentrate on the demands of her body and it was screaming out for satisfaction, a satisfaction only James could provide.

She felt herself being lowered to the bed, her legs parted by hard thighs encased in superfine trousers. While his mouth moved to minister the other breast with the same detail to attention as he had the first, James divested himself of his garments with sure deft movements, only pulling away briefly to pull off his trousers and undergarments.

His fingers trailed down her concave stomach to the apex of her thighs. She let out a helpless moan.

James drew in a ragged breath. "God, you feel so good," he murmured, threading through the triangular thatch of dark hair, and into the slick cavern of her sex. Missy heaved beneath his sensuous quest, clamping down hard on his finger with her inner muscles. James groaned, his pleasure so profound he thought he'd come at that moment before he'd even penetrated her.

Missy's head thrashed on the pillow, her hands working his muscled back and down to the curve of his buttocks. He emitted a harsh groan.

James knew if he didn't take her now, he'd end up spilling his seed on the bed. Using the width of his hips, he held her open and guided his throbbing erection to her entrance, and buried himself to the hilt in one fluid motion. He wanted to scream in pleasure the fit was so tight and so right, working his stiff length in that wonderful milking motion that had him throwing back his head in ecstasy as he thrust wildly, heavily into her.

The feeling of being completely filled was still new, driving Missy mad with pleasure. Every thrust and withdrawal caused a building crescendo that climbed higher and higher, her hips meeting his in a frantic, delicious pounding.

As they neared the edge of the abyss of madness, of pleasure, James swooped his head down and caught her lips in a kiss that was neither gentle nor soft. His tongue stabbed at the seam of her lips demanding entry and gaining it on a breathless sigh.

With her head thrown back, her mouth being pillaged and

plumbed by his marauding tongue, and the throbbing length of him firmly buried in between her silken thighs, she felt him pummel her in wild abandon. Missy glimpsed a piece of heaven before her world splintered into a kaleidoscope of shooting colors. Seconds later, James followed her in the tumble off the edge, emptying himself into her, his expression a mixture of anguish and bliss, his breath labored and spent.

For several minutes, they lay entangled, their naked limbs languid, their bodies sated. The evening air worked to cool their heated flesh. Slowly, James rolled from atop her to rest at her side, his dark chest hairs scraping along the mounds of her breasts, sending a thrill of sensation to their tips.

He pulled her into the curve of his body spoon fashion, his erection, still semi-hard, finding a place in the soft crevice of her bottom. Fingers, knowing and strong, cupped her breasts possessively while he buried his head in the notch between her neck and shoulders, the dark stubble on his jaw and chin lightly scratching her creamy flesh as he nuzzled and nipped.

Like a mindless twit, she responded instantly as if her body had not been long satisfied, reveling in the feel of him and every place he touched.

"We will be married as soon as can be arranged," he murmured.

The alarm bells inside her head, which had been mute, rang loudly. She immediately stiffened under his soothing petting. Grabbing the edge of the sheet, she yanked it over her naked form and twisted to face him and garner some distance.

"Pardon?"

He surveyed her as he would a naughty child, except when his gaze wandered down past her neck, a glint of lust glazed his eyes. "You could be expecting now."

The man didn't have a stitch of clothing on and didn't

look the least bit disturbed by the fact. If it didn't mean she'd have to give up her own cover, she'd have gladly draped the swath of cotton over his lean naked flesh, especially the hard, thick length between his legs. She wrenched her gaze back to his face.

"We are not getting married." She eyed him with suspicion. "Is that why you're here, to get me with child so I will have little choice but to marry you?"

He sent her a look of disgruntlement before he pushed himself to the edge of the bed and began to pull on the garments he had discarded on the floor. His trousers went on first. She breathed a deep sigh of relief. He worked the buttons on his shirt and watched her, his expression determined but decidedly grim.

"We are getting married." He looked in no mood to be reasoned with.

"For the last time, I am not marrying you. Now go, you should not be here. What if my mother were to come?"

He looked at her askance, his mouth partially cocked.

Her forehead puckered and she set her mouth in a mulish line. "Anyone could come in at any moment." She did not care she was being quite absurd as it was the wee hours of the morning and the house stood still and quiet with not a whisper from even the smallest of visitors.

"You didn't seem too troubled about being caught when you came to my chamber that night." The corners of his mouth lifted as if in remembrance, and her face heated at the memory. It was unconscionable for him to remind her of her shameless behavior. She tugged the sheet up higher so it covered her shoulders.

"You have to leave before someone finds you here." She looked pointedly at the chamber door. She made a mental note to make sure she locked her door when she retired to her room for the duration of his stay. She could not afford a repeat of the mistake she made this evening, no matter how tempting. James was playing a game with her heart and it was not one she could afford to lose.

He jerked on his Wellingtons. "I will see you later this morning to solidify the wedding plans. This time it will be done quickly. We will not wait to see if you are with child, for I guarantee you," his eyes seemed to be able to see through her covering, "I will spend every second making certain that if you are not at present, you will surely be by the time I slip that ring on your finger."

His words started a hot throbbing between her legs. Missy had never seen him so determined or felt so weak.

"Mrs. Delacroix has given me the blue room. If you require anything from me, please do not hesitate to come." His tone was suggestive and his eyes, even more so. Before she could blink again, he was gone.

Chapter Twenty-Two

James arrived at Rutherford Manor still in a state of shock the following evening. The shock had occurred early that morning at Stoneridge Hall. That was when the missive had arrived informing him of his father's death. He had been thrown from a horse and broken his neck. That was what it had taken to end the fifth Earl of Windmere's life.

From the moment the note fluttered to the floor from his nerveless fingers until now, everything had been a blur. He was numb, not in shock. Or perhaps he was numb with shock. He barely remembered dressing and apprising the viscountess of his departure, though he remembered quite distinctly Missy had still been asleep when he left and he hadn't been able to even bid her good-bye. He'd had many hours on his coach rides and train ride to think about his father's death . . . and his life.

Reeves, their butler since James was a child, offered his condolences the moment he opened the front door to him, his thin face red, his eyes hollow. His father had evoked loyalty in everyone he knew and who knew him. The servants were especially fond of him. James nodded vaguely and was instructed kindly that his mother was in the music room.

The countess was tall and elegant, her hair a color between

blond and brown. She sat on a small love seat next to the piano quietly sipping tea—or so he assumed from the shiny silver tea service sitting next to her. Her blue eyes fixed on him the moment he entered the room and she smiled. It was a sad smile, the corners of her lips barely turned up.

"I am much too young to be widowed, wouldn't you agree?"

How very typical of his mother. As with everything else, she gauged every event on how it would affect her. His father's death would be but a slight ripple in the sea that was her life, unless he'd left her bereft financially.

"Good evening, Mother. I daresay I thought Father too young to die," he replied dryly, bending to brush a kiss on her cheek before taking the seat closest to her. He noted that she wore a purple gown trimmed in yellow beads. Somehow he hadn't thought his mother would follow the mourning wear for the allotted year which was *de rigueur*. After her own mother had died some ten years back, she'd complained how black made her look sallow and could only abide wearing it on the day of the funeral.

"Your father was a reckless young man and he never changed," she said with a sniff.

"I would hardly call riding a horse reckless." The man was not a day cold and she could still find fault with him. He dropped his head and sighed. Would she allow her sons to grieve their father without her poisonous barbs?

She ignored his response, continuing as if he hadn't spoken. "I'm surprised he was here at all. Your father didn't spend much time here. He preferred to while away most of his days in Town even when Parliament wasn't in session. But then I don't expect he would have stayed long, as he never did."

"The funeral, Mother, when is it being held?" Here sat

the reason he didn't like to come home often. If not for Christopher, he didn't think he'd ever come home at all.

"In two days. I would just like to have this whole thing over and done with."

"And Christopher?

"He is due home tomorrow."

James nodded slowly. His eyes burned and his head had begun a dull unrelenting throb. He hadn't shed a tear and perhaps that was because his shocked senses hadn't the ability to produce them. But right now an emptiness existed inside him and he wasn't sure what was missing.

He hadn't been all that close to his father but a kinship had existed between them. Although not much about the earl's life had ever been altogether appealing, James had quite resigned himself to a life very much like his father's.

At one time, his mother had been happy, smiling, and passionate about life—just like Missy—but that had been when he was a child. He couldn't recall exactly when it had changed, but change it had.

He now took in his mother's remote visage and wondered again what a marriage to the woman she'd become would be like. An involuntary shiver caught him. It might be enough for a man to wish for the tranquility of death or at the very least, to forever lose himself in the arms of other women. And his father had had women. Many women. What else was he to do with a cold fish of a wife?

James rose to his feet. "It has been a long day." *And my father has just died.* But he didn't utter the latter aloud. Instead, he gave his mother a rather pointed look.

"Italy was beautiful," she said, gazing out the bowed window overlooking the front lawn.

James sighed. "Good night, Mother."

Inclining her head in a dismissive fashion, and with her

eyes devoid of emotion, she brought the teacup to her lips again and continued to sip her tea.

The viscountess had canceled the remaining festivities of the weekend rout once James had informed her of his father's death. The partygoers had been most understanding given the circumstances, many of them having known the man personally. In a wave, they had vacated the estate during the course of that day, and the following morning Missy and the viscountess set out for Rutherford Manor.

The slender and efficient-looking butler who admitted them entrance to the grand stone structure heralded their arrival.

Missy had little time to take in the luxurious surroundings of richly colored silken walls, large silver-framed oils and plush carpeting before her gaze was caught and held by James's pale blue-eyed stare.

He stood just outside the drawing room, their arrival drawing his attention. He straightened, and it was only then that Missy noticed Alex and Thomas flanking his sides. He started toward her, his regard never wavering. Missy felt her insides tighten in apprehension and, even while she reminded herself that she was here for his father's funeral, she could not stop the twinge of excitement she experienced at the sight of him. He should have looked entirely too sober in his black mourning wear and the black armband wrapped around his right arm. But if anything, he looked devastatingly handsome.

Her mother was so busy ensuring the footman retrieved every piece of baggage from the carriage, she didn't notice the men until they were almost upon them.

James broke eye contact to greet the viscountess. Missy stood quietly while they exchanged tender hugs of condolences. When he moved to her, Missy could scarcely think.

He gazed down at her with such potency she felt her stomach take a careening drop.

He bent down and, propriety be damned, brushed a feather soft kiss across her warm cheek. "Thank you for coming," he said in a thick voice.

Aware they held an audience that included her mother and brother, Missy murmured a brief, "I'm terribly sorry about your father." She immediately dropped her gaze, the pull of attraction too intense for public scrutiny.

He took a step back and his hands dropped to his sides. He offered her an oddly tentative and intimate smile. "We will speak after the funeral," he said, only loud enough for her ears.

Peering up at him, Missy could only nod her reply. Moments later, she and her mother followed the footman who bore their luggage to their guest chambers.

The late Theodore Rutherford was buried on a family plot some distance from the main house beside his parents, the former Earl and Countess of Windmere. The funeral was a somber affair with many of the most influential of the *ton* attending as well as the local gentry and the men and women who worked the Rutherford land.

While the mourners gathered in the drawing room for food and discussion, James escorted his mother for the reading of the will.

The solicitor, Mr. Clarence Henry, was a pudgy little man. When he walked into the library, he seemed to have to fight for every labored breath. He held a valise, which couldn't be considered small, but certainly didn't look weighty enough to explain the kind of exertion he exhibited in hefting it onto the desk.

The Countess of Windmere sat regally in the blue-ballooned chair, and James was relieved to see she was appropriately dressed in black widow's weeds. He sat in the adjacent armchair while a puffy, red-eyed Mrs. Talbot, their housekeeper of some twenty-odd years, and a stoic Reeves sat on a couch nearby.

Mr. Henry held court in front behind a massive cherry escritoire in a chair that left him quite dwarfed by its dimensions. He shuffled through a stack of papers for a moment, clearing his throat all the while.

Finally, he looked up at the four other occupants and gave one last prolonged clearing of his throat. When he began to speak, James felt his mind began to drift. He heard the drone of the man's voice as he informed them of the bequest to Mrs. Talbot and Reeves for their years of faithful service in the amount of five hundred pounds a year to each for the rest of their lives. Both servants gasped, and James noted the tears flooding the housekeeper's eyes and then amazingly, Reeves's. But then, five hundred pounds was very generous, indeed.

As his heir, there was little else in the contents of the will that surprised him. Christopher, who had arrived home the prior day from Eton, was subdued and taking his repast in his bedchamber. Their father had left him the grand sum of twenty-five hundred pounds a year, which would be held in estate for him until the age of twenty-one. He would then receive the lump sum and then the same amount every year thereafter.

With the countess, his father had been most generous. He willed her an estate in Derbyshire and thirty-five hundred pounds a year for the remainder of her life. A glance at his mother revealed little reaction to his bequest. After all she'd put his father through with her coldness and her severity, she had the temerity to appear not the least bit grateful. He'd seen men with more wealth than his father's leave their widows with far less. James turned his attention from his mother.

"Mrs. Talbot and Mr. Reeves, I believe that will be all. The remainder of the will is strictly familial matters," Mr. Henry said, his small eyes peering over the rim of his wire-framed glasses.

With that, Reeves and Mrs. Talbot gave a deferential nod and a curtsey, respectively, Mrs. Talbot, with a handkerchief clutched tightly to her generous bosom, and quietly departed.

At the loud click of the door closing, Mr. Henry directed his attention to James and continued. It was this last part of the reading of the will that caught and held his attention wholly and completely.

"And for my two daughters, Catherine and Charlotte Langston, I bequest one thousand pounds a year for the rest of their lives. My son, James Rutherford will be the administrator of their fund until they reach the age of twenty-five. If they marry before that time, the lump sum of ten thousand pounds will be the amount of their dowry . . ."

James's mind stopped functioning at that point. He vaguely heard some mention of a boarding school and fees and upkeep, but that was it. He turned abruptly in his chair toward his mother. She regarded him, her visage impassive, but her hands betrayed her emotions, lying white and clenched tightly on her lap. His gaze darted back to the solicitor, whom at this point had stopped speaking and surveyed him uneasily.

"Daughters? My father has two daughters?"

Mr. Henry lowered his gaze to the desk before meeting his own again. He nodded slowly. Then he sighed. "I told your father to apprise you of the fact in the event that you would need to administer their trust but he wouldn't hear of it."

James shook his head as if to clear cobwebs from his brain. Nothing of this made sense. "How old are they?"

"Fifteen."

"Both?" he asked, still trying to comprehend what it was he was hearing.

"They are identical twins."

James collapsed back into his seat. He had identical twin sisters who were close in age to Christopher. Which meant of course—

He swung toward his mother. "You knew," he stated. She had to have known. She didn't appear shocked by the news, and it would explain so much.

Her slender hands unclenched and she regarded him, her countenance blank of all emotion. "Yes, I've known since Christopher was a baby. When I was in confinement, your father took up with a trollop in Lord Townsend's residence."

Mr. Henry cleared his throat rather loudly in protest. "She was the daughter of Lord Townsend himself."

"You mean bastard daughter," his mother said with venom in her voice.

James's brow shot up. "I find it difficult to believe my father would dally with the daughter of an earl, illegitimate or otherwise."

"She wasn't just his by blow," the countess intervened, "she was little more than a servant in his house." She spat the latter in disgust.

James shot a glance at Mr. Henry and his tentative nod confirmed what his mother had just said was true.

"Their mother died thirteen years ago of consumption and, as I said, they have been residing at the Our Lady of Fatima School for Young Ladies since the age of five. Your father has been paying for their living expenses since their birth as Lord Townsend cast his daughter from his estate when he discovered she was *enceinte*. Your father was an extremely generous man," Mr. Henry said, a smile of admiration transforming his plain features.

"Your father was a philanderer of the worst sort. He has

visited shame upon me since the day he took me as his bride," the countess said, her tone biting and laced with bitterness.

Unwilling to become embroiled in an argument regarding his father in front of the family solicitor, James rose unsteadily to his feet.

"If that is everything, Mr. Henry, I believe I can take the matter from here."

Mr. Henry's gaze darted between mother and son, before he stood and began collecting his documents and thrusting them into his valise. "I will leave you with a copy of the will. All of the information regarding your sisters' care is there. I will be available if you require my assistance."

James walked Mr. Henry to the library door and shook his hand briskly. "Thank you, I will do so," he said. With a murmured farewell, Mr. Henry took his leave.

James didn't return to his seat, instead propped himself on the edge of the desk. He stared down at his mother and, for all her hauteur, tears welled in her eyes. In that instant, his heart softened.

"Did you love him?" he asked.

She looked up at him as if startled by the question. After a moment, she nodded and closed her eyes, a tear squeezing out, managing its way down a pallid cheek.

"I loved him once," she said, her voice choked with emotion. "I believed when we married he'd stop all his philandering but I found out soon after the honeymoon that he once again had taken up with his mistress in Town. For years I tried to ignore his behavior and be the perfect wife but when I learned of the twins—" Her voice broke and she swallowed. "After I discovered, I could not do it anymore. He now had children who would forever be evidence of his infidelities. Children of a woman so beneath—"

"Tread carefully, Mother. I know you have been hurt, but they are still my sisters and I intend to treat them as such."

"What exactly are you saying?"

"I'm saying I intend to see them. I'm going to see where and how they are living."

The countess's mouth opened but no words emerged.

Once she'd recovered from the shock of his announcement, she asked, "You cannot be serious?" Her tone was a mixture of affront and disbelief.

"I am."

"You would betray me like that? When people discover, I will be the laughingstock of the *ton*."

"Hardly, Mother, these things occur all the time. If anyone discovered the girls' existence, you would more than likely get their heartiest sympathies. If anyone, it will be Father they will castigate beneath their breaths and in their thoughts and, as he is not here, it will be of little matter."

"But why would you want to associate yourself with them? They do not know you. You do not know them."

"Because they are my family. It would behoove me to at least meet my own sisters," he stated quite simply.

His mother rose proudly from her chair and after sending him a condemning look, swept from the room.

Missy could say she'd left the confines of Rutherford Manor because she wished for the fresh air of the uncommonly cool August afternoon, but she knew she would only be lying to herself. She'd come in search of James. After nearly an hour of sipping sweet tea and nibbling on pastries while making light conversation with fellow mourners, she'd yet to see him again since the service. He had said after the funeral they would talk. Talk about what? Their future together? A real marriage? Well then, where was he? Her stomach churned in anticipation.

She waited amidst the fading beauty of the lush gardens,

the scent of the coming season infusing the air. After another ten minutes passed without not so much as a glimpse of the new Earl of Windmere, Missy thought it best to resume her search indoors. Turning to make her way up the flagstones leading back to the house, she nearly started when she saw the countess standing several feet away.

The paleness of the woman's visage against the cloying black of her mourning dress gave her the appearance of a ghost. As she'd already offered the widow her sympathies at the funeral services, Missy could not think of what else to say.

"I beg your pardon, Lady Windmere. I didn't mean to disturb you. And once again, I am truly sorry for your loss." Condolences always bore repeating.

The widow acknowledged her with a slight inclination of her head. Having no desire to infringe on what had to be a most unbearable grief, Missy dipped in a small curtsey before stepping to the side to beat a hasty retreat back to the house.

"You are in love with my son." The statement chilled the air, as emotionless as the expression on the woman's face.

Halting just abreast of her, Missy's head snapped to the side to regard the dowager's elegant profile.

Lady Windmere met her gaze with a languid turn of her head. "My dear, one thing I am not is a fool. At least not any longer. I saw the way you watched him during the service." A smile infused with warmth enough to form ice lifted the corners of her mouth. "I hope you hadn't intended it to be a secret. And I saw the way he watched you in return. He is like his father in that respect. Quite obvious if one knows what to look for."

Feeling like livestock on the auction block, Missy endured the countess's scrutiny, which commenced at the top of her upswept mane, and ended at the black satin trim of her dress. "And, like his father, he is not a man who can keep his attentions exclusively to one woman. You will indeed be fortunate if he manages the honeymoon without mishap."

Missy swallowed. Her words rang painfully true. James had practically blanched at the notion of fidelity. Apparently, his mother knew his feelings on the matter just as well.

"I hope you are prepared for the children. My son has informed me today that he intends to acknowledge them." She laughed, something shrill, bordering on hysteria. "Perhaps he will decide to raise them himself. Or, worse yet, eventually introduce them into Society as if they were women of quality. My equal. Again, like his father, he is determined to bring shame upon the Windmere name. Upon me."

Missy took an involuntary step back, the revelation landing with the impact of a physical blow to the chest—the heart. A sharp inhalation of breath caused a dizzying rush of blood to her head.

"James has children?" The question was wrung from her throat hoarse and choked.

In that instant, she saw fury banked in the countess's eyes. "Girls. And twins at that. I see he has yet to inform you of the blessed event. As I told you, he grows more and more like his father each passing day. And you," she ran another jaundiced eye down the length of Missy's frozen form, "look hardly equipped to raise children that are not your own."

Missy could scarcely breathe much less speak. It had taken several seconds for the realization to sink in that Lady Windmere wasn't speaking of Lady Victoria. That perhaps she was still under the erroneous conception that Lady Victoria's unborn child was his. But the children she spoke of were already born. Two girls. Daughters.

Hadn't it been only days ago when he'd made love to her and told her he'd marry her come high floods or a swarm of locusts? All of that and he'd never breathed a word of their existence. It hardly seemed possible.

"But—are you quite certain? What I—I mean is—" Missy halted to gain control of her tongue. Her shattered composure.

"I assure you, my dear, this is not something I would ever dare to presuppose, nor anything I welcome, as you can well imagine."

Missy cast a bewildered, sightless look around. She needed to leave, desired it with an unwavering intensity. She must remove herself from the Countess of Windmere's noxious presence. Quit Rutherford Manor. Quit James.

"I—I believe I must be—be getting back inside," Missy said, her voice but a cracked whisper. She struggled to compose her features into a semblance of normalcy, one that didn't reveal the true depth of her pain. The finality of the death of a dream unrealized. Treating the countess to a vague nod, she hastened up the cold flagstones.

Chapter Twenty-Three

The remainder of the day dragged by in a haze. James made a brief appearance at supper that evening. He stared at her frequently but hadn't approached. She hadn't seen him since. Not that she hoped to see him. Every bit of warmth she'd felt upon learning of his father's death had perished under his mother's searing words. She knew she shouldn't feel betrayed, but she did.

With sleep playing elusive that evening, Missy had not much else to do but think as she lay twisting under the linen sheets gracing the bed in the guest chamber. She thought of Lady Victoria and her unborn child. James said it wasn't his but how did she know he was being truthful? He had children—two daughters—he intended to claim. And their mother, who was she? A woman he had cared for years ago? How long ago? Did he have feelings for her still? A piercing pain rent her heart at the nameless and faceless woman who had borne him children. Something she would never do.

A well of tears spilled from her eyes and tracked down her cheeks. Did he make a sport out of impregnating young ladies and leaving them to stew? It had been only by the grace of God she hadn't met a similar fate.

The chamber door glided open and Missy started violently, the feathered quilt pulled up to her chin, her eyes wide. Before a sound passed her parted lips, the light in the hallway illuminated James's unmistakable form before he stepped in and closed the door.

Missy keenly remembered a similar scene from just days before . . . and how it had ended. It was definitely an incident she couldn't bear to repeat.

"I saw your light," he said softly, approaching the bed, his stockinged feet treading quietly across the carpeted floor. He wore a dressing robe, his hair was ruffled, and a day's worth of whiskers shadowed his jaw. He looked sad, weary, and bereft, and for one moment Missy's heart contracted painfully for him. She had experienced the same acute sense of loss of a parent when she was just eleven years. The pain never completely went away no matter the age. Then she remembered. She remembered if she allowed it, this man would break her heart all over again.

"You shouldn't be here," she said, her voice slightly scratchy from recent tears.

He stood regarding her, his lids at quarter-mast, the tightness easing from the sides of his mouth. She recognized the unmistakable signs of arousal as his pupils dilated, the heat sparking in his eyes. Missy's breasts peaked and she immediately scooted over on the bed as if inches or even feet would negate her body's response. James took in her action with mild surprise and amusement.

"I wanted to speak with you without a houseful of people present," he said, his gaze seeming to burn through the pink counterpane she clutched to her chin. "I didn't trust myself in approaching you with others around."

Missy watched him closely, not saying a word or moving so much as a muscle.

"We need to marry," he said, sinking onto the edge of the bed, his body now too close, too familiar.

The silence that followed was deafening.

"Why?" Missy finally asked, in a toneless voice.

His eyes widened a fraction as if surprised by the question. Then he braced one hand on the other side of her tense form and he leaned in, his mouth hovering only inches from hers.

"Because—"

Missy ducked her head underneath his spread arm and scrambled to the other side of the bed, the quilt edging down to reveal bare arms and a translucent cream nightdress.

"Because you may have gotten me with child? Or perhaps you are afraid that my brother will beat you bloody again? What reason do you have now?" she charged.

James straightened, his gaze never straying from her. "I don't give a fig whether you are expecting or not. As for your brother, my decision has nothing to do with him. I care for you more than I've ever cared for any woman in my life. As much as I wanted it to, it hasn't gone away. My feelings have only grown stronger these past months."

It would be so easy to succumb to his words when he looked at her as he was doing now. But she knew what she could expect from a marriage with him. Just as his mother had said, James didn't have it within himself to be faithful. He didn't love her. She would be sharing him with his mistresses. And his children. Would he even tell her about them? As his wife, wouldn't she have the right to know of their existence and that he intended to acknowledge them as his own?

"Just when exactly did these feelings grow stronger? Was it when you started courting Lady Victoria only days after bedding me?" she asked with heavy sarcasm, her brow quirked. "Or perhaps it was when you escorted Lady Willis home after the supper party? No, I am wrong. It must have been when you told me that you didn't love me and all you felt was lust. You said you'd never marry me." By the time she finished her damning speech, her voice was thick with emotion. The truth of her words was even almost too much for her to bear.

James's gut twisted in agony throughout her scathing indictment. When she listed them so succinctly, his actions appeared more than damning and less than caring. But he had been driven by guilt, his own stubborn willfulness, and circumstances beyond his control.

Reaching across the bed, he gave her hand a firm tug and pulled her resistant body close to his. "I was a fool. The situation with Lady Victoria—"

"I do not want to hear about your affairs. The days I cared about what you did, and with whom, are over. The only thing I want you to do now is to leave me alone. You were right all along when you said I was young and too naïve to know about love. I acted utterly selfishly in thinking I could force you to love me." The latter she had learned over the course of the last month.

"No, that is not true. I do love you—"

Missy interrupted with a high laugh, pushing herself up into a sitting position, the quilt forgotten and pooled around her hips. His gaze zeroed in on taut buds pushing up against her nightdress. He felt the familiar quickening of his pulse as his blood rushed thick and hot through his veins and his eager member jumped to attention.

"You don't love me," she scoffed.

Aroused, angry, and not thinking clearly, James grabbed her hand and roughly placed it on the rigid heat of his erection. He felt her fingers' involuntary clench and almost groaned aloud at the searing lust that tore through him like a runaway cart plummeting downhill.

Wide, startled eyes stared up at him through the dusky light. Then her countenance changed and through his silk robe and linen drawers, he felt the sweep of her hand sliding the length of his cock.

"This," she said softly, giving him a brief squeeze, "is a man's reaction to any desirable female." She pulled her hand away abruptly, tucking it securely at her side.

In an ironic twist, not only had she thrown his own words back in his face, but so had she thrown back the only declaration of love he had ever made to any woman. His ardor immediately cooled as he blanketed his emotions behind a mask to hide the searing pain shredding his heart like shards of glass. She couldn't have made herself any clearer than she did now.

Slowly he rose to his feet, ignoring the tight knot in his stomach and what felt like a gaping hole in his chest. "Then I will not bother you again," he said hoarsely. Without glancing back, he departed the room.

After the door closed softly behind James, the first tear was joined swiftly by another, until a torrent ran down her cold cheeks. Laying her head on her pillow, Missy cried herself to sleep, her heart in pieces.

She had left.

James wasn't surprised when Armstrong informed him. Early the following morning well before the cocks had stirred, the viscountess and Missy had set off back to their estate in Devonshire. The viscountess had, naturally, left a note apologizing for their hasty departure but nothing else. No reason. But he knew what the reason had been. Missy.

Determined not to allow the knowledge to weigh on him, he performed his host duties like an automaton. By the end of the day, all of the mourners had cleared the premises. He was alone again.

Two days later, James stood in a small office at Our Lady of Fatima School for Young Ladies. He awaited his sisters on a scarred chair in an office equipped with solid but worn antiquated furniture.

The first glimpse of them had him mildly surprised. They looked nothing as he'd expected. They had hair the color of dark gold, which hung in perfect spirals down their backs. He knew their age to be fifteen but the dewy softness of their cheeks made them appear years younger. And their eyes . . . identical . . . were the purest powder blue he'd ever seen. All in all, they had an almost exotic beauty to them with their dusty rose complexions, high cheekbones, and full pink lips.

Lord, for fifteen years his father had kept them a secret. How he would have enjoyed having sisters all those years. And just like that, he made the decision not to leave them here. They were his sisters, illegitimacy and dubious lineage notwithstanding, and he had the financial means to raise them as proper young ladies. If nothing else, they deserved to be raised in something better than the sterile environment of a boarding school.

"Charlotte and Catherine, this is your brother, James Rutherford, the new Earl of Windmere."

Now, which one was Charlotte and which one was Catherine? James assessed them, wondering how he would ever come to tell them apart. Both stood behind Mrs. Doubletree, the headmistress, their reticence obvious by the nervous flutter of their hands and their peeking eyes.

Mrs. Doubletree gently urged them forward until they came to stand directly in front of him, their expressions anxious. He wanted to ease their fears as much as he could.

With a welcoming, easy smile, he said, "I have never been fortunate enough to have a sister. Now I can claim two." They continued to watch him with those gorgeous blue eyes. "You will both come and live with me at my home in London."

Mrs. Doubletree started and her eyes widened in shock. Her jowls shook gently, her chest heaved—abundant as it was— and James thought briefly she'd keel over on the spot.

She darted him a questioning look and he gave a curt nod in response. "After we're finished here, my sisters shall pack their belongings."

Both girls stared at him wide-eyed, as if they, too, had a hard time taking in the enormity of what he was saying.

"Would you like to come and live with me?" He hadn't even asked them if they wished to live in London with him. Regardless of his title and the blood they shared, he was still a stranger to them. They might not want to leave the familiarity of their school.

His sisters exchanged a look he could not decipher, and then turned and gave him tentative nods. James smiled broadly, relief easing the tension he hadn't known had formed in his shoulders.

"Have you ever been to London?"

Charlotte—or at least he thought it was Charlotte— nodded shyly. "Once, two years ago."

They had lived their entire lives in England and had been to Town only once. Well, by the time they reached the age for a proper come out, it would be as if they'd lived there all their lives. He felt more determined than ever that they would enjoy a life as dictated by their grandfather and father's stations and titles.

"Mrs. Doubletree told us our father is dead." Catherine stated matter-of-factly.

"Yes, unfortunately, that is true."

She eyed him as if she was trying to decide whether she found him trustworthy or not. "We can't remember our mother. Did you know her? Or perhaps you could tell us about our father? We didn't know much of him."

Mrs. Doubletree turned, an embarrassed flush on her face. "Now Catherine, that is quite enough—"

James held up his hand. "No, please, madam, that is quite fine. I'm sorry but I was never acquainted with your mother. However, I'm certain she was a lovely woman. As for our father, he was a very generous and amiable man. It would appear, however, that I didn't know him as well as I thought."

"The girls can have their things packed in no time at all," Mrs. Doubletree said briskly. "Go on girls, your brother is a busy man."

"Do not rush on my account, we have plenty of time," James said smoothly, irritated by the woman's tone.

With two hurried curtsies, the girls departed.

It required precisely a half hour for his sisters to pack. When they emerged from their stark, white-walled chamber, the footman carried only two pieces of luggage out to the carriage. That everything they owned could fit in such small trunks caused his stomach to knot. Most girls he knew could fit but only two or three gowns in luggage that size. But that would soon change. They would have everything girls of their age should have and more.

After his sisters exchanged stilted farewells to the woman who'd been responsible for their care and schooling for the past ten years, the three set off for London.

Chapter Twenty-Four

"James is back in town," the viscountess announced from the bedchamber door.

Missy spared her mother a glance but kept her face expressionless. After a week of absence, she had heard of his return and the two young girls who'd accompanied him—his new wards. But she didn't care. She was on her way to America in two days. Cousin Abigail was due to arrive that evening. Her plans were set; James could do as he pleased. He didn't love her. *He didn't love her*.

The viscountess entered the chamber and closed the door. She stepped daintily over several large portmanteaus and then pushed aside a leather valise on the bed before taking a seat beside her daughter.

"Mama, I don't want to discuss James. What he does and where he goes is none of my concern. I no longer have the same feelings for him as I did once." She held up a silk flowered shawl she was considering for her trip.

No, her feelings were not the same. They had in fact grown into those of a woman's feelings, a woman who was now well acquainted with the sexual pleasures that accompanied true love. But she was sure in time those too would fade. She sincerely hoped they would.

"My dear, he wants to marry you. I would say that says something about his feelings." The viscountess said gently.

To look directly into her mother's green eyes was to reveal all of her heartfelt pent-up emotions. Missy averted her eyes and busied herself folding the shawl to rest it atop the feathered quilt.

"He doesn't love me anymore than he loved Lady Victoria. He doesn't want to marry me for the right reasons. And none of this matters, as I have no intentions of marrying him. I told you as much. The only reason he persisted is because he felt honor bound to do so." She gave the shawl one final pat before glancing over at her mother.

The viscountess gave a small, almost sad smile. "I know you, Millicent, and I know you would never give your heart so easily nor would your feelings change so quickly."

Missy laughed darkly, and then sat mute and unmoving. Her mother did know her too well. She turned to her. "I want the kind of marriage you and Papa had. I saw the way he adored you and you him. I could not bear to settle for anything less than that. Please say you understand my reasons, Mama. You do understand why I was forced to turn him down. How can I settle for anything less than what you had?"

The viscountess's perfectly arched brows rose, her eyes growing wide. And when they slowly lowered, a sigh such as she'd never heard from her mother, slid past her lips. "Oh, Millicent." Her chest rose and fell gently. "Your father and I didn't have the marriage you imagined." The gravity of her tone told Missy that it had required effort to utter those words.

Missy furrowed her brows. "What do you mean?"

The viscountess cleared her throat delicately. "Your father and I were not a love match."

"No, that can't be true," Missy replied automatically, shaking her head in denial.

"Indeed, it is true. When I married your father I was in love with another man, the son of a physician, and your father was enamored with a Vauxhall dancer. Neither of us wanted to marry—well, certainly not each other."

The notion fractured her entire belief system of love. It was an impossibility. She'd grown up blanketed by their love. Not only their love of their children but of each other. How could her mother now tell her it had all been a lie?

"Are you telling me that you and Papa did not love one another?" That was absurd. Even at a young age, their love had permeated the walls of Stoneridge Hall and beyond. Surely that kind of emotion could not be feigned and sustained for years on end?

"No, we cared for each other deeply but that took some time. It wasn't until years before your birth, when Thomas was a young boy, that those feelings grew. We learned not to fight against our circumstances." Her mother's eyes took on a faraway look, a smile edging the corners of her mouth. "We were not falling in line with our parents' plans with regard to marriage, so your grandfathers pushed us together. When I was your age, I didn't have the backbone to stand up against my mother and buckled quite easily to my father's wishes. Your grandfather threatened to leave your father without a shilling when he inherited, so your father relented and we were quickly married."

So it had not been how she envisioned it for her parents. There had been no immediate, passionate, forever love? They had been forced into marriage? Missy drew in a shaky breath.

"Mama, James never once really proposed. He demanded I marry him. He suggested it as if it were the only recourse. He doesn't love me." What he had said to her after his father's funeral didn't count because he hadn't meant it. They had been words merely to bend her to his will. Just words.

"I would never tell you to marry James if you didn't wish to do so. However, I do beg you to think long and hard before you cast aside the man you love." The viscountess reached over and took her hand in hers, her green eyes intent. "Nothing is perfect but I believe one should always strive for a perfectly happy life, just as your father and I did. Your father and I were blessed with four wonderful children, and we did have the best possible life that we could. But it called for sacrifice and compromise and an acceptance of reality as opposed to a dream."

Yes, a dream. The life she had envisaged with James had been built on dreams. The reality, however, was quite different.

"Do you ever think about what kind of life you would have had with your first love?"

Her mother shook her head sadly. "I was not the kind of woman Paul deserved at the time. He required someone strong of mind and heart, and that was something I could not give him. If I could, I would have gone against my parents' wishes and married him no matter the consequences."

"But, Mama, you are all of those things," Missy protested. She didn't know anyone as strong as her mother.

"I wasn't almost thirty years ago. That has come with time."

"Would you marry a man now who did not love you?"

The viscountess paused a moment before she said, "No, not if he didn't truly love me, but I do not know that's the same as your dealings with James. For most, love doesn't come overnight in a flash of fury and thunder. It grows over time." She released Missy's hand after giving it a reassuring squeeze.

"I will leave you to think on that." With an indulgent smile and a brush of her lips against her forehead, the viscountess quit the chamber.

Missy's gaze ran over the portmanteaus and dresses draped

over every fixed piece of furniture, and drew in a deep sigh. What she wouldn't give to have what her mother said be true.

"Lord Rutherford."

James nearly started at the greeting he had been so lost in his thoughts. Glancing across the pebbled path of Hyde Park, he saw Miss Claire Rutland and a young slender girl he assumed by her dress was her lady's maid. Instinctively, he scoured the area for any sign of Missy. When his search came up empty, he vehemently denied that the sharp pain that scored his chest was abject disappointment.

Pasting an easy smile on his face, he replied, "Good morning, Miss Rutland."

She bustled across the path, pushing back the brim of her bonnet with the tip of a gloved finger. "I wanted to personally express my condolences on the death of your father," she said, her hazel eyes filled with sympathy.

James inclined his head. "Thank you."

Silence followed.

"Well, I will—"

"Have you seen—"

Miss Rutland broke off and laughed lightly as they spoke in unison. "I apologize, Lord Ruth—I mean Lord Windmere. Have I seen . . . ?" she prompted, peering up at him from her diminutive height.

He was going to ask about Missy and for a moment thought better of it. But his insatiable curiosity for knowledge of all things Missy got the better of him. "I was going to inquire about Miss Armstrong," he said, feeling exposed and discomfited by his necessity to know.

"Missy is quite well," she said slowly, watching him curiously. "I thought you and Lord Armstrong were close."

James cursed silently. Of course it would appear odd that

he was asking after Missy when he could easily have asked her brother. "Yes, well, I have been out of Town and have yet to speak to him since my return."

In the week since his return to London, he had managed to settle his sisters and hire Miss Bridges, their governess. Initially he had thought her a little too young for the post but she'd come highly recommended and her references were impeccable. The girls were slowly warming to him, though still very shy and tentative, and appeared overwhelmed by their new abundance of clothes. One of the first things he'd done was to have Madame Batiste personally come to his townhouse to fit them for new wardrobes.

"Well, I'm sure you're aware Missy is leaving for America."

The news hit him with such force, he was surprised when he blinked that he was still standing erect. His shock must have shown on his face because Miss Rutland's expression instantly became contrite. "I assumed you were aware."

Still reeling, James could only shake his head, remaining mute. Several uncomfortable moments later, Miss Rutland bid him farewell to continue on her morning promenade.

James started back toward his carriage, his strides swift and urgent. *She is leaving* was the overriding thought in his mind as it worked at a pace fast and furious. Walking away from her had been easier when he knew she remained firmly within his reach. But for months, perhaps even longer, she'd be in America. What if she found an American gentleman who gave little thought to her lack of innocence? She could marry and not return.

The mere thought lengthened long, aggressive strides until he was running. His footman stood waiting quietly by the phaeton as he drew near. No words were spoken, James just gave a brisk nod of his head and bolted onto the high perch as his footman did the same. Soon they were speeding toward the south entrance.

* * *

James took the stairs two at a time and sounded the knocker hard against the door. The moment the door swung open, he barged by a bewildered Creighton and down the hallway where he heard voices coming from the library. Without so much as a preemptory knock, he threw open the door.

Armstrong and Cartwright lounged in the room, each man holding a glass in his hand. Their attention was immediately drawn to him but neither looked terribly surprised by his arrival. Nor did they seem at all surprised he looked a complete wreck, his hair mussed, his neckcloth askew, with a rather frantic and desperate look in his eyes. But James noticed none of this, his mind was focused on one thing and one thing alone.

"Where is she?" His breathing was labored, as if he'd been running—which in fact he had, from the carriage and up the front steps. But what choked him was the anxiety and fear.

Armstrong settled farther back into the winged-back chair, eyeing him, his expression deadpan. "And by she you mean . . . ?" He raised a brow in that supercilious manner that always had the desired effect of making James want to grit his teeth and smash his fist into his friend's perfectly arrogant nose.

James advanced into the room, unclenching and clenching his hands at his sides, his eyes narrowed and stormy. He stopped just short of the ottoman separating him from Armstrong and glared down at him.

"This is not the right time to play games with me, *Lord Armstrong*."

From behind him, Cartwright emitted a dry laugh. James rounded on him, wild and frantic.

"Whoa, no need to take offense." Cartwright held up one hand in mock surrender wearing a grin he tried hard to suppress. "I was merely going to suggest to Armstrong that he ease up on you. It's a historic fact the moment you start calling him by his title, your temperance is all but gone."

James shifted his attention back to the viscount. They could have their fun and amuse themselves all they wanted, just not now and just not with respect to Missy.

"Where is she?" he demanded, his voice breaking.

Armstrong regarded him directly and said, "She's gone." He appeared utterly composed. He raised his glass to his mouth and took a long swallow. As cool as ever, he placed the glass on the side table, still watching him.

James felt the breath leave his lungs and gasped. She had left him. She was gone. He grasped the back of the sofa to steady himself.

"When?"

"Yesterday."

Dazed, James crumpled onto the sofa, his legs unable to support him, his shoulders hunched, and his head hanging low. He felt empty, hollow in his chest where his heart should have been. Miss Rutland had led him to believe that Missy was still here. He'd thought he still had a chance to stop her. For several seconds there was only his breathing, harsh and audible in the room.

He raised his head and glared at his tormentor, his voice accusing. "And you let her go? For God's sake, she's too young to venture so far from home. Do you know the harm she could come to? And who does she have in America? Have you any idea of all the—" His voice broke and he dropped his head again, his eyes squeezed shut.

"You seem to forget Missy is headstrong with an iron will of her own. Look how bloody long she pined for you. But, just as I couldn't force her to marry you, I certainly couldn't keep her against her will. Regardless, I had little choice in the matter as she had the support of our mother. I'd be a fool to go up against the two of them."

James shook his head slowly. Unfortunately, everything he said was true. Missy would have found a way to leave. Even if they had married, if she'd grown unhappy with the marriage, she would have left him.

"I imagined you would be relieved," Cartwright said with only the trace of a smirk. "From everything you've said, I thought you only planned to marry her because Armstrong here threatened to make you a eunuch. And then, of course, with there being no threat of a little Rutherford coming in nine months . . ."

James swung his head toward his friend, blue ice blazing in his eyes. "I bloody well don't want to marry her because of that." He levered himself to his feet, his gaze darting between the two men. "Missy has turned me down countless times and I keep asking. Do you want to know why?" Regarding Armstrong, he said softly, "Because I am in love with her."

Armstrong and Cartwright exchanged a look. No doubt they thought he was mad as a hatter. But he didn't care. He didn't care that they had now seen him at his most vulnerable. He didn't care that he'd just bared his heart.

Cartwright cleared his throat loudly, setting his glass down before coming to his feet. "You will never see love turning me into this kind of blubbering mess. The man is in so deep he can't even see straight." His expression held a mixture of amusement and horror.

"It's our family's curse. We have that effect on the opposite sex." Armstrong reeked of smug nonchalance.

His friends' voices became an annoying buzz. Missy was all he could think of, and it would be like that forever. She was the only woman he wanted to take as his wife, and the only woman who would ever bear his children, and the sooner she came to accept that, the sooner they could start their lives together.

He started for the door, his strides long and urgent.

"Where are you going?" Armstrong was on his feet appearing ill-at-ease.

"Where do you think? To America," James replied without looking back.

"Who is going to America?"

James thought at first he must be hallucinating. He blinked several times in rapid succession. Like a vision in light purple, Missy stood framed in the doorway.

James stared at her as if she'd just risen from the dead. He then turned to glower at her brother.

Thomas's laugh held mild nervousness. "It appears she has returned."

Missy watched the men in confusion. What on earth was going on? What was James doing here and why did he now look like he was about to commit murder?

"You knew I believed . . . and you let me—"

"James came here hoping to speak to you," Armstrong said to Missy. He then turned to Cartwright. "I believe you and I are late for a previous appointment, is that not so?"

"Um—oh, yes indeed. Dreadfully late by the look of that clock."

Bewildered, Missy watched the two men take their leave, Thomas glancing back once to wink broadly at James. James scowled in response.

And then the two lone occupants of the room were greeted by silence. The kind of silence that grew ever more uncomfortable with each passing moment.

"You look disheveled." Missy said with her usual straightforwardness.

James eyed her with the desperation of a man lost in the desert who had just come upon an oasis. "I thought you'd gone," he said in a low-pitched husky voice.

She furrowed her brow. "Gone where?"

"To America. I thought you'd left me." He surveyed her thoroughly, from top to bottom.

Missy knew that look in his eyes—too well—and felt her body's tingling response. She forced herself to look away, knowing just how quickly she would fall under his spell if she allowed herself the luxury of feeling.

"How can I possibly leave you? We are not together," she said in a thick voice.

He closed the distance between them and then cupped her shoulders in his hands.

"You are with me every day," he assured her, staring deep into her eyes.

Missy felt herself weakening and resented him all the more.

"If you think I am expecting because of our—our last time together, you are mistaken." She fixed her gaze on his blue neckcloth, which was unaccustomedly askew. "And this time I am telling you the truth," she added hastily, remembering the last time she lied to him regarding the same matter.

He slid his hands down to encircle her waist, pulling her flush against him. With her nose brushing his neck, every inhalation brought the heady scent that was him. She tried to arch away but he refused to release her.

"Then we will keep trying until you are," he whispered into her ear, and then feathered the soft curve with a kiss. Missy moaned and clamped her thighs tightly together, but that didn't staunch the flood of moisture at her center.

Twisting her head to dislodge his talented mouth, she said, "So that you can then live to regret that we ever met? No, thank you."

Very slowly, after dropping another string of impassioned kisses on the long slope of her neck, he lifted his head. When she tried to look away, his hand held her chin firmly so he could look directly into her eyes.

"I was a fool. I allowed my parents' union to warp my views on marriage. I only recently discovered my father was not the besotted fool I thought he was, and my mother is just a very unhappy and bitter woman betrayed horribly by her husband. I thought I wanted a marriage in which I couldn't lose my heart. Actually, I don't believe I thought I *could* lose my heart to a woman. And then you came along, too precocious and beautiful for my peace of mind. I wanted you when you were just seventeen. Do you know what it was like for me to want someone I considered a child? Countless days of guilt and suffering made worse because you were the sister of my best friend. I knew no matter what you felt, I could never act on my feelings. You deserved better than what I had to offer."

"But what you felt was only lust. You told me so countless times." How she wanted to believe him, but when it came to James, she'd had too many years of disappointment and heartache.

"I did think that's all it was. But I knew the day you told me there was no child and you refused to marry me— I knew I had been lying to myself. I knew then how much I wanted to marry you whether you were carrying my child or not. I knew then I loved you."

"But Lady Victoria—"

"Nothing ever happened between us," he said in somber insistence.

"But—"

Taking her gently by the hand, he led her to the sofa, and then explained what had really occurred with Lady Victoria. Although Missy could understand her desperation, she still didn't take kindly to the woman's rash solution. But at least she now understood what had driven James to do the things he'd done.

"Now that we've cleared up the whole situation with Lady Victoria, I have some news I need to share with you."

Missy tried to withdraw her hand from his, but he held hers fast. She wasn't sure she was prepared to hear about his daughters, and she was fairly certain that was coming next.

"No, don't pull away. I want us to share everything." He traced delicate lines on the back of her hand with his finger, staring intently into her eyes. "Tomorrow I want you to meet my sisters."

Missy sat frozen in place for what seemed like an infinity. For some reason her brain took its time comprehending the meaning of the word sisters. When it finally did, she expelled an audible breath from her lungs.

"You have sisters?"

He smiled. "Yes, twin sisters, Catherine and Charlotte. My father's children with the illegitimate daughter of the Earl of Chester."

"James, that is wonderful," she practically shrieked and launched herself into his arms. There were no daughters. He had sisters. There was no faceless woman in his life who had borne him children. She wanted to jump for joy, but she was more than contented with peppering his face with kisses.

"If I'd known you so wished for sisters-in-law, I certainly would have told you sooner," he laughed, holding her tightly.

"Your mother said—I thought—I thought they were your daughters." Twining her arms around his neck, she burrowed her face into his chest, inhaling him as deeply as she could. Her own personal intoxicant.

"Daughters?" He lifted her chin with his finger. "Was that why you turned me away the night of my father's funeral?"

She gave a hesitant nod. Was he angry? she wondered, taking in his suddenly serious expression. "I was confused, and jealous, and I—"

"Shhh," he whispered placing his finger on her lips. "I understand. I've had my moments of acting terribly irrational because of you." He ended by dropping a kiss on the tip of her nose.

"Sir, did you say something about sisters-in-law," she said in mock innocence.

Missy nearly started when James dropped down onto his knee beside the sofa, and pushed his hand inside his forest green waistcoat to emerge with a sparkling sapphire ring. The brilliance of the stones dazzled her eyes.

James clasped her hand—now unsteady and moist—in his. "Millicent Eleanor Armstrong, will you do me the honor of becoming my wife?" His gaze never once wavered from hers, and the stark emotion she saw in his eyes caused her belly to drop.

"But how—where—when did you—"

"I have been carrying this around with me since the week of your mother's rout. I intended to give it to you the night I came to your bedchamber."

Dumbstruck, Missy could only nod, her hand trembling violently now, tears streaking down her flushed cheeks as he slid the ring on her finger.

She'd never expected anything like this—James on bended knee. So heartbreakingly touching. This was the first time he'd asked and not demanded or coerced. He had asked her with love shining brilliantly in his beautiful blue eyes. He loved her.

"Do you believe I love you or do you still think me a child?" she teased, clasping the back of his head in her hands.

"Believe me, I haven't thought of you as a child for quite some time," he murmured before capturing her lips.

He kissed her thoroughly, with a pent-up, long denied passion. Their tongues tangled and mated in a searing dance of lust and longing. Everything around her faded, leaving in its wake nothing except the touch and feel of him.

His hands scored the rigid tips of her breasts through the silk of her dress, and the prominent swell of his erection prodded her belly. She squirmed in response, her hips undulating in an attempt to ease the building pressure in her loins.

James groaned. Hands shaking, he set her away from him, leaving her to surface from the hazy mist of passion. Her heavy-lidded eyes struggled to open. Instinctively, she reached out to him but he took another shaky step backward, his eyes devouring her even as he denied himself.

"Are you forgetting that your brother is out there somewhere? Even if we were to be married tomorrow, I hardly think he'd approve of me taking you here in the library. In addition, your cries of pleasure would undoubtedly reach the servants' ears, and before sunrise tomorrow, all of London would know you'd been thoroughly debauched and by whom."

Missy opened her mouth to protest his claim, then remembered their last two encounters, and wisely snapped it shut. She had no defense. When he touched her, she became mindless and all consideration to anything else vanished from her thoughts.

"I know you are right but surely a small kiss wouldn't hurt." Her mouth pouted temptingly. She closed the gap between them and slid her arms around his waist. His body tensed for a moment before relaxing as he enfolded her securely in his arms.

Nuzzling her neck, he whispered, "You could never be satisfied with one small kiss."

Missy let out a soft moan. "There is nothing small about anything you give me."

"One week," James said, chuckling against her hair. "That is all I am willing to wait to make you my wife."

"I will tell my mother she has four days."

"That's my girl," he murmured before sealing her lips in a scorching kiss.

Epilogue

"They are quite the most beautiful babies I have ever seen."

Missy knew she viewed them with a mother's bias, but she readily admitted Catherine spoke the truth. Charlotte sat on the bed, peering at Jason over Missy's shoulder, who at only three days lay swaddled in a soft cotton blanket in his mother's arms.

Emily and Sarah had left only moments before to get something to eat, claiming they were famished. James held Jessica, who was only three minutes younger than her twin. By the manner in which he gazed at her, it was obvious his young daughter had already managed to wrap him around her too-tiny finger.

"It is hard to believe I'm an aunt," Charlotte said, tenderly stroking the downy soft tuft of dark hair on her nephew's head.

"You can still hardly believe you have two brothers," James replied, smiling at both his sisters, his affection obvious.

"Which reminds me, when will Christopher be home from school? I hope he will be excused to come home before Christmas." Missy knew from his letters he had eagerly anticipated the birth of the baby and, now that there were two instead of one, he'd be over the moon just as the girls were.

"I sent a message to the headmaster to ask that he be

excused the following week. As Christmas is over four months away, I didn't think it would be fair to make him wait so long. He is already jealous his sisters get to see the baby first—well, babies, but that will be his surprise."

A preemptory knock sounded on the bedchamber door before it was thrust open to admit Thomas, Alex and the viscountess.

Her mother and sisters had arrived a week ago, and would be remaining for a fortnight. This was the first time she had seen Thomas and Alex since the babies' birth.

"Ah, there she is, as fit and as hale as ever," Thomas said. "Thank goodness, because for the last five months, I just thought poor Missy was just the biggest pregnant woman I'd ever seen. If I'd known she carried two babies, I wouldn't have said all of those heartless things behind her back." He wore a broad grin on his face and first stopped by his sister's bedside to brush a loving kiss on her proffered cheek.

"And just where have you been? If you were not aware, I gave birth all of three days ago. More than ample time for you to make your way from London."

"Unfortunately, business matters with Lord Bradford detained us." He grimaced as if that hadn't been the only thing.

Alex verified that in the next statement. "If one can now call matters concerning the marquess's daughter 'business'." His voice was dry as the desert.

James's raised brow and curled lips gave him a decidedly mocking look. "I didn't know your dealings with the marquess were so firmly—uh—linked to the daughter. Isn't that the same chit Missy told me gave you a rather sordid setdown at the Langley's ball last year?" He shot a glance at Missy. "I believe you told me she indicated she was not at all enamored of his professed talents about the Town and didn't she in fact say that—"

"Spoiled, rude, insolent chit. She'll drive her poor father

to an early grave if he allows it," Thomas grumbled, his forehead knotted.

"But isn't that where you come in?" Alex smirked and sent him a knowing look, and by the glowering response he received from Thomas, Missy could tell they shared a secret joke.

"I believe we are here to see my dear sister, my brother-in-law, and my niece and nephew. Unpleasant discussions have no place here."

"And yes, Thomas, I'm doing quite fine. Thank you for asking." She smiled up at his golden visage.

"Mother said you did a wonderful job, and I see that you have."

"Would you like to hold your nephew?"

Thomas stared at the small bundle and cleared his throat, his discomfort evident. "Lord, he's so small I'm likely to drop him."

Alex stepped from behind him, elbowed him to the side and took Jason from her arms after dropping a light kiss on her forehead.

"If all women look as you do after giving birth, I can't imagine that marriage will be such a duty." Alex looked completely at ease holding the tiny infant. Missy thought whenever he decided to marry, he would make a wonderful father.

Thomas took his cue and sauntered over to the other side of the bed to stand next to James. The viscountess had already relieved him of his daughter so he stood like the thoroughly besotted man he was, observing his wife and children, love evident in his eyes.

"I see you're still making her happy," her brother said in way of a greeting, grasping James's hand in a handshake.

"No, I imagine we're both making each other extremely happy," he replied, but he had eyes only for her and she for him.

Thomas snorted in mock disgust. Turning to his mother he said, "If this is marriage, I want no part of it. He can hardly be called a man anymore."

Without looking up from her sleeping granddaughter, the viscountess *tsked* her son. "I imagine you will sing a different tune when your turn comes."

Thomas snorted again. "You'll never see me acting the fool over any woman."

Catherine scrunched up her nose at Thomas. "I want my husband to be exactly like my brother. Which woman wouldn't want a husband who adores her as James does Missy?"

Missy smiled and when her gaze swung to Charlotte, she noticed she was unusually quiet, her blue eyes glued to where Alex stood cooing over the baby. The girls were now sixteen—hardly girls any longer—making them the same age as she had been when she'd fallen fathoms-deep in love with James. Lord, her husband would kill Alex, she thought with a smile, but it would be such a fitting retribution.